Blood on Fire

M. P. DePaul

All rights reserved. No part of this book may be reproduced or transmitted in any form, or by any means, mechanical or electronic, including photocopying, recording, or by any information storage and retrieval system without permission in writing from the publisher.

Copyright © 2012 by M. P. DePaul
Jacksonville, FL
All rights reserved

http://mpdepaul.com
http://facebook.com/mpdepaul

This book is a work of fiction. Any references to real people, events, establishments, organizations, or locales are intended solely to provide a sense of authenticity and are used fictitiously. All other characters, incidents, and dialog are drawn from the author's imagination and not to be construed as real.

Cover art by Heather Scott
http://dragonmun.com

My dedication is to you, reader.

Take it or leave it. It's your choice.

Table of Contents

1: Rebirth in Blood	1
2: Concert for Magicians	15
3: Sorting Matters	34
4: Homeland Security	50
5: Blood-Soaked Fur	66
6: Eyes on Me	82
7: Strange Attraction	101
8: Knowledge Arcana	118
9: Mistrusted Existence	136
10: Tactical Espionage Action	152
11: Food and Family	174
12: Protested Existence	184
13: Wolf's Bane	200
14: Breaking Point	216
15: She's Not Legal	228
16: Taking Charge	244
17: First Kill	256
18: Falcon's Fire	271
19: The Fool's Warning	290

What if everything that you see, is more than what you see? The person next to you is a warrior and the space that appears empty is a door to another world? What if something appears that shouldn't? You either dismiss it or accept that there is more to the world than you think. Perhaps it is really a doorway, and if you choose to go inside, you'll find many unexpected things.

—Shigeru Miyamoto

1: Rebirth in Blood

Some say that every girl wants to make love to a vampire. What a load of crap. Then again, my experience has been a bit different from those generic love stories.

This is the tale of how my life became ridiculous. It all started when one of the teeth I lost grew back, although perhaps I should explain how I lost it in the first place. It'll be useful to know later on. It happened during my freshman year of high school, when I was a tiny and bubbly little 14-year old. Having just come out of my awkward middle school years, I was still wearing glasses that looked grossly oversized on my small face.

It was a Thursday in September before first period, and I was talking to my friend Amelia at her locker. "So have you been talking to Chad much?" Chad was someone we had recently met in our second period. He transferred to another school before the end of the year.

"Yeah."

"Isn't he hot?"

"I know! I wonder if he'll ask me out." He later did ask her out, and they dated for a few minutes, as usual.

Even I had to admit that my best friend, Amelia Marie Valentine, was hot. With shining black hair and bright green eyes, her very appearance was a sight to behold. Unlike some others at our school, she had brains as well as looks, though her grades were somewhat behind mine. Many of our classmates, however, cared little about her mental abilities, viewing her simply as the second hottest girl in our year. Needless to say, I was a bit jealous of her.

When Amelia closed her locker, we began to walk together to our respective classes. A few feet away, my eyes met a flier that someone had taped to the white-painted cinder block wall. It was an advertisement for the wrestling team that listed the names of the members alongside dates for their first several matches. I raised an eyebrow when I saw the name "Emily Rogers" on it. "I didn't know we had a girls' wrestling team."

"We don't." Amelia had dated a guy on the team, so she knew.

I scanned the other names on the flier and noticed that they were entirely masculine, like "Josh" or "Gerald." I scratched my head, trying to think of an explanation for the odd name. "Could it be a guy's name?" Being a guy and having a name like "Emily" would be pretty awkward. None of the members were pictured, only a few images of public domain clip art, one of which was a nude ancient Greek wrestler.

I decided to forget about it and continue heading to class, but I started moving before turning my head. At first I thought I inexplicably walked into a wall until I realized that it moved slightly, indicating instead that it was a person—a person who weighed a few hundred more pounds than I did. These pounds consisted of both muscle and fat. As usual, I lost my balance and fell backward. My clumsiness was something I was never proud of. My own fall was accompanied by the plopping sound of plastic against tile. I could see a giant pair of boulder-like legs turned toward a puddle of what appeared to be some fizzy brown liquid that had a plastic bottle with a red Coca-Cola label lying in it.

The legs turned around and I peered upward. Staring back at me was the largest woman I'd ever seen. She looked like she could split me in half with her bare hands. She had brown hair tied into a pony tail that ended at the base of her neck, and she was wearing a pair of athletic shorts along with a double extra large men's t-shirt and a sports jacket. Her shape indicated that she was a woman, but she seemed more masculine than most of the guys I knew. She didn't look happy that I made her drop her soda.

"What the hell, bitch?" The monster woman had a rather deep voice.

"Um…I'm…uh…sorry." As usual, I had trouble forming words when meeting this new and imposing individual.

"You better be! Buy me a new soda!"

Freaking out and hoping that I would live through this encounter, I reached for my backpack and pulled my wallet from it, which I unfortunately discovered was entirely devoid of cash.

"I'll go grab one," Amelia said, being kind in a way that I definitely needed at the moment. We were lucky that a vending machine was nearby.

Rebirth in Blood

I tried to stand up, but the monster woman forcefully pushed me back to the ground. "Ow! What the...?"

"You're not getting up until I get my soda."

"Here!" Amelia came back with a Coke and practically shoved it in our opponent's face.

The monster woman grunted and unscrewed the cap. Then she pushed me down when I tried to get up again.

"Damn it, let me up!" Now I was both scared and pissed off.

"Hey Emily," said a certain voice I hated, "I see you've got Lamy right where she belongs."

I mentioned that Amelia was considered the second hottest girl in our year. She was second only to Shelly Smith, the beautiful blonde aspiring cheerleader and winner of the Bitch of the Year award for five years running (yes, I made that part up). "Lamy" was her combination of "lame" and "Amy." Isn't it such a nice nickname? She had been the bane of my existence ever since late elementary school, and she was always looking for an excuse to make my life less enjoyable.

Ah, right. I forgot to mention my name earlier. When my parents got married, they thought it was funny that both of their last names, Able and Aulin, began with the letter A. Therefore, when they had their son, they named him Allen Arthur Able. Cute, right? Three and a half years after his birth, Allen's younger sister, Amy Allison Able, was born. Even though I wasn't the first-born child in my family, I was always listed first among my class in any school yearbook. Sometimes the people I knew or met, particularly Amelia, would call me "Triple A" as a nickname ("Double A" if they didn't know my middle name).

"Emily?" I turned to my arch-enemy, who stood above me to my left with a few members of her girl posse visible behind her.

"Yeah, retard. You know, Emily from the wresting team?"

I could taste the irony. Just a minute earlier I had been wondering who on the wrestling team would possibly have a name like "Emily" and then there she was, standing in the way of an otherwise normal day.

"Clean up the mess you made." Emily said, motioning me to get up as the warning bell sounded to signal that one minute remained until class. She stood like a tower, making clear to me the fact that she wouldn't move until I did as she said.

BLOOD ON FIRE

"Have fun with that." Shelly strolled off with a sarcastic grin.

Amelia offered me an arm to help me up and accompanied me to the girls' bathroom to fetch paper towels. "Triple A, as much as I'd like to bust that beast's lip open, I think we should just clean up and get away from her." Hearing Amelia so intimidated was definitely a rare occurrence.

"Agreed."

Once we'd gathered enough paper towels and started sopping up the soda, Emily turned and walked off. By the time we finished, Amelia and I were, of course, late for class and appropriately reprimanded.

That was my first run-in with Emily Rogers. It was far from my last.

A few weeks later I was minding my own business at lunch. I waited in line to get my spaghetti in meat sauce, an entrée seldom partaken by the majority of other students since, apparently, most are on strict diets of burgers, fries, and nothing else. I grabbed my chocolate milk and waited on the line to meet the hairnet-wearing woman at the cash register.

However, I then noticed who was in line in front of me. In fact, how could I not have considering how huge she was?

Crap, I'd better keep my distance. This was all I could think. The last thing I needed was even a glint of recognition from her, let alone actual interaction. I started to panic when I spotted two figures entering the line behind me. They were Shelly and her boy toy at the time, whose name I never bothered learning.

"Stop holding up the line, Lamy." Shelly recognized the distance I was keeping behind the Ogre Queen, which was a nickname that I thought of right at that very moment. Taking her tray by one hand, Shelly nudged me slightly, and I walked a few steps forward, still trying to keep my distance. "Move it!" She pushed me harder.

I was afraid of this. My balance was always bad, and Shelly wasn't exactly the weakest girl around. Her douche bag boyfriend gave a low chuckle. I was sure that she knew exactly what was about to happen to me.

I fell forward, impacting the floor hard. I found that I was clean aside from some scant dirt. The Ogre Queen, however, had a back covered in spaghetti.

"Ooh, Lamy, trying to get revenge for when Emily embarrassed you?"

I quickly scrambled to my feet as the Ogre Queen turned to face me, a look of raw rage on her face. "It was Shelly's fault!" I was desperate to get out of this situation somehow.

Rebirth in Blood

"Can you buy me a new shirt?" The back of the one she was wearing was covered in warm marinara. In truth, I couldn't buy her a new shirt. I still had no cash. I was going to make my lunch purchase using the account the school kept for me, which was funded by checks from my mom.

"But, I, it was..." I was too flustered to form a coherent sentence.

"Leave her alone already!" Apparently Amelia had noticed what was going on and now came up behind the Ogre Queen, looking quite pissed. "She hasn't done anything wrong."

"She ruined my shirt." The Ogre Queen didn't even look at Amelia. The lady at the register and the other students around were annoyed that the line wasn't moving.

"Just because you're bigger than everyone else doesn't mean you can boss them around, dyke!" Amelia was definitely brave.

"What did you say?" Now Ogre Queen turned to Amelia.

"Big girl on campus has to push everyone else around. My dad knows about you." Amelia's father was a local policeman. I would too many run-ins with him later.

"Shut up!"

"You want people to be afraid of you."

"I said shut up!"

"You think doing the popular girl's dirty work will actually make you worth something."

The Ogre Queen roared with rage and shoved Amelia, sending her falling backward to the ground.

"Amelia!" Seeing her being pushed like that filled me with determination. With the Ogre Queen's enormous back in front of me, I took the bravest action I had ever taken up to that point. It was also the stupidest.

I punched her. I punched the Ogre Queen on the back in the remains of my pasta. My wrist hurt. Horribly.

Suddenly two huge hands grabbed that wrist, and I found myself swinging around and then slamming into the ground face first. At the moment, I didn't feel like I was in pain.

Before I knew it, four different administrators were dragging the Ogre Queen away. She violently struggled with them. Amelia and another of my friends, Will, helped me up. Shelly just stood back and laughed to the point of asphyxiation.

Blood on Fire

When I was on my feet I tried to speak but only coughed. I could taste blood. I quickly covered my mouth with my one hand that didn't feel dead. Blood now covered that hand, along with something else. I examined it and found it covered in blood and holding two odd whitish objects. One was flat and rounded and the other pointed. Then I realized exactly how much my mouth hurt. I felt like I was going to faint. This confrontation had left me with broken wrist and two missing teeth. Amelia and Will tried to comfort me on the way to the nurse's office, escorted by an administrator—I was in too much pain to remember which one. I would later need to go to the hospital to have my wrist wrapped in a cast. As I suspected, my parents weren't happy. They ultimately refused to get me false teeth as a reminder of my mistake (they also wanted to avoid potential complications). As I lived with that huge gap in my mouth, I never expected that one of those teeth would grow back.

No, it wasn't a baby tooth. Remember when I mentioned vampires earlier? Yes, that was important. Even though I had friends, I wasn't exactly high on the social totem pole. I managed to stay away from the Ogre Queen for the next two years until that fateful week when my life changed in so many ways.

I woke up one morning during my junior year of high school from what felt like the best sleep of my life. I couldn't remember having any sort of dream, but if I did, then it must have been good. However, I felt curiously tired and just didn't want to move. I struggled to open my eyes as a blurry world appeared before me. I reached for my glasses, which had much smaller frames than the ones I had during my freshman year, from my nightstand and put them on. Even that small amount of movement was exhausting.

"Damn, what happened last night?" I felt like I had a hangover. "Have I been drinking?" Then I remembered that I had no idea what a hangover felt like since I wasn't one of the cool kids who illegally drank. I tried to remember the previous night's events. I had gone to see a movie called *The Adventures of Space Bear* with Will and Amelia. It was a weird movie about a bear mauling people in space. Then I came home, and then...that was where I was stuck. Somehow I couldn't remember anything at all past that point, which bugged me.

As I fought my body's desire not to move, I glanced at the clock by my bed, finding out from those glowing red electronic numbers that the time was 11 A.M. "Aw crap! I'm late!" I scrambled upward and flung open the door to my bedroom. "Mom! Why didn't you wake me up?" But mom wasn't there. In fact, the house was empty and eerily silent. "Mom?" None of the curtains on the

Rebirth in Blood

windows had been drawn either, so it was surprisingly dark for that time of day. My father's absence was normal since he would have left for work hours ago. My brother would also be absent since he had long since moved off to college and was only really around at Christmas time and parts of the summer. My mother, though, only worked at night, teaching remedial writing classes at the local community college, so she should've been home.

I went to the front window that overlooked our driveway. We had too much crap stored in our garage, so mom usually parked her car outside. It would have been gone if she were absent since she most likely would be using it to run errands.

I drew the curtain aside, but as I did, the sunlight that poured in was blinding and excruciatingly painful. My skin felt like it was on fire. I quickly forgot about how tired I was and instinctively closed the curtain. I backed away, wondering what had just happened. The sun had never done that before. I had always sunburned easily all throughout my childhood, but that was nothing compared to what I just felt. The pain quickly disappeared, but now I was very confused.

"The sun...why can't I look outside? What's going on?" I spoke out loud because I hoped in vain that someone might hear me, only to be reminded that I was very much alone. Then I felt an awful pain in my stomach. I mean, of course I had felt hunger before. Who hasn't? Granted, hunger for a middle-class American is nothing like that of someone living in a Third World country, but that's beside the point. This hunger felt as if I had a ferocious beast inside of me that yearned for sustenance and would do anything to get it. I ran to the kitchen, having to duck around a skylight along the way, and flung open the door to the refrigerator. My eyes met with the pizza that mom, dad, and I had shared very recently, at least according to my memory, which was made with plenty of cheese and garlic, just the way I liked it. I had always loved garlic. Hardly thinking, I grabbed a slice and stuffed it into my mouth.

It tasted disgusting, like I was eating sand covered in battery acid. I started gagging uncontrollably. Dropping the pizza on the floor, I ran to the sink. I closed my eyes and let out a torrent of projectile vomit. I apologize for that image, but I'm not sure how else to describe it. My head hanging, I opened my eyes and looked down.

"What the hell?" I backed away from the sink, which was full of blood. *Why blood?* I knew that in any medical situation, vomiting blood is an extremely bad sign. My glasses had become lopsided, so I nervously adjusted them, but then I caught sight of the skin tone of my hand, which was nearly pearl white. I had always had pale skin, but never this pale.

I spat several times to clear my mouth of as much blood as I could, but as I did, I felt something that shouldn't have been there. *My canine tooth?* The Ogre Queen had knocked out my left canine and my leftmost incisor. The incisor was still gone, but the canine was back. I ran my tongue along it, and it was much longer than it was before being knocked out. It also had a syringe-like point at the end of it. I then felt for the canine that hadn't be knocked out and found that it too was longer and pointier than usual.

Though math was never my best subject in school, the factors now seemed to add up in my mind. *Blood…sunlight…pale skin…fangs… could I be a…* I couldn't believe that this thought was actually crossing my mind …*vampire?* The properties of vampires are common knowledge considering the wealth of literature available about them. Let's face it, the only way I wouldn't have known about them is if my parents had locked me in a cage and given me no mental stimulation. Only one test remained, and I needed a mirror to confirm it.

I rushed over to my bathroom, which had been mine alone for a while after my brother moved out, and stood in front of the mirror inside. "What?…Am I a vampire or not?" I had expected to see nothing, but my reflection was right there in front of me. I supposed that it was a stroke of luck, though, since I could examine how I had changed. My body structure and facial features were all intact, as was my long, straight, light brown hair that was the same color and length it was supposed to be, reaching just below my shoulder blades. However, my skin was a deathly shade of white and the eyes behind my glasses were clearly blood red in color instead of their previous brown. I then opened my mouth wide and saw my pointy new teeth.

I kept examining my face, growing increasingly more certain of my conclusion, though I tried to convince myself that vampires weren't real and that I was just having some bizarre dream. Isn't that usually supposed to be the case? Only then did I notice my clothing. I wasn't wearing my pajamas but rather the T-shirt and jeans that I had worn to the movie theater, but unlike that night, they were covered with what looked like rancid brown rotting blood.

"Ew!" I smelled my shoulder, which stank with a sickening odor of death. "Gross!" I tore my clothes off and leaped into the shower. I thoroughly washed every inch of my pale body, careful to not miss any spot. Though I never kept my room very organized, I always valued cleanliness. When I was finished, I dried my body off and smelled myself again. The stench was gone.

Relieved from my new cleanliness and wearing my towel as a robe (it was big while I was small), I walked into the living room, sat down on the couch, and grabbed the remote control for my family's enormous HDTV, which was surrounded by pictures of my brother and me and my mom's various trinkets that she inherited from her parents and other family members. Normally I didn't really watch the news much at all, but I figured that maybe I could find out something about how in God's name I became a vampire. Of course it was a long shot, but I figured that it was worth trying.

I tuned in to the cable news stations like CNN, MSNBC, and Fox News, but they all just reported the usual economic, political, and social gloom and doom. Luckily though, the local news happened to be on as well.

The first station I tried was Channel 3, whose anchorman had hair like a wax mannequin. "Welcome to Channel 3 News, Orlando's finest." (Orlando, Florida was the major city that housed the local stations for the county I lived in even though Jacksonville was closer.) "This is Niles Granite reporting. For our first story this afternoon, the town of Palm Coast is still trying to solve the cases of the mysterious chain of three murders that occurred there recently, all of whom were females between the ages of 15 and 18 and were found in their bedrooms seemingly drained of all blood. A similar murder happened in Jacksonville. To further add to the mystery, all the bodies disappeared before coroners were able to perform autopsies. There are no leads as to who could have taken them away. Authorities have yet to release the victims' identities."

This was worrying. I couldn't help wondering whether I was one of those girls, especially since the anchor had said that their blood had been drained, which I knew was something a vampire would do. I mean, vampires are undead, so I figured that I must have died, which, as I thought about it, worried me even more.

I needed more information, so I decided to check Channel 7 to see if they had anything to add or another angle to give. A doll-like woman who gave her name as Delta Stone appeared on screen and partly reiterated what the guy on Channel 3 had already said until she came to "All the victims were found with odd circular intrusions in their necks. The cause of these wounds is currently unknown." Circular intrusions? To me that sounded like lot fang wounds.

Blood on Fire

I figured that maybe Channel 45 and its host Rock Rivers would show something different: "The local liberals have done nothing to prevent the murder of our young women." Okay seriously, even I, a mere teenager, knew that this probably wasn't a political matter. I then checked the remaining Orlando stations like 2 and 9. They had little else to add. I had heard what I needed to hear, at least for the moment, so I shut the TV off.

I walked back to my room but I didn't sit on my bed, noticing dried blood just like what was on my clothing. Other than that, my room looked as it should have with the Pokémon and Final Fantasy posters on the wall, the small TV with my game consoles in the corner, and my desk covered in old homework. I sat in my desk chair, deep in thought. *So here I am, an undead blood sucker. What exactly happened?* The thoughts raced through my head. I was still so hungry, and I was afraid to try eating from the fridge again, suspecting that drinking blood would be the only way to quell the beast inside. My general exhaustion also still hadn't let up at all.

I looked around my room for clues as to what may have happened, but the only thing I spotted was my cell phone. I picked it up only to discover that the battery was dead, so I plugged it in to charge. When I was able turn it on, I took a look at the screen. The date on it said November, which was the correct month, but it also said Saturday. I had gone to the movie theater on Monday night. Apparently I had missed out on a chunk of my life…or death…or unlife…or whatever. It also said that I had 22 missed calls—15 calls from Will, 6 from Amelia, and 1 other from an unknown number, which was probably a wrong number. I figured that my friends had been worried about my disappearance. I also had voice mail.

"You have three new messages. First message."

"Hey Amy, it's Will…I know we just went to the movies yesterday, but Amelia just got three tickets to the Lupia concert Saturday night, and we just wanted to know if you want to come along. Also, why weren't you in school today? Uh…anyway, talk to you later, bye!"

"Next message."

"Hey Amy, it's Will again. We're getting a bit worried about you since you've been missing and nobody can get in touch with you. Are you okay? Call back please."

"Next message."

"Triple A, it's Amelia…where the hell are you?"

Rebirth in Blood

"End of new messages."

Suddenly the doorbell rang. I rushed toward the front door purely out of habit, ready to greet the visitor, whoever it was, but then two very important thoughts crossed my mind. The first was that I was a vampire with a weakness for sunlight, which would inevitably pour in through the door. The second was that I was only wearing a towel.

Another ring came, but I ignored it, heading back into my room. I opened my closet, searching for proper attire to match my new vampiric nature, but the best I could find was my red tank top and black skirt. Though I always thought I looked better wearing dark colors, I'd never been much of a Goth, so I didn't have anything more befitting of a vampire. I also figured that black and red would be colors that, with a little luck, wouldn't show blood very well.

After dressing, I had a crazy idea. I rushed over to the freezer. Desperately digging inside, risking frostbite of my now dead fingers, I found an unopened pack of steaks that were originally bought fresh. It was lying sideways, and it had frozen blood collected at its side.

I looked at it, sickened at what I was about to do. It was a great idea, just a very disgusting one. I tore open the package and bit off some of the blood, letting it melt in slowly in my mouth, which took much longer than I expected due to my complete lack of body heat. It also didn't taste how I expected it to; instead, it seemed more like how I would expect a below-average undercooked burger to taste. Eating frozen beef blood felt strange, but it was oddly satisfying to a new vampire.

The blood barely relieved my hunger at all—I had a huge appetite for more, and the little frozen blood I could get from the rest of the meat in the freezer would do nothing to help. I also didn't feel like waiting for the meat itself to defrost. I threw it back into the freezer.

Then I heard my cell phone start sounding off its usual *Super Mario Bros.* theme. I rushed back to my bedroom and grabbed the device. Will was calling. This was it. I wondered whether I would sound any differently on the phone. After all, this would be my first interaction with a human since becoming a vampire and having been missing for several days. I nervously accepted the call. "Hello?"

"Amy? Is it really you?" Will's voice showed that he was both surprised and excited.

"Um, yeah, who else would answer at this number?"

BLOOD ON FIRE

"Amy, you've been missing for the past four days. In fact, Amelia just dropped by and rang your doorbell in person and she said that there was no answer." Well at least I knew who was at the door.

"Yeah, sorry about that."

"What have you been doing all this time?"

I had to think for a second. Should I tell the truth? How much trouble would a lie cause? Should I have even answered the phone in the first place? "I've been...sick." It was a standard response.

"With what? You could've just answered your phone to say so."

"Um...it was a really bad virus."

"Then why didn't your parents answer the door? We would've understood if they just sent us away."

"The doctor said no outside contact at all."

"That's...weird. You were quarantined?" He was definitely suspicious. I could tell that knew something was amiss with my explanation. "But now you're okay?"

"Yeah, I'm fine, and I don't really want to talk about it anymore." Perhaps I shouldn't have snapped at him, but whatever.

"Sorry, it's just that it's not like you to suddenly disappear. Your friends were worried about you. On top of that, considering the recent murders, how could we not have been concerned?"

"You have a point."

"So what exactly did you catch?"

I couldn't think of a real sickness on the spot. "I'll, uh, I'll tell you soon, okay?" I could only think of how to stall at this point.

"...Okay..." He seemed to accept that, at least temporarily. "So...I was wondering if you wanted to—"

"That Lupia concert tonight, right?"

He sounded shocked at my knowledge. "I see you got that voicemail I left Tuesday night."

"Uh...yeah..."

"...Would you like to go?...Amelia and I still can't find anybody else to take the third ticket."

"How did she get the tickets?"

"She says that they just arrived in the mail this week. Apparently she won a contest she doesn't remember entering. We checked. The tickets are legit."

Rebirth in Blood

"Oh…cool…" I paused, unsure of how to continue.

"…So do you want to go?"

I needed to think. I didn't exactly want to worry my friends any more than I already had by declining this very rare offer, but I had to figure out if I would be in any danger if I accepted. Sunlight was my first concern. "What time is the concert?"

"It starts at 8:30 but we should probably get there by 8:00."

The sun would be down by then, so that wasn't a problem. Next was the matter of blood. "How many people do you think will be there?"

"It didn't sell out, but it'll be pretty crowded."

Crap…what should I do? I didn't know what sort of vampire I was, so I wondered about whether or not I would go crazy on a blood-drinking rampage around so many people. It was very possible that this whole thing would go horribly wrong.

"Amy…are you still there?"

"Um…yeah, I am."

"…So are you up for it?"

Still not wanting to feel left out among my friends, I decided that I needed to find out how I would act around people eventually. "Sure, I'll go."

"Great! So…do you need us to pick you up?"

"I could always take my mom's car." I said this jokingly.

"Hell no!" Will was serious. He knew about the problems I had driving. Auto insurance for a 16 year old with a learner's permit was expensive enough, and my parents didn't want to take the chance that I would make the price any higher by being terrible at driving. "Amelia can drive both of us, it's no problem."

"Alright, fine, she can drive." I was hoping for him to suggest that anyway.

"Thank God." I heard Will say this under his breath.

"What was that?"

"Oh, nothing."

I yawned. Being awake in the daytime was continuously tiring my out. "Well, I have some stuff to take care of, so I'll see you then, okay?"

"Alright, be ready at 7:15."

"Sure."

"See you later."

"Bye."

BLOOD ON FIRE

I ended the call. I figured that perhaps I just needed to be up at night instead. Though my bed was filthy, my pillow looked untouched, so I grabbed it and a blanket from my closet and staggered lethargically into the living room as I set my phone's alarm for 6:45 PM. Then I passed out on the couch.

2: Concert for Magicians

Normally, a young girl's best friend (forever), or BFF if you will, will be another girl. Such was the case for me and Amelia. However, I suppose that I did have another best friend.

Will, obviously, was a guy. When I first learned that his full name was William Melchior Jadis, I couldn't help remarking that only his first name was halfway normal. Let's compare it to mine, Amy Allison Able. Amy and Allison are nothing special. I mean let's face it, how many other girls have those names? Then again, I suppose few of them would have initials like A.A.A., and Able is uncommon but not unexpected. Anyway, to this day, I still don't know where Jadis came from and Melchior isn't exactly normal.

Will was a great friend of both me and Amelia, but he curiously never asked either of us out. It crossed my mind once that he might perhaps be gay, but I quickly realized that he definitely wasn't. He had male friends just like any guy, and he was definitely interested in girls—he just never asked any out.

As I said, I was always at the beginning of the yearbook, but Will was always at the top of the class. While my grades in school were nothing to scoff at, his put him far ahead of everyone else. Will's appearance, however, was fairly average. Though I always found him at least a bit attractive, he didn't really stand out. He was thin and neither particularly tall nor muscular with bushy brown hair as well as some awkward scruff on his face that seemed to never go away.

Will is excellent at recounting events to me, so here's what he did after that phone call.

"That was strange…even for her." He shut the two halves of his outdated phone and stepped out of his bedroom. The tension of that conversation had made his throat dry, so he went to the kitchen, for a glass of water. He found his mother there examining a collection of cards with various designs on them as she puffed on her usual cigarette.

"Hey mom…are you doing a tarot reading or something?"

"I…suppose you could say that." Her tone told Will that she was hiding something, as she often was. She was an intelligent middle-aged brunette notorious among her extended family for not telling the whole truth.

"Right." The sarcasm in Will's voice was obvious. He grabbed a glass from the cabinet above the sink and dispensed ice and cold water from the front of their refrigerator.

"Hey, don't take that tone with me, young man." Minerva Jadis turned to face her son with a stern look.

Will took a long sip. "Mom, over the last few weeks, you've been in and out of the house at weird hours."

"Will, please just leave me alone for now." She turned back to her cards.

Will gulped the rest of his water, left his glass in the sink, and uttered under his breath, "Dad was probably sick of this crap."

"What was that?"

"Nothing." He walked back to his bedroom through the living room, but he stopped when he noticed an odd cardboard box on the couch. He took a look at it. It was small, cube-shaped, and full of packing peanuts. It was, naturally, addressed to the very house it was currently in, but the return address surprised him. It came from the nearby BioLogic research lab—only about a half-hour's drive away. It was a strange thing for him to find. "Huh, doesn't Amy's dad work for that company?"

My father had earned his Ph.D. in biological sciences relatively quickly and had risen through the ranks of university research until he was hired by the higher-paying private firm. He was usually so busy with his research that it was nothing short of a miracle that he actually managed to meet his wife and raise two kids.

"What are you doing?" Will's mother came away from her work and stood by the doorway to the kitchen. Her face said that she was disappointed at her son.

Will sighed. "Mom, have you been exploiting our family's knowledge for a few quick bucks?" It was the first conclusion he could arrive at considering the facts in front of him.

CONCERT FOR MAGICIANS

"I wouldn't call it that," she said calmly, still puffing on the cigarette that quickly became almost too short to smoke, "but God only knows I'm not getting anything from that other dead end job." She worked as a waitress at a mediocre local restaurant and hated every minute of it.

Will shook his head. "Don't you think that it might be a little dangerous? I mean, didn't our family almost die out for that reason?"

Minerva put out her cigarette butt in a nearby ash tray and immediately lit up another. "Will, nobody remembers that crap. Just relax, okay."

Will didn't answer, only giving his mother a frown as he retreated to his bedroom.

"Oh, Will."

"What?" Will was hardly in a mood to continue their conversation.

"Have fun at that concert tonight, but don't make any moves on those girlfriends of yours. You can't afford child support."

Will didn't reply; he only continued on to his room and grabbed his cell phone. Now that he had gotten in touch with me, he needed to make another call.

Though Will found Amelia attractive—I'd even go so far as to say he wanted to have sex with her—he may or may not have been the only guy who could be content with just being her friend and nothing else. She had a new boyfriend every week, sometimes literally.

Amelia was in her room dealing with on some precalculus homework (she was amazing at math) that was due that coming Monday. She wanted to finish it relatively quickly since she was going to a concert that night and was going to spend Sunday afternoon with her current boyfriend, Doug. The third concert ticket didn't go to him despite my absence since he had work that night. She was interrupted, however, when her iPhone chimed the chorus of one of her favorite Lupia songs.

"Hey Will, what's up?"

"I've made contact! Amy's alive!"

"Really?" This perked her interest. "Where has she been? Perhaps she disappeared with a new boyfriend or something?"

"That's something you would do."

"Hey, maybe she took the hint."

"She wasn't very clear on what happened to her, but it's good to know she wasn't murdered."

Blood on Fire

"You've been really worried about those murders, haven't you? Maybe you have a thing for Amy?" I was surprisingly slow on the uptake that these two joked about this subject when I wasn't around.

"Oh come on, you were worried too."

"Yeah, but the likelihood that it would be her was low. Besides, nothing about Triple A surprises me. She's always had really weird things happen to her. Remember that time when she arrived to school late because she had to dry off her homework after accidentally bringing it into the shower with her?" Amelia always remembered some of the most embarrassing aspects of my life. What else are friends for?

"How could I not remember?" Will felt bad for laughing, but remembering me in that situation was simply too funny. "Anyway, is it okay if you pick both me and her up later for the concert?"

"Not a problem."

"Alright, I'll see you then."

"See ya."

Will ended the call. He was looking forward to the concert that night—it was a chance to escape from everything related to his mother. However, now he was bored. He had finished his homework the night before—he was one of the very few high school students to actually do homework on a Friday night, a merit that I, unfortunately, didn't have. With his mother poured over her cards, he knew that making too much noise would be bad, so his best option was reading a book.

He walked through the door next to his bedroom, which contained the library passed down through the generations of his family. In his childhood, he had spent countless hours in this room immersed inside of its endless tomes.

His family possessed a ton of textual knowledge, much of which was unavailable in a normal library, such as strange topics like ley lines and Gozerian destructor forms. Most of the important books were either in that one room or strewn about the house. The rest were in multiple storage units. He took one at random—he had read most of them anyway. Its cover said:

Bram Stoker

Dracula

"Eh. It's a bit standard, but whatever." It was an original edition, one of the newer volumes in the library at just over a century old. He read fast enough to finish half of the book by the time Amelia picked him up.

Concert for Magicians

Luckily, November brought night on earlier than, say, July, partly thanks to the switch from Daylight Savings to Standard Time. My phone's alarm woke me just as the last rays of sunlight were dying outside. Pushing myself up from the couch, I noticed an obvious difference from that morning, which was the distinct lack of any sort of tiredness. I stood up and walked over to the front window—the same window that earlier that day had repulsed me with blinding light. I drew the curtain aside again, but now I could stand it. The small amount of sunlight remaining outside was irritating both to my skin and my eyes, but I felt that I could easily walk in it without much of a problem. I also discovered that my mother's car was still outside, which meant that my parents were definitely still missing. Where could they be all day on a Saturday? I was extremely worried, but the impending concert was higher on my list of priorities (shamefully so, might I add).

I needed to clean off my glasses and straighten out my hair and clothing, figuring that I should look my best to distract people from noticing that I had become a vampire. I couldn't be sure of how obvious the change would be to others. I tested how far I could open my mouth without revealing my fangs. Concealing them was difficult since they were so long and pointy. They seemed to be noticeable every time I spoke. I hoped that I was just being overly self-conscious.

Next, I took out some makeup. I knew the importance of looking my best, but I was usually just too lazy to bother applying more than just a tiny bit of makeup unless it was for a special occasion. I attempted to make myself look less pale and had little success. "Great...now I look like a dead hooker." I removed some of what I applied, hoping that just a little bit of blush would make me look alive. A thought then occurred to me: *if vampires aren't supposed to see themselves in mirrors, how are they supposed to look their best?*

Right as I was almost finished, the doorbell chimed. "Just a sec!" I rushed to make a few last second adjustments to my appearance. I then grabbed my Sonic the Hedgehog messenger bag and stuffed my wallet, cell phone, Nintendo 3DS, and Lupia CD (I figured I could perhaps get it autographed) inside it. (I preferred this bag over a backpack or purse because it could fulfill the role of both.) I then slapped on the best pair of tennis shoes I had but I failed to tie the laces on the left one correctly. Apparently being a vampire does nothing to relieve one's natural clumsiness. I rushed to the front door and tripped, hitting my head with a loud thud. "Ow!"

I had actually broke bones in the past from mundane tasks. Just thought I'd put that out there.

Will and Amelia heard the impact from outside just as they were becoming sick of waiting. I wasn't sure if my hearing had become better, but I could hear every word they said.

"Wow...she sounds excited," Amelia said.

"You think she's okay?" Will asked.

"Knowing her, she will be in a few minutes."

Will knocked on the door. "Amy, you okay?"

Back on the other side, I, purely out of habit, held my head from the pain I would normally feel until I realized that I actually wasn't in all that much pain at all. All that fall did to me was knock my glasses off center. Now this was something that I knew I could get used to. "Yeah, I'm fine!" I stood up and grabbed the doorknob. *Maybe mom and dad will come back while I'm gone,* I hoped, *or maybe something will come over me and I'll go on a killing spree.* Honestly, at that point, I had no idea what would happen. I unlocked the door and opened it.

So there I was, doing my best to greet my friends with a sprightly, closed-mouthed smile. I could tell that Will noticed something strange, though. He looked me over like a doctor greeting a patient would, and he seemed particularly fixated on my eyes. I hoped that maybe he would just think that I rubbed them too much and turned them red, although they hardly looked that way.

Amelia didn't seem to notice any change in me at all. She had her phone out and was sending a text message to her boyfriend. This behavior was normal for her. Although I was her best friend, her whirlwind of romances usually stole first priority in her mind.

"So guys, what's going on? We ready for this?" I tried to sound enthusiastic despite my creeping feeling of dread at what might happen that night.

"Amy, is something wrong with you?" Will just had to ask.

I peered at him, straining for a response as his grey eyes pierced into me, but I could only think about the red liquid of life coursing inside of him, bringing sustenance to every cell of his body with every beat of his heart. Now...and now...and now still. I could almost feel his heartbeat...

"Amy?"

"Huh? Oh, sorry! Must've spaced out there. Nah, I'm fine." I tried to give the best artificial smile I could to hide my terror at the way my mind just wandered. The remaining sunlight was also really starting to irritate me, so I wanted to get moving as soon as I could.

"You seem like something's bothering you." Will couldn't leave me alone.

"Bothering me? What do you mean?"

Luckily, Amelia had just finished her text messaging. "Sorry to interrupt your flirting, but unlike mine, yours can continue while we're on the road." Amelia wasn't dumb enough to text while driving. "We need to get going." She jumped into the driver's seat of her bright red Chevrolet Camaro parked in the driveway next to mom's blue Ford Taurus. Amelia's parents treated their daughter quite well—well enough to buy a 17-year-old a Camaro. I found this fact surprising myself since her father was so strict when he did police work.

Will and I shared one last awkward glance, him curious and me nervous, before getting into the car, Will in the passenger seat and me in the back.

The concert hall was in the city of Daytona, approximately half an hour away. The conversation on the highway was awkwardly quiet. Clearly, Will still suspected that I was hiding something from him; in fact, I figured he suspected that I was hiding a lot from him, and, well, I was. I wasn't ready to tell him, but I was ready for his blood. Inside of him was a treasure trove of red gold that I just wanted to sink my fangs into and...

"So Triple A." Amelia broke my trance.

"Uh...yeah?"

"Why have you been so hard to reach this past week?"

"I...uh..."

"I mean, you've been missing while others have turned up dead and then here you are, and it seems like you're just fine."

"Well...you know..."

"Not really," Will said, "you said you were sick but you didn't offer much beyond that."

"Look..." I gazed at my feet, avoiding the car's mirrors which reflected my friends' eyes "I...I just don't feel like talking about it now, okay?"

"Oh come on," Amelia said, "We're your friends."

Blood on Fire

"It's a secret."

Amelia sighed. "Fine, have it your way."

"So, uh, Will, how much farther have you gotten in *Devil May Cry 3*?" I needed to change the subject, so I decided to bring up video games—one of Will's favorite subjects, second only to the written word in book form.

"I'm still stuck on the first fight against Virgil." (That's a character.)

I was lucky that my distraction worked and kept Will talking for the rest of the ride. Amelia only spoke at the mention of *Resident Evil*, one of her favorite game series. For some reason, Amelia loved anything with zombies. I was sure that she would have loved to either fight or become the undead.

Finally, we arrived at the auditorium. I could see a long line leading out of it with people impatiently waiting with their tickets to get into the glass-covered building that was essentially shaped like a fancy box surrounded by a desolate parking lot. The bouncers at the entrance were large and imposing, wearing sunglasses despite the sun having completely disappeared into the night.

Will took a long look at the line before entering it. "It's times like this that I wish I brought my DS with me."

I reached into my bag and pulled out my Nintendo 3DS and smiled at him tauntingly, showing my teeth. Of course, that was a big mistake. When I realized it, I faked a cough and covered my mouth. Will looked like he had noticed something strange, but I guess he decided not to question it.

Waiting in line was simple enough for Will and Amelia, but it was a tortuous experience for me. My battling Pokémon within weren't enough to distract me from the adults, teens, kids, men, and women, all of whom could feed the hunger that constantly threatened to overwhelm me. All of them were peach, tan, brown, or black on the outside but red (or blue, scientifically) on the inside. They all looked so delicious, and I was starving.

"May I see your ticket please?"

What would my fangs feel like just cutting through that outer covering to savor that sweet liquid inside?

"Ma'am, may I please see your ticket?"

I knew it would be far more desirable than melting beef blood.

"Your ticket please!"

"Oh, sorry! Here." I handed the large male bouncer my ticket. He looked back at me, menacingly annoyed. *Come on...get it together...get it together...I*

CONCERT FOR MAGICIANS

need to stay focused...and not on blood...delicious blood. I knew that this time around, grabbing a Snickers wouldn't relieve the hunger.

"Triple A, there are people behind you, and they want to move," Amelia said.

"Aw crap!" I almost ran forward, trying to get out of their way.

Will and Amelia each stopped by the concession to get soda and candy.

"Do you want anything, Amy?" Will motioned toward the stand, extending an offer.

"Uh, no thanks."

"Are you sure? You look like you're starving. What about those garlic potato chips you love? I think they have them here. I'll get you some if you don't have any money."

This was one offer that I absolutely had to refuse. "No, really, I'm fine, thanks."

"Okay then."

Even when we found our seats and had the ability to rest, I was still ailing from hunger. Will led the group through the stands followed first by Amelia closely and then me slowly and awkwardly. We took our seats, Will on the right, Amelia in the middle, and me on the left. The audience was quite crowded. Lupia's fan base seemed to be growing. The stage we faced was set up in a minimalist fashion for a concert with only microphones, drums, cymbals, amps, and speakers visible at the moment.

"Hmm...there's still 10 minutes left," Will said, "I wonder if Lupia's going to have anyone open for her."

"Most of the details of this concert are a secret," Amelia responded, "which, if you ask me, is something she pulls too often."

"Yeah, secrets get annoying after a while." This was a fact that Will knew all too well. Then something amusing must have crossed his mind. "Hey Amy, remember that time you..." Looking over at me, he had a reason for not finishing his question.

Blood...blood...blood... My mind had just one focus

"Amy, are you okay?" To him I must have looked like I was having a psychotic episode.

Will...blood...Amelia...blood...

Amelia had also noticed. "Triple A?" She shook me, but I made no reaction.

"Amy, come on, what's wrong?" Now Will was more worried than ever.

BLOOD ON FIRE

Blood...blood...blood...blood...blood...blood...

"Amy, answer me! Come on!"

"Are you all ready to see Lupia?" a man's voice said from onstage. Nearly everyone in the audience stood up and made a deafening cheer, creating a rather chaotic atmosphere.

Will kept examining me while Amelia kept shaking me. That was the moment that I broke, the very moment that my relationship with my friends changed permanently.

Sparklers flared onstage along with smoke. Will couldn't help glancing away to see the booming spectacle. It was always cool in video form, but seeing it in person was different.

When he looked back to me, he was surprised at what he saw: I looked like I was hugging Amelia, which I guess would be accurate in a sense. I was grasping her tightly. Seeing me hug her wasn't unusual, but Will couldn't think of an explanation for why I would suddenly hug her right at that odd moment. He peered where my head was buried next to Amelia's. My hair was covering my face, but he could see a thin red stream emerging from underneath, which was nothing short of alarming.

I bit her because she was the closest to me. What Amelia felt was a blissful relaxation. Of the few cares in the world she had, they just seemed to drift away in a calm release. Her mind was focused on one person, and only one person.

As for me, I tasted chocolate. Specifically, it was milk chocolate, my favorite kind. I had tasted human blood before whenever I got a cut in my mouth or when my teeth were knocked out, and I remembered it tasting more like metal than chocolate. *Why chocolate?* I felt like I was taking a piece of Amelia into myself, a piece of someone who mattered to me. Whereas I felt so little after eating that beef blood, with Amelia I felt invigorated and full of a strength the likes of which I had never known before. The feeling of her skin against my teeth, against my tongue, as I held her ever so close to me was just an indescribably amazing feeling. Then I realized exactly what I was doing.

I released my fangs from Amelia's neck quickly and sloppily, splashing blood all over my own hair and on Amelia's clothing. As I did so, Will could see my blood-covered fangs clearly. He now knew what had become of me, especially as one so well-read in the occult. He definitely knew that I was a vampire, as would anybody who saw what he saw. Amelia slumped downward in her seat as the crowd all around us continued cheering, unaware of what had just happened.

The show on stage continued without a hitch. Lupia wasn't her real name, only her stage name. None of her fans knew her real name—she kept it hidden well even while working as a performer. Luckily for her, she wasn't popular enough to be targeted by tabloids. She knew the drill; after all, performing on stage was what she loved more than just about anything else in the world. She was one of the few musicians who could actually spread an environmental or spiritual message with subtlety, so she avoided limiting her fan base to the usual hippies to whom the blatant versions of her messages usually applied. In fact, the messages in her songs were sometimes so cryptic that many of her fans didn't even pick up on them, liking her mainly for her value as a musical artist (or in the case of many of her male fans, because she was hot). She had her critics—a ton of them—but on that night she was surrounded by fans.

"Okay Daytona," came her sweet voice, "prepare yourselves...because I'm going to rock you to your very soul!" As the smoke cleared, her tall, dark-haired figure became visible. Her femininity was accentuated by high-heeled boots, fishnet stockings, a mini-skirt, and a tank top that showed very visible cleavage, all of which were subdued shades of blue and purple. Isn't it amazing how female musicians can make dressing like an expensive prostitute look so awesome and stylish? She held a shining red electric guitar (unlike many environmentalists, acoustic just didn't suit her), which she immediately started shredding on, filling the air with sweet sound.

"Amy, what the hell happened to you?" Will had to yell over the music. Lupia had switched to vocals as the band with her took over the instrumentals, obscuring any real chance of conversation.

I just awkwardly stared at Will with no idea of what to say or do. I took a look at my victim next to me, seeing Amelia slumped over and seemingly devoid of life. I covered my mouth, horrified, and I could only think, *Did I...did I kill her?*

Will, seeing my horror, which apparently revealed to him that I was no longer a threat, bent over Amelia and pulled her hair aside for a better view of where I bit her. The entry points of my fangs had immediately healed, leaving behind circular red marks. However, I had spilled a lot of blood over her neck and shirt. Will direly felt for a pulse along Amelia's wrist. "She's alive!"

BLOOD ON FIRE

I let out a sigh of relief. "I'm sorry! I'm really really sorry!" I was desperate to not lose Will's friendship.

Will arranged Amelia into a more comfortable and natural-looking position, making her unconsciousness look less conspicuous. "Just act natural for now! We'll deal with this later!"

I couldn't look toward either of my friends; I just felt terrible. I had been unable to control myself, and I was scared about what might happen if I were to lose control again. I was also scared about what Amelia would think after she regained consciousness. I looked toward the stage and Lupia's graceful movements that went along with her lyrics. I wondered why someone like her couldn't be in my position. After all, she was much prettier and even taller than me (I was about 5'1" while her website listed her as 6'0"). She was even much better endowed (and, in fact, so was Amelia). I always thought that the prettiest of girls were supposed to be the ones who ended up as vampires. I thought Lupia would probably be much better at handling my situation than I was.

When the lights onstage flashed as part of the performance, I noticed a smudge on my glasses. I removed them to wipe it off but then noticed that it was a drop of blood. Instinctively, I licked it off. *Aw damn it!* Now I was more disappointed at myself. I was barely even paying attention to Lupia's performance, despite her doing one of my favorite of her songs.

Will did his best to avoid even looking at me, trying to focus on Lupia instead. Amelia, meanwhile, was sleeping peacefully—which, in fact, made me feel even worse because I was causing her to miss a show that I was sure she was excited about. Moving her was impossible; people would see the blood on her and think that she was murdered. I also might have been tempted to lick all that blood off (it was still fresh, after all).

Lupia had gotten into her usual groove at this point. To her, this was one of her better performances. She had just finished her song "Meltdown," performing her vocals perfectly and practically tearing up the stage with her guitar, and now she was getting ready for something to completely blow the audience away.

"Okay!" Lupia shouted, her microphone broadcasting her voice from all directions, "I don't think I've encountered this much awesomeness from an audience in any other city I've been to!" Her statement was met with loud cheers from her fans. "Well, I do believe that all of you have heard these songs before." She received some more cheers, with one guy yelling "I love you!" as loud as he could. "But I've been working on something new for the past few weeks and I just finished it in time for tonight! Do you want to hear it?" The audience returned great enthusiasm.

A new song? I thought. Finally, something had caught my attention in a good way.

"I can't hear you! Do you want something new?" It was hard to imagine the auditorium becoming any louder than that. "Alright! Here we go! Hit it Joe!" (She addressed her drummer, a young man). Joe moved his hands deftly to start the beat.

However, Lupia found herself upstaged.

Suddenly, several rows ahead of my own, a girl stood up and leapt onto the stage. I think I should clarify that: she leapt onto the stage, meaning that she didn't get up, run to the edge of it and jump on it; no, she actually leapt from her seat right onto the stage. Needless to say, the members of the crowd were silent as they fixed their gaze on this strange figure.

She looked only slightly younger than me, though she had a fuller figure (of course). She had blonde hair and was wearing a tight black body suit like some kind of secret agent from an action movie. The skin visible on her head and hands was deathly pale—like mine.

Lupia was speechless for several seconds before asking "Who are you?" Her microphone allowed everyone to hear her. "Answer me!"

The mysterious girl walked forward to the microphone of Lupia's rhythm guitarist, who backed up at her approach. Her voice sounded human enough, but its tone filled me with a sense of dread. She didn't sound like a girl that age should have. Her voice seemed soulless and machine-like. "Greetings, Lupia and fans. You may call me the Tower."

"The Tower?" Will turned his head quizzically. Apparently, this girl's bizarre name meant something to him.

It meant nothing to me. "She doesn't look very tall."

"I am here only for one purpose. My master, the Fool, desires to meet you, 'Miss' Lupia." She put a strange emphasis on "Miss."

Who the hell would choose 'the Fool' as a name? It wasn't very flattering.

"The Fool?" Lupia clearly had no idea who the Fool was and she definitely didn't like this visitor. "Who are you talking about?" Lupia displayed a surprising amount of courage.

"I'm afraid that you will have to meet him to find out."

Blood on Fire

"And what if I refuse?"

"Then I am afraid that I must take you by force. The old order must be cleared away for the new, as old forms must change into new. You, of all people should be able to appreciate this form." Her cryptic words were worrying enough, but what she did afterward was downright terrifying. She clearly was no normal human when she transformed. Without any warning, Lupia suddenly had the most enormous wolf ever in front of her. The transformation was instantaneous. At one moment, the girl was there. At the next, the wolf was there. Right where the girl had been before now stood this huge hairy beast on four-legs, bearing its teeth ferociously. Seriously, who goes to a concert expecting a girl to storm the stage and transform into an angry wolf? Nobody, that's who (although maybe insane people would, but they don't count). Her new form was certainly more wolf than anything else, but it still retained somewhat of a human shape amid its feral mass. The audience was split in its reaction. Some were scared out of their wits and rushed to escape while others thought it was some kind of crazy publicity stunt and stayed in their seats, watching. As for Lupia, what's a girl to do when confronted with a werewolf in an auditorium full of fans who were potentially in danger? She backed up and brace for the animal's approach.

"Shape shifting?" Will stared at the stage, entranced by the supernatural events.

Only mere seconds had past, but my mind was in a flurry. Could I do anything? No video game, superhero movie, or even Japanese anime series I had experienced could have prepared me for something like this. Someone was in trouble, and the only way I could react was to instinctively demonstrate futility by pointing my right hand toward the huge werewolf, focusing all of the energy in my body into it while yelling "STOP!" as if the beast would actually listen to me.

A small fireball flew out of my hand and hit the stage in front of the werewolf, causing it to stop its advance and return to humanoid form. Lupia, her attacker, and everyone in the audience then stared straight at me. I didn't feel any heat at all, but the ball's point of impact was singed.

I, however, just stared at my hand. *What did I just do?*

Will, from his seat nearby mine, scratched his head. "Amy…you know magic?" he whispered, hoping those around us wouldn't notice, even though they probably did.

Concert for Magicians

"...I know magic?" I also spoke quietly, though I truly had no idea what had happened. "Wait...magic?" I had always thought that magic was something only found in fantasy movies, role-playing games, and children's birthday parties.

"Yeah, you know, magic?" I stared at him, confused. "Did you know magic before?" I was still confused. Will then hung his head, frustrated by my lack of answers.

"Who is this who dares to pose a challenge?" Our private moment was broken by the shape-shifter onstage, who now was back at her microphone.

I glanced at Amelia, who was still unconscious. I had no idea what I was doing, but the fact remained that I was now a vampire. If I could somehow make fire with my hand, then I could probably do things that nobody else could. "Will...get Amelia out of here," I said, concerned with the safety of both my friends.

"Amy, what are you going to do?" Will wore an expression that seemed to say "Don't do it."

"Just take care of her, okay? I have some business to take care of." Was what I was about to do a stupid idea? Probably.

"Amy don't!"

I leaped off of the chair in front of me, discovering that I was far more agile than I used to be. I flew forward over the heads of the audience below me, moving downhill along with the seats I passed. It felt awesome; it was really like I was flying. However, I mistakenly caught my foot on one of the chairs I passed and started rolling across the stands instead. People had to duck to avoid me. I hit my face on the edge of the stage, leaving my glasses on top of it and landing on the floor below it, missing my target. Had I still been human, I'd probably be dead.

"What, may I ask, was that?" My opponent was not amused. The audience was speechless, though they would be laughing about at my blunder later.

I reached up and grabbed my glasses from the stage, putting them back on. I climbed upward and faced the shape shifter. "That...was the poorly executed entrance of the one who's going to put you in your place...bitch." I figured the insult at the end would make me sound tougher, but it didn't seem quite as effective as I thought it would be. Although I wasn't talking into a mic, the sound system still managed to broadcast my voice across the whole auditorium, causing a low hum from the remaining audience members as they started questioning this turn of events.

Lupia's attacker sniffed the air in my direction. "I can sense the blood inside of you, and it is similar to mine…our masters are one and the same. You have undergone a similar change as I. Why do you stand against me when we could just as easily join forces?" I figured from her words that she was also a vampire.

But wait, I thought she was a werewolf. I looked at her, skeptically. "Me the same as you?" I would have tried to transform into a werewolf, but I realized that I had no idea how to do that. "So you're a vampire?"

"Why yes. A vampire created by our great master."

"Buy you just turned into a wolf. Doesn't that make you a werewolf?"

"I am, but at the same time, I am not."

"What the hell does that mean?" Her answer made no sense to me.

"Are you unaware of the Fool's work?"

"And who the hell is the Fool?"

"Do you not hear his glorious voice within your thoughts? Does he not guide your every action? He guides all of us to a higher existence as we help him destroy the old order to build up the new, and I, the Tower, am the one to set these events into motion."

"You're speaking awfully highly of someone dumb enough to call himself a Fool." I heard no voice in my head other than my own and I certainly knew nothing about some new order. I wanted to know the identity of this Fool since it could shed some light on how I had become a vampire.

"He has been dead for centuries, yet he will never die…and he will soon rule over this world."

"But who is he?"

"You are the Magician, are you not? His name should be clear to you."

"I'm the what?"

"The Magician."

"The what?"

"Are you not the missing member of Project Arcana?"

"Project what?" It was all going completely over my head. "Fool? Tower? Magician?"

CONCERT FOR MAGICIANS

"I see. I was informed that you might turn up, Magician, and I received instructions from the Fool about what to do with you." She transformed again, but this time the huge wolf was facing me.

The creature snarled to intimidate me as it approached, but I had to stand my ground. *So she called me the Magician,* I thought, *that definitely means I know how to use magic, right?* I stretched out my arm like I did in the audience before, ready to take on the beast's onslaught. "Okay...magic!" Nothing happened. "Um...Fire!" Nothing still. "Aw crap!" I could've sworn that I shot a fire ball before, but what I didn't know was how I did it.

The wolf seemed far bigger than it had from far away. It pounced on me and pinned me to the ground with its massive strength, and at that moment I realized that I had rushed into that fight with no real idea of what, exactly, I would do. I felt a bit stupid.

The paws pinning me down felt like boulders being forced onto my shoulders—boulders with claws on them that dug into my skin. *Is there anything I can do?* The beast's drool dripped onto my cheek as its fangs drew ever closer. *I have to do something!* I was determined, but all I could do was desperately try to push the thing away.

"Get...the...hell...off!" Shutting my eyes and shouting as loud as I could, I mustered all of the strength inside my body, struggling in a seemingly vain attempt to push the beast off of me. I was certain that I was royally screwed. Just imagine my surprise when it worked.

"What the...?" That great weight was gone, so I opened my eyes. I was still flat on my back, but I was free. I stumbled upward, still unable to fathom what I just did. The creature was in front of me, quickly regaining its balance. I clenched my right fist tightly. Something was different about it, as if it were the strongest fist I had ever made, and that's when I remembered a key power commonly attributed to vampires—super strength.

When the wolf was back on four feet, it suddenly transformed back into the vampire girl. "You choose to put up a fight, yet you have no control," she said, "You should allow the Fool to guide your actions instead."

"This Fool crap is really starting to tick me off. Look, just leave Lupia alone and then I won't have to tear you apart and send you back to the Fool in pieces." I was trying to sound brave, but my voice faltered as I was unsure of whether I really had a chance.

"I have my orders, and I cannot abort them unless the Fool tells me such."

BLOOD ON FIRE

Lupia, not moving from where she stood on stage when the madness began, tried to interrupt this conversation. She had put her guitar aside. "Look girls, um…could you two…uh…take this outside or something?"

"Quiet! I'm trying to rescue you!" I yelled to her, my voice still faltering. "And I love your music! I want an autograph later!"

"Neither of you will leave," said the other vampire, "unless you will leave to see the Fool." She transformed again, but this time I was ready.

I dashed to the largest of the speakers onstage (I was amazed at how fast I could move) and grabbed it from behind. It was taller than me and I could just barely fit my arms around it. I lifted it up and hurled it in my enemy's direction. Tossing something that heavy that easily for the first time felt incredibly awesome. It was so awesome that I had hardly noticed the fact that it missed the wolf, who had dodged quite easily. The speaker knocked over the drum set before landing face down. The wolf dashed straight toward Lupia, who, oddly enough, had an easy time avoiding it. It slammed into the nearest wall but quickly recovered its bearings. *I guess the Fool sucks at navigation.*

"Amy!" My focus was broken by Will's voice, which came from nearby in the row of seats in front of the stage. I glanced in his direction to find him there holding the still unconscious Amelia as well as my messenger bag in his arms. "Imagine the fire in your hand!"

"Imagine the…What are you—?" I couldn't finish my question since the wolf came at me right at that instant, gripping me with all of its four sets of claws, holding all of my limbs in place to keep me pinned to the ground. Apparently it also had superhuman strength. I couldn't move, and it felt strong enough to tear me apart; however, Will's words lingered in my mind: *Imagine the fire in your hand!*

What had caused the fire before? I had had no idea that it would happen. It just sort of did when I expressed a strong emotion, a strong desire to help. Now I needed to help myself. If only I could feel that heat in my hand one more time right when I needed it most. I could feel the blood inside of me pulse. It wasn't like a heartbeat, but more like a pulse of energy. I needed to win; I couldn't let this beast tear me apart. My blood pulsed, and I focused the strongest, most burning desire for freedom I had into my right hand.

I could feel the heat coming off of the wolf as it let go and I stumbled to my feet. The creature flailed wildly, on fire. Thinking fast, I used this opportunity to run up to it and punch it in the face with all the strength I had. It barely knew

Concert for Magicians

what hit it. I could hear shouts of encouragement from the remaining crowd—apparently the audience was cheering me on.

My opponent morphed back to human form when she hit the ground half the stage length away from me. She didn't seem to have expected this turn of events.

The vampire-werewolf straightened herself out and reassumed her previous demeanor, though I detected a hint of fear of me in both her voice and her face. "The Fool has instructed me to leave you alone for now, but you haven't defeated me. I'll tear down that will of yours and make you join our ranks." What happened next was strange as she quickly seemed to melt away into mist and float up high into one of the air ducts on the ceiling.

I could only stare as she escaped. "Well," Lupia's voice came from behind me, "you're a vampire too, right? Why don't you turn into mist or a bat or whatever and go after her?"

I still just stood there, but I thought about what she said for a moment before replying, "Because I have no idea how to do that." I tried to imagine myself becoming mist similar to how I imagined myself producing fire, but nothing happened. Then I suddenly felt woozy, and my consciousness began to fade. I started losing my balance.

"Amy!" I could hear Will yell my name as I hit the ground.

3: Sorting Matters

Where was I?

I was at home.

But wait, why could I see myself? It was a strange feeling, but there I was in front of me, less pale, with average brown eyes behind those familiar glasses. Mom was there too.

Amy had just arisen from bed, which was clear from the fact that her pajamas were still on. The pajamas themselves were nothing special, mere soft baggy pants with an equally soft T-shirt. These were exactly the pajamas I wasn't wearing when I woke up as a vampire. Amy opened her mouth to release a drawn out yawn, showing off her perfectly normal canine tooth. She had only one. Then she rubbed an odd pair of scars on her neck. She did so unconsciously, as if some outside force drove her to touch them. The scars themselves were a pair of red rings around white skin

"Are you okay?" mom asked.

"Yeah, just a little groggy." Amy was never a morning person, but she seemed unusually lethargic. She had an almost dreamy look on her face.

"Come in and get some breakfast."

"Sure." Amy ate an entirely normal bowl of Frosted Flakes, needing a decent dose of sugar for the day ahead. "Where's dad?"

"He had to go to work early. Dr. Acula called him for an important meeting. He left about an hour ago." It was 7 AM, meaning that Dr. Acula had called dad before sunrise.

Dr. Acula. That name sounded so out of place yet so familiar to me. Amy seemed to instantly recognize it. The name was apparently one that she had come to associate as belonging to someone who worked with dad.

Sorting Matters

After Amy dressed herself, she jumped into mom's car for a ride to school, which mom gave every weekday morning and then returned home to grade papers and make lesson plans for the classes she taught at night.

When Amy arrived at school, she hopped out of the car and dreamily waved goodbye to mom, soaking in the warm sun of the morning with nary a burn appearing on her fair skin. Her school day began normally enough. As usual, before her first class, she went over to the area where the buses let students off to meet Will and their mutual friend James. James was a bit of an absent-minded fellow who did fairly well in school but had little common sense otherwise. Will had met him in middle school, and though he and Amy weren't really that close, they were still friends.

"Hey," Will gave the usual greeting when he and James came across her amid the flood of various students exiting the yellow school buses—their color and shape always reminded Amy of cheese logs.

Amy didn't make much of a response, simply giving a quick nod while still playing around with those odd spots on her neck.

"Dude, what happened to your neck?" James caught sight of Amy's unusual marks and couldn't help pointing them out.

"Huh?" Amy suddenly seemed more awake. "What do you mean?"

"On your neck!" James pointed shamelessly, though luckily none of the other students were paying attention. Will also scrutinized the strange marks.

Amy tried to check where James pointed, but her vision didn't extend that far. "Let me take a look." Will and James followed Amy through the nearby hallway but stopped when she entered the closest girls' bathroom. Inside, she proceeded to the first mirror she came across and peered at her neck. "What the...?" She didn't have any explanation for that pair of circular marks.

"I guess something must've bit me," she said upon exiting the restroom. Will seemed suspicious but decided to let it go. The rest of the morning went normally until the three of them split up to head to their respective classes. Amy's first class was Algebra 2 with Mr. Royal. Most of the other students were in class already, including Shelly. Few students noticed the marks on her neck; James was typically more observant of those small details, though he overlooked others.

Shelly, from a few desks away, sneered at Amy. "I see you like to let your clients give you hickies when you whore yourself out. I guess somebody likes those itty bitty titties." Ever since Shelly developed sizable breasts, she insisted on poking fun at Amy's lack thereof. Amy responded simply by showing her enemy her middle finger.

Once the bell rang to signal the beginning of class, Mr. Royal called everyone to order. As he did so, an unfamiliar face walked into the room, a girl so plain she barely stood out from the crowd even though everyone was looking right at her. She had brown hair, pale skin, and a widow's peak along with a blank expression on her face. "Yes class," Mr. Royal said, "allow me to introduce our newest student, Ella Spawn. Say hi to everyone, Ella." The girl hardly made any gesture at all before taking an inconspicuous seat at the back of the room. Most of the students seemed to care greatly about her presence for some unspoken reason. Amy didn't.

"Now," Mr. Royal continued, "Principal Cooper has asked me and the other teachers to alert all students that a freshman named Carla Evans was found dead in her bedroom last night, and he would like anybody with possible information as to what may have happened to her to go to the front office so they can relay that information to the police."

Amy had no idea who this Carla Evans was, having never met her before. Apparently this was also the first that any of the other members of the class had heard of this disappearance, as nobody had any information besides the usual ridiculous assertions based on lack of evidence given.

"We all must now observe a moment of silence."

All in the room fell silent.

"I noticed a difference in her eyes and skin before we left her house for here," Will said.

Wait, Will didn't have that class with Amy, and why would I hear Will's voice during a moment of silence? Will wasn't inconsiderate enough to talk at such a time.

"I also thought I saw a glimpse of her fangs earlier, but I didn't know for sure until she bit Amelia."

I wasn't in class at all. I was lying on my back in a cool, air-conditioned room, and I could feel the soft cloth of a couch beneath me.

"Then there were those marks on her neck that James pointed out last week. I guess it just didn't occur to me that they were fang marks."

"But why did she bite me?" I heard Amelia's voice then, though it lacked its usual calmness and really didn't suit her. "I feel so...I don't know...I wonder what Doug would think." I wondered why she would suddenly think

SORTING MATTERS

about her boyfriend in reference to a vampire bite. "So what's the deal? Is she going to kill us now or something?"

"Doubtful," Will said. "She obviously craves blood, but rescuing Lupia doesn't seem like something an evil vampire would do."

"I need to thank her for that." Hearing Lupia's voice without the magnification of a microphone was weird.

"Furthermore," I heard Will's voice again, "look over at Lupia's mirror. You can see Amy in it, can't you? That goes against a bunch of vampire legends."

"Will," Amelia said, "how do you know so much about vampires? Aren't they just...mythological creatures?"

Though I had been unconscious for most of the conversation, if Will was telling them about vampires, then I also wanted to know where he got his information. I opened my eyes, lifted my head up, and spoke: "I'm wondering that too, Will." The battle had drained my energy, and I had to work to say anything. "And where are my glasses?"

Lupia handed them to me. Looking around, I saw Amelia glaring at me. She seemed to regard me with an emotion somewhere in between fear and rage, though I thought I sensed a bit a pity. She had removed the shirt that I had stained with her blood and was now wearing a Lupia T-shirt. Lupia herself was now wearing shorts and a plain white shirt, though her hair was still that pretty wavy mass it was during the concert. Her gaze was also fixed on me, though she was neither scared nor angry. Will also faced my direction, deep in thought. The room was small and tiled with open closet space and a seat in front of a large, well-lit mirror. I was on a couch that had some other chairs and a small coffee table near it, presumably for performers to convene and discuss the show.

"So you're awake," Will said. "I don't think you're used to your new body yet."

I shrugged. I honestly had no clue as to how my undead body worked, so I took his word for it. "But how do you know this vampire stuff?"

Will sighed. "Let's just say that I've read a lot of books about vampires. Some of them even contradict each other, so I must admit that to me it's pretty cool meeting a real one—I can discover what's real and what isn't."

This explanation still seemed a bit strange. "And where did you find these books, anyway?"

Blood on Fire

"I suppose this was going to come up eventually." He seemed reluctant. "I probably should've kept my mouth shut, but after tonight, Amelia definitely deserves a proper explanation." He looked at me and then at Amelia. "Have either of you ever wondered about that room in my house that I've never let you into?"

"How could I?" Amelia said, "You never keep anyone in your house for long because you're afraid of your mom meeting any of your friends for some reason."

"Um…right…well, one of the rooms in my house is actually library where we keep all the books that our family has inherited, and that's where I spent my childhood."

"So you're saying that you're a bookworm who owns a book that contains the workings of a vampire's body?"

"Several, actually, and not all of them agree with each other."

"What about werewolves?" It was Lupia who asked this question, unprovoked.

"Yes."

"Zombies?" This was Amelia's question, appropriately

"Yes."

"Chupacabras?" This was my random question.

"Um…I think there's a mention in one or two volumes."

"What about sasquatches?" Certain cryptids intrigued me.

"And this is exactly what I'm talking about." Will turned to the others. "This shows that there's a very low chance that she's become a full-on monster."

"Wait, what?" That didn't make sense to me.

He turned back to me. "I'm talking about the fact that you, as a newly-turned vampire, can think of anything other than drinking the blood of the living, which proves that you're not just a mindless monster."

"Well, she did do something really evil." Everybody turned to Amelia. "She made me miss an amazing concert!" Amelia stomped over and grabbed me hard by my left shoulder. I made no effort to resist. Her hand felt like a vise, but it didn't hurt. Then she balled her other hand into fist and held it to my face. With the exception of jerks like Shelly or the Ogre Queen, getting on Amelia's bad side was difficult for anyone, and I had never before found myself there before. Being there, though, was scary.

SORTING MATTERS

I looked back to her with wide, sad eyes. "I'm sorry..." My words were genuine.

After a second or two, Amelia released me. "I can't stay mad at you." Then she started breathing hard, struggling not to faint.

"Take it easy." Will helped her into a nearby chair and then turned to me. "You really took a lot from her."

"I...I..." I felt like I was on the verge of tears. "I couldn't control myself."

He turned back to Amelia. "Look, just a few days ago, Amy's eyes were brown, and now they're red. She even grew one of her missing teeth back as a fang. I'm sure that drinking your blood was as much of a shock to her as it was to you." The fact that Will had been looking into my eyes intrigued me, but I decided not to pursue it.

"Right..." Amelia said between strained breaths. "...Right..." She sat down in a nearby chair, struggling to stay conscious.

"Anyway," Will now addressed everyone, "the point I was trying to make is that Amy's mind seems to be completely free from outside influence. Newly-turned vampires are almost always under the complete control of whoever turned them, but Amy is acting entirely like herself. If she were really like that vampire-werewolf-thing from earlier, then the two of them wouldn't have fought. They probably would've worked together."

Lupia smiled at me. "And I must extend my deepest gratitude to you for not doing that, Ms. Able. Such a kidnapping could have compromised my career." She spoke calmly. I could tell that her thankfulness was sincere.

"Um...it was no problem," I said.

"Why was that that other vampire trying to kidnap you, anyway?" Will asked.

"I...don't know."

"Are you sure?" He sounded like he suspected that she might be hiding something.

"Will!" Amelia called, "leave Lupia alone! She's...she's..." Amelia couldn't complete her sentence while she tried to catch her breath.

"Sorry," Will said, "but we really need to figure out what's going on. Lupia, you also didn't seem very surprised at seeing two vampires. Have you run into vampires before or something?"

Blood on Fire

She took a few seconds to respond. "I've seen some crazy crap in my life." She stared into the mirror as she spoke. Her voice carried the sense that she had hidden baggage from her past that she preferred not to mention.

"What do you mean?" Will looked at her inquisitively, as did Amelia and I. Despite some speculation from different forms of media, few people knew anything of Lupia's life before she started her music career.

"Let's just leave it at that, please." We were all disappointed at her response. "Anyway," she continued, "I think this Fool or whatever has something to do with this."

For some reason, hearing mention of the Fool dredged up the name Dr. Acula in my mind. I knew it had some connection to my father. "Hey guys, have you ever heard the name Dr. Acula?"

"Can't say that I do," Lupia said.

"Never," Will said. "Why do you ask?"

"When I was out cold just now, I recalled a really hazy memory."

"Of what?" Will asked.

The idea of having fang marks on my neck seemed like a new concept to me even though I apparently had been well aware of them being there. "Will, you remember when the fang marks first appeared on my neck?"

"Yeah."

"My mom mentioned something about my dad going to meet someone named Dr. Acula. I don't know why, but for some reason I feel like that name's connected to this whole thing."

"I see. Can't you remember anything else?"

I tried picking my brain for any other information, but everything else related to that part of my life was blank. The only other thing I could remember was going to the movie theater. "No...that's it."

"You mentioned your mom. Where is she now?"

I looked away since I had no idea how to answer that question.

"Missing?"

"Yeah."

"And your father?"

"Same."

"...Guys..." Amelia said between strained breaths.

"What?"

Sorting Matters

"A while ago, my brother mentioned the name 'Dr. Acula.'" Amelia had two younger brothers, one in middle school and one in elementary school.

"He did?" This intrigued both Will and myself. "Why?"

"It was a nickname for Dracula."

Will slapped himself on the head. "How did I not pick up on that? I don't think your brother was talking about the same person, though." It was mere word play: "Dr. Acula" is simply a manipulation of the letters in "Dracula."

"Wait, wait, hold on," I was having trouble wrapping my mind around this. "Are you saying that we might be dealing with…Dracula? Isn't he just a fictional character?"

"Well…yeah," Will didn't sound entirely sure, "but there was a historical Dracula, namely Vlad the Impaler." All of us just looked at him curiously. "You know what? We don't have enough information to make any conclusions. All we know is that someone calling himself Dr. Acula is somewhere out there and someone calling himself The Fool sent some kind of vampire-werewolf hybrid to kidnap Lupia. Everything else is still a mystery."

"My father was sent to Eastern Europe about a month ago," I said, remembering that fact and that Dracula would be from that area as far as I knew, having never read the book.

"Like I said, we don't have enough information."

I really wanted to know more about the situation, but I just noticed Lupia staring at herself in the mirror the entire time. "Hey Lupia, is something else wrong?"

Lupia turned toward me, sighed, and then said, "It's just that I got into music as my escape because I wanted to express to people how I truly feel inside, and yet there are so many people who have a problem with what I do. Sometimes I just wonder if I've done the right thing with my life."

"Aw, come on, Lupia. You're one of the few music stars I actually like. You're smarter than those dumb pop stars and you can rock out while still being cute. Right, guys?" I've always had a huge disdain of the popular celebrity train wrecks.

"Oh yeah," Will was really a more casual Lupia fan, so he hadn't expected the question.

Amelia looked a bit calmer than before, but she nodded instead of saying anything.

Lupia looked away at this statement and softly bit her index finger, deep in thought.

I slipped myself off of the couch and stood up. "Where's my bag?"

Will pointed to floor on the side of couch. I grabbed my bag and pulled out the CD I brought. The digitally-enhanced face of Lupia showed clearly behind the plastic cover, admittedly prettier than she looked in real life. I turned to Lupia and said, "I begged my mom to buy me this album instead of just downloading the songs from the Internet. I'd appreciate if you could sign it for me."

Lupia slowly took the case, smiling. "Should I just make it out to 'Amy'?"

"Sure."

She carefully wrote:

Dear Amy,
Thank you so much and keep on rocking!
Your friend,
Lupia

I eagerly watched her finish. "This is so going eBay," I said playfully.

She knew that I was joking. "Thank you," she said with a smile, "that cheered me up."

I quickly returned the plastic case to my bag.

"Though...I think there's somebody else who needs cheering up." Lupia turned to Amelia. "It's past midnight now and you look like you need a good night's sleep. How would you like to stay in my suite tonight? I have an extra bed."

Amelia's face lit up. "A suite? With Lupia?...Of...of course I'd like to."

"Won't you need to leave in the morning?" Will asked.

"I'll actually be in the state for the rest of the week. I have shows in Orlando and Jacksonville to do, so I have time."

Will seemed to approve. "That'll do Amelia some good. Amy and I will search for clues around this building and back at her house. We need to figure out how she became a vampire and what danger anyone may be in. However...Amelia...do you mind if I drive your car? We don't have a ride otherwise."

Sorting Matters

Amelia took out her set of keys and threw them to Will. She knew that as long as he returned it in one piece, her parents would be none the wiser that he drove it. "Don't get any blood on the seats," she said, giving me one last look that showed mixed feelings. I could see two marks on her neck just like the ones I saw on my own. She very lightly rubbed both marks with her right index finger. I wondered exactly how my vampirism would ultimately affect our friendship.

"Will you two be alright here?" Lupia asked. "The police are probably searching around right now."

Will nodded. "That's a risk I think we should take. We really need more information."

"Well, if you insist. Come on then, Amelia." Lupia led Amelia out of the room as she dialed her phone to have an attendant pick them up, but at the door she turned to me and said, "Oh, and don't worry about the speaker you wrecked. We have insurance." Then she left. I hadn't thought about the speaker's cost. In fact, I felt embarrassed about it. Apparently, unlike action movies, collateral damage is a very real worry in real life.

"To be honest, I'm still pretty freaked out about all this." I walked over to the mirror and stared deeply at my pale reflection. My lips were much redder than they were earlier, almost as if I had just applied some lipstick. My clothes and hair were roughed up from the fight, but otherwise all features I observed earlier that day were still there. Those red eyes still stared back at me. "I just hope that I didn't freak Amelia out too badly."

"I think Amelia took you biting her rather well, actually." Will seemed sure of this statement. "A lot of people in her position wouldn't want to be in the same room as you." He came over to me and placed his hand on my shoulder, which oddly made me shudder. "Just don't worry about it, okay? We know Amelia; she'll be fine."

"I hope so." We were silent for a moment until I thought of something important: "Will, could you promise me something? Please keep it secret that I'm a vampire. If any others find out, it could be a problem."

He gave me a strange look. "You should've thought of that before storming the stage."

I took a second to think about what he said. "Crap." I didn't have much of a secret.

"I warned you."

"Right...well, I'm sure that thanks to wolf bitch everybody would've known about vampires anyway, right?"

"Probably."

Will and I exited Lupia's dressing room and proceeded down the hallway in the opposite direction of Amelia and Lupia. We could hear the sounds of newscasters and police making a ruckus as the two of them tried to escape while dealing with as little trouble as possible. The hallway led to the stage's back entrance, allowing performers to bypass the audience in order to make a grand appearance on stage. It was a metal door surrounded by white cinder blocks.

I reached for the handle on the back door, but Will stopped me. "Not yet," he said as he placed his hand on the door itself and closed his eyes. I had no idea what he was doing, but he was concentrating hard, and he did so for what seemed like over a minute. I could think of no explanation. "I sense people intently searching. They want more information, but they're not turning up anything." He took his hand from the door and opened his eyes.

"Will, what did you just do?" To me, Will looked as if he read the door's mind. Do doors even have minds?

However, his response made me think that he was ignoring me: "There are probably police on the other side. If we want information, we'll need to be careful about it."

I gave up on asking for an explanation. "So should we leave or just go in or what?"

"It'll be difficult..." Will searched his left pants pocket.

"Um, what are you looking for in your pocket? And please don't say a rocket."

"A better conduit." He pulled out a sheet of paper that he unfolded, revealing the strange characters of a language I had never seen before.

"A what?" Now I was becoming annoyed. The way that Will kept talking to me made me feel as if I should've known what he was saying when in reality I had no idea. I watched him place the unfolded paper on the door and hold it in place with his hand. The symbols on the sheet then started glowing in an eerie blue light.

"I'm detecting that they're pretty much at a loss as to what happened and the only clues they have include the accounts of audience members and videos that people took on their phones. Other than that they have only a few strands of animal hair, some of which are charred. It doesn't look like we'll be able to find out anything we don't already know."

"And I'd like to find out exactly what it is you're doing." Now I was annoyed to hell and back. "But for some reason you refuse to tell me."

Will removed his hand from the sheet, making the light disappear, refolded it, and returned it to his pocket. "I suppose now that I know your secret, it's okay to use mine to help you. Mages hardly ever discovered anything new by keeping to themselves, after all."

"You have a secret?" I was intrigued. "If I'm a vampire, what are you? The Creature from the Black Lagoon? A troll? A burly bear?"

"A what?" He was confused by my last suggestion. "No, I'm a witch. What you saw was witchcraft."

"A witch?" I thought about his claim for a second. "So have you been a witch for the entire time that I've known you or did you suddenly become one like how I became a vampire?"

"I've been one this whole time."

"How could you hide it from the rest of us?"

"Do you need witchcraft in your everyday life?"

"Touché." Now I thought more closely about the exact word he used. Something was off. "Wait, wouldn't you be a warlock? I thought only women could be called witches."

"That depends on your definition of witch and warlock. Warlocks are typically evil, and 'witch' is not actually a gender-specific term."

"So there are good witches?"

"There are probably more good witches than good vampires."

"And can I just call you a warlock?" Calling a man a witch bothered me.

He shrugged. "Whatever." He didn't seem to like it but he was willing to accept it.

I was astonished. "So I just became a mythological creature while you've been a warlock the entire time that I've known you. I have officially lost faith in everything I ever knew before."

"So you never suspected it?" he asked.

"You did a great job at hiding it...although you've always known things that someone your age wouldn't, like I remember you once talking about the composition of metals in the Magic Mirror on the Wall from *Snow White*. That was weird."

BLOOD ON FIRE

"I guess I let it slip there, didn't I?"

"And then there was your knowledge of vampires in Lupia's dressing room just now."

"Uh...yeah."

"So are you into the whole spiritual Wicca thing or what?" I figured it was a sensible question.

"Those Goth girls at our school who claim to be Wicca really have no idea what they're talking about. There's just more to witchcraft than what the masses know."

We had turned away from the door to the stage but now we heard it subtly creaking behind us. We turned to see a woman who looked more like a doll in a beige overcoat that ran from her neck to halfway down her legs. She had dark brown hair that looked like she had had a perm every day since she was seven years old. She also wore stiletto heels that made me cringe just from the sight of them (with my brand of clumsiness, wearing high heels is suicide). Behind her was a balding man in a stained white T-shirt and jeans who carried an enormous video camera.

"I thought I heard some people talking back here," the woman said as she and her cameraman slipped in through the door quietly. "The police over there are really anal. They're not even cooperating when I'm trying to gather information. So, who might you two be?"

I was taken aback by this woman's sudden appearance. The possibility that she might end up attracting others who could get in our way also worried me.

"What brings you two backstage?" she asked. "Are you willing to give an interview?"

Will and I were frozen in place, unsure of what our next move should be.

"Wait...pale skin, long hair, glasses, short of stature...you're one of the vampires, aren't you? Hey Ron, start shooting." She motioned to her cameraman, who activated the huge device he carried. She grabbed a large microphone from a strap on her coat, turned to the camera, and started talking in that artificial news reporter voice. "For Channel 7 News, this is Delta Stone reporting. I'm here today with one young person supposedly claiming that she is a vampire."

Stone kept on talking as the camera rolled. "Do you know any magic spells to shut her up?" I quietly whispered to Will.

Sorting Matters

"Not without hurting her, but as a vampire you should be able to hypnotize her by thinking."

This suggestion was something that I hadn't thought of. Hypnosis is a power very commonly attributed to vampires. With that fact in mind, I thought at the reporter and the cameraman fiercely, but nothing happened. "What the hell are you talking about? By thinking?"

"It should work. Is something wrong?

"So," Stone turned to us, "have you any comment to make about your battle tonight?" She practically shoved her microphone into my face. Surprisingly, she barely paid attention to Will. I guess the news isn't concerned with people who seem normal.

"Uh...I...uh..." The interview was all so sudden, so I didn't know quite what to do or say. "Look...helping Lupia just seemed to be the right thing to do, so I...did."

"Oh yes indeed." Stone looked satisfied that I said anything at all. "Could we perhaps get your name?"

I could sense that Will was bothered by this whole situation, but I didn't know what he was doing. I gave him a quick glance. He was facing away from the camera, and was likely out of its range of vision since it was focused on me. I thought I saw his mouth moving in some kind of chant.

"Come on, please give us your name. You have no reason to be afraid."

I really didn't want this interview to go on. I wanted to remain low key and this woman wasn't giving me the chance. *Should I just take some of their blood and run? No, then they'd catch that on camera. What if I took the film?*

As I thought about my situation, I noticed that the cameraman ·looked woozy. His whole body began swaying as Stone kept talking "Do you drink blood and are your victims—What?" Stone was caught off guard as her crewman tumbled on top of her, camera and all.

"It's time to get out of here." Will immediately turned around and started running. I decided to do the same, seeing our opportunity for escape.

"Hey!" Stone was angry. "Where are you going, vampire? Damn it, Ron, get off me!" I didn't hear any response from the cameraman.

It took me a while to notice, but I was running faster than I ever had before. It just felt like a natural running speed to me. Will had to struggle to keep up. I wasn't running with super speed like the Flash or Sonic the Hedgehog, but I was certainly going fast. "Amy wait," he panted. I slowed down my pace so that he could catch up. "You're a vampire, remember? I can't keep up with you."

The most vigorous exercise that I normally had aside from gym class involved playing *Dance Dance Revolution* on my PlayStation. Athletics weren't my strong suit. "Um, sorry, I guess I'm just still getting used to my new abilities."

"Just get back to Amelia's car; we'll talk some more there." We dashed out the side exit of the auditorium, where in the distance toward the front we could see some vans from various news outlets. Someone near those vans pointed at us, and still somebody else, presumably a reporter, started running toward us. "Just keep running!" Will yelled. While I was fine, I knew that he was quickly tiring out. He was nowhere near a star athlete, but he was determined to keep running.

We went far into the parking lot before the man running after us, who wore a Channel 45 jacket, came anywhere near catching up. Amelia's car was one of the very few remaining, so it was easy to find as we practically leapt through the doors, Will in the driver seat and me in the passenger. "Gun it!" I didn't even have to say it because he did it anyway. However, besides the fact that he was pretty much speeding, something was strange about Will's driving, as if his focus wasn't entirely concentrated on the road. "What are you doing?"

"I'm obscuring their vision of the space around us so that they can't see our license plate."

"With your warlock powers?"

"Yep."

"Good thinking." He seemed to be on top of things. His did get us out of that jam with the reporter, so I figured that I could count on him.

Since the last thing we needed was police interference, Will did his best to drive safely.

"Whew, we made it." I said this without the slightest hint of fatigue in my voice.

Will, on the other hand, sounded exhausted. "These spells…and all the running…really take a lot out of me."

"If you just calm down and concentrate on the road, I think we'll be fine." I looked out the window, watching the seemingly endless numbers of trees and buildings go by. Even though it was dark outside, I could see everything just fine. My eyes seemed to be adjusted for environments with lower light even though I still needed my glasses to see details properly. This chance to rest also gave me the chance to think. "I don't think I'm quite ready to face the media yet, but I suppose we haven't seen the last of that reporter, huh?"

"Of course not."

"And we'll probably see others, won't we?"

"Yep."

I dreaded the threats to my privacy that I was going to have deal with soon enough.

4: Homeland Security

Our drive continued in relative peace. "So Will, what's the deal with your witchcraft, anyway? Can you make fire from your hands like I can?"

"I'm not that lucky." He had a hint of jealousy in his voice. "The spells I know relate only to fortune, deception, and surveillance. Shooting fireballs and using magic for the purposes of battle is something else entirely. While human sorcerers have had such power before, it's rare."

"So what else can I do with it?" I was interested to know the full extent of my powers.

"I really don't know. Vampire magic in lore isn't consistent. You don't seem to have psychic powers or the ability to transform into anything like that other girl."

"So unlike her, I'm not a werewolf."

"Probably not." None the answers he could give me were definite, and he ashamed of it. At school, I wasn't sure if I had ever seen a teacher call on him and not get a correct answer in return. "If you don't mind, Amy, I want to go over to your house right now. If that's where you were when you woke up as a vampire, then we may find some clues."

I had been too tired to do much searching for clues during the day and I hadn't had time at night. "Alright." Then something else interesting crossed my mind: "Wait, Will, don't you only have your learner's permit? You're not supposed to be driving."

"Do you think I care? The fact that I'm 16 doesn't mean I'm an idiot."

My birthday was April 8, Will's was March 12; we were practically the same age. Amelia's birthday was September 14 the previous year.

"I'm required to wait a year after getting my permit, which my mom wouldn't let me get until I was 16." This fact annoyed him. "Amelia's a good driver, and she's slightly older than us, so of course she'd have her license by now."

"Unlike me." I frowned.

"I'm sure you'll learn to drive correctly...someday." He couldn't help holding back a chuckle.

"Yeah, laugh it up. I wonder what your blood tastes like." I said it as a joke, but I was curious.

"You shouldn't really overeat; I mean, you've already had dinner."

Both of us chuckled, though I had to suppress a worried sigh because of Amelia. "Speaking of tastes," I said then, "Amelia's blood didn't taste anything like iron like it should."

"What did it taste like?"

"Chocolate."

"Interesting." Will was intrigued "I've read a lot about vampires, but it's mainly been accounts written about them by humans. I've never encountered anything about how a vampire's sense of taste works."

"So you have no idea why I tasted chocolate, do you?"

"If I had to guess, I would say that you taste the magical properties behind the blood, not the physical ones. That taste could even be exclusive to you, or her, or the combination of both of you."

"Magical, huh?" My mind drifted back to that taste of chocolate and the feeling of Amelia in my arms. I shuddered.

I looked at Will as he drove, thankful that I had someone willing to look out for me and to expose his arcane knowledge like this. Then Will noticed my gaze fixed on him. "You're not thinking of biting me now, are you?"

"Um, of course not." I turned my head back to the window.

From that point the ride passed in an awkward silence until we arrived safely at my house, where we got out of the car. With only dim street lights I could see every detail of my blue and white house as well as I could during the daytime previously.

"Thanks for bringing me home."

"Don't forget, we're here to look for some more clues. You have your key, right?"

"Of course." I pulled it out of my bag and unlocked the door. We both walked in and Will turned on one of the lights, though I didn't really need it to see. The house seemed just as I had left it...until Will and I both sniffed the air.

Blood on Fire

I didn't realize that I had an enhanced sense of smell. I just knew that something unbearably smelly was in the house. *It's like feces from the anus of death itself.*

"Amy, does something smell rotten to you?"

*Wait...*I opened the door to my bedroom and found my blood-covered bed teeming with flies and even at least one cockroach. "Oh God!"

Will peered in. "Let me guess, you woke up covered in blood this morning, right?"

I nodded.

"I read somewhere that blood from a vampire rots quickly when the vampire isn't around."

"So wait, who did this blood come from?"

"Whoever made you a vampire, whether or not it's Dracula. He probably fed you his blood while draining your own right here."

"Wait..." an image entered my mind of me being held in place by a mysterious male vampire, his arms tightly gripping my shoulders, forcing me to do things I'd have never done of my own will. I shuddered at this figment of my imagination, pushing it out of my mind quickly. I was a virgin after all, and that was hardly the type of thing I wanted as my first halfway sexual memory.

I then checked my bathroom. The clothing I had removed there looked similar to my bed—something was moving in the pile. I ran over to the kitchen sink and grabbed one of several pesticide sprays. Then I doused the area where the flies were buzzing. I promptly stomped on the cockroaches. The force of my foot put a slight crack in the floor.

"Will, could you help me get this stuff into the washing machine?" He did as I asked. "This will actually clean them, right? Or do I need magical detergent or something?"

"Regular detergent should work."

"Thank God."

"Amy, do you think this house is safe?" He kept looking around curiously.

"How do you mean?" I had never felt unsafe in it before.

"The magical resonance here doesn't feel right. I think a magic-based being other than yourself has been here recently—probably the one who made you a vampire."

"That would make sense."

Homeland Security

"The problem is that—" Will's cell phone started ringing, making the victory theme from the *Final Fantasy* series. He discovered his mother's name on the flip phone's outer screen. "Aw crap."

"Go ahead and take it."

Will lifted the phone to his ear. "Hello."

"Where the hell are you?" His mother's voice buzzed clearly through the speaker loudly enough for me to hear it. "You better not be screwing around with those friends of yours at this hour!"

"No mom." Will remained calm. "Something happened at the concert. You can probably find out about it on the news tomorrow."

"Look, you had me worried sick. Just get home as fast as you can." The call suddenly ended. Will closed his phone and looked down in embarrassment, trying to keep his composure.

"Um, Will," I said, "if you need to go home, it's fine. I can take care of myself here."

Will looked back at me. "Are you sure?" If any other vampire was invited in here, then he could possibly come and go as he pleases."

"Even in the daytime?"

"I'm not sure. I guess I should research a warding spell to keep people away in the mean time just to be certain."

"Go ahead and do that. I'll be fine here on my own, okay?"

He was definitely reluctant to leave. "Alright, but call me if you notice anything weird."

"Will do!" I put on the cutest face I could muster as I waved goodbye to him, but all the while I was thinking, *Why does he have to leave at a time like this?* I didn't want to be alone.

Will weakly waved back as he exited through the front door.

I thought about looking for clues, and I searched around the various rooms of the house to look for anything that may be out of the ordinary, but I soon realized that I really had no idea of where to begin. After some hesitation, I settled on my parents' bedroom, which looked as pristine as if mom had just straightened it out recently (in fact, I think she did). I figured that if Dr. Acula really was connected to these events, then I should search for clues about my father. I searched all of my his drawers and under his side of the bed, but the only secret I found beside some old receipts for boxes full of soil, which I could only assume he needed to for work, was his stash of pornography. I had never expected dad to be into cute Asian girls (I was around teenage boys often, so that sort of thing is hardly appalling to me).

Desperate to find something, I started searching my mother's side, and, oddly enough, in one of the first drawers I searched, at the very bottom one on her dresser, I found what appeared to be a journal of some kind, but it was mostly burnt. *Why would mom have a burnt journal?* The pages were almost completely black, so I could hardly read any of it, but one word stood out: Dracula. *There's that name again!* The pages were right next to what appeared to be an extremely old typewriter. I wanted to ask Will about the burnt journal, but calling him would probably piss his mom off, so I would just have to wait.

I moved to the couch in the living room and turned the TV on. I tuned the channel to CNN since, as I was up so late at night, the local news channels wouldn't be broadcasting anything useful. Nothing about the concert incident was mentioned. I supposed that the news of the existence of vampires wouldn't reach the national level so quickly.

At this point, I really just wanted to get away from my problems. I wanted to lose myself in something. I walked back into my room and fixed my bed with a new set of sheets since I'd definitely be going to sleep as soon as the sun rose.

As I worked, my eyes caught the boxes of various PlayStation 3 and Wii games on my desk. One cover depicted two male martial artists, one with dark hair wearing white and the other with blonde hair wearing orange. It was a *Street Fighter* game, and I was one of the few girls around who played it, albeit casually. Another cover featured a plumber named Mario with a red cap, red shirt, and blue overalls. Yet another cover was a *Final Fantasy* game that featured a woman with strawberry blonde hair wearing an odd white and brown clothing that made her look both like a soldier and an adventurer holding a sword that doubled as a gun.

I wonder... I carried my game consoles out to the superior TV in the living room. All of these characters had one thing in common: they all shot fireballs. Having found my muse in video games, I set out to master my fireball. After getting some ideas from gameplay, I tried practicing those ideas in real life.

What was I practicing on? Well, I found several items in the refrigerator that were several days old, and I could tell that they had gone bad. When I ran out of bad food, I used the logs for my family's seldom-used fireplace (who really needs one in Florida?), which I split into multiple pieces by simply breaking them with my bare hands (it still took a bit of effort). I positioned the items in the back yard on top of a folding table and kept the hose on standby in case I lit up anything I shouldn't have. Needless to say, the table was destroyed by the time I was done.

Despite my success in perfecting my fireballs, my spirit was still down since I had no idea where to look for clues for my parents' whereabouts. I fell asleep as soon as the sun started rising

When I did, I could see him. He was there. I was there. Amy was there. She was wearing a familiar-looking shirt and jeans—clothing that was now sitting in the dryer—without a speck of bloody taint.

He told her to do something, but I couldn't hear what.

"Um…if you say so, Acula," Amy sounded like she wasn't interested in whatever he said.

He said something else.

"…Right…" She seemed to just want him to shut up. "I'm going out now." She headed to the front door. Amelia was on the other side of it, waiting for her.

I slept for the entirety of Sunday's daylight hours. I yawned as I stepped out of bed and stretched my arms. *So I met Dr. Acula? Why am I having these weird dreams?*

After showering, I looked at myself in the mirror closely. My eyes were still red, my skin was still pale, and my canines were just as sharp. *So I'm still a vampire. Yesterday really wasn't a dream.* I then properly dressed myself and decided to call Will, figuring that he had kept himself busy that day.

"Oh…hey…this is awkward." I detected hesitation in his voice.

"What's awkward?"

"I've been at your house for the past three hours."

That was not something I expected to hear, and I didn't quite like it. "Where are you?"

"Front yard."

I put my phone down and proceeded to the front door. I found Will on the driveway behind Amelia's car holding a container of Morton salt. It was open. "Why are you on the driveway with a container of salt?"

"You didn't lock the door, you know. I used your parents' bathroom an hour and a half ago." I was asleep at the time.

"You didn't answer my question."

Blood on Fire

"I'm casting a warding spell. Seriously, you're lucky no one tried getting into your house in the daytime. I'd better finish this before any more weird stuff happens." He was absolutely right. Not locking the door was a big blunder, but my mind was more focused on what he was doing.

I sniffed the air. "Do I smell…pork?" Any scent associated with blood really stood out to my vampire nose. I wasn't sure exactly how I knew it was pork. That was simply the first thing that came to mind.

"Uh…yeah." Will motioned toward a brown paper bag adorned with a green rectangle with the letter P cut out of it, the logo of the Publix grocery store chain, sitting on top of Amelia's trunk. "I need some pig's blood for the spell."

I raised an eyebrow. "This is all really weird. I hope you realize that."

"Uh…just give me another half an hour…and it'd be better if you didn't watch." He didn't explain why, and I didn't feel like asking.

"Don't let the neighbors see you." I retreated back into the living room and started playing *Final Fantasy XIII*. I was still far from done with the game. An hour later (yeah, he said half an hour), the front door opened and Will strode in.

"I see you let yourself in—without my permission—again." I didn't really mind it all that much; it was just the principle of the matter that bothered me.

"Lock the door next time." He sat down on the couch next to me.

I kept my eyes fixed on the screen, not at him. "You couldn't have rung the doorbell or called my phone for me to let you in?"

"I did."

"Oh." If I ever needed to get out of bed for whatever reason, my mom was usually the one to wake me up. I seemed to be at a major disadvantage without her.

"It doesn't matter anymore, though. Thanks to that spell I just cast, unless you invite them in, nobody's getting past your mailbox."

"Why the mailbox?"

"Don't you still want to receive mail?"

"Oh, right." I didn't think of thanking him at that moment, mostly because the whole concept of magic was still just so weird—and also because the fact that he was in my house while I was asleep was a little creepy. Inwardly, though, I was glad to not be alone.

I continued playing. He watched me. "Why do you keep casting Fire?" Indeed, among a few other attacks, I was mainly commanding the character I controlled, the tough female soldier on the cover, to repeatedly cast Fire spells, regardless of the enemy's weakness.

"Because." I didn't bother following up.

"Because what?"

"Because you'll find out soon enough. So what did you do all day today?"

"Research and shopping…using Amelia's car."

"Didn't she want her car back?"

"She said to keep it until she was done hanging out with Lupia tonight. She just didn't say what time she'd be back."

"She must've cancelled her plans with her boyfriend. You were researching and shopping for that spell, I take it?"

"That and my mom left a note for me to buy wood polish for some reason. She wasn't even home today and she was in bed when I got back last night. I have no idea what's going on with her."

I wasn't sure what to say about that, so I changed the subject. "Was anything on the news about what happened last night?"

"They released the name of that vampire wolf girl."

I paused the game. "Really?" Now I was interested.

"It's been confirmed that she was one of the murder victims." He handed me a sheet of paper. On it was the name "Carla Evans," some basic facts about her, and an address—one not too far away.

"Will…how did you get this address?" I wasn't sure whether to be unnerved after the way he entered my house.

"Facebook."

"So she was dumb enough to put her address on Facebook with no privacy settings enabled?"

"All too many people are." Seriously, it's a bad idea.

"What about those other murder victims?" I wanted to know of other possible opponents.

"Their names haven't been released yet."

I kept looking over the page. "So she was a freshman from our school…I wonder…" I could vaguely remember Mr. Royal mentioning her murder in first period. "I wonder if the other victims also came from our school."

"Possible, but the police are keeping their names hidden until they can confirm what's going on. Carla Evans was the only one given out to the general public because she's considered a criminal."

Blood on Fire

"What about me?" I was part of that fight as well, after all.

"Nobody's identified you yet."

"Well, I say now that we have her address, we should go check it out!" I smiled deviously.

"Are you sure? We could run into another fight. You also never know when a vampire hunter will show up. You're safe as long as you remain here."

I rolled my eyes. "*Final Fantasy* may be interesting, but seriously, I need to know what's going on so I can find my parents." I unpaused the game and guided my character to the nearest save point.

"I thought we were going to search for clues about your parents here."

"Why search here when we can find that wolf bitch? Once we find her, she can lead us to them."

Will held back a laugh. "Gee, most kids our age would use the excuse of missing parents to raid the liquor cabinet and throw a big party."

I stood up and shut off my PS3, which sat vertical on the coffee table looking like a big dark monolith. "I'm not that cool. Now let's go."

Will had no further objections, but he did give a warning as we proceeded to the car (I made sure to lock the front door this time). "Just remember: you may be near-immortal now, but you certainly aren't invincible. Vampires may not die easily, but they can still die."

"Just start driving."

The drive didn't take long at all. By 9:00 PM we had already arrived. Carla Evans lived in a quiet neighborhood. The streets were well-lit with most of the houses illuminated by lamps and the moving lights of TVs inside. The area was heavily forested, with thin slash pine trees in between and behind all of the houses. Overall, it was fairly quaint, similar to so many areas of Palm Coast.

Bearing much less association to the vampire in question, Will agreed to ring the doorbell, but I hung around nearby, just in case something went wrong. The plain white house's garage extended outward well past its front door, so I waited in front of it. We were both aware of the possibility that we might be attacked, so I was ready to defend both of us, should the need arise.

Will hesitated, nervous about the bizarre social interaction that would inevitably ensue. Slowly, he moved his right index finger to the doorbell button, ready to press it, but the door suddenly opened in front of him.

A tall middle-aged blonde man stood in the doorway, giving one of the meanest looks to ever appear on a human face.

HOMELAND SECURITY

"Who're you?" The man spoke angrily in a heavy southern accent. "Another heckler here to make fun of my family? Saw my daughter on the news, did you? Well Carla ain't no vampire, ya hear?"

"Sir," Will put on a calm, respectful visage to disguise the intense fear he felt, "I'm just one of her classmates and I want to know if she's safe. Her friends are worried about her."

Mr. Evans became angrier by the second. "You shut up! I know your kind, and I'm sick of you! It's been all day with you reporter types, constantly! You have the nerve to show up this late at night? That's it!" He slammed the door in Will's face. Will was speechless.

"Well that was unpleasant," I said.

Will stepped away from the door and turned around. "Somehow I knew something like that would happen."

"Oh well, we tried. At least he didn't try to shoot you or anything."

I shouldn't have said that. Suddenly the door opened again. Both Will and I turned to it, hoping to see something positive, perhaps someone willing to give a lead about Carla Evans. Instead we got her father again, but this time he was carrying a sawed-off shotgun.

I put myself between him and Will, who backed away. I held both my hands up to show that I didn't have a weapon (not that it mattered). "Look, man, we didn't come here wanting any trouble! We just wanted information!"

"I recognize you." He took aim at me. "Yer that girl what tried to kill my daughter. Yer some kinda fire monster girl."

"Um...I wasn't trying to kill her...just trying to defend Lupia."

"What the hell is a Lupia?"

Now that I thought about it, I had no idea what her name meant. "A friend. Look, we'll just be on our way and we won't bother you again."

"If I kill you, people'll think I'm a hero." This I didn't want to hear.

"Uh, there's no need for that, sir, trust me." I backed up.

"Die monster! You don't belong in this world!" Those were his exact words when he squeezed the trigger. I flew backward against my will, landing flat on my back in the soft grass.

I never knew the pain of a shotgun wound before. It was far from pleasant. My torso felt like it was full of holes. *I've been shot...am I going to die?* The pain quickly subsided, and I realized that nothing was wrong with me. I sat up in the grass and inspected the wound. My light blue shirt was full of holes that had tiny blood stains around them, but my skin looked and felt untouched. The shotgun pellets rolled off of my body and onto the ground. *I have enhanced healing, don't I?* I was sad to see my shirt so damaged. I hoped to avoid further clothing loss.

I didn't have much time to count my blessings, though, as Mr. Evans' assault continued. He pulled out a necklace that he had tucked in his shirt. It was a small crucifix. He held it out while standing above me and chanting "The power of Christ compels you! The power of Christ compels you!"

I looked up at him, wondering what I should do. *Am I supposed to fear that?* I knew that vampires were supposed to be adversely affected by holy objects, but I didn't feel any different after he took that cross out.

He pulled the cross off of his neck, destroying the chain that held it, and threw it at me. I instinctively blocked my face with my arms just in case it was harmful. It bounced off my elbow and landed on my torso. Nothing happened. *Huh…so I'm not harmed by crosses.*

I picked it up. It had no effect on my hand whatsoever. "Do you want your cross back, sir?" I was trying to show him that I wasn't a threat.

"You shut up, demon!" He threw his shotgun aside and pulled a pistol out of his shirt.

I heard Will behind me, near the car. He shouted some incomprehensible words. The ammo magazine simply fell out of Mr. Evans' gun. Two more magazines fell out of his shorts, as if he had a hole in his pocket. My attacker looked down in bewildered confusion.

I took this opportunity. Using my strength to propel myself forward, I pounced on the magazines near Mr. Evans' feet and grabbed them. He kicked me, but it only hurt a little bit. I rolled backward and staggered to my feet, holding up the ammo.

"I have no problem with the Second Amendment, but you're taking this crap too far. We just wanted to talk to you."

"Shut up! Shut up! Shut up!" He ran at me, swinging his arms wildly.

I decided that I had long overstayed my welcome and dashed back to the car. Will had already jumped into the driver's seat and started it up by the time I got inside. I was still holding the magazines in my hands. Will hit the gas and we zoomed away.

Suddenly we heard the sound of glass shattering. Will kept driving while I turned around to check. The back window was very much broken. An ammoless pistol lay below the back seat amid the blunt chunks of shattered safety glass.

"He threw the gun through the window." I was absolutely dumbfounded. "He was that determined to kill me."

Will seemed to be deep in thought as he drove. "In retrospect, this was a very bad idea."

"Yeah, let's never do this again. Good thinking with that ammo-removing spell though."

"It was actually just a bad luck spell. I couldn't really predict what would happen."

"Still, good job." He really did come through for me. I didn't quite like the thought of being full of bullet holes.

I now had a gun and some ammo for it. I thought I had a crucifix as well, but I must have dropped it. "So that cross had no effect on me."

"Holy objects are weird. They only work for some people and only harm certain demons, monsters, and evil humans."

"So wait, God is real?" This was a logical conclusion to me based his statement.

"Hell if I know. But holy magic is real, so…probably."

At least I knew that we had escaped from Mr. Evans. "You think everyone's going to greet me like that guy?"

Will paused to think before speaking. "He just saw his daughter become a monster, so he was likely ready to shoot anything that moved. We can only hope that others are different."

I wasn't feeling entirely confident. I peered at the back window once again. "How the hell are we going to explain this to Amelia?"

Speaking of Amelia, she and Lupia were having problems of their own at the same time, which they would explain to me later. Here's what happened.

"That was surprisingly fun." Amelia had a big smile on her face.

"I'm glad you enjoyed yourself." Lupia gave an assured smile back. "Frankly, you've been one of the best autograph assistants I've ever had. You even managed to take the eyes of some of the creepier guys off of me for once."

"I'll take that as a compliment." Amelia was always proud of any success her looks could grant.

"No, seriously, I usually have guys helping me, so having a pretty girl like you broke the usual flow of ogling that I have to deal with."

Blood on Fire

"Aw, thanks."

Amelia and Lupia had become good friends since the night before, and they were packing up from the late-day autograph signing session that they had run at the F.Y.E. in the Volusia Mall. The workers in the store were shooing away the last stragglers as they went about closing up shop.

Lupia lifted up a box of extra CDs. "This is a big improvement over last night."

Amelia sighed. "I still wish that I could've actually seen the concert and the fight." Two circular red and white marks were still very clearly visible on her neck.

"Are you okay now? You did lose a lot of blood."

"I'm fine, don't worry. And I'm not mad either. It's just…" Amelia looked away. "It's just weird, you know. On the one hand, I feel like she violated me somehow. On the other, it's not like I really care that she did."

"Perhaps you two should just talk it over."

"Maybe. Triple A and I have been best friends for God only knows how long." Amelia kept caressing her neck. "But she did step out of line. Anyway, Will explained how he knew so much about vampires. How do you know so much about them?"

"Speaking of vampires," Lupia changed the subject quickly, "we should probably get out of here in case any more show up."

The suggestion made sense to Amelia. "Hmm, you're right."

The pair worked on packing the last of Lupia's possessions, but soon they could hear several people running by the bars that now blocked off the entrance to the store. Amelia walked over for a better look. She could see several men with khaki uniforms standing nearby. One was dragging along a wheeled metal cage while another had a pole with a sort of wire loop on it. The patches on their uniforms made their profession clear. Amelia turned back to Lupia. "Animal control…why would they be here?"

"Why don't you ask them?"

She did. "Someone just sighted a wild wolf in the Mall," one of the men said.

"A wolf?" Amelia was surprised. "I didn't think there were any wolves around here."

"They're actually endangered in the area, but apparently one of them just wandered in."

Homeland Security

"Is it dangerous?"

"Yeah, but we can handle it; just go out of that store the other way, okay?"

Amelia turned back to Lupia. "We should probably get out of here soon."

Lupia, however, was frozen, staring off into space, wearing a disturbed expression.

"Lupia?" Amelia was concerned. "What is it?"

The musician sniffed the air. "Something is very wrong."

"What do you mean?"

"We're not safe here."

"What?"

A booming growl came from outside the store. Amelia turned to see the Animal Control officers facing off against what was definitely a beast. "Whoa, that doesn't look like any wolf I've ever seen." She had been unconscious when Lupia was attacked. It wasn't the same wolf, but it was bigger than any canine creature that Amelia had ever seen before. It bore its teeth at the men.

"Okay Rover, come on over," one of the officers said in a cocky voice as he tried to loop the beast with his pole tool.

The wolf was unfazed by Animal Control's efforts. It roared at the man with the pole and leapt straight as his face, knocking him down and sinking its teeth into his nose.

"Oh my God!" Amelia stared in horror at this brutal display. A man's face was being mauled right in front of her, blood dripping onto the floor.

Another officer pulled out a small pistol, which Amelia could tell probably shot tranquilizer darts, but he never had the chance to fire it, as another wolf pounced on him and started tearing at him as well.

The third officer was too scared, bolting at full speed in the opposite direction, but he was soon taken down by yet another huge wolf.

"W—what's going on?" Amelia slowly backed up. She was separated from the beasts by the metal cage at the front of the closed shop, but she still feared for her life at this moment.

Lupia powerfully shoved open the door to the back storage room of the shop. "We need to get out of here now!" But Amelia just kept staring, unable to believe what she was seeing. "Amelia! Get over here before—."

Lupia found her words drowned out by a collection growls as the wolves let go of the injured men and an odd cloud of mist permeated the metal bars and formed into two figures. Lupia recognized one of them, though she was a mystery to Amelia. Carla Evans had changed little since the previous night. The other figure was clothed similarly in a black body suit. She had the same hauntingly pale skin with cropped brunette hair. She looked slightly older than the first.

"So Tower," said the new vampire, "this is the pack's target, correct?" Her voice had a bloodthirsty edge that any normal human's wouldn't. She would definitely show no mercy to her prey.

"Yes, Strength. The Fool does desire 'Miss' Lupia's apprehension." Again, Tower put an odd emphasis on "Miss."

"Come on Amelia!" Lupia needed to run.

Amelia knew vampire skin tone from seeing me, but my eyes, despite also being blood red, lacked the ferocity that these vampires had. Amelia turned and ran to Lupia, and both escaped into the storage room, which had another door in the back of it. They ran to the next door knowing that the vampires would follow quickly. In fact, the mist cloud was already close by.

They found an open alley behind the store used for unloading the delivery trucks that stocked the various stores in the mall. The light of the gibbous moon and the electric lights in the area made seeing the three growling wolves making their slow and imposing approach easier. Amelia did know how to defend herself, but she had no weapon that would be useful against these opponents.

Lupia quickly looked around to find some outlet of escape, but all that she could see was one plain white van with long painted-over windows toward the back. It was probably used for a delivery. One of the windows was left open.

"Come on!" Lupia effortlessly lifted up Amelia with one arm by the waist and rushed at an almost Olympic speed through the open window.

Amelia was amazed at Lupia's physical abilities but had no time to comment about them as she found herself on the empty floor in the back of the vehicle. The only seats inside were the two in the front.

"You have a phone, right? Call for help." Lupia then immediately moved to the driver's seat, tore the front console open and started working with the wires inside. Amelia had one person in mind.

We were almost back at my house when my phone rang. I was actually glad to see Amelia's name on the screen—it meant that she was definitely willing to talk to me again. I was a bit nervous, though, as I answered. "Hey Amelia, what's going on?"

Homeland Security

From the second she started talking, her voice sounded desperate. "Amy, Triple A, look, I forgive you for what you did last night, but I—Lupia and I—really need your help."

Now, I was worried. "My help? How so?"

She hastily explained the situation.

I couldn't believe what I was hearing, and I didn't like the fact that I couldn't do anything about it from where I was. "I'll be there as soon as I can."

"Thanks Triple A. We'll try to—oh shi—" I heard a loud crash and then only silence.

"Amelia?"

No response.

"Amelia!" Words couldn't express how worried I was. "Will, we have to go to Daytona now!" Not only was one of my favorite musicians in danger again, but my best friend as well. Somehow, I felt like it was my responsibility, and in some way, as a vampire, my fault.

"What, why?" He had no idea what was going on.

"It's Amelia. She's in trouble and she needs our help. Lupia too."

"What's going on?"

"Just turn the car around and I'll explain!"

Will sighed as he did what I asked. "This better not be another idea that could potentially kill us."

"It probably is, but they need our help!" Will liked to play things safe, but he understood the sense of duty that I felt. That was something I liked about him.

5: Blood-Soaked Fur

By the time we reached it, the mall was in a state of chaos. Will had to park several streets away just to be sure that the car would be safe. I stepped out and stared in the direction of the commotion. Even from a distance, I could hear the sounds of the ensuing brawl. I heard the growling and barking of wolves accompanied by gunshots.

I tried calling Amelia along the way, but I didn't receive an answer. The time was now well past 11.

The moon was clear in the darkened sky above. "Will, why is this happening to me…to all of us?"

"I may be smart, but I'm not that smart."

I didn't look at him, instead continuing to gaze toward the mayhem. "I became a part of all this without even knowing it. I could just stay home behind your protective barrier and try to achieve some semblance of my old uneventful life, but here I am rushing out to where people try to shoot me and giant wolf vampire monsters try to harm my friends. Am I stupid for rushing into danger?"

"No, you're not stupid. You're just trying to handle a bad situation."

I grabbed the pistol from the back seat and shoved in a magazine. I examined the gun. It was something I had never actually held in my hands beyond mere toy representations. "That guy may not have liked us, but he did leave us a nice present." I shoved the gun into the right pocket of my shorts and the ammo into the left. "Wait up for me!" I rushed toward the battle as fast as I possibly could.

"Amy!" I could hear Will calling after me before yelling "Crap!" I didn't want to put him in any danger, so I left him behind.

Blood-Soaked Fur

I didn't take very long to reach the mall. Its parking lot was mostly empty as I made my approach. The many cars that would have been there during the day had all long since left.

I soon heard the sound of vicious growling behind me. Looking back, I found two wolves baring their teeth and making their slow approach.

"Um…nice doggies…" I didn't quite know how to handle this situation. I'd always liked animals even though my father had never let me have any pets. (He never gave me a good reason, but I personally think it had something to do with his test subjects in his work as a biologist.) These beasts, however were much scarier than any dog I'd ever met before.

Without any other warning, one of them leapt at me. "Oh crap!" Luckily, the wolf quickly found itself several feet away as I reflexively pushed it back with all of my strength. It landed back-first on the concrete.

I pulled out the pistol. "Freeze!" I frantically yelled at both wolves, which made no reaction at the sight of the weapon. "Just stay back!" My arm shook. Something made me afraid to pull the trigger. *I—I've never fired a gun before.* Wielding a lethal weapon in real life for the first time is a strange feeling indeed.

Having animals for opponents was a very disconcerting experience. Unlike Tower, they weren't monsters, but unlike a human, they didn't communicate much to me and I couldn't try reasoning with them. I figured that they were under the control of someone, but I had yet to meet who.

One wolf leapt at me again, and my first reaction was to squeeze the trigger. In an instant, the creature lay in front of me, blood dripping out of a hole in its head. *I killed it. I actually killed it. It's dead.* I hardly noticed the pain in my wrist from not properly taking the gun's recoil into account—the sight of death in front of me was just too horrifying. Tiny insects notwithstanding, this was my first exposure to actual, real-life, in-person, not-acted-out death—besides my own undeath, of course.

The remaining wolf, angered by the loss of its pack mate, started howling. I had seen enough movies and documentaries to know that it was calling for help, so I ran forward and punted it, sending it halfway across the parking lot. Despite my lingering horror, the kick was oddly satisfying.

I turned away from the corpse. I figured that I should advance before the beast's friends showed up, so I ran in the opposite direction, but I found yet another wolf right as I turned the nearby corner. It sank its teeth into my ankle before I could dodge.

BLOOD ON FIRE

"Get off!" I shot it. Its blood and fur splattered on me and the surrounding ground. "Alright, fine. Bring it!" Any regrets I had about killing these animals disappeared, as did my bite wound. *These aren't animals; they really are beasts.* I tried to convince myself of their monstrosity so that I wouldn't feel bad later.

After turning that corner, I could see a group of police who had made their stakeout in front of the mall struggling against the surrounding wolves.

I wanted to help the police, so I started running through the parking lot toward them, but I failed to notice the puddle of oil that had dripped earlier from a parked car. "Crap!" I slipped and tumbled forward, landing face-down in the pavement. Falling down is just what I do best, unfortunately.

I quickly managed to stand up, but as soon as I did, gunshots started flying at me. Apparently, those who were not already busy dealing with the wolves had now set their sights on me. "What the hell, guys? I'm a friend!" They couldn't hear me. They probably were just ready to shoot any pale teenage girl they saw. Luckily, I saw an entrance nearby, so I ran for it.

The entrance was lined with metal and glass doors that opened by pulling, but all of them were locked at the moment. Of course, the mall had been closed for a while, and I hadn't accounted for how I would get in. I desperately searched for an unlocked door. The officers had stopped firing at me for whatever reason, but some more wolves approached.

"Damn it!" When I came to the last of the doors and found it locked, I pulled on it, letting my frustration get the better of me. I pulled it off of its hinges. It hit the ground, useless, behind me. "I hope I don't have to pay for that later." The wolves now came dangerously close, so I rushed inside.

I entered the food court, which several wolves were tearing apart. They left pieces of hamburgers, fried chicken, and pizza everywhere. Condiments covered the floor. For a few seconds I stared in awe of their ravenous appetites, jealous of their ability to eat normal food, but I had little time to reminisce since my attackers weren't far away. With their coming, the wolves in the food court also turned their attention to the same target: me.

I turned to the ones behind me first. "Okay, you growling freaks, you want to see a cool trick? I stood firmly and formed my hands together, quickly focusing my blood and the power it contained into the right physical form. "Hadouken!" The fireball flew swiftly, lighting up the pair following me and causing them flail wildly in pain. *Thank God for Street Fighter.* I then spun around to see three more wolves approaching. I grabbed the pistol. I had to aim fast. I had nearly emptied the clip before finally hitting just one of my attackers. *I guess my aim isn't as good as gun games on Wii make it look.* I decided to dash further into the mall rather than battle the remaining wolves. They chased.

As I passed by multiple stores and kiosks, the wolves kept close behind. With wolves as my opponents, however far I ran really didn't matter. They would follow my scent anywhere. However, the clash of paws against the tile floor behind me suddenly ceased as the wolves stopped dead in their tracks. Slowing down, I took a look at them, seeing that they had not stopped out of fear, as they still looked forward with pure aggression in their eyes.

When I turned back around again, I found a strange sight—mist actively forming into a human a short distance in front of me.

"Look what the pack brought in." A girl about my own age with obviously vampiric features came out of the mist, giving me the same aggressive and hungry look that the wolves did. If not for that look, she probably would have been pretty.

"So it seems the bitch from last night wasn't the only other vampire after all." Again, I tried to sound tough, but my voice faltered. "Or are you a werewolf?"

"I am a vampire whose link to the wolf is strong." It was a cryptic answer, but clearly she was the one in control of the wolves.

"So what's your name?" It's always nice to have a name to attach to anyone, even enemies.

"Strength." This was only word she said.

I found myself just as confused as when I talked to Tower. "That's a weird name. What did your parents call you?"

But she didn't immediately answer this question. "So the Magician still has ties to personal identity. If you had become part of the Pack, then you may have accepted your place simply as the Magician."

"The last one of you I met called me that too."

"That is your new and true name."

"I may be able to use magic now, but that doesn't define who I am."

"So you truly don't understand your role, the purpose of your new name. Let the Fool guide you. You will realize your true potential."

"And what role does your name give you?" I knew what the word meant, but I wanted her to explain it.

"Strength…the ability to overcome false human emotions and reach enlightenment. I know that true enlightenment comes from embracing the beast inside all of us."

I sighed. To me her explanation sounded like just another version of what Tower already said. "That's cool and all, but what did your parents call you?" I wanted her real name so I could confirm whether or not she was a murder victim later.

"Parents? I no longer have any need for such trivial birth tools now that I have my pack. If you must know, however, I was known as Bethany Davis throughout my pitiful and false life."

"I wish I could say that it's a pleasure to meet you, Bethany, but I'd be lying. My name is Amy. I don't care where you're getting this 'Magician' crap from. That isn't me."

"The Fool has issued orders to capture the Magician as well as Lupia. If you come quietly, my pack mates and I will have no reason to harm you. You may even be allowed to join us."

"I don't think so." Did I want to become another pawn? No. "Just tell me one thing. Does this Fool of yours go by the name Dr. Acula?" I needed to confirm whether the name from my dream was connected to these events.

"Our leader goes by many names. That could be one of them."

"But you don't know for sure?"

She ignored this last question. "You have killed my pack mates, and it is clear that you will not come willingly. Therefore, I must take you by force."

"Of course." I nervously rolled my eyes. I knew that I was in another fight.

Strength and her wolves moved at a swift pace toward me. I hesitated, looking for the easiest way out of the situation. My aim wasn't good enough to make the gun useful, so I tucked it away, but I spotted a small cart parked near a platform of various green plants underneath a now dark skylight. It was this cart that filled me with a bit of hope. *Let's conduct a little experiment. Maybe they'll work on an evil vampire.* I barely dodged my attacker by quickly moving sideways and scampered toward my new target. The cart contained variously colored and ornately decorated crosses, multiple depictions of Jesus Christ in different forms, and frames with inspirational religious sayings inside of them. The frames were useless—the crosses were what I was interested in. I quickly grabbed two of them and held both to my opponent, saying "The power of Christ compels you!" The vampire just stopped and simply stared at the crosses.

Blood-Soaked Fur

"Advantage Amy! You can't come near me now, can you?—OW!" One of the wolves bit me and was tearing at my thigh.

"That symbol holds little power in your hands, Magician." The vampire still would not approach me but did not appear afraid.

"Get off!" I dropped one of the crosses, balled my right fist and slammed it into the attacking wolf's head. I could feel its skull cracking under the force of my hand. Strength cringed at the impact. *So she's harmed by crosses, but not if I'm the one wielding them. Good to know.* I then kicked the creature away and fixed my gaze on the next wolf approaching, which was readying itself to pounce. I kept the cross in my left hand, which I held toward Strength while bracing myself for the wolf's oncoming attack.

Suddenly and unexpectedly, a familiar form flew head first directly into the wolf, both bodies landing limp a decent distance away. The form was that of the huge wolf creature from the previous night, and it transformed back into Carla Evans. I could hear another sound of claws hitting the ground coming from the direction that she flew from, only I could tell just from the sound they made that these claws were obviously very large.

The creature they belonged to, which ran at a blistering pace across the open mall, cracking the tile floor as it went, was neither all wolf nor all human. *Another wolf? What is the big deal with wolves?* The other wolves I had seen before, even Tower, all stood on four legs. This one stood on two. I stared at it in horror, frozen in fear. Was this yet another opponent for me to fight?

The werewolf stopped in front of the cart, stood up straight on two legs and let out a deafening howl. It was in that moment that I saw it. How do I word this? I guess I could say that, without a doubt, this was a male werewolf, and he was very naked. "It" was huge, like a furry's fantasy come true, but enough about that. Otherwise, he had a huge and muscular form, covered from head to toe in dark brown fur. The shape of his body was more human-like, but his face was definitely that of a wolf.

"So you failed to subdue him, Tower," Strength said.

"The Fool had did not anticipate a transformation without the presence of a full moon." Tower had recovered her bearings and was now facing the werewolf, ready to move as soon as she needed.

So werewolves really don't need a full moon in order to transform? An intriguing thought.

Blood on Fire

The beast in question turned to me, much to my surprise and fear. "The women's dressing rooms in Sears." His voice was deep, masculine, and almost feral. "Go there."

"W—what?"

"Just go—I'll handle these two."

"Um...okay." Apparently the werewolf was on my side. "You're not also going to kill me as well just because I'm a vampire and you're a werewolf, are you?" I had often heard an old cliché about vampires and werewolves being mortal enemies of each other, so I couldn't help asking.

"Just go!"

"Alright, fine!" I didn't want to take any chances with making this thing angry. The more help I had, the better.

I ran. Sears wasn't very far away—I could, in fact, see it from where I had been with the werewolf, in addition to a set of three more wolves approaching. "Hadouken!" Luckily they were heading toward Strength, so one Hadouken did the trick to keep them away from me.

Sears had been closed off much like the rest of the stores by a cage-like metal gate, but it now had a gaping hole in it, which looked to be the size of the werewolf I had just left behind. The department store was normally a fairly bustling place, but seeing it so dark and quiet just felt eerie. The fitting rooms weren't difficult to find. The women's clothing section was rather large, filled with everything that would possibly be expected of it, and letters saying "FITTING ROOM" were clearly visible from behind the racks of clothing.

"Um, hello? Wait, who am I looking for?" I had never been told. "Amelia? Are you here?"

"Triple A?" The call came from one of the fitting room stalls toward the back wall.

"Amelia!" The sound of unlocking came from one of stall, and the door opened by just a crack. Amelia's green eyes were visible to me even in the dark store.

"Triple A!" Amelia fully emerged from behind the door. She ran over and gave me a tighter hug than she had ever given before, which sent a shudder down my spine for some reason. Holding her safely in my arms was a great feeling. She was soft and warm. She looked scared but seemed relieved at the sight of a familiar face, even if that same face was one that bit her. After releasing me, she nervously grabbed hold of her fang marks. I wasn't sure if she did it unconsciously or not but seeing her do it was strange. She held her hand there the entire time we spent at that spot.

"I'm here to save you. Let's go!"

"No…" This was an odd response.

"What? But…"

"Lupia's still here."

I thought for a second. "Amelia, I haven't seen Lupia. I figured she'd be with you."

"She tried to get us out of here by hotwiring a van but the vampires got in the way…They just kind of stopped it with their hands. We bailed out and broke into this store. We got away from the vampires and she told me to hide in here. I don't know where she went after that."

"Wait," I said, "You broke in? What about security?"

"For some reason, there was no alarm."

"Well, Lupia has to be around here somewhere." I turned my head to look even though I knew I wouldn't find her right there. "I mean, the vampires wouldn't still be here if they had gotten her, so she must still be around."

As I said that, I could hear a sound increasing in intensity behind me. One of Strength's wolves was in the store, sniffing around. "Damn it!" I pulled out the gun and shoved in a new magazine. I took aim and fired a shot. I missed, hitting a rack containing lingerie instead. The wolf turned and started coming toward us. I shot again and again and kept missing.

"Let me show you how that's done." Amelia tried to pry the gun from my hand, but found dislodging it from my absurd grip difficult. I trusted her, so I let go of it. Within a second, the wolf was lying on the ground, a hole in between its eyes. She made this shot even with only a few emergency lights remaining on in the store.

I looked at Amelia in amazement. I had never seen her do anything like that before.

"What?" She said. "My dad's a cop, remember?" She smiled. "He brought me to the shooting range every once in a while. Most of the officers were surprised that a little girl could hit most of the bull's-eyes better than them."

"Little girl?" I found it odd that she worded it that way. "How little were you?"

"I was six the first time he took me."

Blood on Fire

My eyes widened. "So you've been shooting guns for ten years?" I started to feel incredibly inept compared to her.

"Eleven years."

"Right." My math tended to be slightly off

Her smile increased in size. "No matter what the size of the target, I can shoot it down." This new knowledge revealed why she was so good at any game that involved shooting. Even though she wasn't suddenly telling me that she was a witch, I felt almost as surprised as when I found out about Will's secret.

"Wow, you really seem like you're not scared at all anymore." Any fear that seemed to possess Amelia when I found her or when she called me was gone.

"Because now I have a gun and a strong ally." Perhaps many people felt this way.

Then both of us heard the sound of several things, likely racks of clothing in the general vicinity, being knocked over and of something large coming our way, accompanied by growls.

"Uh-oh." I expected the worst. Quickly, the familiar hulking wolf form of Tower came into view, knocking down racks of clothing as it approached. It growled at both of us. "Oh of course there's something even more deadly coming at us." I kept my view fixed on the enemy but spoke to Amelia. "Do you think you can hit a bigger target?"

"I'll see what I can do!" Amelia started firing off shots rapidly. Each shot penetrated skin and made the beast approaching us flinch, but it still kept on coming.

"Damn!" I handed her the last magazine so she could reload. I needed to do something as well. In an instant, a thought came to mind. It was my training with *Final Fantasy* the night before.

I quickly focused the energy of my blood into five separate charges in my right arm. Each one felt like a ball, the first in my hand, the second near my wrist, the third farther up my arm and so on. "We'll do this together!" I shot the five charges of my fire one by one near the same spot where Amelia's bullets hit. When I ran out of charges, I quickly queued up five more and shot them out.

Under the stress of the constant onslaught, Tower was unable to maintain her wolf form, reassuming human form. When she was just about the reach us, she stumbled from the constant pain and fell down. She was burning.

"Alright!" I was so happy that I held up my hand for Amelia to give me a high five. She followed through.

"Ow!" I moved my hand a little too hard for that high five, and Amelia held her wrist in pain.

"Whoops, uh, sorry about that." I was embarrassed to say the least. "Now for you!" I pointed at the vampire on the floor only to discover her absence. "What? Where'd you go?" I scanned around the room and saw noticed mist, this time the color of smoke, entering the nearest air vent above. I ran after it to no avail. "Damn!" She escaped. I punched a rack of bikinis in frustration. It fell over, bent. "When you get back to Dracula or whoever you work for, tell him you suck!"

A tall female form suddenly appeared next to me. Thinking it was Strength, I immediately moved my fist in her direction. Luckily, I managed to stop it in time.

"Woah, woah, hold on, it's me!" Her voice was high and feminine. It was Lupia.

"W—where did you come from?" Amelia was relieved to see her but still shocked by her sudden appearance.

"I was going to locate some crosses or garlic to stave off the vampires but it turned out that I didn't need to. A werewolf got to them first."

"A werewolf?" Amelia's eyes widened in disbelief.

"I saw the werewolf. He was the one who told me to come here. He had a really huge—" I never got a chance to say it.

Lupia quickly interrupted me. "He could probably smell Amelia in here and knew that she needed help, so he told you to go get her."

That seemed reasonable, at least. "Well one of the vampires escaped him, but we took care of her. Right, Amelia?"

She nodded enthusiastically.

"What did the werewolf do with the other vampire?" I hoped that Strength wasn't still nearby.

"She retreated soon after he attacked. Both vampires had apparently come prepared to fight you, not him. He disappeared while chasing after her. I saw you run this way so I just followed when I was sure it was safe."

"Wait," something was wrong with that statement, "I didn't see you on the way here."

"I was hiding."

BLOOD ON FIRE

"There weren't very many places to hide out there."

"You'd be surprised about that."

Something still didn't seem right with Lupia's explanation, but I just decided to leave it alone. "Anyway, we should probably get out of here. I really don't want to deal with the police. It's pretty obvious that they don't trust me yet."

Then we all heard a loud sound from nearby. It was a fire extinguisher, and Will, who none of us expected to show up, was using it. He dowsed several racks of clothing that Tower had passed on her way to me and Amelia. "You know, you should really put out the fires you cause. All this collateral damage is more than enough; do you really want to burn the place down as well? You're lucky the smoke detector didn't go off."

I was almost as surprised to see him there as I was to see the werewolf. "Holy crap, how did you get here?" I could have sworn that I left him behind at the car. The answer was obviously magic. I realized that after I asked.

"I found an unguarded entrance that's pretty well hidden. We can get out through there." He threw the fire extinguisher aside when he was finished with it. "I hid the car across the street, and we need to move fast if we want to get out safely. The police are shooting wildly at anything that looks like a vampire or a wolf." Will motioned for us to follow him, and we kept close behind.

We managed to reach the car unhindered. This time, Amelia was back in the driver seat, having been reunited with her beloved Camaro. "I still can't believe what you guys did to my car." We drove along the dark highway. "My parents aren't going to like this…"

"I would think your parents would be more concerned with the fact that you've been caught up in vampire attacks twice." Will was sitting next to her in the passenger seat.

"But how am I going to explain the gaping hole in the back window to them? You two had better be willing to pay for this." To be clear, when Amelia spotted damage on her car, I was completely honest with her. She only had that pistol in her possession because Tower's father had thrown it at us.

"Amelia," Will said in a serious tone, "Amy's parents are missing and my mom and I are poor. That guy was an absolute psychopath. If anything, your parents should ask him to pay for it."

"But then I'd probably have to give up this gun, and I'd like to have it in case of another attack."

"It's not going to kill a vampire, though," I said. "How else do you think I got these holes in my shirt?" I figured that Amelia had noticed the holes but not asked me about them.

"But it'll help." Amelia then sighed. "I'll try to think of something to tell my parents and see if they'll pay for the damage." Amelia's parents probably would; they often enjoyed spoiling her and her brothers.

I was in the back seat on the driver side staring out the window and watching everything go by as we passed. I wasn't sure what emotion I should feel. Was I supposed to be proud of fighting off the vampires? Should I have felt ashamed that they escaped? And where were my parents? I still knew nothing about what happened to them. "Amelia," I said.

"Yes?"

"Could you tell your father to keep an eye out for my parents?"

"I could, but the police are going to want to know who your legal guardian is."

"Oh…crap." I didn't have any family living in the immediate vicinity, and I didn't want to live in foster care, at least not when I was less than two years away from turning 18. "I suppose I could designate my brother, but he's kind of an ass." I considered my very few clear options. "You know, give me a bit to think about this. In the mean time, we'll keep searching for my parents."

"Alright. We'll go to the police together when you're ready, okay?" She tried to sound reassuring. She succeeded.

After a few seconds of silence, Amelia decided to address Will. "How did you get in and find us, anyway?"

Will didn't want to answer Amelia's question, so he changed the subject. "Lupia, have you thought at all about why these vampires are after you?"

"I can't really say…" Lupia's voice trailed off. She said in the back seat next to me.

"Do you really not know?"

"I…don't…"

"Speaking of not knowing," Amelia interrupted, "you never answered my question. How did you get into the mall before?"

"Well, I…" Will hadn't thought about having to explain the matter to Amelia. "I snuck in by…" He couldn't complete the sentence.

That was when I decided to just clarify things in the simplest way possible: "Will's a warlock." Yes, I said it. "He probably hid himself with magic." My personal belief is that a very thin line exists between when it's best to tell the truth and when it's best to withhold it. Maybe I should have done him the courtesy of not butting in, but I didn't see any need for friends to withhold secrets from each other.

"A warlock?" Amelia tried to keep her eyes on the road, but she was clearly distracted now.

"Amy, what the hell?" He certainly didn't address me with a friendly tone. He really didn't want to tell Amelia about how he really had used magic to make himself unnoticeable to all but the most keen observers. That's the wonder of magic—it can be as subtle as it can be blatant. He had a hellish time avoiding the persistent wolves with their powerful sense of smell. Despite its usefulness, however, magic was something normal people didn't usually accept.

"So you get to keep a secret but I don't?" I said in retaliation. "If Amelia deserves to know that I'm a vampire, then she also deserves to know that you're a warlock." That was my reasoning this time.

"Wow, a warlock." Lupia sounded enthusiastic. "That explains a lot."

"Amy, everyone knows you're a vampire because you revealed it in front of a crowd." I couldn't argue with that. "You made that mistake yourself."

"If you're so willing to reveal your secret in front of me, though, I think you should be able to trust Amelia as well. After all, it's only because of me becoming a vampire that she has those scars on her neck. I'm sorry, by the way."

Amelia shrugged. "Don't do it again unless I'm feeling kinky." That was a weird thing to say.

"And how about Lupia?" I looked toward the musician, who gave me a confirming nod. "I never said that I'd tell anybody else besides them; they're our friends!" Lupia smiled. I think she appreciated hearing that. She seemed to like being around us even though she only knew us for less than two days.

"Amelia, please don't go blabbing about this like Amy just did." Will sounded desperate.

"Why would I tell anybody?" Amelia seemed hurt at Will's lack of trust. "I'm not telling my parents about everything that happened these past two nights."

"Um, they'll know about Saturday night and probably tonight from the news. That much is certain."

"Well, we'll see what happens."

"Gee, Amelia, you're so...accepting." Now that Will said so, I was also surprised that Amelia accepted these supernatural happenings so easily.

"Well, I just figured that I'll have to accept that the world is filled with vampires, warlocks, and werewolves. Weird crap happens." She lifted a hand from the steering wheel and touched her bite marks.

"Lupia, are you willing to keep my secret?" Will had to ask her too.

"Trust me, I'm good at keeping secrets." Lupia spoke in a somber tone, looking out the dark window.

"Hm?" Something about the way Lupia had said that had triggered some curiosity within me.

"What is it?" Lupia smiled at me again.

"Oh, uh, nothing." I knew she was hiding something, I just couldn't figure out what. After all, a girl that pretty had to be hiding something. (I could say that I felt the same way about Amelia, and indeed, she was hiding her marksman skills.)

"Although I do wonder how people will feel about the vampires at school tomorrow," Amelia said.

That one statement, a statement Amelia made with hardly a second thought, broke me. It completely broke me. My eye started to twitch at the realization that dawned on me. As soon as she had said that one sentence, I was filled with the most horrified feeling I had ever experienced. From the moment I woke up as a vampire to the moment I discovered the existence of werewolves, I had forgotten just a few of the normal aspects of her human life. "Um...s—school?" That word was the scariest word in my vocabulary at that moment.

"Yeah, school. Remember, we go there every day other than Saturday and Sunday?"

"Um...every...day...right..." I could barely form a coherent sentence.

"Triple A?"

"Oh, I get it," Will said.

"Get what?" Amelia was still confused.

"Amy forgot to plan for going to school."

"Um...school...during the day...in the sun...with other people..." It was all coming to me so suddenly.

"Well..." Will considered his words before speaking. "If you don't want to risk it, you're old enough to drop out and do night school for a GED instead. Hell, you could even do it online and not even go to class."

Blood on Fire

"A GED?" My eye twitched even more. I was instantly appalled at the idea. "How am I going to go to a decent college with a good scholarship if I get a GED?" Now, I have nothing against people with GEDs; I was just very much on track to get a real high school diploma and wasn't ready to accept anything else.

"Hey, I'm just trying to help out here. What do you even want to do with your life, anyway?"

"Um..." I really hadn't given much thought to career plans. I excelled at most subjects, though mainly ones in which my clumsiness and absentmindedness didn't really matter. I planned on going to college but didn't really know where I would go or what I would major in. "Um...would colleges accept a vampire?"

"How should I know?"

"You know everything!"

"Hardly."

"Damn it! My life is over!" My social standing at school sucked enough as it was, but I could just see the whole vampire thing ending horribly.

"Please don't turn this into a teen drama." Will tended to hate complaining of this nature.

"It's already a teen drama!"

"What?"

"We're teens and there's drama going on. Therefore, this is a teen drama."

"She has a point, you know," Amelia said.

"Your life technically ended already when you became undead. You do know that, right?"

"Yeah, yeah, whatever." I still felt like I was in a dire situation. "Anyway, just tell me if there's anything I can do to survive at school!" Even though I wasn't human anymore, I definitely could still feel the human emotion of desperation.

"Well, if you keep yourself covered when you're outside or near a window and if you don't go into sunlight for more than five minutes at a time, I think you may be able to make it through. You'll do even better if you can convince your teachers to close the windows."

"Can I defend myself once others know what I am?"

"You should have weaker versions of your vampire abilities."

BLOOD-SOAKED FUR

"Hey, Triple A." Amelia sounded like she really wanted to tell me something. "You may have drank my blood, and that's pretty sick, but you did come to help me today, so, well, if you need any help tomorrow…"

I knew what she was getting at and she seemed overly excited to offer me her help. "Thanks…I think I'll need all the help I can get."

Once we arrived back in Palm Coast, Will instructed Amelia to drive to my house. When he suggested it, I simply figured that they were dropping me off first to let me figure out how to prepare for school. However, that was not the only thing that he was planning.

When Will got out of the car, he immediately went over to Lupia and spoke to her in a hushed voice. She nodded. Will then turned around to face me and said, "Well Amy, is it alright with you?"

I had no idea what he was talking about. "Is what alright?"

"As I've stated, your house is magically protected from unwanted invaders, right?"

"So you've told me." I had yet to see any proof. "What are you getting at?" I had a hunch, however that I knew where this was going.

"I'm suggesting that perhaps Lupia should temporarily live in your house."

My eyes widened in surprise. Ever since I became a vampire, my life had simply changed so much so quickly, and here was yet another change coming to me.

Amelia stood by the driver's side door of her car and simply said, "Lucky." She definitely knew Lupia better than either Will or myself, as the two of them had discussed music all day.

I had trouble giving a coherent answer because of the surprise. Of course my answer was "yes."

And then I still had to prepare for school.

6: Eyes on Me

I was definitely scared out of my mind. Part of me thought that maybe Will's suggestion of a GED would have been a better idea, but the rest of me was determined to get through school. It was just a scary thought: a being whose weakness is sunlight must venture forth into it in order to gain this a piece of paper that says she has the initiative to accomplish four years of secondary education.

I also had another lingering fear: that others would react like Mr. Evans.

I was never exactly the type to not graduate high school. I mean, nobody in my family ever really doubted that I would get my diploma. My sudden change just put me in a situation that, quite honestly, I didn't know how to deal with.

For once I could actually say that I truly hated the fact that I lived in Florida. I mean, it's the freaking Sunshine State! I would just have to bear it. Luckily, nights in November are fairly long. I would dread the spring months (summer mostly wouldn't be an issue since school would be out).

Will told me that as long as I stayed mostly covered up, I might be fine. Yeah, he only said "might"; he didn't say "would." Uncovered, I could go about five minutes without burning to death. Covered, I could survive for about 20 minutes outside or indefinitely but uncomfortably in a room with a window that I was sitting far away from. If the room had no exposed windows, I could go around uncovered without any risk. The numeric figures he gave me were only estimates, of course, and I had no idea what he based them on.

I had to go to bed well before sunrise, meaning that I lost hours of darkness that I could potentially have utilized for something worthwhile. My new roommate occupied my brother's old bedroom, the walls of which were lined with pictures of cars. She went to bed soon after we arrived home that night, and she went right back there after waking me up at 6:45 (as a human, I woke up at 6, but I didn't need to eat breakfast anymore). I couldn't blame her. I always hated the fact that school started at 8. I didn't like imposing on Lupia, but I always just turned off alarms without waking up. I suppose I really should've gotten used to not having my mom wake me up, although it definitely is hard for a vampire to wake up in the daytime, so I really did need Lupia's help.

I wasn't wearing my usual skirt or shorts and tank top or shirt combination, which I wore even in November since Florida never became very cold except during spurts between October and February (I didn't really mind cooler weather all that much, unlike others who bundled up at the slightest chill). I decided to save my usual airy clothing for the night time. I played it safe with jeans and a long sleeve shirt under a hooded sweatshirt and a wide-brimmed hat that I had to borrow from Amelia. Wearing so much clothing made me feel like some kind of strange alien in disguise as a human, but it was all necessary to keep Mr. Sun away. On top of everything else, I also had that same general lethargy from Saturday morning, so I just felt generally unpleasant.

Mom wasn't around to bring me to school, and taking the bus would be a huge risk with all the idiots who usually rode it, so Amelia agreed to come pick me up.

I finished packing everything into my Sonic bag and replaced my glasses with my prescription sunglasses, putting my clear ones in the bag for use in a darker place later. I felt lucky that I had those sunglasses even though I never really used them enough before.

The doorbell rang and I took a deep breath. Less than a month before, during Daylight Savings Time, sunrise might not have occurred yet, but the dawning sun was right outside, waiting for me.

As I opened the door, the sunlight poured in, and it was, well, horrible. Even through the sunglasses, Amelia resembled Jesus appearing in a burst of bright light.

She tilted her head. "Are you okay?"

"Uh, yeah." My voice was weak. Getting used to my situation was really going to take a ton of effort.

"You're shaking." Amelia was clearly worried as she grasped the spot where I bit her again. "Are you absolutely sure you want to do this?"

"Yeah, I'll be fine!" I lied. Even through the clothing, my skin was starting to hurt.

Blood on Fire

"You should probably get in the car before you burst into flames." I quickly nodded to agree with her and jumped in the passenger seat.

Unfortunately, drivers need to see their surroundings as they operate their vehicles, so cars are naturally loaded with windows. I felt like I was inside of some torture cell as I tried to keep myself shielded from every angle. Indeed, the sun was cruel to this creature of the night. Perhaps if I were evil I would hatch a plot to get rid of it altogether.

I made a mental note for subsequent car rides that I should bring a blanket. One would certainly have made the trip more bearable.

"Be careful, Triple A" Amelia said. "I mean, I wasn't very scared of you, but I'm weird." Though the guys were all over her, she was still an oddball. "People at school may be terrified of you, and you probably won't even have to bite them." Even in the car's blinding light, I could see that she had one hand on the steering wheel and the other on her fang marks. I really hoped that no one else would think too much of them, for both of our sakes. "But I think if everyone manages to get used to you, you should be fine."

I still had to struggle through the pain to get any words out, so I only nodded even though she should've been concentrating on the road as opposed to looking for a response from me. At this point, I felt like I had moderate sunburn all over most of my body. Despite living in the Sunshine State, I had never really spent that much time in the sun, hence the fact that I was used to being pale. With all said, though, I had never actually disliked the sun, but now I hated it.

The drive felt like it took forever to end. I just wanted to get out of that car. Fortunately, all car rides eventually end and we arrived on campus. Unfortunately, being a junior, Amelia couldn't park in front of the school but instead had to go into the underclassmen lot, which was a bit far away. I knew it would be one hell of a run—or, rather, walk, as running was forbidden for some reason (though I guess it makes sense considering my propensity for falling down)—in order to get inside the school.

As Amelia pulled into the parking space, I noticed that the time was 7:39. That was lucky. I had a few minutes to sneak into my first class before the massive number of students who came via school bus would flood in at 7:45. Neither Will nor Amelia shared that class with me, so I would be on my own.

As soon as Amelia shut the car off and unlocked it, I jumped out of it—into the even more open sunlight. Amelia took one look at me and said, "Triple A?"

Eyes on Me

"Yeah?" I was getting ready to rush to class, so I was barely paying attention.

"…You're smoking."

When she said that I sniffed the air, which smelled oddly like barbeque, and then I noticed a thin veil of gray smoke coming right off of me. My skin felt like it was literally being fried. "I'm off to class!" I ran as fast as I could, despite school rules, to the nearest source of shade—the covered walkways between buildings. Using one of said walkways, I made my way to the nearest building, which contained the cafeteria, the library, and most of the freshman classrooms. As my luck would dictate, this building was not where my class was, but it had very few windows, giving me a much needed escape from the outside.

I quickly stepped inside and turned a corner away from the entrance, which was when I saw a young freshman picking at the contents of his locker. I was breathing hard (I wasn't sure whether it was necessary or not for a vampire), so he must have heard me come in as he turned around to look at the overdressed figure before him. He quickly shut his locker and rushed away.

Freshman guys scare so easily.

I found a girls' restroom nearby, so I decided it to survey the damage. I went in, stood in front of the mirror, took off the hat, pulled down my hood, and switched my sunglasses for my regular ones.

My face was charred. It felt like sunburn but it looked like someone had lit me on fire. It was still clearly my face, but the damage to it was unmistakable. However, the burns slowly faded and my face began to return to how it was supposed to look. I decided to stay covered for the present time unless I wanted to freak anyone out with my overcooked face.

As I rushed through the circular hallway, I passed by other early arriving students here and there. They all seemed a bit disconcerted at my strange fashion.

After crossing another covered walkway through the accursed sunlight, I finally reached the correct building (while crossing, I found that I would need to switch to my sunglasses every time I went outside). After a quick dash up the stairs (the elevator in that building was always inaccessible for some reason), I finally reached the classroom I needed to be in. The textbook I needed for this class was one that I had brought home anyway, so I didn't need to stop at my locker.

Blood on Fire

I wasn't really all that terrible at math, I was just always on the upper end of the "average" spectrum, so while Will and Amelia were math geniuses enrolled in Precalculus and going for their chance to enroll in AP Calculus, I was stuck there in Algebra II—and not the Honors version, might I add. Though I had tried, I could make Honors for everything other than math. I understood the subject and I even sometimes found it fun, but I couldn't get above a B in any math course, and the one time I tried taking an Honors level one...well, that's what grade forgiveness is for. I could almost always get straight A's in every other subject—gym, where I was a safety hazard, would've be an exception, but all the coaches really cared about was wearing a uniform and attempted participation.

The door to my first class was unlocked well before class began, which I never had known before since I'd always taken my time getting there. I jumped through the doorway, much to the surprise of the teacher, Mr. Royal, who was writing his usual mathematical jargon on the black board. His piece of chalk snapped in half the second he saw me.

"Are you a member of my class?" He wasn't sure what to do, still holding his chalk in place while blankly staring at me. "Who are you?"

I sighed. I was sure everyone I met today would react in this fashion. I removed my hat and hood to reveal my face. "One of your students."

He turned away from the board and came just a bit closer to me. "Amy Able? My God, what happened to you?" I was probably still burned from so much sun exposure. Speaking of the sun, the windows on the side of the classroom were only a constant nuisance and not a source of certain death because of the cage-like structure on the other side of them that I guess kept kids from falling out. Could high school students really be that dumb? Probably.

"The sun."

"The sun? How prone to sunburn are you? Miss Able, you should know to take better care of yourself! Some people believed that you may have been one of the girls who disappeared...wait." He examined me carefully. I think he noticed my skin's rapid healing. I knew what he was thinking.

"Were you at a concert this past Saturday?"

"Yes."

"Was that concert supposedly attacked by some kind of vampire-werewolf?"

"Yes."

Eyes on Me

"You were on the news the other night. I thought the good vampire looked like you, but I just wasn't sure. What happened to you?" Now the hallway was starting to fill with random echoey voices and the stomping and skidding of footsteps. I had very little time before other students came in.

"I'm not even sure myself. I just woke up Saturday morning with no memory of what had happened since Monday and suddenly I was a vampire. I really have no idea how it happened."

"You're not here to suck my blood, are you?" I wasn't sure whether he said it jokingly or if he was afraid, but at that moment, the door swung open and in came a student I didn't recognize offhand, though she seemed familiar. She froze as she took her first look at me.

I think it's time for a little background about my relationships with my classmates. By this point, it should be obvious that I'm a bit of a geek. Okay, so I'm not "a bit" at all; rather, I'm very much a geek. I had friends in school, but I wasn't exactly one of the "popular girls." Many saw me as that scrawny little nerd who was barely even worth remembering.

However, this new girl seemed to see me differently. "Good morning, Miss Spawn," Mr. Royal said.

She barely batted an eyelash at the teacher, instead looking awkwardly at me as if she were taking in every detail of my appearance. "Um…I'm sorry, do I know you?" I asked.

"Miss Able," Mr. Royal said, "this is our new transfer student, Ella Spawn. You met her last week, though you were both only here together for one day." Then I remembered that dream I had after I passed out. This girl was in that dream. She barely stood out at all, which was why I took a while to remember her. She could pretty much be a stand in for almost any other girl. Her presence told me that I must have remembered actual events in that dream.

She didn't say anything to me. In fact, I got the vibe from her that she was waiting for me to talk first, but what was I supposed to say, really? Still, she just kept staring at me as if something were wrong with me (although I suppose something was). "Um…could you please stop staring at me? It's creepy." She then retreated to her desk, showing no emotion. I hardly knew this girl and already I disliked her.

I rolled my eyes and stepped over to my own desk just as three guys walked in and stood confused at the sight of me. Royal returned to writing on the blackboard but continued to repeatedly steal glances.

Blood on Fire

I wasn't sure whether Royal accepted my new condition, so I just had to ask him, "Um, Mr. Royal, do you have any problem with me being here? I mean, I'm not here to suck blood, just to finish my education."

"While I will admit that it is strange having a vampire in my algebra class, throwing you out may get me fired for discrimination—that and I don't really give a damn either way. Just be careful with the other students, okay?" This last piece of advice couldn't be more important. I don't think that I saw a single person who walked into the room and didn't flinch at the sight of me. I hoped that I would have better luck after all of my skin healed. I thought, perhaps, that removing the hoodie would also help. From what little I could see, the color of my skin was still more ashen than its usual pale.

Still, nobody could take their eyes off of me. Some looked scared while others looked curious. Still others were staring at me in a rather creepy manner, as if I were some kind of odd celebrity. My attention was torn away from them, though, just as the bell rang to signify the start of first period and a certain other of my female classmates walked in.

Shelly took one look at me and had the gall to say, "Lamy, that's a good look for you. Going for the 'I'm a poser' style?"

"And are you going for the 'I'm a bitch' look?" I had to return the ill will.

"Only an idiot like you would believe in the whole vampire thing." Whether or not she believed it didn't matter to her. All that mattered was that I apparently did (and why wouldn't I?). "You need to stop reading dime novels and just accept the fact that no guy would ever go for you and your microboobs." Ironically, she was the one more likely to read those books.

I didn't respond to her verbally, instead just showing her my middle finger.

"Alright class, settle down." Mr. Royal motioned for everyone to take their seats as he moved to his preferred spot at the chalk board and began his lesson. Shelly gave me one last pompous smirk before assuming her place next to Ella. She seemed to be treating Ella like her best friend ever. Ella seemed awkward around her. Somehow I had the feeling that she would seem awkward around anyone.

I tried to focus on the class as best as I could but was distracted by the combination of my tiredness, my four days of missed class, and the gaze of every eye locked onto me. I had the feeling that a bunch of them wanted to say something to me, but Mr. Royal never stopped talking. He seemed determined not to allow any sort of distraction to occur in his class. He even gave a pop quiz. Said quiz, of course, turned out to be disastrous for me.

I knew that it was going to be a very long day. For a while, I was in a daze, barely paying attention to the veritable chaos ensuing around me. I barely knew what went on during the rest of that period. During my next class, which was art, I got the odd impression that everyone thought that I wanted to paint my canvas with their blood. Then I had gym, and I had a ridiculously hard time convincing the coach to let me take that day off.

"Able, why aren't you in uniform?" Coach Bellows spoke in a heavy southern accent. He looked me over with his squinty eyes. The sleeveless shirt he wore barely covered the wrinkles all over his otherwise intimidating muscles. "I need you dressed out and on the field playing softball with the other girls."

"Outside?"

"Yes."

"In the sun?"

"Yes. It's the healthiest place for a sickly pale girl like you to be."

"Sir, I don't think you understand."

"I understand perfectly. Youth these days don't care about sportsmanship and teamwork anymore. You're all obsessed with painting your nails and eating Taco Bell and posting on the FaceSpace or the MyBook and playing your Guitar Bands and Call of Halo on your WiiBoxes."

I was so stressed out that his ignorance barely fazed me. "Sir, if I go outside, I'll burn."

"So rub some sunscreen on your body and get over it."

"No, I mean I'll catch on fire because I'm a vampire." I showed him my fangs.

"Take those ridiculous things out and put your uniform on."

I pulled on my fangs to demonstrate that they were definitely attached to my mouth.

He ignored my demonstration. "Come on, you need to get outside and start hitting balls with a stick." He was always wording things in an erotic manner, which was the main reason why I thought he was a pedophile.

"Sir, for my own health, I am declining to dress out."

"Do you have a doctor's note?"

"A what?"

"A doctor's note. I want proof that you have a condition."

Blood on Fire

"Should I just stand outside and burn for you? What the hell do you want from me?"

"Without a note, you're losing credit for today, little lady." He wrote something in red marker on the clipboard he held.

So he wanted a doctor's note to prove that I was a vampire. The fact that I burst into flames when I stepped outside apparently wasn't proof that I shouldn't be in the sun. That coach was a bastard. I just sat on the bleachers, waiting, until lunch. Luckily, hardly anybody in gym class bothered me since most of them were outside.

At lunch, I simply stared straight down at the table. The built up strain of the day in general continuously took its toll on me, but being around some of my friends somewhat brought me to my senses. Will and Amelia were there as well as James and Doug. A few of the friends we sat with were nowhere to be found, though, in particular my friends Vanessa and Kim, among some others.

"Dude," James said to me, "I didn't know all this crap happened to you. I never watch the news or anything. I just heard about it from someone who does this morning. I guess those marks on your neck last week were bite marks. Do you at least have any cool vampire powers?"

"Oh, the usual," I said without lifting my head, "super strength, shooting fire from my hands."

"Can you turn into a bat?"

"No...at least I don't think I can."

The cafeteria was loaded with a huge human population with people of all races, sizes, and high school grade levels. The thing that most of them had in common, though, was the distance that they kept away from me. I felt like I had a force field around me that only certain people could pass through. With what limited vision I had, I could see many people around the cafeteria lean in toward one another to whisper. I knew that they were talking about me. While I was never popular before, I was also never a pariah.

I didn't budge my head, but I soon heard the voices right behind me. "Ella," came a male voice that tried far too hard to sound dark and convey a sense of hidden pain behind it, "you don't know what I am." I lifted my face up and turned see Ella Spawn and the school's resident attractive weirdo, Buford Mullen. They were both holding lunch trays, and Buford's was loaded with meat.

Eyes on Me

"Why are you so obsessed with me?" Ella spoke in monotone but seemed worried about something. I had no clue of what it was.

He quickly hid that face under his shoulder. "Don't look at me, Ella! I have the face of a killer. Your blood smells so delicious!" Buford was one of several adopted children of a local doctor, and the collection of them usually kept to themselves, so I really knew little about him other than the obvious fact that he was aloof, although he was at least good looking. This interaction with the new transfer student was certainly unusual for him. The two soon moved out of earshot, Buford taking his place with his family and Ella with Shelly and the rest of her preppy friends.

"So Amy," Will turned to me, "you haven't told us anything about your day."

I looked up at him, scowling, and said, "How the hell do you think it went?" My voice was weak. The day wasn't even half over. I was sitting far enough away from the cafeteria windows, so most of my proper paleness had returned though some burns still remained. "If they're not desensitized to everything like James over here then they're staring at me like some circus freak."

"I heard about you being a vampire from Amelia," Doug said. "I actually thought it was pretty cool that my girlfriend knows a vampire, though I guess I didn't really believe her at first." Doug and Amelia then quickly and almost silently discussed this disbelief before lapsing into their usual public display of affection.

"I tried to warn you last night." Will took another bite of his taco. "I told you that today would be crappy."

"How is that taco anyway? I think I already miss eating actual food."

"You're not missing much." Will kept eating regardless.

I looked all around the room. As my skin had continually healed that day, a certain urge was returning to me. "Maybe I could use a snack."

"Don't even think about it." Will was extremely adamant as he said this.

"Right, sorry." *But I'm surrounded by blood at every angle.* I was thankful for the consideration that the rest of my classes likely wouldn't require too much sun exposure. Still frustrated with my life, I resumed my position of staring straight down at the table, my nose pressed against the artificial wood, my glasses resting on the matted surface.

Blood on Fire

"Cheer up, Triple A." Amelia tried to sound sprightly. "I'm sure that eventually everyone'll be like me and they'll just learn that shit happens to some people, right?"

"Hey vampire!" A random guy's voice called me out from a nearby table. "I got some blood for you...in my dick! 'Cuz it's hard, yeah!" Hardly anybody at that guy's table laughed, but that was mostly because his joke was incredibly lame.

"Eventually." Amelia sounded less sure of herself.

"Well," Will said, "if it makes you feel any better, I'll be with you next period in English." Will, in fact, shared the same English and computer classes with me while Amelia had the same biology and history classes. Knowing that I wouldn't be as alone gave me a small sense of comfort in the rest of the day.

"Hey, don't forget me!" James said. He was also in the same computer class.

"James, you'd probably somehow end up killing her." Will said this jokingly. Then, though, he noticed someone approaching who he wasn't expecting. "Amy," he whispered, "weirdo at six o'clock."

I didn't budge from my position. *What the hell does that even mean?* I then felt a cold hand on my shoulder. "Amy Able." I turned to see that man I didn't really pay much attention to, Buford Mullen. He stood tall above me, his pale skin framed by his overly bushy hair. *Why is he here? Why is he talking to me?* All the other girls were probably jealous because of how much they wanted to do him. I wasn't very interested.

"Um...hi..."

Our eyes met. His were an eerie shade of yellow, which was a strange sign, though he also looked like he may have been wearing contacts—or maybe he had jaundice. "So, I heard that you too have a dark secret." I detected a false sense of pain in his eyes and voice that almost made me sick.

"She's not keeping it secret, dumbass." Amelia rubbed the fang marks on her neck again. Doug looked at her oddly, wondering why she was rubbing her neck. Had he noticed the marks? I wasn't sure.

Buford ignored Amelia's outburst of logic. "You must keep our secret for the sake of everyone." He then returned to his seat.

I turned to Will. "What did that mean?"

He shrugged. "I swear, he needs to be dragged onto the street and shot." I think he may have been jealous that the ladies were so interested in Buford.

Eyes on Me

"He doesn't seem to know anything about anything. And then there's that transfer student he's so obsessed with. She's one of the most boring people ever."

"Hey, go easy on Ella," James said, "give me some time with her and I'll set her straight." His tone gave away his sexual attraction to her.

"Tough talk coming from a virgin." Amelia said snarkily.

"Burned," Will said.

James knew Amelia was joking, but he took some offense. "Hey, you're one too, Will."

"Whatever." Will wanted to brush away the subject. "Anyway, he's just a moron."

As bells would be difficult to hear in the noisy cafeteria, the booming, amplified voice of one of our assistant principals signaled the end of lunch time. Doug gazed into Amelia's eyes longingly. She gazed back at him, though not with the same intensity. "Lunch just never lasts long enough," he said before forcing an "I love you." The pair gave a long kiss with Doug clearly dominating in lip strength (Amelia usually did) before the two headed in separate directions. Amelia was oddly in a rush. I had thought that she would probably stay around to make sure that I could reach my next class without trouble, but she just left. Perhaps I just selfishly expected too much from the situation.

"I'll see you guys soon." James waved as he headed his own way. I didn't really expect much out of him anyway. Everybody in the room was moving quickly to reach their next and varied destinations, resulting in a sense of chaos all around.

Will beckoned me forward. "We'd better get going before somebody tries to do anything to you. You never know what some of the people in this school are thinking."

"Right." But as I was about to move, the deadly rays of the sun from outside disappeared slightly. I shielded my eyes and could see a group of students gathered outside, circled around somebody in the middle. With the sun so strong, I had a hard time making out what they were looking at. "Hey, what's going on out there?"

"Stay put; I'll go check." Will also had no idea what it was.

I made sure to put my hoodie and hat back on as he went to investigate whatever was happening outside. I tried to move a bit closer, shielding my eyes as I did so, and I passed by the table that Buford had been sitting at. My eyes spotted something quite unexpected. "Phosphorescent glitter paint?" Those were the words that stood out to me. It was apparently an art supply that was supposed to make things sparkle. It was in a plastic container that looked like it was intended for children, and it was nearly empty. I picked it up to examine it more closely

Will burst through the cafeteria doors, looking like he had just witnessed something inexplicable. "It was Buford Mullen..." He paused, staring at the ceiling while trying to figure out how to word his next sentence. "...He was..." Again, he was almost speechless. "...sparkling in the sunlight." He looked down from the ceiling and spotted the container of sparkle paint in my hand. "Well, that explains the sparkling, but...why?" We were both clueless as to why Buford would want to sparkle in the sun. It was simply something weird that nobody had ever done before and which seemingly nobody would have any reason to do. I just couldn't explain it.

Suddenly one of the school administrators who regularly patrolled the cafeteria came up behind us and said, rather degradingly, "You two little blood suckers better get on to class now or ya'll will be late." He made sure to keep a short distance away in case I attacked.

"Well, Amy?" Will wanted to make sure that we had no more business there.

"Yeah, let's go." As we ventured out the door into the dangerous sun, I couldn't only think, *Why sparkling?*

As Will and I arrived at our junior honors-level English class, we noticed our teacher, Mrs. Perth, standing nervously at her podium at the front of the room and fiddling with some of her books. She looked up and found me there, which only seemed to increase the tension she so obviously experienced, making her shake awkwardly.

"What do you think is wrong with her?" I asked Will, concerned.

"Unfortunately, I'd have to say that it's you." He sounded sorry to say that. I could only shake my head sadly in response as I removed my hat and took my seat, which was on the other side of the room compared to Will's due to Mrs. Perth's preference for seating charts.

"Wel—uh—welcome, c—class," Perth could barely get any words out. I had never noticed her stutter at all before, let along this much. "Well, I—as um,

Eyes on Me

you all sh—should be aware...I, um." Seriously, she sounded as if her heart were going to explode.

"We—we should have been..." she was breaking out into a cold sweat, "starting to read *The Great Gatsby* today, but..." her voice trailed off as she thought. "But...but...I thought..."

I wanted to tell her to calm down but I figured that she might go even crazier if I said anything at all. *Easy now, I'm not going to hurt you, though I might bite you so you can take a much-needed nap.* I found myself imagining what her blood would taste like, a thought that I quickly tried to suppress. The hunger inside of me was constantly growing, but sucking someone's blood in school would attract all the wrong kinds of attention. The shock of doing so probably would have also killed this teacher.

Perth finally managed to say what she wanted to, though she had to yell loudly to convey it: "I thought that with current events we should study vampire literature instead!" The entire class stared at her, seemingly awed by her raw display of anxiety, which even spread to several of the students, who repeatedly glanced at me with alarmed expressions.

"I—I planned today's lesson without knowing that there would be a v—v—vampire in the class, so, um, please forgive me if my selection was a bit h—hasty." She staggered over to a table lined with books.

"N-n-n-now, I—I've requ—quested copies of *Dracula* from the English department and I w—want all of you to r—read it in full. Hopefully we will a—all...gain a greater understanding...of the vampire in fiction." The class looked around at one another. Some were actually eager. I suppose they felt the time had come to read about something like vampires instead of the usual rich people of the past that so much classic literature is about.

There were hushed and incomprehensible discussions all around the room, and I think I heard my name along with Dracula's as almost everyone in the room soon began to stare blankly at me. I was really getting sick of being singled out all day. Did they find me creepy? I mean, I certainly found them creepy with the incessant staring. I looked to Will. He was clearly unsatisfied with the reaction around the room, rolling his eyes with discontent. Sometimes teenagers just act all too idiotic.

"P—please take a copy of *Dracula* from the front table here." She made a weak motion to the table in front of the first row of desks to tell everyone to grab one of the many books.

Blood on Fire

Will then put his hand up. "I have my own copy; can I just use that?" Of course he would say that, being a warlock with a huge library. Thinking about that fact was still extremely weird. In a sense, knowing that he was a warlock the entire time that I knew him was even odder than suddenly finding out that I had become of vampire.

"Y—you may." The other members of the class began standing up to retrieve their copies from the table, so, naturally, as a member of the class myself, I stood up as well. I didn't exactly have a mysterious library of my own in my house.

Many of my classmates still stared at me as I approached the front of the room, and the guy I waited behind seemed a bit more anxious than he should have been. The line steadily moved and I found myself at the front with a book within easy reach. I grabbed the freshest looking of the bunch remaining, with the fewest visible tears and creases. I still await the day that public schools can finally afford books that aren't at least three decades old.

When I retrieved the book, I lifted my gaze from the pile and saw the face of pure anxiety fixed straight on me. It was then that I finally felt that the situation was getting ridiculous. I mean seriously, why should my English teacher be so afraid of me, who just a few days ago was her second best student?

Sick of the crap, I decided to speak up. "Mrs. Perth, is there a problem?" The dull hum of conversations around the room faded as quite literally everyone in the room—including Will—turned to the nervous student-teacher face off.

"I—I—I—I—I—I—I—I..." that was all she could say.

"Well?" I said it forcefully. Perhaps I should have been a bit easier on her, but I was really getting frustrated.

"V—v—v—v—v..."

"Vampire?" Of course I knew where this was going.

She nodded slowly, afraid that the slightest movement of her head would suddenly set me off onto her neck to suck her dry, though I had to admit that it did look tasty. Thus, I had to banish any such thoughts from my mind; they were just too dangerous at present. I needed to feed. I wasn't dying of hunger like I was on my first morning as a vampire, but I feared being at that point in school.

Eyes on Me

I sighed. I felt like all I could do was declare the truth to the world and hope that the world would listen. "Mrs. Perth, I'm not going to eat you!" My raw frustration made me sound harsher than I should have. "I'm just here to be a student! Does it really matter if I'm a vampire? Stop being so afraid of me!"

She was unable to make a logical reaction to my outburst. In any normal situation, a student yelling at a teacher would be inexcusable, but I suppose she was unfairly treating me differently from the others.

As Perth and I were locked in our faceoff, an odd question came from one of the guys in the room—I think his name was Dean: "Um, so, you're a vampire…do you, you know, have super strength or something?"

It was a question that wasn't related to me being an unholy monster and someone other than James asked it. It took me by surprise. "Um…yeah, actually I do."

"How much can you lift?"

I thought for a second, the only thing I could think of was the speaker I threw at Tower. "I can throw a theater-sized speaker. I can probably do more than that, but I haven't tried."

I heard some more incomprehensible discussion around the room. I could have sworn that I heard one guy say "cool."

Now a girl, I think her name was Nadine, asked the next question. "So…like…I think I saw you on YouTube, and you, like, shot fire at this girl my little sister was friends with and who turned into a giant wolf?"

One of her sister's friends, huh? "Yeah, that was me." Even more talking ensued. Some of my classmates were still staring at me in fear but now others looked at me with absolute bewilderment, as if my very existence were one of the wonders of the world. Then again, I suppose it was. In particular, Will actually looked confused for once. Apparently he hadn't thought that any member of the student body would respond to me with any emotion other than fear, so he was watching and waiting to see what would happen next.

The next question came from one of the goody two shoes students. Everybody knows the type. I may have been made fun of throughout elementary and middle school for being a geek, but this guy was the type who was picked on for being completely spineless. However, I could tell that the question he asked and the statement that went with it were potentially dangerous to me, so I had to think very carefully about how to answer him.

Blood on Fire

"Have you been drinking human blood?" he asked, "Because that's disgusting and you should go to prison for taking people's blood against their will!"

Everybody, especially Will, shot me look of alarm. While I didn't agree with this guy, he had a point, and the law might not see it my way. I had tried consuming that beef blood out of the freezer, but it didn't feel satisfying at all. It wasn't like human blood. Just a bit of what's inside of one person provides satisfaction that lasts a long time, but I had enough sense to know that not everyone would be as willing as Amelia to accept the fact that I drank human blood.

The rest of the class and even Perth leaned forward. Apparently they all wanted to know how I would respond. I tried to steal another glance at Will, but I couldn't catch him in my sight for very long without others being suspicious. I thought I saw him shake his head for me to not tell the truth about this, but I couldn't be sure. Or maybe he shook his head to say that drinking human blood wasn't illegal. Whatever the case, I determined that the best course of action was to be cautious.

Would lying be a good idea, though? Would they be able to see right through me? And what lie should I tell them?

"I've only done it once, and it was consensual." I inadvertently made it sound like sex. I also lied. It wasn't consensual at all, but they didn't have to know that. "Nobody died." I figured that I should add on one comment that wasn't a lie.

"How can we believe you? Who did you feed on?"

"Is it really any of your business?" It wasn't. I didn't see any reason to bring Amelia into this.

What I actually could never have imagined was what would be said next. "So you're not a vegetarian vampire?"

Vegetarian? What was she talking about? Ella, who I only now realized was actually in the class, just completely took me by surprise. "What do you mean 'vegetarian'? Like as in drinking tomato juice instead of blood?"

"Buf—" I could tell that she was about to say "Buford," but she stopped. "Certain other vampires only drink animal blood instead of human blood so no one gets hurt."

Her sheer idiocy made Will need to speak up. "I think the vegetarian community would prefer a term that implies the fact that such a vampire

Eyes on Me

drinking a meat by-product, which isn't 'vegetarian' in any way." I was glad that he brought that up.

"But it must be so much less fulfilling. You know, like being a real vegetarian must be."

"Vegetarians are generally quite fulfilled by their choice of diet." Will's tone was downright biting. He wasn't a vegetarian; he was just intelligent.

Ella didn't say anything else.

The next question didn't come from another student. "S—s—s—s—so you're going to f—fend off the evil vampires like...Dracula?" Perth looked at me almost like she was begging me to reassure her that she would be safe. She was almost cute.

I could also finally go back to answering honestly. "Well, Dracula's just a literary character—I think—but if he went around killing people, you can be sure that I'd kick his ass." I gave the kindest and widest smile that I had given in entirely too long, which actually showed off my fangs, and luckily it did seem to reassure her, at least somewhat.

Now about three-quarters of the class looked to me enthusiastically, while the remainder still looked put off. Perhaps one of them had another question waiting, but Perth had something to say. "Alright, alright, I—I...I'd like you all to start reading *Dracula*. I'll be in my office. Please...please just be quiet for now and read." I suppose she needed a few moments to cool down, but as soon as she retreated into her office, I received at least five more questions.

"Hey, you heard our teacher." I didn't always follow everything that a teacher said, but I also needed a breather just to realize the scope of everything that had just occurred. Furthermore, I had never read *Dracula* before, so I wanted to know some more about it. "Seriously, just leave me alone." People still whispered to each other, but nobody asked me any further questions.

I started reading Bram Stoker's novel, finding the beginning filled with the journal of Jonathan Harker. I would describe it, but you should probably just read it yourself.

The bell rang soon enough, and I quickly returned my attention my classmates around me. I may have gotten more reading done than I did if not for the fact that I was completely exhausted.

Perth made one last attempt to act as a teacher as everyone started picking up their belongings to leave: "Please read the first three chapters of *Dracula* by tomorrow!" I was surprised that she didn't stutter there, but even that wouldn't change the fact that hardly anyone would actually bother to get the reading done.

Will walked up to me as I packed. "Do you think they believed you?" He kept his voice low.

"I'll have to wait and find out."

"Well I hope this doesn't all go wrong."

"Will, I'm doing my best. I don't exactly see very many options at the moment, so I'm trying to be as straightforward with people as I can. It's not like I can just alter their minds into suddenly accepting me. I already tried doing that, remember? It didn't work."

"All I'm saying is that the G.E.D. option is still there."

I was suddenly annoyed by his mention of that accursed piece of paper. "You can take that G.E.D. and shove it up your A.S.S.!"

He seemed hurt. "Jeez, you don't have to be such a bitch about it." I realized that I was harsher than I should've been.

"Uh, sorry…just don't mention that again."

Will looked as if something else, something that my outburst had dredged up, was bothering him, but he didn't say anything about it. "I'll…see you later." He walked out of the room, leaving me as one of the last students.

Oddly enough, Perth then decided to speak to me, "A—A—Amy…"

"Yeah?"

"I'm…sorry. Things haven't exactly been going well for me lately." She seemed to have something in her personal life bothering her. I figured that I wasn't any of my business.

I gave her a thumbs-up. Let's face it, I couldn't blame her. "No…p—p—p—problem." I used a fake stutter to lighten the mood before heading out into the hallway. The break between classes was winding down, so I decided that I needed to head to biology.

As I made my way through the hallway, I got all the usual stares, but a few of the people who had been in my class and those they had talked to during the break stared at me just a bit differently—enough to make me feel like just a bit less of an outcast, but only a little bit.

7: Strange Attraction

"So, have you seen *Vampire Hunter D?*"
"I always meant to but I never got around to it."
"How about *Hellsing*?"
"Ditto."
"What about *Blood+*?"
"Blood what?"

"Gee, for a vampire you really haven't studied up on yourself, have you?" I didn't have much time before biology, but I found myself facing my old friends, Vanessa and Kim, who had been mysteriously absent lunch. "Are you really not just cosplaying?" Vanessa wouldn't quit with the questions.

"Why would I be cosplaying as myself as a vampire at school?" For those who don't know what "cosplay" is, the term was adapted by the Japanese from the English words "costume" and "play," and it describes a common practice among the otaku subculture of dressing like one's favorite characters. Now, for those who don't know what "otaku" means, well I don't do it much justice with such a simple explanation, but it generally means someone with a great interest in Japanese animation, or "anime." Vanessa and Kim were most definitely a pair of otaku. Was I an otaku? A bit. I wasn't nearly as into anime as these two.

Vanessa looked at me, sizing up how serious I really was. She was a tall, heavy-set girl with cropped black hair. Next to her stood Kim, a short (about my height), slightly chubby girl with thick, wavy brown hair and decrepit glasses that looked like they hadn't been removed from her face in a few years. Vanessa wore a ratty ankle-length skirt and a *DragonBall Z* T-shirt while Kim wore her usual jeans and solid-color shirt with a black cloth jacket. These two were not representative of all otaku—they actually vary widely.

"I think it'd be a cool idea," Kim said. She was relatively soft-spoken.

Blood on Fire

This conversation seemed a bit ridiculous to me. "Look I don't know how this happened, but I'm pretty sure it has nothing to do with anime."

"We didn't say that," Vanessa said. "We just thought you might be cosplaying."

I opened my mouth and pulled on my fangs. Unlike Coach Bellows, they were convinced.

"Wow, real fangs? That's awesome!" Vanessa smirked while Kim had a gleam in her eyes.

"Wait...so you guys aren't afraid of me?" I was confused.

"Why would we be?"

"Well, you weren't at lunch today."

"That was because Kim and I were drawing yaoi in the courtyard." For those who don't already know what "yaoi" is...that's probably at good thing.

"Typical." I rolled my eyes while the two of them chuckled. I glanced in the direction of my biology class, as I had mere seconds before I would be late, but these two didn't seem to care. "Look, I need to go to class."

"Alright fine, but you're going to show us your vampire powers later."

"Yeah, sure, whatever." After a quick wave of goodbye, I dashed to the door of the class, crashing into said door when I didn't realize it was closed. "I'm okay!" I said this to no one in particular.

While math was hardly my strong suit, I'd always been pretty good at science. The classroom was set up in the usual fashion—fire-proof tables, petri dishes, gas lines, and microscopes. I entered right at the nick of time while the bell rang, and everyone in the room stared, which could have been either because of my vampirism or because of my fall. "What?" Everyone immediately turned away. This class had no assigned seats, so I went over to sit with Amelia since Doug didn't have this class and she had broken up with her previous boyfriend who did have it. He was still sulking in the back of the room.

Buford Mullen sat in front of us doing nothing important until Ella walked in, passing by the fan in the front of the room, reveling in it as if she were caught in a supernatural burst of wind. Buford stared at her as he fidgeted uncomfortably until Ella took her seat next to him.

When I came up to her, Amelia was lightly stroking her neck again. I finally decided to ask her something about it: "Are you okay?" If anything were wrong with her neck, it would have been my fault, after all.

She answered as if she didn't even notice her own action. "Yeah, why?"

STRANGE ATTRACTION

I decided to let it go for the moment since I didn't want to attract any unwanted attention to her. "So what have we been studying lately?" After all, I had missed four days of school in every subject.

Amelia scratched her head, trying to remember. "We started the circulatory system on Friday...I think we're continuing it today."

"The circulatory system, huh?" My eye twitched as a sense of fear grew within me.

"What?" Amelia hadn't thought that anything would be wrong with that subject.

"Um...you know what the circulatory system carries, right?" My voice was shaky.

"Blood. But what would that...?" She paused. "...Oh." Now she understood.

"Amelia, all the sun damage I've healed today is really making me need to..." I looked around at the other students. Everyone was still staring at me, but those who had been in English class didn't look afraid anymore, though they didn't seem to entirely trust me, either. If I suddenly bit someone, it would be a problem because then nobody at all (except maybe Amelia) would trust me.

Mrs. Butcher strolled in out of her office, took one look at me, and uttered what I thought was a strange word: "Nosferatu."

I turned from Amelia to the teacher and tilted my head questioningly. I had no idea what she said.

"Nosferatu," she said again.

Butcher was her married name. It was fitting since she was a biology teacher and loved dissections, but it didn't fit her Romanian accent (regardless, her English was quite good). She had married an American man with a love of "exotic" women. I can't say whether or not she was really exotic, but she was definitely out of the ordinary.

"We have a nosferatu in class today." She addressed everyone in the room.

I didn't take long to realize that she was using that strange word to describe me. "Um...Mrs. Butcher...what's a nosfertutu?" The word was so strange that I couldn't help mangling it.

"You. You are the nosferatu. I will excuse you for being absent."

"Well, thank you, but what *is* a notfortaco?"

"Is Buford also a nosferatu?" Ella wondered to herself at what was close to a whisper. Buford shot her a dirty look

Blood on Fire

Butcher heard her. "No." A simple answer. "Okay." She went over to the chalkboard. "We were talking about the circulatory system last week." She had ignored my request for a definition. Considering the context, I could only guess that "nosferatu" meant vampire.

Amelia whispered to me. "Sometimes, I think that Butcher might be clinically insane."

I turned to her and shrugged. I also noticed that she had yet to let go of those fang marks.

"Blood is pumped through the arteries to its destinations around the body and then is returned to the heart through the veins. You should all know this from elementary school." Butcher was focused on her teaching, as if she had forgotten the fact that she had a vampire in her class.

Amelia then assumed what was pretty much a normal position for any high school student suffering through a class lecture—she had her elbow on the lab table with her head resting in her hand. Her other hand finally left her neck; it rested in her lap instead. I could clearly see the bite marks.

"The red blood cells are the ones that carry oxygen on their hemoglobin molecules to the cells around the body."

Red blood cells...the mere name of a component of that which gave me energy was enough to start driving me crazy. My eye kept twitching. I looked at Amelia again. She was still fixated on the front of the room, head in hand. I then that I noticed just how pronounced the vein running from her wrist up the rest of her arm was. I could bet that it was loaded, just loaded with that chocolate that I tasted before. She also had such nice, soft skin around it, which she definitely took good care of.

"I have some slides of red blood cells for you to observe, but we are short on microscopes, so you will need to share them."

On that note, Amelia turned to me. "What is it?" She had noticed the way that I stared at her arm.

"I...uh...nothing." I turned away, embarrassed. If I could still blush, I would have. Ogling a friend's blood vessels is certainly an awkward thing to be caught doing.

"The microscope"

"M—microscope?"

"It's...next to you."

STRANGE ATTRACTION

"Oh." I looked to my left, and surely enough, sitting there on the counter, amidst several other tools of high school science, was a light microscope. I picked it up, but my arm shook. Amelia stared at me, waiting for me to finally move the device. I couldn't look at her. I could smell it: that subtly sweet blood within her had an amazing chocolaty scent.

"Triple A?" I could never get anything past Amelia; she knew something was wrong. I put the microscope on the table, trying not to look at her.

Butcher came by, dropping the various slides of blood cells and the sheets on which we would complete our assignments on the lab tables as she passed, I think she saw how uneasy I looked. "Don't worry, nosferatu, all will be fine."

Amelia had the microscope in front of her. She placed the slide in the viewing area awkwardly. She looked through the viewing lens at the top of it, and then she made notes on her worksheet. I just watched her. I couldn't look away. The soft skin of her hand held the microscope steady as the pure green of her eye peered inside—that is, until she noticed my gaze.

"Um, uh, here." She slid the microscope and the second piece of paper Butcher had put down (my own worksheet) to me. "Sorry for, uh, hogging it." Her tone indicated that she was uncomfortable.

In all the time that I'd known Amelia, she'd always been the calmest and most collected individual I knew. This awkwardness was an entirely new experience.

After hesitating for a second, I broke my visual lock on Amelia and peered into the microscope, though first I needed to adjust the light on it since it almost blinded me. I could see little red discs, oriented in almost random ways, seemingly floating in suspended animation. They were bright red, a color that I could hardly look away from. These little discs were my life, my sustenance, and I craved them. I needed them.

I couldn't move. I didn't want to look away from the cells. I started breathing faster. I needed blood, even if I had to break the microscope slide open and lick it off the glass. I needed to stay calm. If I went into a feeding frenzy, my life would be utterly ruined and I probably wouldn't be allowed among normal humans ever again. But it was right there. What I both wanted and needed was right in front of me.

"Triple A…" Amelia's voice broke me out of my trance. "I—I know what you need." She spoke nervously.

I wasn't in any state to respond.

105

BLOOD ON FIRE

She held out her hand, bending her wrist and showing the blue vein beneath her delicate skin prominently. "Just take a bit."

I was speechless.

"Quick, before anyone notices." She hung her head, and her dark hair covered her eyes, but I swore that I could see red on her cheeks. Was she blushing? I looked around quickly to make sure no one else was watching. Butcher was typing on her computer at the front of the room while Ella and Buford were busy ogling each other strangely. The other students were either doing their work or goofing off with one another, but most of them stole a glance every so often. These glances had a chance of exposing what I was about to do.

If I didn't accept her wrist, I would have had to risk randomly biting someone else, but if I did accept it, I might betray myself immediately. Then Amelia did something ingenious. She positioned her wrist over my worksheet. "Act like you're working and I'm helping you."

Upon that suggestion, without a second thought, I dug right in. Again, I felt the ecstasy that came from her blood. I could taste that sweet chocolate. It felt so immensely refreshing and energizing after the stress of that day. That taste was the only sensation I needed. *I just want you, Amelia.*

I opened my eyes and released my fangs even though I knew that I hadn't drawn nearly enough blood to quench my thirst. Why did I suddenly have such intense feelings for Amelia? Why did I feel that I didn't want her to leave my side? I hadn't ever felt any such emotion toward her before, so why did I feel it now? I felt weird, extremely weird. *What just happened? Am I? No, I couldn't be.* I was confused. The first time I had bitten Amelia, I was too overcome with hunger to really notice any feeling of the sort.

Amelia didn't pass out, but her voice sounded weaker than it did before. "Is that all? I figured you would want more." Her hair still obscured her face, but it was all too obvious that she was blushing.

"I...uh...I'm...uh...done, yeah, I'm done." Hesitation's a bitch. It just makes awkwardness even more awkward. I pulled my worksheet toward me and hastily began writing in answers to the questions on it. I wasn't even sure whether or not they were right. I tried my hardest to ignore Amelia's presence. *I need to figure out what's going on.*

I detected disappointment in Amelia's voice as she turned to her own assignment: "Alright. Just...just let me know if you need another fix."

Strange Attraction

"I can't be your lab partner anymore!" Buford's random outburst stifled my worry over Amelia somewhat. Even Ella looked surprised after it happened. "I can't read your mind, so I must switch into a different class!" He ran out of the room.

Butcher peered in Buford's direction after he ran out. "He is definitely not the nosferatu." Meanwhile, Ella spent the short remainder of the class quietly asking herself why that "strange and beautiful" guy who was all over her before would suddenly run out, making no secret that she had become obsessed with him.

"Alright, it is time to collect the worksheets." Butcher rose from her desk and began moving through the aisle between the lab tables, taking the presumably completed assignments away from the students as she passed. When she reached me and Amelia, I quickly grabbed my sheet and shoved it into the pile she held, but only at the very last second did I notice the mark that I had accidently left toward the bottom of it.

It was a small red streak.

I gaped in horror at that streak. However, Butcher simply took one look at it and said, "lunch time has passed, nosferatu." She continued her collection.

Not long later, the bell rang and Amelia stood up. She lightly put her hand on my shoulder, which gave me a very slight, and very disturbing, thrill and said, "See you later, Triple A."

I could only watch her walk off, shaking her hips the graceful way she often did, before I could stand up.

I had my own troubles in biology class, but little did I know of what was brewing outside.

It was Rock Rivers' first lead, and he wanted to see it through. "You know, boys," he said to his cameraman and gaffer, one of whom drove the van they were in, "we're bringing the truth to these fine people. We'll find those vampires and expose them for the monsters they are. My only regret is that one of our rivals met one of them first." He adjusted his mustard yellow tie, making himself more comfortable in his brown suit. He had yet to discover that I was the only vampire in school.

His crew glanced at one another. The driver spoke up. "Sir, don't you think there will be a problem if we just show up to a high school unannounced? Hell, do we even know if these vampires go there?"

Blood on Fire

Rivers scowled at him. "What the hell do you know? Someone reported sighting a vampire at Flagler Palm Coast High School. That's the only information we need. You know, I pity you. You're just a lowly cameraman while I'm the big name TV personality. Soon everyone will know my name and the entire region will turn to Channel 45 for their news." His crew just rolled their eyes, weary of his constant hubris. "Hey, there it is! Stop there!" The driver pulled into the high school's parking lot, unashamedly parking across two handicap spaces. They spotted the front entrance, which was nestled behind a long walkway and a pair of flower beds surrounded by concrete.

Rivers swung open the van's back door. "Alright boys, we have a story to catch!" He lifted his fist to the air, proud of his self-appointed status of one of the news industry's greats.

"What do you think you're doing here?" The words came from a soft-sounding female voice to Rivers' left. There he saw the already up and coming reporter, Delta Stone, dressed in her signature beige ensemble. She stood next to her Channel 7 van, which was parked in a similar fashion to the Channel 45 van.

"Well excuse me, princess, but I was just about to bring the story of the killer teenage vampire to America."

Stone stared back at him, the anger brewing across her face. "Um, I don't think so. I'm the one who already knows the vampire and confirmed her existence to everybody."

"And you totally failed."

"We were here first, so this story is mine, a Channel 7 exclusive straight from the mouth of the lovely Delta Stone."

Rivers' tone became demeaning "More like Delta 'Stoned,' right guys?"

"What's that supposed to mean?" Stone became angrier by the second.

"Look babe, you can just go perpetuate your liberal bias across the street while the great Rock Rivers brings the people the real story."

"Me biased? Speak for yourself, you backwards right-wing nut job!"

"Hey, we only bring people the truth. If we discover that truth to be on the right, then so be it."

Then the two reporters heard a third voice that caught both of their attentions: "This is Niles Granite reporting for Channel 3." They both looked behind the Channel 7 van to find one for Channel 3 sitting across three parking

STRANGE ATTRACTION

spaces with a dark-haired man in a grey suit practicing his lines in front of a camera. He had yet to actually start broadcasting.

"Oh hell no." Rivers rushed toward the group from Channel 3, who paid little heed to his approach. "What are you communists doing here?"

Granite gave a confident reply. "We 'communists,' as you so wrongly put it, are going to have a little interview with the vampire and ask America what they think about her on Twitter."

"You have to be freaking kidding me." Stone had rushed over herself, careful not to trip in her high heels across the asphalt parking lot. "Well the gang's all here, so who's getting the story?" She scowled at both of her competitors.

"Well obviously it's going to be me because I'm amazing," Rivers said.

"I was here before any of you," Stone said.

"I've already gotten started," Granite said.

They locked their stares onto each other. "It seems we're at a Mexican standoff," Rivers said.

"What's a Mexican standoff?" Granite asked.

"That was a racist remark!" Stone sounded like she was pouncing on an opportunity, "Someone write that down! Channel 45 is racist!"

"You're racist you liberal bitch!"

"This is Niles Granite reporting for Channel 3 at the school of a young vampire where a fight seems to have broken out among our competitors."

Both Rivers and Stone turned to Granite and yelled, "Go to hell!"

As the three further discussed who would be able to take on the deadly vampire, they were not without their witnesses. Will's History class was fairly normal except for the usual vampire paranoia that was ever present throughout the school that day, but now Will found himself walking across the front of the campus near the main parking lot, holding a complicated form and a hall pass, having volunteered to take the form to the school's main office. For him, it was a chance to take a walk and clear his mind.

Two things pervaded his thoughts. The first was my plight, as I was so intent on avoiding a GED that I would put my own life in danger. My decision just didn't make much sense to him. He wondered whether he should even keep helping me.

Then he also had a problem with another woman in his life. He just couldn't shake the feeling that his mother was up to something questionable.

BLOOD ON FIRE

He hadn't actually spoken to her since Saturday. She was either asleep or entirely absent any time he was home.

He stared forward blankly, paying little heed to what was in front of him, but then he heard what sounded like a set of voices arguing loudly from the direction of the parking lot. He didn't like what he saw when he looked in that direction. The presence of news vans could only mean trouble with a supernatural creature in school.

Will took a look at the form that he still had yet to deliver. He decided that his errand could wait. He wanted to help me, but he didn't want to involve himself directly. He decided to invoke the same invisibility spell that he had used at the mall, so he looked around for any possible witnesses who would compromise his invoking of the spell. He found one.

The end of the current class period was near, and Buford Mullen was fresh out of biology, having randomly rushed out in horror. He still had paint on his body, so he glistened in the sun.

"You!" He caught sight of Will.

Will checked his left and his right, hoping that was someone else was around for Buford to single out. Nobody was.

"You are the friend of the other vampire, right?"

Will nodded very slightly, not wanting to actually say anything.

Buford strangely hesitated for several seconds before blurting out "We must protect our secret!" and running straight toward the news vans.

"Crap." Will didn't like the idea of Buford's involvement, so after checking around himself again and keeping clear of windows, he activated his invisibility. Hidden from unaware sight, he made his way to the ensuing argument.

"Who the hell is this kid and why is he sparkling?" Rivers and the other reporters were clearly unfamiliar with the inexplicable sparkles. "Look, punk, unless you have information about the vampire, you should just leave and let the grownups handle this."

"But you don't know our true nature. The true pain of being a killer. The awkward pained look on his face made Will have to keep himself from coughing, lest the sound reveal his position.

"So you're saying that you're a vampire too?" Granite asked. "The only vampires we have a positive ID on are Carla Evans and Bethany Davis. There's a rumor about someone named Amy Able. No one said anything about any males, though"

STRANGE ATTRACTION

"I will never reveal my secret to you." Will was excessively confused about Buford's odd behavior.

"What's the deal with your sparkling?" Rivers asked. "Do vampires sparkle or something?"

Will still had no explanation for the sparkling. Buford didn't answer this question.

"What are the vampires in this school after?" Stone asked.

"We are not after anything. Leave us alone. Leave all of us alone. If we let the secret of our existence get out then we will never survive."

"What do you mean? I came all the way out here to find that girl!" Rivers became more and more furious by the moment. "It was hell going through all those emails."

"Yes, that's right," Granite said, "email is a good way to contact your news providers. You know, you can also contact us at Channel 3 through Facebook, Twitter, and a number of other services."

"Oh can it, you socialist hack!"

"Well if you think we at Channel 3 are being too socialist; please let us know on Twitter or Facebook."

Buford looked deeply in the face of Niles Granite and said, "You do not need to be here. You can get your information elsewhere."

Granite was silent for a moment. "What are you trying to tell me?"

"This is not the best place to be." Will knew that what he heard was imperceptible to anyone who wasn't attuned to magic. He heard another voice over Buford's. A woman's voice said exactly the same words as his. "There are better places you could go." No woman other than Stone was present in the area, and the voice certainly wasn't hers.

"You're right!" Granite was ecstatic. "We don't need to be here. Okay everyone! We're done! It's time to pack up!" He immediately started preparation to leave.

Buford turned to Delta Stone, and, with the same unnatural echo, said, "Interrupting an educational institution will inevitably be trouble for the integrity of your network."

"You're right. I should really rethink this." Stone walked off toward her van, deep in thought.

Blood on Fire

Rock Rivers stared at the sparkling young man in front of him, confounded by what had just happened to his competitors. "Little boy, I don't know what you just did, but you're never going to make me abandon this scoop."

"There are some liberals causing trouble across town."

"To the Channel 45 Mobile!" He ran off at an Olympic speed, jumped into his van, and then ordered it to drive off immediately, almost leaving a cameraman and some equipment behind.

Buford stood still for a few seconds before spinning himself around to and making his way toward the main office to switch out of his biology class.

Will found a hidden crevice near the main entrance to the school where he could undo his invisibility magic unseen by any others. He then checked his watch. Less than 5 minutes were left in the class period. He rushed to the office to deliver the form and then return for the last seconds of his class. Now yet another mystery consumed his mind.

He was later able to report his findings to me during our next class.

"Whoa, dude!" James sounded baffled, though his face was hidden in the side of an open computer as he made a few adjustments to wires attached to its motherboard. "So, like, what you're saying is that there were news vans, and they left just because he told them to? If you're telling the truth, then that's crazy!"

"Curiosities aside, what's more important is that there must be something supernatural about him, though he probably isn't a vampire."

"Maybe he and Amy are secret vampire lovers." James gave a sly smile with his joke.

"I doubt it. He's all over Ella Spawn, right Amy?" Will turned to me, but I was busy connecting a monitor to an old machine's VGA port. In case it isn't obvious, this was a computer class. It was a rarity in most high schools, but the idea of the class was for students to make outdated computer hardware work again. It basically saved the school some money that would otherwise be used to pay technicians. I took the class because I was interested in learning how computers worked, having had a lackluster education in the subject in previous years of school. Ten workstations were divided into two sets of five on either side of the room, with a small web design class working on the left and my class on the right. Our teacher's workstation and tables full of computer parts took up the middle. Other than the teacher, Mrs. Kavon, I was the only female in the class, at least during that particular period. I worked slowly, my mind in deep thought.

"Amy?"

I jumped backward, my focus broken suddenly. "What?" I yelled out.

"Woah, Jesus, calm down!". Everyone stared at me again.

"Uhh...sorry...sorry everyone." I made an effort to calm down, but James and Will still looked at me in utter confusion. "What was your question again?"

"Amy, why are your lips so red?" Will obviously knew the answer, but he hesitated to ask.

"I...uh..." I stupidly tried to cover my tracks: "I felt like applying some lipstick. You know, a girl's got to look her best."

"You never wear lipstick." He had me there.

I really didn't want to tell him about what had gone on in biology, but I knew that he had already figured it out. I disliked keeping secrets anyway. "Well...um...all the time I've spent in the sun today...made me kind of desperate."

Will shook his head. "I knew coming to school today would be a bad idea, but you wouldn't listen to me." He sounded like an authority figure.

"Come on, not this again" I really hoped that he wouldn't mention the letters G, E, and D together again. "Some of us are worried about getting into a decent college."

"So...who was it?" James asked, deciding to step out of line.

The thought of Amelia immediately invaded my mind. "None of your business."

"Okay, okay, jeez." I was glad that he decided to drop the topic.

I still felt the need to feed, though. I hadn't taken enough from Amelia, and the day still wore on. Even when staying out of the sun I still spent far more energy than I did at night. Just moving was starting to become difficult.

"Look," Will glanced around and then kept his voice down, "you can't just bite people whenever you feel like it. You know, vampire bite victims have usually—"

"Hey, hey, Amy?" James interrupted Will while sounding as if he had a crazy idea, which the look on his face confirmed.

"What?" While James was mainly Will's friend, I had still come to know him quite well. I just had to hear what ridiculous scheme he had come up with this time.

BLOOD ON FIRE

James looked around, making sure that the others around the room had returned to their work. "Are you still hungry?" The weird look on his face showed that he was definitely serious.

Will and I just stared at him, surprised. "Well...yeah." I wondered whether I should go along with what I thought he implied. Will shot an angry glare at me.

"I want to know what it's like to be bitten by a vampire. I'm just curious."

I was hungrily fixated on his neck, unable to respond. I needed to confirm something: would I feel the same connection with all of my friends that I had felt with Amelia or would this be a different experience? James was giving me the opportunity to figure out how feeding really worked.

Will checked around the room again and said, "Everyone can see you; don't do it," but no one was listening to him. James positioned himself to look like he was staring down into the open computer he stood over while I stood behind him, my hair spread outward, which (I hoped) made us look like we were peering at the same thing awkwardly.

Will observed in horror, as if I had practically just committed suicide. One of our classmates looked up and seemed curious about what was going on. "Don't worry, they're just examining a short circuit on the motherboard. The student shrugged and resumed his work. People seemed to be tired of being suspicious of me as the day wore on.

Bacon was the taste that registered in my mind as I drank deeply of James' blood. *Really really salty bacon. Tasty.* It was a fitting taste for a joker like James, whose sole purpose in life was screwing around and who was notorious for eating (or at least joking about eating) bacon lattice sandwiches. I don't think I've ever seen him eat a healthy snack. He wasn't fat, but he did have a bit of a belly. As for that connection, it wasn't quite the same. I could feel that his intentions were good and that I could trust him, but he lacked something that Amelia had. I couldn't figure out what that something was. Amelia had this spark in her that he didn't. Now I was even more unsure of my feelings while drinking blood than ever. I released my fangs, careful not to let any loose blood collect either on James or on the computer. I lifted my head away from him. "You just keep working with that. I'm sure you'll find the problem." I then casually moved away, acting like nothing significant just happened.

STRANGE ATTRACTION

Will breathed a sigh of relief. He was glad that we hadn't been caught, though he would have much preferred if we hadn't done it at all. "That was a very bad idea."

"Would you rather I go crazy like at the concert?" I was lucky that I had that pretty much universal excuse.

"Well, no, but you're not going to hear the end of it from him now."

"Wait, why?" That was a strange thing for him to say.

His expression made him look like he was stepping up onto his intellectual soap box, saying "Amy, why do you think there are so many vampire romance novels out there?"

"Um..." This question seemed to come out of left field and I didn't quite know how to respond.

"Your fangs are a magical adaptation. Some witnesses of vampirism, especially of older vampires, make no mention of them at all."

"Okay..." I followed him so far.

"Those vampires usually killed their victims, sometimes eating their flesh."

"Right..."

"Your fangs work a lot like the feeding appendage of a mosquito."

"Ew..." Living in Florida, I'd learned to hate mosquitoes, so I wasn't happy that he compared me to them.

"Though I don't know exactly how they work, I know that they dull lingering pain and cause quick healing."

"I see..."

"So in the same way that a mosquito's bite can cause swelling and itching, yours could potentially cause..."

James started to stir. "Dude..." he said while lifting his head up, "that was awesome! Do it again!" His face was lit up like a kid in a candy store. He looked at me pleadingly.

"Attraction." I whispered it to Will, understanding finally what he was driving at. It made sense, considering Amelia's reaction earlier and her constant rubbing of her fang marks. I wanted to let James down easy, so to him I said, "Uhh...I've had enough and you need some time to make some more blood." In truth, I only took enough to supplement what Amelia already gave me. "Another time, okay? It's not you, it's me."

"Just let me know when you're ready." James returned to his work, beside himself with pride.

Blood on Fire

"You alter the emotional state of whomever you bite." Will peered at James, who had a dreamy look on his face and shook his head. "It won't necessarily cause sexual attraction, but something will happen. Now that that matter's been resolved, did you hear what I was telling James before about what happened outside?"

"I got the general gist of it, yeah. Buford apparently used some kind of mind trick to get some jerk journalists to leave me alone, right? I guess I should thank him."

"If anything, we should keep an eye on him."

Before either of us could say anything else, the bell rang to end that period and begin that day's final transition between classes.

"Well, good luck in history." Will usually had to leave quickly since his class was on the other side of the school.

"So Amy, I'll catch you later, okay?" James made his way out of the room looking all too satisfied with himself.

I had little trouble in the hallway I got the usual stares, but nothing particularly significant happened.

Honors-level American history was taught by Mr. Europe, who was neither European nor a specialist in European history; as I just stated, his preference was in American history. Normally he had the ability to take control of the class, but as soon as I arrived I found him struggling to keep order.

I normally would've thought that Europe could handle an argument, but when two of the most forceful girls in the school go at it, nobody can do anything about it. Add in the fact that they were arguing over me and of course things would just be crazy.

Amelia glared at Shelly, who sneered back. These two hadn't ever liked each other. Guys loved Shelly because of her blonde but not dumb (though I would disagree) cheerleader persona while Amelia just had that natural charisma that made men shudder (and boobs that I would never stop being jealous about). She was also less of a nerd than me and far less than Vanessa or Kim, who were just outright extreme. Speaking of Kim, she sat in the back corner of the room concentrating on her habitual drawing, barely paying attention to the argument.

"So? She's a vampire and she's my friend. I really don't see the problem." Amelia was on my side.

STRANGE ATTRACTION

"Lamy has always been a dramatic slut. She's just making crap up again." Shelly was not.

"Haven't you seen her burn in the sun outside?"

"Nope."

"Are you blind?"

"Nope."

"Well maybe if you spent as much time paying attention to what's right in front of you as you did being a complete bitch, then maybe you'll end up somewhere in life other than barefoot, pregnant, and unemployed in the kitchen with seven screaming kids around you while making dinner for a man who's just going to beat you when he gets home!" Amelia was normally forceful, but right now she was downright intense.

"Now uh, girls," Europe tried to speak up, but he quickly realized that he wouldn't get anywhere with these two, so he grabbed the phone on his desk and called the school's main office.

"At least I'm better than Lamy who will probably die by tripping over her own toes." Shelly always enjoyed informing the entire school of my clumsiness.

"Leave her alone!" I can't really say it any other way: Amelia was pissed off.

"If you love Lamy so much, then marry her, dyke!"

"I'm gonna knock your teeth out!" After promising to do the same to Shelly that she had indirectly done to me, Amelia pounced on her, slamming her and some desks onto the ground. The two were locked in a rather violent cat fight until members of the school administration came to cart them off and reestablish order in the class.

"I'll call you when I get to the car!" Amelia made sure to tell me this before being pulled out the door.

Shelly also had to add something "Lamy, just give it up already. You're not fooling anyone!"

Europe then did his best to give a real start to class, though he was clearly unable to focus, as were the rest of us, who were in the final class of one absolutely crazy day.

117

8: Knowledge Arcana

Amelia.

That name played through my mind over and over.

Why her? Hadn't I first bit her just because she was the closest to me at the time? We had been great friends before my vampirism. Were we simply just better friends now? Or was I missing something else entirely? The very thought made me shudder. What was I feeling? Why was I feeling it for her? What was she feeling for me?

I knew that I was definitely a vampire, but the possibility of being a lesbian never crossed my mind. Only at this time did I realize that as a human, I had rarely given sexuality much thought. My parents never actually talked about dating to me, not that anyone ever asked me out—or if they did, I hadn't realized it (though I was pretty sure they didn't).

Amelia always had a boyfriend. If she were ever attracted to me, she would've come forward at some point, but maybe the attraction arose only because of my bite. I couldn't be sure.

I asked Mr. Europe if I could stay in classroom after the final bell until Amelia called so that I wouldn't be lost in the ocean of people flooding the hallways to leave school. When she was finally released from her reprimanding, our shared drive home passed in relative silence. I didn't really know what happened to her after going to the front office, but she said little, giving off the aura that she was pissed off—though I was definitely sure she wasn't pissed at me.

"Thanks a lot for all your help!" I ran through the sun and into my house, leaving her outside in the driveway. I didn't stick around long enough to see her response. Shelly and Amelia had argued over me. What did I do to deserve this sort of attention?

Knowledge Arcana

The day certainly wore me out. I lay in bed restlessly, trying to sleep for as long as I could. Amelia was constantly on my mind. *Why her? Why now?*

When I opened my eyes, I glanced over at my clock, seeing the illuminated numbers of 8:37 PM. *Just four more days until the weekend.* I cringed at the thought of the standard five day week. Though I was determined to succeed at finishing high school, I still dreaded the amount of time that I would inevitably need to spend in the sun to do so.

Overall, since night had fallen, I felt better than I had in the morning, but I still didn't want to get out of bed. I eventually forced myself to do so, showered, and dressed myself in something simple before heading out into the living room, where I found Lupia, whom I had all but forgotten about during the chaos of the day, staring out of the front window. She was dressed casually in pajama pants and a T-shirt. I could also hear the television over in the living room, which sounded like it was playing one of those talent search shows networks often play during primetime. I shook my head in order to find the inner coherence to talk. "Um…is there a performance going on in the cul-de-sac or something?"

She was startled by my voice. "Oh, hey there. No, there's no performance out there, but this guy's been coming and going and just staring at the front of the house. It's…weird to say the least."

"Is he still there now?"

"No."

"What did he look like?"

"Pale skin, thick brown hair, about your age. He was kind of a looker if I may say so myself."

I could only think of one possibility. "Maybe it was Buford."

"Who?"

"Buford Mullen. Something was up with him at school today."

"How do you mean?"

I told her about his insistence on being a vampire, his sparkliness, and the weird mind control that Will told me about.

"I see. So he's probably not a vampire." Lupia was intrigued.

"He may just be a byproduct of all the insanity going on."

Then the doorbell rang. Lupia had looked away from the window after our conversation, so neither of us had seen anyone approach. "I wonder if it's…" Lupia's voice trailed off.

"I'll answer the door," I said. "If it's Buford and if he's in league with the other vampires, then he's probably after you."

Lupia nodded as I approached the door. I made sure that I would be ready to attack if an opponent were to jump through, preparing myself to punch. I turned the knob slowly but then opened the door quickly to more easily counter the possible attack that could be waiting, I started to punch but stopped myself quickly when I saw that an attack was unnecessary.

Will jumped a few feet backward from the door. "Woah! What did I do to deserve this?"

I relaxed my arm, embarrassed. "Um...sorry. I, uh, thought you might be...uh..."

"Yeah, yeah, I know." Will deliberately stepped inside. "Something wrong? You look like you just got out of the shower."

I hadn't yet brushed my hair and it was still soaking wet. "That's because I did. How did you get here, anyway?"

"Amelia said she was busy, so I walked." This was a feat since Palm Coast was designed with driving, not walking, in mind. Neighborhoods were always far apart. The roads winded around with no rhyme or reason, and few streets had sidewalks. The walk from Will's house was one of the easier ones at just under a half mile.

"I'm impressed, but what brings you over here at this time, anyway?"

"I came by to check on you because you didn't answer your phone."

"I didn't?"

"I could hear it ringing from in here," Lupia said.

"Why didn't you wake me up?"

"I figured you really needed to sleep."

"I guess I must've really been tired."

Will sighed. "That should go without saying. Anyway, has anyone tried to get into the house?"

"According to Lupia here, the only person who's been by was likely Buford staring at the front door."

"Really?" Will was surprised, "No one else? No news people?"

"None," Lupia said. "It's been pretty quiet today to be honest"

"Did Buford try to get inside?"

"He never stepped past the base of the driveway."

Will smiled. "I guess that means my warding spell worked."

KNOWLEDGE ARCANA

Lupia nodded.

My mind was still stuck on a different matter entirely. "Wait, if I didn't answer my phone, why didn't you just call the land line?"

Will thought for a second. "I guess I'm too used to calling you instead of your parents."

"My parents..." I still had no clue about what had become of them.

"Oh, sorry." Will felt guilty for bringing up a touchy subject.

"Wait a sec...my parents..." I suddenly remembered something interesting. I didn't know whether it was important or not.

"What?"

I ran over to my parents' room and came back holding the charred paper I found. "I completely forgot about this, but you finally reminded me to ask you about it right now." I handed it to Will, who examined it closely.

A curious expression formed on his face. "Strange..."

"I can only make out a few words," I said, "and one of them is 'Dracula.'"

Will scanned the ashen pages. He seemed to see something that I didn't.

"What is it?" I wanted to know.

"There's another name here that I think you overlooked."

"What is it?"

"Mina Harker."

"Who?" Having begun to read *Dracula* in class that day the name Harker now meant something to me, but only when it came after the name Jonathan. Other than maybe a passing mention that I overlooked, I hadn't yet come across a Mina Harker.

"She's a major character from *Dracula*."

"Yeah, I remember," Lupia said. I just shrugged, still left with no referent to that name.

"Let's see..." He examined the pages more closely, careful not to tear any of the already weak paper. A few pieces of ash fell to the ground. "I think I found something." He cleared his throat. "Here's one passage: 'Over eight years have passed since our fateful battle with Count Dracula, yet I fear that I have once again begun to feel the effects of the vampire's curse. It has been painful hiding this from Jonathan and little Quincey, but I am truly afraid of worrying them.' And here's another: 'It is for these reasons that I fear our great enemy may still be lurking about.' That's all I can make out."

"So what do you think this means?" I had no clue.

BLOOD ON FIRE

"If I had to guess. I'd say that this used to be draft of a sequel to *Dracula*."

"Um...okay." I supposed that his assertion was sensible enough. "But why would my mom have that?"

"I have absolutely no idea. Was there anything else with these pages?"

"Only an old typewriter."

"Can I see it?" I led Will and Lupia into my parents' room and opened the drawer with the typewriter. "That's certainly old."

"It looks to be from the 1800s," Lupia said.

"Is there any magic on it or anything?" I asked.

Will put his hand on the typewriter and closed his eyes. "Nothing."

"What about on the burnt pages?"

He did the same with those. Then he shook his head.

"Damn." I felt defeated. "I wish I could ask mom about this."

Will shrugged. "You know, it's probably not important."

"But don't you think it's an odd coincidence that my mom would have something in her possession that talks about Dracula while our enemy apparently is Dracula?"

"Our enemy is the Fool. We don't know anything beyond that."

"Whatever." Then I grinned sarcastically. "So not even the super-intelligent Will, the man so well-read that he has his own library, has any explanation for my mom's strange literary possession. Is the world ending or is this just a fluke?"

Will sneered back at me. "Hey, without a witch by your side, you'd be screwed." I stuck out my tongue at him. It was just friendly banter, after all.

Lupia interrupted our sarcasm tournament. "Why don't we search the house for more clues about it? It could be useful."

"Clues?" I said, "You mean about Mina Harker? Shouldn't we actually be focusing on stopping the vampire werewolf people trying to catch you? Besides, I just did that the other night and the burnt pages and typewriter were all I found."

"Maybe Will and I will find something you didn't."

"Eh, why not? If you guys would do that for me, I'd really appreciate it. It seems you're even more awesome than I thought, Lupia."

"Well, thanks. Let's get searching." The way Lupia girlishly blushed after I complimented her reminded me of Amelia and her sweet blood. Those thoughts would be a distraction.

KNOWLEDGE ARCANA

Before searching, I glanced out the front window again. "What the hell?"

"What is it?" Lupia and Will both looked concerned.

"He's there!" I was talking about Buford Mullen staring at the front of the house from the driveway. "Holy crap that's creepy."

"Wow, that is strange." Will looked disturbed.

"I wonder why he's not doing anything."

"The warding spell won't let him pass that point of the driveway."

"Is it like some kind of wall?"

"It's more like he just finds himself unable to pass that point. It's a mental effect."

"Is he going to have any way of getting around it?"

"Even if he were a vampire, it wouldn't be likely. It would take a powerful mage to…" He trailed off.

"'It would take a powerful mage to' what? Will?"

A thought that filled him with dread had just crossed Will's mind. "Amy, does your father keep things from his work here in the house?"

"Sometimes."

"I see. My mother received a package from BioLogic the other day, and she hasn't been home much lately, so I wonder if I can find any clues to what she's been up to."

"What would BioLogic have sent your mom?"

"I don't know. The box was empty. But I have the sneaking suspicion that she might be involved in some way with what's been going on." He looked as if this thought consumed his mind. "It's all too much of a coincidence, you know?"

"Well, I already gave you the okay to search the house, so go ahead." I watched as they commenced. "I wonder if he's still out there," I said as they scoured deeper under the scores of otherwise useless items.

"Likely." Will dug through the BioLogic records that my father had kept.

"We probably shouldn't search anywhere else but inside of this house until he leaves, right?"

"Right."

I watched Lupia work. She went through some of my mother's possessions. I thought I saw her sniffing the air, as if she detected an odd scent in the area. Then she pulled out something—another set of burned pages attached to what appeared to be a wedding ring—out of my mom's jewelry box.

"That isn't my mom's wedding ring." The metal was tarnished, and the gem looked ready to fall out.

"Maybe it belonged to Mina Harker," Lupia said.

"Give me that, please." She did as I asked. I scanned the page for anything of interest. "'The sun was high and bright that day, and I found myself wanting to return to the shelter of my home as soon as possible.' I can definitely relate to that. Think she was turning into a vampire?"

"Perhaps." Lupia pushed her hair out of her eyes. It apparently became unruly without a stylist around. "Can you read anything else on there?"

I checked the remainder of the document, but it was burnt worse than the one before it. "Damn it, this sort of investigation is just annoying, you know? We find clues that could relate my family to Dracula and it's all been destroyed by fire." I thought about my own pyrokinetic ability, deciding to try my best to avoid catching books in any blast I create.

"I found something!" Will sounded happy. I went over to where he was, curious. "It's a receipt." Will pulled the slip of paper out and examined it again. "Your father spent a lot of money on shipping from Europe."

"Shipping of what?"

"Boxes of dirt."

This was actually something that I had already discovered on my own. I had thrown the receipts aside because the matter sounded irrelevant to me. If my father had dirt, then it most likely involved botany in some way. "You call that finding something?"

Will explained to me that in the original novel of *Dracula*, the titular vampire has to transport graveside soil from the previously hallowed—and subsequently desecrated—ground from beneath his castle in order for him to be able to rest and rejuvenate his dark powers. In fact, such was the case with all vampires

"But wait, I don't need graveside soil."

"That's probably because you were never buried. Judging by the bloody filth you threw in the laundry the night before last, you probably died in your own room. I think you just need something from that room in order to rest somewhere else."

"Hey guys," Lupia said, "I need to call my agent. I forgot to cancel tomorrow night's concert. I'll be right back." I nodded to her as she left the room.

KNOWLEDGE ARCANA

"Damn, where are my parents? They left me too much to figure out. Their daughter's dead and they're not around to comfort her."

Will, hearing the dejection in my voice, could only awkwardly try to reassure me: "Well, just because you're not 'alive' doesn't really mean that you're 'dead,' per se. I mean, you're talking and thinking right now, aren't you? At least you're not a zombie."

"But what if I am?" I stood up, outstretched my arms, and slowly shambled toward him, saying "brains...brains..."

"Oh my God, a zombie!" Will acted like he was pumping a shot gun and firing off a blast at me. I fell backwards onto my parents' bed, pretending that my head had been splattered all over it.

I tilted my head up to face him again. "Do I have a morbid sense of humor?"

"Only if you believe that I'm an axe murderer."

"Wait, what?"

"Hmm?" He pretended to not have said anything. "Anyway, in all seriousness, the arcane powers keeping you alive—or, rather, undead—right now are so complex that nobody completely understands them. I can get you a book that sort of explains it, but I don't think it'll do any good."

"Um...okay." I wasn't quite sure what to think about that comment. Everything he said brought something else to my mind. "Will, there's something else I'm curious about. I'd imagine that there's any number of arcane subjects that you could take the time to read about. Why vampires? What made you so interested in them."

Will had to consider my question for a few seconds. "I guess what's most interesting about them is the fact that they were once human, and I guess they really still are. They have this sense of character behind them that other such beings just lack."

"Human..." My brain slowly processed what he said. "Do you think of me as human?"

"Amy, don't be silly. I knew you before you became a vampire." He answered the question as if he didn't even have to think about it.

"So...do you think of me as a monster at all?" I was looking for a little bit of assurance that maybe I wouldn't always be considered an outcast by all others I came across.

"Well, a bunch of people in our class probably don't think of you as one either. Many of them seemed indifferent or positive around you."

Blood on Fire

"So...I'm human?" I awaited his answer with nervous anticipation.

Will moved over to me and sat down at my side on the edge of my parents' bed. He lightly put his hand on my shoulder, which made me shudder. "Look, I've spent my entire life simply reading about beings like vampires, so, I mean, seeing this happen to you...well, I guess you could call it a dream come true."

What does that mean? I turned to him, my eyes wide.

Will realized that something he said was off. "Wait, that sounded weird. I—I mean that meeting a vampire, or anything else I've read about, has always been something that I've been waiting for. But when you became one just a few days ago, it was like a world that I could previously only imagine had come together with the world I had lived in before. My opinion of you of a person hasn't changed at all, but I guess you being a vampire now just makes you all the more special. I also figured that this whole thing would be causing you a whole ass load of trouble, so I wanted to help you out."

We gazed at one another. *What is this? What he said was downright weird, but I feel like he really cares.* Our eyes drifted subconsciously until our gazes locked with one another.

I couldn't say how long our eyes were locked, but the urge was back. I had felt it so clearly with Amelia earlier that I had begun to question my sexuality. Now, however, here I was with yet another person whom I had previously only considered a friend. The feeling was the same, despite Will being a different person whom I hadn't yet bitten. Did I just not have any drive toward romance before becoming a vampire? Or were sudden feelings like these just normal for a 16 year old? What was happening to me, really? I couldn't tell.

Our lips drifted closer together. I could feel him breathe slowly and deeply, which made me quiver in anticipation. Closer and closer we moved, slowly.

"Um, guys?"

Our gazes broke and both our heads whipped around to see Lupia standing at the room's doorway. I could almost literally feel my soul sink in disappointment at the breaking of that intimate, albeit strange, moment. I even felt like I was blushing, which I wasn't sure was even possible. He definitely was. My first kiss would have to wait.

"Well..." Lupia also blushed, obviously embarrassed at breaking that scene "There's something on TV that you might want to see."

Will and I stole one last glance at each other as we reluctantly stood up and followed Lupia, silently.

KNOWLEDGE ARCANA

A familiar face sat at the anchor desk for the evening news. "Good evening, I'm Niles Granite. Vampires walking among us. You have probably heard mere rumors of their existence on the news recently, but we at Channel 3 now have an exclusive interview with a few of them."

"What?" This new turn of events made me forget all about what had just almost happened.

"Yep, I have a very bad feeling about this," Will said.

"Well that's the understatement of the year."

Lupia remained silent.

"Strangely, the group was invited in by a member of our news team when they arrived. They are a group of young women who—hey what are you doing?" Suddenly Granite found himself forcefully pushed away by someone all too familiar to all three of us.

"Oh no." I was definitely distressed at the sight of her. "Not her again." Seeing the face of Carla Evans would inevitably mean a whole load of trouble for me. I rolled my eyes in anticipation.

"We'll be taking it from here," Tower said as two others joined her. I recognized one of them as Bethany Davis, the one I met at the mall. The third was a new face. She looked slightly older than the other two, likely by only a few years, and she oddly bore a heavy resemblance Ella Spawn, at least to me, although she was many pounds heavier. "Greetings, Florida, the first of many states and eventually nations to fall to make room for the new world order that we will create. You may or may not have seen us recently on the news, but we are known as the Dark Arcana. The three of us you see right now were once known by the now-irrelevant human names of Carla Evans, Bethany Davis, and Melanie Steyer."

The new name didn't sound familiar.

"However, we are not better known as Tower, Strength, and Devil. We are the future that will replace you, but for now we mean none of you any harm—"

"Fat chance," I said.

"—if you meet with a very simple demand."

"I think I know what they're talking about," Lupia said.

"We want you to turn over the musician Lupia to us. Whether or not she comes by choice doesn't matter, as long as she is brought to us within 96 hours. You will find us within Palm Coast, Florida. You may be wondering why we want her, but that is for us to know and you to find out soon. So please, just return 'her' to us." Again, Tower put an odd emphasis on "her." "If you do not meet with this demand," Tower now looked sternly into the camera, "then we are afraid to say that the town of Palm Coast will be erased from the map. All of its people will join their ancestors in hell."

"Or those who are capable can become like us as part of our pack," Strength said.

"Or those who are beautiful enough can join my cast of characters," Devil said, speaking for the first time. Niles Granite walked back onscreen, this time seemingly in a hypnotic trance. He came and put his arms around Devil sensually, a look of bliss on his face. I could only assume her main power was mind control. Dealing with a power like that would be scary. Such a power also explained how the group managed to take over the TV station so easily without breaking in.

Tower resumed her monologue. "Even should you manage to escape the town before our attack, our friend, Chariot, will reduce all of your houses to rubble. Some of you may have once called her by the name Emily Rogers."

I suddenly shook violently. "Will, what name did she just say?" My voice was weak as I overflowed with dread.

"She said Emily Rogers." He spoke with a similar, though not as extreme, sound of fear.

"I don't get it," Lupia said, "who is Emily Rogers?"

"Chariot!" Strength called out off screen. "Show yourself to these people!"

The sight I saw on the TV made me shudder with a sense of fear the likes of which pulled my soul right into my throat and made me gag. Not only had these enemy vampires suddenly showed up in my life, but now a ghost of my past stood at the forefront of my TV screen, making a public threat alongside the other vampires.

The Ogre Queen's enormous mass hadn't changed much, and she looked very different from the relatively pretty female forms of her allies. That mass of muscle and fat that I knew all too well was still there, only it was covered in the same body suit that the others wore. Now her skin was pale and her eyes seemed to glow bright red. She spoke no actual words, only letting out a deafening, high-pitched roar. Her long fangs were prominently visible as she made this sound.

KNOWLEDGE ARCANA

"You have been warned, 'Miss' Lupia." The image of the four vampires and Granite slowly disappeared as Devil waved her hand at someone off screen. The TV was blank.

I just continued staring at the screen, my mouth agape. I eventually managed to move enough muscles to say "God damn it." The thought of possibly confronting that beast once again consumed my mind.

"Do you have some sort of history with that last girl?" Lupia asked.

I still shook. "I'm supposed to be missing two teeth," I pointed to the gap next to my left fang, "but one of them grew back just a few days ago. That monster was the one who knocked them out in the first place."

"Don't worry," Lupia said as she hunched her head downward, staring at the ground with her hair obscuring her face, "you won't have to meet her again."

"Huh?" What she said confused me.

"Because...I'm going to turn myself over to them."

"What?" The mere thought was appalling. "You can't do that!"

"And why can't I? Isn't it the only way to save countless lives? You've seen how ruthless they can be. They're going to do exactly what they said they would."

"But...but...come on, Will, can you help me talk her out of it?"

Will had remained silent throughout most of the announcement, aside from when the Ogre Queen came onscreen, quietly considering what was going on. "Well, let's seriously go over the possibilities here. On the one hand, Lupia could turn herself in and everything would be fine for the rest of us, end of discussion."

"Will!" I didn't like what I heard.

"However, on the other hand, we don't know why they want Lupia in the first place. Turning her over could end up causing something far worse than what they're threatening. Furthermore, they could be lying about not destroying the town if they get Lupia and would therefore just destroy it anyway. We don't exactly know how trustworthy they are. If you ask me, that's two to one in favor of Lupia not turning herself in."

"You see, Lupia? You see? You have no reason to turn yourself in."

"But I..." She sounded like she wanted to say something that she couldn't. "It's just...Everyone has always..."

"Everyone always what?"

129

"I...just need to be alone for a while." Lupia quickly stood up and went back to her guest bedroom.

I turned back to Will "What do you think she was trying to tell us?"

"Whatever it was, I'm sure we'll find out soon enough." That was all Will could think of saying at the moment. I couldn't tell what went through his mind.

I sighed. "So we have 96 hours. That gives us until Saturday night."

"Friday night."

My math was off again. "Right. Damn it, why can't they wait for the weekend?"

Will shrugged.

Something else crossed my mind. "Will, there's still one thing I'm wondering about. I kind of figured that the other vampires would want me to turn myself over as well. I mean, both Tower and Strength said that I need to be captured."

"I really don't know, but we still have time to find out. We need to figure out what to do as soon as possible."

"But where do you think we should start?"

"Well apparently, you've had a visitor standing outside and staring at this house."

"I wonder if he's still out there." I decided to actually go and check at the front window, and surely enough Buford was standing at the base of the driveway, simply staring at the front door. "I'll be damned if that's not creepy."

"He's there?"

I turned away from the window. "Yep. Thanks a lot for that magic barrier, really." I smiled at him. I could see him blushing.

Will muttered something under his breath. I thought I heard him say the word "mom."

"What did you just say?"

"Um...uh...nothing."

"Have it your way." From what he mentioned earlier, I knew about his problems with his mom, and I assumed that he was thinking about her in reference to being a mage who could potentially remove a barrier. I decided to change the subject. "I'm curious about something else."

"What?"

"The names. They called me Magician, and then they were named Tower, Strength, Devil, and Chariot. They called their group Dark Arcana or something

KNOWLEDGE ARCANA

like that. What do any of these names mean? Shouldn't the Ogre Queen be Strength, you know, because she's strong and all?"

"You don't know?" He seemed surprised.

"No. What does it mean?"

"It's all a reference to Tarot cards. The vampire names are all Major Arcana, or cards with special meaning. Chariot represents keeping emotions in check to accomplish great things, and, well, from what we could see, I think that beast has only one emotion now. Strength represents rising above that which weakens us, which that vampire accomplished by spurning humans for wolves. Devil represents the darkness inside that drives us toward negative actions. The Tower represents a sudden and life-altering change."

"Is the Fool a tarot card?" It was a logical conclusion.

"Yes. The Fool is the wild card, representing the uncertainty of beginning a journey. It's actually quite a powerful card, despite its name."

"What about the Magician?"

"The spark that accomplishes change."

"The spark, huh?" I thought about what that meant with regard to my status as a vampire. I didn't know much about tarot cards, though I had previously heard of them and knew that they were associated with the arcane, so it made sense to me that Will would know so much about them. I looked back through the window again to see Buford there. An intriguing train of thought then crossed my mind. "Hey Will."

"What now?"

"Now humor me for a second. Let's assume that Buford is a vampire. Do some vampires have immunity to sunlight?"

"Yes. They're called daywalkers."

"Could anything within Tarot possibly represent complete immunity to sunlight?"

"I suppose the Sun would, but that's a bit too literal."

"The Sun, as in that thing that kills me, is a card?"

"Yes"

"That's it! He must be working undercover! His vampire name must be Sun!" I admit that maybe I was a little bit delusional from the combination of my day of school and what I had just witnessed on TV.

"I suppose that's possible but we don't have any proof." Will sounded skeptical.

"Proof?" I clenched my right fist. "The proof is right there. He must be waiting for his chance to strike."

"Which is why we should stay here until he finally leaves."

"Or until he figures out how to get in. Don't you get it? The vampires on TV said nothing about me because they knew he would come here to take me out—and maybe even figure out where Lupia is! I can't let him do that!"

"Wait, Amy! No!"

I decided that I would fulfill my role as "The spark that accomplishes change" as I quickly made my way to the front door. Will tried to stand in my way, but a light push fixed that. The door was soon wide open, as I took in the fresh night air under the soft moonlight. It was so refreshing after spending so much of that day in the sun.

Very quickly, Buford noticed me and started spouting his crap like "Yes, Amy, fear not, we vampires have to stay together and never allow our secret to get out. I think I…"

He kept talking, but I didn't listen to him for very long. The other girls at school were so crazy about this guy, especially because even before he (presumably) became a vampire he always acted pained and aloof. They thought I was insane for being disinterested.

I tightened my right fist as he spoke, each word driving me closer to doing what I had stepped out to do. When I finally had enough of him talking, I jammed my fist upward, directly into that firm jaw of his. It was truly an odd feeling for me to feel his bone cracking under the pressure of my dainty little knuckles. Still, it was absolutely exhilarating. In just a few days' time, I had learned the joys of violence. The strength that my new form gave me was just so amazing. So much power was now packed into such a feeble-looking package, and mere days beforehand I really had been just as feeble as I looked.

The force knocked Buford off of his feet, both flew upward. Then I grabbed them and swung his whole body around in a few circles. Again, this felt amazing. He obviously weighed far more than me, yet here I was swinging him around like a lasso. I finally flung him away. I'd have listened for a thud sound in the distance, if letting go of his weight hadn't knocked me off balance and flat on my ass. Strength does nothing to relieve clumsiness.

"Well that takes care of that stupidity." It was almost midnight, so it wasn't likely that any witnesses would be around to see that spectacle. I retreated back into the house, locked the door, and looked triumphantly toward Will, who was speechless. He had watched the whole thing through the front window.

He searched for something to say, but nothing came to him. I just continued smirking at him.

Lupia emerged from her room, a confused look on her face. "Did something just happen?"

"Amy, she just..." He was still speechless.

"Punched a stalker vampire in the face so that he'll never think of coming back here." I felt a ton of pride.

"You mean that guy who was outside before?"

"Yep. He's very much gone."

She seemed to not quite know what to make of what happened.

"Anyway," she had actually come out of the guest room to say something, "you guys have a point. I shouldn't turn myself in. I realized that if I want to truly get my messages across to people, I need to stand up to these vampires." Her voice faltered a bit.

"I'm glad to hear you say that."

"I—I'll just wait it out here in this house for a bit." Lupia looked to her side and then looked toward me. "Oh, and Amy, please try to be careful. You can't always rely on a werewolf to get you out of tight situations."

Why would she bring that up now? "Well anyway Lupia, you won't need to worry about that guy getting in."

"Why thank you." She smiled. I was glad that she appreciated the effort I put out for her.

"You know..." Will finally managed to say something, "if he really wasn't a vampire, his family could press charges. And considering how far you threw him, he could be...dead."

While I will admit that what he said broke the high that I was experiencing, I was sure that I had made the right decision. "He had to have been a vampire. Why else would he have been standing out there?"

Now, please forgive Will for what he said next. He later learned better than to say things like this, and it's understandable why he would say it, as he was around friends and he really never liked Buford Mullen. This is what he said: "Well, let's just hope that faggot will leave us alone for good."

133

Blood on Fire

Lupia violently twitched when he said it, causing both of us to turn and face her. She furrowed her forehead and hid her face in her hand. "Don't say that word."

Will looked to me, confused, and then back to Lupia. "Um, which word?" His voice was shaky, and he sounded like he really didn't know which word had caused a problem. He likely had uttered that sentence without even thinking about it. However, he was intelligent, and he was soon able to figure out what he had done wrong. "Was it...faggot?"

She had another spasm. "Just please...don't...say that." She choked on her words as she slowly retreated back into the guest room, shaking slightly with every few steps.

"I wonder what her problem was." The only women I had ever seen offended by that word simply disliked it due to the idea behind its usage. It was also just universally offensive. I mean, I wasn't exactly a fan of it myself, but never had I seen anyone so disturbed by it as Lupia.

"I really didn't mean to set her off like that." Will was worried. "You know that, right?"

"I know, don't worry." I could easily forgive him for saying that word, since, let's face it, friends very often throw random obscenities around one another. It certainly wasn't the first time that he had said it.

Then Will let out a prolonged yawn.

I glanced at the nearest clock and noticed that it was past midnight. Of course, I, as a creature of the night, was fine, but he, as a human, would need proper energy for school the next day. "Will, why don't you just go home? I'm sure everything with Lupia will work itself out on its own."

He yawned again. "I hope so."

"Look, thanks for all the help you gave me today." I looked at him expectantly, secretly hoping that we would have some sort of a follow-up for what had happened between us earlier—though I simultaneously dreaded that same possible moment. Would it be great or would it be awkward to kiss a friend? I wanted to know, yet I wanted it to remain a mystery. What was up with my mind?

But that moment didn't come. He simply nodded to me and said "I'll gather information on BioLogic tomorrow after school. It should be easier without...him... around." He tiredly stepped out the door to go home, weakly waving to me, and I found myself alone.

KNOWLEDGE ARCANA

I thought about visiting Lupia in the guest room, but would doing that be a good idea? I decided to leave her alone that night unless she came looking for me, which she didn't. I guessed that she just had a lot on her plate and the whole faggot thing just pushed her over the edge. I tried to continue my homework, but I was too distracted by Amelia, Will, Lupia, Mina Harker, Dracula, Tower, Strength, Devil, and the Ogre Queen.

9: Mistrusted Existence

Despite the seeming turmoil of her emotions the night before, Lupia still came to wake me up that Tuesday morning. She didn't stay in my room for very long before immediately returning to hers.

Even though this was my second time waking up on a sunny weekday morning as a vampire, pushing myself out the door wasn't any easier. Amelia was there to pick me up again. Like the previous afternoon, the drive passed mostly in silence. At least this time I thought of bringing a large blanket—an old, pink, seldom-used comforter originally intended for the short periods of cold weather in Florida—which made the whole experience halfway bearable. I wanted to know what caused Amelia's silence, but I also wanted to conserve my energy.

I eventually reached Mr. Royal's class, where I found my teacher in his usual spirits—neither high nor low.

"Ah, Miss Able. Early to class again? How is our favorite vampire doing today?"

Still exhausted, I pulled my hood down. Again, he couldn't avoid cringing at the damage to my face. "I'm doing fine, but I'll only accomplish great things at night." I was mainly referring to what I did to Buford Mullen in that statement, but I wasn't going to let him know.

"Did you see that announcement last night?" I immediately knew what he was talking about, and I panicked a little.

"Y—you know that I wasn't a part of that, right?"

"You weren't on the screen, so I believe you. That and you're here today and were here yesterday when Emily Rogers wasn't."

Mistrusted Existence

Emily Rogers... "Wait a second, was the Ogre Queen one of your students?" I used my nickname for her without thinking about it.

"Why yes, she was in my sixth period. I teach a senior level class then. She often had to miss class in order to meet for wrestling practice. She was on the boys' team, you know."

Trust me, I know that too well.

"Vampire or not, though, missing class is inexcusable, right?" He peered at me, expecting a positive answer.

"Of course." Can anyone really blame me for sucking up?

A few seconds later, Ella Spawn stepped into the room and took her seat, looking sad. I decided to be a bitch. "Anything wrong, Ella?"

"I can't find Buford today. I think he might be avoiding school because of the sun." That logic definitely didn't make any sense. The sun that day was the same as it was the previous day, when it had no effect on him whatsoever aside from fueling his sparkles.

Of course, I knew the truth of why he was absent that day. "Aw, I'm sorry about that." I tried my best to feign empathy. "I'm sure he'll turn up soon. He obviously can't get enough of you."

"I think he hates me!"

Holy crap, this girl's an idiot. "If you keep telling yourself that, then he will."

She didn't reply, quietly sobbing instead. I felt a deliciously evil sense of satisfaction for what I had done. For once, I actually made a difference in the high school drama that I so disliked.

Shelly then walked in and took one look at me. "Still devoted to the whole vampire thing, Lamy?" I shot two middle fingers at her.

Several more students walked in. About a quarter of them were appalled to see me present at all, even if they had been indifferent the previous day. I suspected these individuals to be the few high school students who actually bothered watching the news. The rest, however, unlike the previous morning, didn't give me quite the same negative reception. On the whole, people were still wary of me, but I felt that if I could distance myself from the message of the evil vampires, I might be in a better position than I was before.

The bell eventually rang to start off the new day and Royal began teaching "Alright, hopefully last night's homework taught you all that irrational numbers are more rational than you might think." He started yammering onward about math stuff. Any math fans who are disappointed that I'm not going into more detail should know that I have far more important things to talk about.

After a fairly normal class lecture (that was one thing that I could always count on Royal for), first period ended and I decided to rush to my next class just in case anyone got the idea of messing with the vampire. However, I suddenly found myself shoved against the nearest locker. I staggered for a second or two but managed to remain standing. I turned in the direction of the shove and saw Shelly standing before me. "I want to know something, Lamy." A few students gathered around, curious to see what the popular girl would do to the vampire geek.

I didn't respond. I just tilted my head while scowling. I wanted to know what she would ask, but I also didn't really care to talk to her in general.

"What are you trying to pull associating yourself with Emily?"

"What do you mean?" It was a strange question.

"You're both pretending to be vampires. Why are you two so buddy-buddy all of a sudden?" Ah, the logic of the ignorant.

"I have no idea what you're talking about. A better question to ask would be why you had her try to kill me two years ago. Why would a varsity cheerleader have her as a friend? Wouldn't she be a liability to your popularity?" The same could be said of Shelly if she were friends with me. The cliques that she was a part of weren't exactly very easy-going with regard to who could be friends with whom.

"She wasn't my friend!" She suddenly became defensive, yelling in my face and spitting all over it. "Just an acquaintance…and it's really none of your business." She seemed ready to punch me.

I was curious as to why she reacted that way, but I knew that I wouldn't find out any time soon. "Shelly, I'm not working with that ogre, and even if I were, it's really none of your business." I said those last six words exactly as she did, just to emphasize her double standard.

"Everything is my business." She spoke through gritted teeth.

I turned and walked away. She didn't follow. The spectators who had gathered watched me walk. I didn't know what to think about that exchange. It was so out of character for Shelly. Her usual interaction with me involved hurling insults and spreading rumors. This was the first time that she had ever asked me anything with the intention of getting an actual answer.

Mistrusted Existence

Along my trek to art class, I was accosted by all too many of the people I passed with the questions regarding the vampire ultimatum:

"Why weren't you on TV too?"

"Hey, why do you vampires want to capture Lupia?"

"Did you invade Channel 3 too?"

"Are you going to kick the asses of those vampires?"

"How is Niles Granite in bed?"

"You're not going to kill my grandma, are you?

"Are you Tower or Chariot?"

I didn't answer any of them.

Art class and gym didn't go much differently from the day before, but the nature of the stares I received from others was more mixed. The next unusual thing happened during lunch.

"Wow," said a voice that was absent the day before, "all this vampire stuff sounds like this crazy anime I saw."

"I know, Vanessa." I didn't even know which one she was talking about. Kim was next to her, drawing as usual.

"So has today been any more difficult for you?" Will seemed genuinely interested in knowing.

I shrugged. "Not really. I mean, some people think I'm associated with the other vampires, but overall it hasn't been all that different from yesterday." As I jealously watched everyone else eat, I could feel some slight pangs of hunger myself. "Although…" My mind immediately turned to my odd exchange with Shelly. "For some reason, Shelly seemed really intent to know what my connection to the Ogre Queen is. She even stopped me in the hallway to talk. Yeah, that's right—talk, like a person, except she was still a bitch."

"That skank." Amelia clearly wasn't happy about my mention of Shelly. "I still owe her an ass whooping from yesterday." Shelly wasn't a fighter; she normally functioned best in social combat. However, she would be ready to defend herself against someone feisty like Amelia.

"I didn't hear much about that." Will wasn't present and I hadn't mentioned it to him. "What happened?"

"Well…" Amelia was about to explain it, but with Doug around and Amelia's awkward attraction to me, I felt that I had to stop her.

"Amelia helped me out when Shelly tried to turn the class against me." I nodded to Will and then to Amelia and gave a smile. Amelia nodded back.

Blood on Fire

"Hm, okay." Will understood, although he clearly suspected something more.

Then I noticed that next to Will was James sitting in his usual spot, but his eyes were completely locked on me. I leaned to the left, and his eyes followed me. I'm not going to lie—it was immensely creepy. I looked back to Will to see if he had noticed, and he quickly caught on. Will waved his hand in front of James, whose only reaction was to look around that hand to keep his view on me.

Amelia noticed. Always willing to stand up for her fellow sisters against any sort of objectification (though in this case her action was likely also fueled by her own apparent attraction), she stood up, walked over to James, and gave him a hard backhand slap to the back of his head. It was truly a pimp smack.

"Ow! Dude! What the hell?" He broke his gaze and shot Amelia a dirty look. He then turned to the lunch in front him, which consisted of his usual cheeseburger and fries. I shot Will a look to indicate that I may have screwed up when I bit James. He rolled his eyes and shook his head.

Suddenly I felt a tapping on my shoulder. It wasn't cold like Buford's hand—it was definitely the hand of a normal human. I turned around and found the pot belly of one of the school's several assistant principals, Mr. Aft, who immediately pulled his hand back, likely afraid of me biting it. He was a chubby man with a thick goatee and was always a fun guy to talk to under normal circumstances. "Miss Able...the principal would like to speak with you."

"The principal?" I turned my head inquisitively. He took a few steps back. "Why would the principal want to see me? It's not just because I'm a vampire, is it?"

"You're not in trouble...he just really wants to talk to you." Aft motioned for me to follow him. I looked back at my friends. Will shrugged. Amelia seemed like she couldn't stand the idea of me leaving and looked like she was about to jump up to follow me. James had resumed his creepy stare.

Luckily, the principal's office was in the same building as the cafeteria, so I didn't have to cross any sunlight along the way. In the middle of lunch and class periods, only a few people were in the hallway, but upon my arrival in the main office, I received awkward stares from all of the secretaries behind the front desk there, including Ms. Turner, with whom I had previously had some fun conversations.

Mistrusted Existence

I got much the same reaction as Ms. Turner's upon passing offices with open doors. Instead of reacting, I just simply kept following Aft, who made sure to keep his distance in front of me. He left me when finally we arrived at the principal's office, which had a rather welcoming open door with a poster on it of a mouse wearing a top hat and a monocle decreeing the greatness of a well-balanced education.

"I've been expecting you, Miss Able. Please, close the door behind you." Mr. Cooper was a kindly middle-aged man with straight, symmetrical brown hair and a thick brown mustache. He was tall and relatively well-built, and he spoke with a strong Texas accent. "Have a seat, if you would." I detected no change from his usual demeanor.

I fell back into one of the cushy chairs behind me. I mainly knew Mr. Cooper's personality from the announcements he would make over the school's intercom and the way in which he acted around the student population in general. I had never actually been inside of his office before. Looking around, I mostly saw artifacts from Texas, which was where he spent most of his life before entering the Florida educational system. Countless objects were adorned with the symbols of the Dallas Cowboys or anything related in some tenuous way to the beef industry, including numerous magazine clippings extolling the wonders of propane and propane accessories—it's a clean burning fuel. Overall, it was a nice and cozy office, though I had to shield my eyes from the window behind the large desk.

"Now, I know that there's been a lot of talk about vampires at school nowadays."

"Well, considering I've become one..." I didn't really intend to finish my sentence.

"Of course, of course. Miss Able, can I call you Amy?"

"You may." I preferred being called that over my last name, and especially over Magician.

"Now, I don't know how much stock I should really put into this whole vampire thing. I see you shielding your eyes. Would you like me to close the blinds?"

"Yes, please."

He did as he offered, making the atmosphere significantly more relaxed for me. "Now, Amy, we need to talk about a few things here. As of yet, you haven't done anything wrong. From what I hear, you claim that any blood drinkin' you've been doin' has been consensual. I don't know what the law says about such things, but you haven't been drinking people's blood in school now, have you?"

I panicked a bit inwardly. I didn't know whether I would be punished if I told the truth. "O—of course not." I didn't like having to lie.

"That's good, that's good, but are you sure you can't just take animal blood instead? It would probably be much safer. I don't know if those fangs of yours can spread disease or not, and I wouldn't want to have you ostracized from the other students, I tell you what."

As if that hasn't already happened. "I suppose I could buy some steaks and give them a chance." I wasn't lying. I still had yet to really test the extent of what I could consume.

"Now little lady, I can appreciate a girl who knows the value if a nice piece of beef. I suppose propane wouldn't do you any good since you'd probably like your steak as rare as possible, right?"

"Umm…okay?" I didn't really know what he was getting at.

"But I digress. The reason why I called you here was to let you know about some complaints we've been receiving here about the fact that we allow vampires on campus. Even though you weren't on the TV yesterday, people are associating your presence with theirs." He paused.

The situation didn't feel like it would bode well for me. "You're not…expelling me for being a vampire, are you?"

"Oh no no, of course not." He shook his head to try to reassure me. "Personally, I'm not even sure if I should even believe in vampires. It could all be in your head."

Is the crackling of my flesh as I'm cooked alive by sunlight really all in my head? Nah.

"Anyway, if you believe you are a vampire, then that's your right, and far be it for me to kick you out of school for doing so. Let me tell you, our county may have been one of the last in the United States of America to allow Blacks the same quality of education as Whites, but we have come a long way since then and we now have a strict non-discriminatory policy, whether you're Black, White, Latino, Asian, Muslim, Jewish, Christian, Hindu, Buddhist, Communist, gay, lesbian, Texan, or vampire." He smiled in hope that the humor he injected into that list would help calm my nerves. "For this reason, so long as you do no harm to any of our student population, the administration will take no action

Mistrusted Existence

against you. I want to trust you, but if you do step out of line, you will be dealt with just like anyone else. The safety of my students is my number one priority. Now, do you swear to me that you haven't bitten any of my students without their consent?"

I tried the best I could to suppress any instinct to tell the truth. "I do, sir."

"That's good, that's good. Alrighty then, I think I've kept you away from your friends for long enough. You are free to go back to the cafeteria, though I guess there ain't much time left."

"Thank you sir." I stood up, but something still bugged me. "Um...Sir."

"Yes?"

"Exactly who has been giving you complaints about me?" My curiosity was killing me.

"I can't name names."

"Of course."

"But several of our students have come forward anonymously, and we've received some telephone calls from parents."

"What about the girls who appeared on TV last night but haven't shown up to school? I heard that at least two of them were students here."

"All but one of them were. Melanie Steyer is from Jacksonville." His voice and his face were both now very grim. "Something went wrong that we at this school had no control over, yet everyone is blaming it on us. Honestly, I want to trust you. You are my student, after all, and you have made the effort to come to school, but in order to attempt to please everyone, I have to at least keep my eye on you." His kindly tone had disappeared. I didn't receive the impression that he meant me any ill will, but rather that I should take his words as a warning.

I nodded to Mr. Cooper and began to step out. "Oh, Amy." He stopped me just as I was about to get away. "I actually have one more thing to ask you."

"What is it?"

"How do your parents feel about this whole vampire business?"

My parents—in all of the madness of the past several days, I hadn't told anyone other than Will, Amelia, or Lupia that they were missing. *Oh crap, I forgot to contact the police.* The same concern about my lack of a legal guardian, which I had already discussed with Amelia, returned to my mind.

Blood on Fire

"They're okay with it." I still didn't know enough about my situation, so I lied yet again. "I may have become a vampire, but I'm still their daughter." My bad karma just kept growing.

"That's good, that's good." He seemed to accept that explanation, though I got the feeling that he suspected I was hiding something. "Alright, go ahead on your way."

"Thank you, sir." I proceeded through the door. He kept his eyes fixed on me until I was out of sight.

Meanwhile, back in the cafeteria, Amelia was strangely annoyed at my removal. The wounds on her neck still hadn't healed, but she didn't mind. They weren't bleeding and they didn't hurt even when she touched them—in fact, touching them actually made her feel better.

Doug gave Amelia a quick nudge, much to her surprise. She had forgotten that he was even there. She liked him, but as her seventh boyfriend, it was becoming clear that her interest was dwindling in normal guys. She wanted a reason to love him more. "Baby," he said, "you want to go see that new movie, *Islands of Paradise*, with me tonight?"

"I'll think about it." She really didn't feel like going.

The doors leading outside from the cafeteria suddenly burst open, letting in the afternoon sun in all its glory. A figure stood amid the light, his appearance obscured by the brightness around him. He almost seemed to shine like diamonds.

"Buford!" Ella Spawn yelled loud enough for the entire cafeteria to hear as she went to embrace her vampiric hero.

"I have returned," he said in a calm voice.

Once their eyes adjusted, Will and Amelia could see Buford quite clearly. Will in particular noticed the same sparkle paint on Buford's skin from the day before. He also noticed that Buford had no injuries. "Wait…This can't be right…"

"What is it?" I hadn't yet told Amelia about what I did.

"Amy's going to have a cow when she hears about this." Will sounded weary.

I did have a cow. "WHAT?" I clenched me fist in frustration. I didn't witness Buford's return, but who was I to call my friends liars? Lunch was almost over by the time I was done talking with Mr. Cooper. I met Will near the entrance to English class. "But I…but he…but what?"

Mistrusted Existence

"He was just fine." Will spoke with his arms crossed.

"Are you sure he's not a vampire?"

"I really have no idea what to say. You got rid of him and now he's back. Still, you should probably be glad that he's not dead."

I sighed. "Damn it, you have a point. He'd better not be staring at my house again tonight."

"If he is, what will you do?"

"Well nothing's going to stop me tonight. We need to find my parents before things get too crazy. If he's there, then I'll…I'll."

"You'll what?"

"I don't know."

"In any case, for your parents, I'd say our best lead is BioLogic. Like I said, I'll look more into that tonight. Now let's go to class." Time was wearing thin.

Admittedly, not much happened during English class. One of the common substitute teachers, Mr. Jacobs stood at the head of the class, his bald head glistening in the fluorescent lights. "So your teacher, Mrs. Perth, has actually decided to quit teaching here and move elsewhere."

"What?" Some of the other students chattered about this turn of events, but I was particularly confused. She seemed to be doing well by the time I left class the day before despite how she acted when I arrived. "Did she say why?"

"She didn't give us a reason, but not to worry. The administration is currently interviewing her replacement as we speak." That wasn't very reassuring. "I've been told that you needed to read Dracula. Fitting." He glanced at me with that last word, making no effort not to single me out.

The class consisted of an innocuous writing assignment to prove that we did the reading, and I had done a fair amount of it, making it easy overall.

I met with Will again after class. "So Perth is gone? I just can't believe it."

He shrugged. "I guess she was just too afraid of vampires after all."

"Well damn it." I didn't like the thought that I had scared someone off, so I changed the subject. "I know I cracked Buford's jaw. I could feel it crumbling and dislocating." I got a twinge of ecstasy as I spoke, much like I did when I committed the act. Even the thought of the power I had was just so invigorating. "I think I also threw him about three blocks away." I smirked. Then I thought of a potential problem: "He didn't call me out for throwing him away, did he?"

"He didn't say anything about you. He was just his normal self floating around and saying random crap as usual."

BLOOD ON FIRE

"Well that's just..." my body suddenly made a spasm as spoke, and I felt a bit more woozy than usual.

"Something wrong?"

The hunger was setting in again. The fact remained that I hadn't fed since taking James' blood the day before. I shook my head to regain my bearings. Will didn't want me feeding at school, so I felt that I needed to make up a lie to throw off any concern. "Sorry, I just had a bit of a brain fart."

"Because you're hungry, right?" Will said this sarcastically, though he clearly knew he was right.

Damn it, I can't get anything past him, can I?

"We really need to find a solution for that, if you're so insistent on coming to school."

"Couldn't I just...you know...with James." I was hopeful that the same solution from the day before would work.

"For one thing, that's a bad idea for the same reasons it was yesterday. Furthermore, for God's sake, give him some time to make some more." I assumed that he was talking about blood. His tone at that last statement was somewhat playful, and I appreciated his attempt to lighten the mood. Then for a second he looked into my eyes, and I thought something might happen like the night before, but he simply said "Well, I'm off to class; good luck!" He waved and walked off. I was a fool for having such expectations at school.

I ran into Vanessa and Kim in the hallway again, but this time, I just waved before continuing on my way. I arrived in biology class and sat alongside Amelia once again, tiredly pulling out the necessary materials to get through the class.

The class, a continuation of that of the day before, served only one purpose: to make me hungrier. Truly, this would be a daily problem.

Amelia looked at me, concerned and caring. "Do you need another fix?"

"Amelia, I love you..." Her face perked up, apparently hopeful. "...like a sister..." That perkiness only somewhat faded. "...but I can't keep this up. You need your blood more than I do." My decision disappointed her.

"Miss Nosferatu!" The call came all of a sudden, and it nearly gave me a heart attack, if that were even possible.

"Uh...uh...yes?" No other teacher had yet called on me after I became a vampire, so Butcher was the first.

Mistrusted Existence

"Can you tell me, and I ask specifically you, who should know better than the rest, why blood has the taste that it does?"

Blood's taste? Well that depends on whosever blood it is, doesn't it? That was what crossed my mind. Amelia's flavor was chocolate and James's was bacon. The flavor differed depending on the type of person the blood came from.

Then I realized how ridiculous that sounded. Butcher and the students knew nothing of my taste of blood. Luckily I knew the answer offhand: "Because of the iron in hemoglobin."

"Indeed." Butcher was apparently satisfied with my answer. "Become used to that taste."

Is she trying to drive me crazy? I rolled my eyes when she turned around and went back to the chalk board. I also gave another nervous spasm that I hoped went unnoticed.

"Blood does taste...irony." Buford said, struggling to insert that last word, which, might I add, was incorrect.

However, Buford's statement got me thinking. *Wait...I thought I established that he's a vampire. Wouldn't he have the same experience with drinking blood that I've had?* Indeed, were he a vampire, he certainly would have already drank blood, and I was sure that he wouldn't have tasted mere iron. *And another thing*, suddenly another, stranger thought entered my mind, *I've never actually seen him drink blood, but...I have seen him...eating food.* I thought back to lunch time on the previous day, when he had a big plate of meat. *Damn, if I'd only thought of this at lunch. But wait, I did try eating when I first woke up on Saturday morning...but that pizza had garlic on it, so it didn't really count.* I was definitely hungry, and the principal didn't want me biting anyone in school. The thirst for blood was ready to show itself full force within me. Maybe some food would calm that hunger? I thought about the taste of Amelia's blood. It was the same as something that she usually carried. "Amelia, can I have a kiss?"

"Excuse me?" Her voice sounded slightly appalled at my sudden question, though her face betrayed excitement at such a proposition.

But that wasn't what I meant. In actuality I had only just remembered that Amelia usually kept a supply of Hershey's Kisses in her purse to occasionally snack on. I then wondered if her love of chocolate was what flavored her blood, but I suspected that the real explanation would be more complicated. Those kisses were potentially the only source of nourishment in that classroom other than blood. "A Hershey's Kiss, you know, one of the ones in your purse."

"Oh, okay, alright." She seemed both relieved and disappointed as she awkwardly took the bag of candy from her purse and pulled out one silver-wrapped treat that she then handed to me.

I unwrapped it silently so as not to arouse the suspicion of the teacher, which was the concern of just any normal student trying to eat in class, and sniffed it. It smelled exactly as chocolate should have, which, of course, is delicious, but I found that I had no desire to eat it.

Amelia stared at me, curious as to what I was about to do. I was sure that she thought that vampires couldn't eat normal human food. In fact, I was sure of that conclusion as well. With her watching, I decided to take the plunge and shove the piece of candy into my mouth.

Never before did I think that a piece of chocolate could taste so much like sand. Chewing it was an arduous process that must have been accompanied by a look of suffering on my face, judging by Amelia's fearful reaction. When I swallowed it, I couldn't help gagging as my chest convulsed in rejection. I coughed loudly a few times, making sure to cover my mouth as I did so.

"Miss nosferatu, is there a problem?" Butcher turned from the board to face me, wondering why I would cough the way I did.

My voice was strained. "Nope, no problem at all." I kept my hand over my mouth as I spoke.

"Hm." She turned back to her teaching, letting the matter rest, which was lucky for me.

Everyone else stared at me, though.

I took my hand away from my face and found it covered with a mix of blood and chocolate, which I then could feel dripping from my bottom lip down my chin. Amelia handed me some tissues, also from her purse, to dry it up. Human food was definitely out of the question. *Unless...Buford was eating meat. Maybe that still works.* But I didn't have any meat around, so that really wasn't an option at the moment.

I stared at Buford, who faced the board in front of me. How did he stay sustained as a vampire? And how could he eat food? At the very least, it was clear to me that he wasn't the same type of vampire as me, and most likely he wasn't a vampire at all but something different entirely.

Mistrusted Existence

But if he is a vampire, how does he survive? Where does he get his blood? Blood...blood...I need some blood. The desire for blood played over and over strongly in my mind. I had one of my hands under the lab table, and it shook unconsciously out of the sheer stress I was experiencing, as if blood were rushing into it.

Then the strangest thing happened. The air between me and Buford looked as if it had suddenly become red hot. It was subtle, appearing like small waves in the air that were a very pale shade of red. My arm continued to shake as I felt a power surging into it. It was a very odd sensation, both refreshing and exhausting.

I peered under the table and saw something that I doubted anyone had ever seen before. In my hand was a sphere made of blood that grew. I jerked my arm back, reassuming control over it, and calmly bent downward to shove the sphere into my mouth. It melted into liquid immediately as I swallowed it. It tasted like nothing at all. The waves between Buford and me were gone.

I could see Buford nodding off and struggling not to fall asleep, which oddly didn't perturb Ella's nonstop staring at him.

I, on the other hand, experienced an odd mix of sensations. I felt both refreshed by the blood and exhausted because of the means by which I obtained it. It was like eating a feast after running a marathon (not that I were ever in the sort of physical condition to be able to do that). I had to struggle to stay awake even more that I usually did during the day time, and I had trouble even sitting up in an upright position. Ultimately, I ended up resting my head on the table.

Just like my initial use of fire, this was a brand new spell that suddenly responded to my need in a specific situation. It allowed me to obtain blood without having to touch anyone. However, I would feel completely exhausted for the rest of that day. It wouldn't be as taxing at night, but using it could still be a liability. I would later discover that it removed all taste from blood.

"What was that?" Amelia whispered to me. The presence of other people in the room had slipped my mind, so I was almost startled when she addressed me.

"Um...I'll, uh, explain later." I just wanted to sleep, not think. Then I glanced around to catch any signal that somebody else may have seen me. I couldn't be sure about the majority of the students in the class since none of displayed any reaction of having just seen something out of the ordinary besides just the basic fact of a vampire's presence.

Blood on Fire

The bell that ended that period seemed to me like it was sent by God. I just had to get out of that room. "Tomorrow we will be doing an experiment using the material we discussed today," Butcher said. She then poked Buford to wake him from what looked like an odd trance. He just stared at Ella, not moving. Ella just stared back. *He's probably asleep with his eyes open.*

I rushed into the hallway after hastily packing my bag. I then had to struggle to not collapse when I arrived outside. I supposed that it was better to be tired than hungry, all things considered.

Amelia quickly caught up to me, appearing and sounding worried. "You look...exhausted. So would you tell me what happened?"

"Magic."

"Magic? That's right, you were shooting fire from your hand at the mall, weren't you?" Amelia had been so caught up in the moment during our tag team against Tower that the unusualness of pyrokinetics had hardly registered to her. "What did you do this time, exactly?"

I mentioned that the spell activated spontaneously and that it seemed to allow me to take blood, which was all I knew at the time.

"So you don't know about all the abilities you have?"

I nodded.

"This is all...so weird." She started rubbing her fang marks.

"Yeah, well, Will and I are going to get to the bottom of this tonight." Between yawns, I explained what he and I found the night before and our plans to investigate BioLogic.

"I want to help too." She seemed eager.

I shrugged. "The more the merrier, I suppose." Not in any state to give the matter any further thought, I slowly staggered to my next class.

I was actually a bit disgusted that I actually had some of Buford's blood inside of me, and I hoped that he wouldn't develop the same sort of obsession with me that James and Amelia had. Taking all into consideration, however, he already seemed to be obsessed with me, as shown by his weird staring at my house.

In history class, Shelly and Amelia kept their distance from each other. I still didn't know Shelly's real motives for confronting me earlier that day.

Amelia was definitely in a better mood during the drive home. She had had enough time to cool off after her fight with Shelly. I'd have said more to her during the ride if I weren't trying to keep myself covered. "For the love of God,

Mistrusted Existence

get a darker tint for your windows." Amelia and Lupia had to help me get inside my house, as my exhaustion from the spell and my sun damage together were just too much to handle.

10: Tactical Espionage Action

Even more so than the night before, I didn't want to get out of bed. Will stopped by my house at night before I did. Apparently, Lupia let him in and left him in the living room before retreating back to her guest room. I found him playing my PS3—without my permission, might I add.

"Don't you have a house of your own?" I felt sarcastic.

"I did what I needed to do there."

"Does your mom know you're at a girl's house? I heard her on your phone; she seems to hates girls...despite being one."

"Amy, my mom hasn't spoken to me since Saturday. She's either asleep or not present at all."

I crossed my arms. "At least you've seen her. Asleep is better than nothing. Anyway, what'd you find out about BioLogic and their role in this?"

"Other than the location that your father works at, nothing." He handed me page he printed out from Google Maps. "It was on the return address label of my mom's weird package."

I gave it a quick glance. "I guess we'll need to go there, won't we?"

"I suppose so."

"And you just assumed that I didn't know the way to my father's place of work." He didn't bother consulting me to see if I would know.

"I printed the directions out just in case." We were actually lucky that he did because I forgot the address.

"Alright." I made a fist to show my determination. "We're going to go storm BioLogic and find out exactly what Dracula's been up to!" I spoke enthusiastically. The prospect of making some headway toward solving this mystery gave me a bit more energy.

Tactical Espionage Action

"Don't get ahead of yourself." Will rolled his eyes. "It might be dangerous." He didn't acknowledge the fact that I said "Dracula" instead of "the Fool."

Suddenly our ears were filled with the Super Mario Bros. theme song. I had shoved my cell phone into my cargo skirt's right pocket. The screen showed Amelia's name. Will patiently stopped talking as I answered. "Joe's Crematorium: You kill 'em, we grill 'em." I felt like being random.

"Excuse me?" Amelia hadn't expected that answer.

I chuckled. "Just kidding. Hey Amelia."

"Hi there Triple A," she sounded both relieved and amused. "Should I head over to your place right now?"

"Well, uh, hold on a sec, we've kind of decided to go on an adventure, so let me ask Will." I lifted the phone away from my ear and turned to Will. This situation felt a bit awkward. "Can Amelia come with us?"

"I hope she realizes that we might run into other vampires and God only knows what else. I mean, I'm not necessarily opposed to her coming along, but she needs to realize that she may need to defend herself. You and I have supernatural powers; she doesn't."

"She knows how to use a gun, remember?" Then I addressed my phone, "You're okay with carrying the gun that broke your window again, right?"

"Of course. I stole some ammo from daddy's stash. If you need a shooter, I'm your girl!"

Let me interrupt this conversation just to give a public service announcement: Amelia was highly practiced in firearms. That doesn't mean that anyone should play with them just to be as cool as her. Seriously, guns are not to be taken lightly. Normally high school students have no real use for packing heat (unless they intend to murder). Our situation was far from normal.

Will didn't look entirely thrilled. "Well fine, she can come along. It'll be good for us to have a proper driver anyway." (Will's intent had been for us to use my mom's car.) Then he whispered to me. "Just please try not to distract her too much." I assumed that he was talking about the effects of my bite.

I nodded and then addressed Amelia. "Come on over."

"Sweet! I'll be right there, Triple A!" Amelia sounded delighted to be a part of our little adventure.

"I hope she knows what she's getting into." Will rolled his eyes.

Blood on Fire

"Amelia's not dumb. She's just as much a part of this as you are. Just give her a chance." I wasn't sure if Will had witnessed our glorious tag team attack on Sunday night.

When Amelia came to pick us up, we all said goodbye to Lupia, who barely made any reaction. She was the last one in the house when we left. In fact, she hadn't left the house for two days, and it was starting to wear on her. Whenever I was out or asleep, she only had the TV to keep her company.

As the last program she watched ended, she went to her room and grabbed her pill bottle. She needed to take one every night to maintain the health of her feminine body. She went to the kitchen to pour herself a glass of water to help the small capsule go down.

She didn't like the fact that she had to take this pill, but she knew that it was necessary. She set the bottle down next to the sink after taking out one dose, which she then gulped with the entire glass of water.

"Welcome to Channel 45 news at 10!" A voice came from the living room TV. "This is your very own Rock Rivers reporting. Exclusive! We have reports of a vampire in one of our local high schools!"

Upon hearing Rivers' claim, Lupia dropped her glass on the kitchen counter and rushed back into the living room. The report didn't seem like one that she should miss.

"An anonymous tip has turned in info to us that one Amy Able has been attending class for the past two days at Flagler Palm Coast High School in Flagler County. While she was not among the three vampires making public threats on our competitor, Channel 3's, newscast last night, authorities suspect that she might be a threat to the other students in the school." The news then switched to various interviews with local parents:

"It's an outrage that such a monster would be allowed in one of our schools."

"I don't want her spreading her vampire ways to our kids."

"I don't know...she hasn't done anything wrong and there's a YouTube video showing her saving that missing musician from one of the other vampires. I think we should give her a chance."

"Stay tuned to Channel 45 News for more updates on the vampire menace. "And now we move over to the coming week's weather forecast."

The camera panned over to another member of the news team, who stood in front of a computer-generated map of Florida. "Expect partly cloudy skies all over the state tomorrow. You'll still get a great view of that full moon tomorrow night—if you want to risk going outside with those vampires around."

Lupia switched the TV off, knowing that the next day would be a bad day for everyone.

Meanwhile, In Amelia's car, I had taken notice of something I hadn't in the daytime. "When was your back window repaired?"

"Daddy took care of it yesterday after school. He knows a guy who owes him a few favors. We had it covered with plastic before that but you were too busy trying not to die to notice."

"Okay, cool. Now, there's something else I'm curious about." I wanted to ask her about her strange behavior and my strange feelings, but doing so would just be too awkward, so I asked something else. "Are you sure a gun really gives you all the courage you need to fight vampires?"

"Not really. I need both it and something else."

"What else?"

"You." I didn't expect her to say something so blunt in return. She gave her usual cool smile. "I may have amazing aim but I know I'm not invincible. Oh, and having Will around helps too." She seemingly didn't want to leave him out.

"I guess the Second Amendment really isn't enough to make people feel safe." I liked the idea of being useful to others.

Traffic was light, though the road wasn't exactly empty. Amelia didn't drive any differently even despite getting herself psyched up about what we were going to do. I was in the passenger seat this time. Will was in the back seat. He seemed to be deep in thought.

"I remember this area..." I examined the surrounding landscape with my night vision. I was navigating because I was the only one who could read the directions Will printed out in the dark. "There it is!"

I knew what the building looked like. I had gone there several times with my mother anytime we needed to bring my father something or pick him up from work (if, for instance, his car were undergoing repairs, etc.). For a biological research outpost, it was pretty plain and unremarkable, consisting of a beige building with a flat roof. It didn't have any sort of logo in any visible position. I remember my dad telling me that the building was inconspicuous so that protestors couldn't find it on the off chance that the company did something that a group didn't like.

Blood on Fire

"Don't park right at the actual building." Will wanted us to not appear like we were breaking in, despite the fact that we were.

Amelia instead parked at an apartment complex three blocks behind our target. It was still earlier than midnight, so several of the surrounding windows were still lit up. With Amelia carrying a weapon, we would have to stay hidden. Luckily, Will had us covered, waving his hand and chanting under his breath to invoke a spell to obscure the vision of others. Cars still passed by on the main road, but the surrounding area was otherwise empty. Still, being safe never hurt anyone.

We came up to the small BioLogic building. No cars were around it in the parking lot, so we had hardly any cover aside from the bushes surrounding the property, which we hid behind.

Will led the operation. "Well Amy, you have the best night vision. Take a look around." His voice was business-like, as if he did this sort of thing regularly.

Admittedly, I was getting into the moment. I was about to break into a laboratory, albeit a small one. It felt like I was in action movie. To make sure my view would be clear, I wiped my glasses on my T-shirt (which was black, as was my longish skirt, to go along with our current attempt at espionage). Then I peeked my head above the bushes and peered around the area.

Darkness still wasn't an issue for me. No people were around; that was certain. But the distance confounded me. I could swear that I saw movement, but I couldn't tell what was moving. I could sense that something was there— perhaps multiple somethings. I squinted, trying to gain a better focus. "Something's moving."

"What do you mean?" Amelia asked. The look on Will's face asked the same thing.

"I can't tell exactly what it is. Any way you can use magic for a closer look, Will?"

"I could create a window if I had a puddle and some time." The area hadn't had rain for about a week, so that was out of the question.

"Can you make me invisible?" It was a question worth asking.

"I can only make myself invisible. All I can do for you is obscure vision for others in the area around you."

"That'll have to do."

TACTICAL ESPIONAGE ACTION

A few magic words and some hand waving later, I crept on the ground between two bushes incased in a cloud of obscurity. While on the ground I made a mental note that short sleeves and a skirt weren't the best for sneaking through coarse mulch. I stayed close to the curb against the parking lot, and I squinted again. This time I could see that the movement came from two creatures right up against the building. I saw them sniff the air, knowing that they could smell us. I ducked back through the bushes to face Will and Amelia. Will waved a hand to disperse the veil. "It obscures sound as well," he said, implying that I wouldn't be able to say anything with the veil in place.

"I can see some wolves" I said, "they're just smaller this time and they're black to blend into the darkness."

Will considered the fact before speaking. "One of our enemies controls them, right?"

"Right," Amelia and I said at the same time.

"So what should we do? Should I just light them on fire?" I cringed when I said that. Despite my experience two nights before, I still disliked killing animals.

"That might cause some collateral damage that we don't want. No…what we should do…?"

"Can you get rid of them with magic?"

"I already told you that I don't know any offensive magic." He then glanced at Amelia. "Maybe bringing you along wasn't a bad idea after all, Amelia. You can sharp shoot, right?"

Amelia took out her pistol and spun it around in her hand before holding it in a normal position. "How would I ever survive the zombie apocalypse if I couldn't?"

"Wait a second." I thought of something important. "There's no silencer on that gun. Won't that give away our location?"

"Now that's where magic comes in." Will said some obscure words and made a fancy hand flick toward the gun. "Go ahead, try shooting it."

With a curious expression, Amelia pointed the gun upward toward the sky and away from anything that might be harmed and fired off a shot. It made a noise, but not much of one. Only sound was suppressed; the weapon appeared as it should have.

"I can adjust these sensory veils to mute certain aspects." Will seemed proud. "Not muting sight gives better muting of sound."

Blood on Fire

"Well done," I said.

"One problem." Amelia sounded worried. "I can't see anything in this darkness. How am I supposed to aim?"

Time was a factor; I could hear the sniffing of the wolves getting closer. I signaled to my friends to keep quiet since sound would only attract the beasts faster.

Will looked around for something usable. By sheer luck he found a dead tree branch nearby. He carefully picked it up one end of it and then signaled to me to light it on fire.

I nodded and then concentrated, focusing the blood into my hand in order to ignite it, but I did so very gently since I wasn't making an attack.

Will struggled not to cry out in pain. The fireball was only a tiny bit bigger than I intended, so I didn't hurt him much, but it was still an error. All that mattered, though, was that the branch was on fire. Will uttered a few more incomprehensible magical words and then let go of the branch. Instead of falling, it floated in mid-air. The flaming branch illuminated Will, and I could see him holding out his arm toward it as he kept up a continuous low chant. He directed his hand upward and then forward to quickly move the branch over the bushes and stop it above the wolves, which were much closer now.

They didn't like what they saw, and they instinctively ran forward toward us.

"No you don't." Amelia stood above the line of bushes, quickly aimed, and fired twice. Her movements were almost instantaneous with deadeye precision. Soon, two dead wolves lay around that branch, and nobody heard anything. I stood wide-eyed with my mouth agape. Even having seen her do it once before, I still found her skills amazing.

Will then magically moved the flaming branch to the middle of the concrete parking lot where nothing would catch on fire to let it fizzle out on its own.

Amelia turned her aim toward me. "Hey, don't shoot me for fun," I said, knowing that it would hurt though not kill me. She did shoot, but she didn't shoot me. Another wolf hit the ground a few feet away. "Damn, you're good."

"We should get over toward that wall." Will moved forward. "It looks like we'll need to keep an eye out for any more of them."

We snuck around the side of the building to the back entrance, where we didn't see any more wolves. We came upon the back door, which looked seldom-used at best. I tried turning the knob. "Of course it's locked."

Tactical Espionage Action

"I've got it covered." Will kneeled in front of the door, putting his hand on the lock while starting another chant. "Both of you keep watch."

Amelia pulled out her iPhone and loaded its flashlight app, which caused the small light underneath its camera to glow with a blinding white light. She used it to better see any oncoming attackers. It seemed like an inefficient source of light to me, as it didn't exactly illuminate much a distance in front of her. I stuck up my right index finger and concentrated. After a few seconds of flares that I had difficulty controlling, I managed to create a small, stable flame on my finger. It didn't hurt at all; it just felt like I was holding a lighter. My skin didn't take any damage. I tapped Amelia on the shoulder with my other hand and showed her the flame. She gave me a big smile and put her iPhone away. I extended my arm outward while she stepped behind it next to me, staying unusually close. I kept watch in the other direction.

Will's magical lock picking skill wasn't exactly fast by any means. "Got it." After enough time waiting, Will finally managed to open the door.

My impatience got the better of me. "That's great, but you'll need a better time before you earn the honorable title of the Master of Unlocking."

He rolled his eyes. "Is the sarcasm really necessary?"

"Yes." Amelia chuckled. She definitely got the *Resident Evil* joke.

We crept inside. It would have been much darker if not for those ceiling lights that are impossible to turn off. So many office buildings and educational institutions have them. I guess those lights stay on in case of an emergency or something despite the power they waste when nobody is there to use them. I don't really know. What I do know is that they enabled Will and Amelia to see properly without turning any more lights on, which was good because we were able to stay relatively stealthy. The building consisted of both offices and labs, and the room we entered was both an office and a storage room for lab tools.

"Well, we've got the usual stuff here." Will looked around. "Beakers, test tubes, Bunsen burners."

"This is stuff we'd find at school." Amelia examined the available items. "It's not stuff vampires would use...I think." To me, these were simply just tools of the trade as I was accustomed to seeing my father use them.

Will turned to me. "Amy, do you remember where your father worked?"

"He would oversee the various labs, but he had an office as well."

"Where's that?"

Blood on Fire

"Let me see." I slowly opened the door out of that back office and into a long hallway with windows that looked into a large laboratory on one side and offices and storage rooms on the other. The walls, ceiling, and tile floors were all white, befitting of a place of science. I looked left and then right, and the coast seemed clear. No wolves were around, in any case.

I motioned for Will and Amelia to follow me, but Will grabbed my shoulder. "Wait." Then he pointed outward into the hallway at what looked like a security camera. He motioned to Amelia to shoot it, which she accomplished easily. "Just because there are no wolves around doesn't mean that we can relax quite yet."

With that said, I led the team to where I remembered my father's office to be, and luckily my memory served me right. "Maybe we'll find something about his whereabouts here." It was a tiny office with no windows, but it had a small desk and a bookcase full of research journals. On his desk were pictures of mom soon after he and she first me, my brother back in his high school soccer days, and myself when I was but a tiny elementary school student in a frilly green dress and Coke bottle glasses that were so obviously too big for my little face. Dad really needed to update his photos. Nothing was on his desk that would give any indication that he was doing anything unusual. "It looks like he hasn't even been at his desk for a while."

Will was far from giving up. "The fact that there's nothing in here doesn't mean anything. We just need to keep looking around."

Amelia kept watch at the office door. "What about that lab over there?" She pointed to a set of double glass doors.

"Seems like a good bet to me," Will said.

The doors were made to keep a definite separation between outside and inside. It was not a clean room, however, and by that I don't mean that it was dirty but that it was not the sort of lab that requires workers to wear hazmat suits in order to prevent dust, dirt, and bacteria from entering—or leaving, for that matter. Rather, with this facility being a mere branch office for BioLogic, my father rarely ever worked with particularly deadly diseases that would require a larger facility. With a little effort, we managed to slide the doors open and enter.

"Cool…It's all full…of science," Amelia said in a playfully ditzy voice.

Suddenly I encountered a smell that was instinctively familiar to any vampire. I sniffed the air very deeply. "Blood…" Most normal people don't usually think of blood as having a smell, and to this day and I still haven't thought of how I would describe it. I couldn't tell whose blood it was, just that it was blood. I knew the smell of Amelia's blood. This smell wasn't tied to any person in particular. It didn't smell like any particular food; it just smelled delicious.

"Blood? Where?" Will sounded afraid of what I might do in the presence of blood but interested in why I would smell it.

As Toucan Sam would say, I followed my nose, and it led me past all of the various tables toward the back of the lab where we found a very large metal door, presumably leading into a large refrigerator. I sniffed some more. The smell definitely came from inside. It wasn't locked despite it having a loop for a padlock, so I went ahead and opened it. Will and Amelia came over to stand behind me.

Just as I smelled, blood was inside. Tons of it. Probably every specimen jar in the building was filled with it, and when whoever filled them had run out of specimen jars, they started using plain old mason jars. The shelves lining all of the walls in this giant walk-in fridge were loaded to the brim with jars of blood.

I pulled one of the jars off of a shelf and stared at its contents. Something was off about the blood, but I couldn't tell quite what it was. Even in a sealed jar, the smell coming off of it was intense. I decided that a little taste was in order.

"Wait, Amy!"

"What?" I turned back to Will, who looked desperate to stop me from taking a sip. Amelia stood behind him, curious about the whole situation.

"Hand me that for a sec." I reluctantly did as he asked. He took the jar and concentrated on it for a few seconds. "There's a huge magical resonance coming off of it. This isn't normal blood."

"Then what is it?" I wasn't sure what he meant.

"If I had to guess, I'd say it's vampire blood. Amy, if you drink this, you might have a chance of becoming the slave of whatever vampire it came from. The same goes for either of us." He resealed the jar and put it back on the shelf. I had to fight the constant craving, but the last thing I wanted was to become a slave.

"So did somebody just run a bunch of vampires through a juicer?" Amelia had a vivid imagination.

"Probably not," Will said, "though I guess it's possible."

Blood on Fire

"Are all of these jars filled with vampire blood?" I didn't feel that the little blood I took from Buford was quite enough to keep me going through the next day.

"I wouldn't take a chance if I were you."

"Damn it." Little else was in the refrigerator besides the countless jars of blood. Most of the rest of the contents consisted just of various chemicals used in scientific procedures. As my friends started shivering (I was uncomfortably cold, but my body didn't react that way), I noticed that another door was inside, much like the one we went through to initially enter this cold storage room. I pointed it out to the others. "Hey, where do you suppose that goes?"

"Probably a freezer," Will said.

"I wonder…" I grabbed the door's handle, which looked like it needed a huge amount of force to be pulled open. Luckily, opening it wasn't a problem at all for me. Afterward, though, I wished that I hadn't opened it.

"Oh my God!" This was my reaction.

"What the…" This was Will's.

"Sweet mother of…!" Amelia could finish her sentence.

All three of us shrank backward when we saw this sight. It was a corpse, but not a human corpse. "Is—is that a werewolf?" Only once had I never laid eyes on such a creature, but never in this state. The body was definitely female and covered from head to toe in grey fur. However, her body was shriveled up as if she had been completely drained of all blood. Her human-dog face was contorted into a horrified and tortured expression.

Amelia couldn't take the sight for long. She turned away, leaving a puddle of vomit in her wake.

I didn't like what I saw. I never wanted to see anything like that ever again. I slammed the door shut. "What the hell is going on in this place?" I shook my head in vain to try to strike that image from it. I noticed Amelia trying to get the taste of vomit out of her mouth by spitting into the puddle. I tried to lighten the mood a bit. "You know, you'll probably see far worse in a zombie apocalypse."

"Just…give me a minute."

We didn't have a minute, though, as we heard something entering the lab. It sounded like paws moving slowly across the tile floor accompanied by the sound of a dog sniffing the air. We knew what was coming for us, especially when the creature's low growl came within earshot.

Tactical Espionage Action

"Amelia, enough with the puke." I spoke in a whisper. "We need you." I hid myself near the refrigerator door, as did Will, who did a quick chant to renew the sound suppressing spell on Amelia's gun. I hadn't closed the door, and closing it now would make our presence too obvious.

Amelia shook her head quickly to regain her bearings and set up her aim. Within mere seconds, the wolf lay dead on the fridge floor on top of the puke, a bullet lodged in its brain. Seeing another dead canine broke my heart even more.

"Now would be a good time to leave," Will said. Amelia and I nodded in agreement. Quickly and quietly, we made our way out of the lab and back into the hallway. Because of the path we took to reach dad's office and the lab, we would reach the back entrance faster by taking a path we hadn't used before. After shooting out another camera, we passed by more offices and a much smaller lab filled with microscopes. That was where we heard voices. Will, Amelia, and I all looked at each other to make sure that we would all remain against the nearest wall, silent and still.

"I can feel it...something has been killing my pack mates." Strength's voice sounded angry. "Why has the Fool commanded us to stay in this room? What's so special about the things in here, anyway?"

She received no response, but she spoke as if someone else were in there.

"I can't disobey orders, but I must know why my pack keeps sensing danger and then disappearing. Do you have any ideas?"

Again, no response came from whomever she was talking to. At the head of our trio, I was closest to the doorway. I peered inside and could see Strength pacing back and forth nervously. I couldn't see the entire room, meaning that I couldn't tell who else was inside. It was a room lined with counters of light microscopes with a huge and expensive-looking electron microscope recessed into one back corner and a colossal, long wooden box that had dirt collected around the base of it in the other. Exactly what the pacing vampire could possibly be guarding was anyone's guess.

"Commanding us to stay in this room while only my wolves guard the building...does the Fool even know what he's doing? Where did he even bring Tower and Devil, anyway? And why has he cut off mental contact to us?" I wasn't thinking about exactly who else was in that room, keeping my eyes on the vampire I could see, but I knew that not all of our enemies were present. "I don't even understand any of this! When are we going to claim our territory?"

Blood on Fire

She picked up an object from a nearby counter and started examining it. I never knew Bethany Davis when she was still in school, but I could guess that she was probably a free spirit. Ultimately I would never come to know what sort of person she really was. "I should trust in the Fool's judgment." She sounded like she was trying to calm herself down, but she wasn't successful. With a scream of enraged annoyance, she threw the object across the room, close to the doorway. The sound it made when it hit the ground gave the impression that it was long and lightweight. She stood facing away from the doorway with her head down.

Will pointed to object with a finger over his mouth to indicate to keep quiet and then made some hand gestures that I figured indicated that magic would be out of the question at that moment, likely due to the chanting involved.

To be quite honest, I was scared to death of being spotted, especially with two friends by my side who didn't have any sort of supercharged healing factor.

I crept slowly, making as little noise as possible. I only needed to move a little bit farther, but it felt like miles. No matter what, I had to pick up that object. I couldn't even guess what it was or what it did, but I could only hope that it would give me an edge in straightening my life out again. With just a few more steps, I was right there. Then I just had to bend down a little bit, just enough to get my hand on the item. As difficult as it was, I succeeded. All that was left was to slowly back out of that room as quietly as I could, object in hand.

That was when the Super Mario Bros. theme played, seemingly louder than it ever had before, from my skirt pocket. I stood frozen with the object, which felt to me like a huge pencil, as Strength spun around to face me. "Intruders." She had the sound of murder in her voice.

Then from the shadows toward the room's side came the individual Strength had been talking to, a figure I dreaded too much seeing in person. It was Chariot, or, as I preferred to call her, the Ogre Queen. She let out the same deafening roar that he had on TV.

As the two came closer to me, I quickly grabbed my cell phone to check it so that I would know what name to associate my impending doom with. The letters clearly stated "Allen Able."

What could I possibly say about my brother besides the fact that he was nothing more than a constant thorn in my side, more so than Shelly could ever hope to be, during my time growing up? By the time I was born, he was already three and a half years old, and he asserted his power over me in every way possible, which was usually through punching or kicking. He was consistently much bigger than me, which was due to many factors, not just age.

Naturally, with a three and a half year difference between us, while I was 16 and in high school, he was 20 and in college. He would usually call us in Palm Coast one or two times per week. My parents would put me on the phone to talk to him, but I hardly ever had anything to say since we didn't have much in common after he "grew out" of the one common interest we did have, which was video games, and I was never very interested in cars or sports. I was really getting used to a new life of freedom without him around.

Despite having nothing to say, though, talking to him on the phone was never really an unpleasant experience since the separation of distance cooled our sibling hatred of each other. However, one time when I genuinely didn't want to talk to him was when I was standing right there in front of those two vampires. I felt so stupid for not turning my phone off.

This call came at what would be an unacceptable time were I not a vampire. I estimate that it was about 11:30 or so. One might wonder why my brother would call me so late. Wouldn't he have classes in the morning? Shouldn't he have been sleeping? The truth of the matter was that he was a normal college student in a few respects, such as scheduling all of his classes in the afternoon and partying and drinking (yes, he was underage) well into the night alongside his fraternity brothers in Gamma Alpha Upsilon. Therefore, calling his sister so late on a Tuesday night, even though she would probably be asleep were she still human, wasn't out of the question for him.

"Hey! Was that you on TV?" His voice was nonchalant.

Mine wasn't. "I'm sorry Allen, I'm busy, I'll talk to you later!" I literally screamed into the phone as I ran. Amelia and Will struggled to keep up with me.

"Don't destroy the building!" Strength yelled to the Ogre Queen when she burst through the wall of the microscope room. "The Fool has ordered it!"

Somehow we outran them to the back door, but as we made it there we saw a tiny wolf trot by holding a set of keys.

"The door's locked?" Amelia sounded horrified, "How the hell did a dog lock the door?"

"I'll try to unlock it!" Will was ready to use some magic.

"Screw it!" I pushed him out of the way and rammed the door at full speed with the broad side of my right arm, putting all of the strength I had behind it. It easily fell off its hinges. Stealth was already out of the question, so why bother with subtlety? "Let's go!"

By the time we made it outside, our enemies weren't far behind us, and being outside meant that nothing was around to be destroyed, making their job of catching up that much easier.

With a colossal arm, the Ogre Queen grabbed Amelia from behind, lifting her off the ground while grasping only her right shoulder. "Help!"

"No!" I turned around. I couldn't just leave her in the beast's hands. In the mean time Will had put up an invisible barrier around himself to fend off the wolves that Strength sent at him. Amelia did manage to get one arm free to squeeze out a few rounds into the Ogre Queen's neck, but the bullets did little more than annoy her.

"Put her down!" I dashed toward the Ogre Queen and plunged my fist into her torso.

Amy used Mega Punch. It's not very effective.

It was like punching a boulder and seemed to have no effect whatsoever. In fact, I it did more damage to my fist. Completely ignoring me, the Ogre Queen grabbed Amelia's legs with her other hand and was ready to start pulling, intending to split my friend in half. Knowing I had little time left and with my hand already in place, I went with a different tactic.

Amy used Flamethrower. It's super effective!

Through later research, I would learn that burning and beheading are the only two ways to kill vampires. Incineration works regardless of whether the source is sunlight or any source of normal fire. A stake to the heart only paralyzes the vampire, although it makes killing much easier. Holy symbols only leave scars that take an extremely long time to heal and may damage the vampire's psyche (though I may not have had to worry about that). Garlic is merely an inconvenience. I could turn my hands into very powerful weapons.

The Ogre Queen stumbled backward in pain after my fireball's impact, dropping Amelia in the process. I burned a hole in her body suit, exposing pale skin that was stretched tightly with the muscle and fat underneath it. She was badly singed. *I damaged her!* The two times I had punched her—once a few years before and once less than a minute before—had done nothing to her. Although I was still afraid of her, I knew that I had a much better chance than I did before.

Tactical Espionage Action

When Amelia hit the ground, she immediately shot Strength in the head, which caused her to fall backward. The wolves attacking Will flinched as she lost control of them. Amelia and Will took this opportunity to make a mad dash to the car.

Keep in mind that I was still holding that strange wooden object that I had picked up from the floor when my brother called me and screwed everything up. I held the object tightly in my left hand, refusing at all costs to let go of it. The punch and subsequent fireball had come from my right hand. Since I could run faster and take a bigger beating, I decided to hang back and provide a distraction while my friends escaped.

I tried to shoot another fireball at the Ogre Queen but she instantly punched me, sending me flying several feet away. I thought some of my ribs cracked, though they immediately started healing.

Strength got back on her feet using only her heels, looking as if she were supernaturally resurrected, which was pretty creepy. The bullet wound in her head had completely healed. "Why do you still defy us? Join our pack, and we can help you become more powerful than you could possibly imagine." The Ogre Queen stood still as her comrade spoke. Apparently, though she could no longer form words, she had manners when other people were talking.

I decided to play along. I had a feeling that stalling would give me a chance to wait for my friends to come and pick me up. I just had to give them time. "That's what you keep saying, but what exactly can you offer me?" I skirted around the two of them slowly, hoping that they would turn to follow me. It was my goal to have my back to the BioLogic building so that they would face away from the direction Will and Amelia ran in. I wanted to make sure that my friends wouldn't be chased.

"The Fool will provide you with everything you need. You will never need to hunt for blood again. If you would only comply and turn over Lupia, you will learn everything you need to know."

"What do you need Lupia for anyway? What could you possibly want with a musician?"

"Isn't it obvious? Have you not figured it out by now? It is because—" Strength stopped mid-sentence, and I knew why she stopped because I could hear it too. A car was coming. In fact, I could see its lights glaring right behind her. I made sure to dive out of the way as a familiar red Camaro came from behind Strength, braking rapidly from an insane speed. Strength was sent flying forward, her face slamming into the BioLogic building. The car had to veer sideways to avoid crashing into the building itself.

Keep in mind that while vampires have super strength, they only weigh as much as any normal human. Therefore, of course a vampire would go flying when struck unexpectedly by a car.

The Ogre Queen roared with anger and started running after the Camaro. For the safety of everyone, I couldn't let her reach it. I dashed after her. I then leaped onto her back. My feet were well off the ground, and I grasped her shoulders, hanging. It was satisfying to know that I could accomplish such feats of agility. I slowed her down as she tried to grab hold of me, but I managed to leap off before she could, avoiding any more loss of teeth.

I knew my escape was in my grasp. All I needed to do was land on that car and I would be free of vampires for another night. Unfortunately, I misjudged the distance (since I didn't take into account that my target was, indeed, moving) and missed the car by about a yard, falling flat on my face in the pavement. *I really hope my glasses aren't scratched.*

The car stopped as I scrambled onto my feet, knowing that both my opponents would be ready to strike. Will lowered the window, yelled "Get in!" and then promptly raised it again. From that call I could only assume that the doors were unlocked for me.

Right behind me, roaring more furiously than ever before, Chariot was ready to knock me right out of the way and smash the car, but I immediately spun around, put my hands together, yelled "Hadouken!" and shot out the biggest fireball I could within those few seconds. Mere inches away from pulverizing me, she stopped and flailed in pain, a good portion of her front engulfed in flame. I made another 180-degree spin and dashed to the car. I leaped into the back right seat, relieved that I had actually reached safety.

Amelia slammed on the gas pedal just as a bunch of wolves surrounded the vehicle. We ran over two of them. After making some dangerous turns that would have made a lesser 17-year old girl crash and burn in the worst way possible, we were quickly back on the main road.

I laid across the back seat flat on my back, still coming to grips with what we had just escaped. I dropped the object (I still hadn't had a chance to check what it was) right below the seat. I was in too much of a shock to worry about it at the moment. "Guys, we've been through some crap in the past few days, but that was ridiculous."

Tactical Espionage Action

Will sounded winded. "Whatever is going on, I guess we really do need to do something about it." He didn't like having the responsibility of dealing with such dangerous opponents, but he recognized that we needed to take action. "I mean, let's face it, the police can't handle THAT."

Amelia declined the comment. She kept a trance-like focus on the road, though she gripped the steering wheel with only one hand. The other gripped her neck scars.

Just as Amelia allowed the car's speed to relax to levels that would be acceptable to the speed limit, I sat up and decided to take a look out the brand new rear window, just to reminisce about our daring escape. That was when I saw something that I simply couldn't believe. It had to be my overactive imagination playing tricks on me because what I saw couldn't possibly happen. I lifted my glasses and rubbed my eyes, hoping that the horror would just disappear. It didn't. The realization then dawned on me that we were in some major trouble. "Speed up the car."

"What? Why?" Amelia apparently had yet to notice what I saw very clearly.

"God damn it! Just speed up!" Fortunately, we were on a well-lit street, so when Amelia finally checked the rear-view mirror, she saw what I saw, and she promptly floored the accelerator.

Apparently, the fact that we had wheels didn't mean that we didn't still have to worry about the Ogre Queen. She chased us on foot.

Will was legitimately afraid. "With the amount of strength packed into those legs it's going to be hell outrunning her." I never imagined that her legs would be that powerful.

"She's gaining on us!" I vigilantly kept watch out the back window. *Damn it! Why did it have to be her?*

"It won't go any faster!" Amelia struggled to keep the car straight at that ludicrous speed. We approached a traffic light that just happened to be red. Amelia, breathing hard, was about to make the legal choice and stop.

"What are you doing? Run it!" For once Will didn't act as the voice of safety.

"But..."

"Damn it, woman, we don't have time to argue!" Amelia did as he said and by sheer luck narrowly avoided a car passing at a normal speed on the intersecting road (even that late at night, a bit of traffic was still around). The car's driver slammed on the brakes, honked his horn, and gave us the finger (I was the only one who could see that last action). Unfortunately, the driver wasn't entirely lucky as the Ogre Queen, seeing the car as a mere obstacle in her path, literally flung it out of her way, flipping it over onto the side of the road. We couldn't tell whether or not the driver was safe.

Damn it...what can I do about this? I was desperate to end this chase before any other horrible things happened. "Will, do you have any spell that might help right now?"

"Not unless I can touch the road or the wheels or put myself within range of her."

"What about one of those veils?"

"She can already see us; it won't do any good."

She was mere feet away from our rear bumper, and she looked ready to grab it. I searched all around for any possible option that I could utilize in getting us out of this mess. I wouldn't be able to get a clear shot at her out of the side window. Then I saw the answer to the problem. "Amelia, open the moon roof!" We were lucky to be in a sports car. She didn't argue, trusting in my judgment even though I never really did have the best judgment in the past.

Curse my small ass... I had a hard time getting steady on the roof. I practically sat on Will's head before assuming the awkward position of lying across the back part of the roof by my chest and torso with my legs dangling back into the car. I had to hope that Will didn't have any strange fetishes.

Seeing me on the roof only made the Ogre Queen angrier, and now she was close enough to strike the car with her arm, causing us to veer off course, which Amelia had to struggle to correct. Thanks to my strength, I managed to hold on.

I needed a strong enough blast to get her off of us. I focused hard. I had to concentrate enough power into one hand while using the other to keep steady. Wind was also a factor. I aimed as carefully as I could and focused as much energy as I could under that kind of stress. I also wanted to be careful not to melt any part of the car.

Come on... I formed the biggest fireball possible in my palm and shot it directly into the Ogre Queen's face and chest, although it also singed Amelia's spoiler pretty badly. I cringed since I damaged her clothing from the waist up and what it revealed wasn't a pretty sight. She roared in pain, but she didn't slow down much. When she managed to hit the car with her arm again, I knew that this effort would be in vain.

Tactical Espionage Action

Far ahead of us, Officer Maurice Freeman was bored. He was stuck in his police car for another two hours "Man, why does Valentine always give me all the worst shifts? It's like the man's always got to keep a brother down. Damn it. I gotta take Tiffany to pre-school tomorrow morning." Officer Freeman was a relative rookie on the Flagler County police force. With only about a year of experience under his belt, he struggled to gain recognition as a capable officer while also trying to take care of his family. His peers complained that he was too soft on those who broke the law, but as relatively new father and husband, he valued understanding above all else while performing his duties. However, the other officers mainly disrespected him because he screwed up too many of his cases, which only reflected negatively on his reputation.

Despite his boredom, he was about to receive a colossal surprise. "The hell is that?" A car approached his position at a breakneck speed, but it wasn't the speeding car that was unusual. It was what was behind the car. "Is that someone...on fire?"

The car and flaming figure zoomed past, registering 125 MPH on his radar gun. "I don't know what's going on, but I'm finally getting some action!" He flipped his siren on and joined in the chase.

"I couldn't shake her!" I shouted from the moon roof, simultaneously disappointed and scared out of my mind. I could see and hear her too clearly, still on fire and screaming in pain. Over that scream, though, I could hear a sound that I didn't know whether to interpret as good or bad. "I think I hear a police siren!"

"Uh-oh." Amelia sounded even more scared, "Did I pass by a police car? I was too busy trying to keep us alive to notice!"

The Ogre Queen clearly heard the siren as well because she started violently shaking her head at the sound as if something—or someone—inside of her was telling her to avoid an encounter with the police. Shaking off as much of the remaining fire as she could, she dove off of the road into the surrounding woods. This section of the road was relatively empty of homes and businesses, so it was pretty easy for her to get away, although her path of destruction among the forest's pine trees wouldn't go unnoticed.

"The police scared her off!" Will definitely wanted us to stop. "Stop the car!"

Amelia gladly slammed on the brakes. Keeping control of the car at that speed the entire time was hard enough, and doing so became even harder during

Blood on Fire

the process of braking. "Wh—whoa crap!" I roughly slid off the back of the car, banging my head on the spoiler and landing on the pavement face first, my spine contorted in a shape it had never been in before.

And that is why everyone should always wear a seatbelt when in a moving vehicle. I stress the word "in" because no one should ever be "on" one at all.

The police car stopped right in front of me. "Oh my God!" Officer Freeman rushed out, disturbed at the shape of the young girl in front of him. "I—I'll call an ambulance!"

Will stepped out of the car. "Don't bother." He didn't say this casually. While he did sound like he was worried about me, the fact that he told the officer not to call an ambulance when I was clearly very, very hurt was a little bit insulting. "She'll be fine."

I knew I'd be fine. I knew I had quick healing, but that didn't mean that it didn't hurt. Horribly. "Owwwwwwwwwwww! Oh Jesus that hurts!"

Amelia rushed out of the car to help me stand up. Officer Freeman looked on with a mix of both horror and awe as I stood up—if such could even be called standing with my body bending in various directions that it should never have. Slowly and with a ton pain and effort, I managed to bend myself back into the correct shape. "Oww!...Owwwwww!...Damn it! My glasses are scratched..." I took them off and took a closer look. A huge scratch stretched across both lenses.

Officer Freeman stepped backward at the horrific sight. "Wh—what the hell are you?" I made sure to take a good look at him so that I might remember him. After all, I wanted to be on the good side of the police if at all possible. He was a tall, thin black man who was neither muscular nor out of shape. He had soft features and thick, curly hair.

Will sighed. He really didn't want the police involved in our whole matter. "She's a vampire."

"A vampire?" He sounded amazed though quite familiar with the concept. "And you two? You're both vampires?"

"Nah, they're human."

"What about that flaming thing chasing you? What was that thing?" The officer ran his fingers through his hair. He seemed to shake.

"A vampire."

"But you two don't..."

"It's...a long story. Didn't you see the news last night?"

Tactical Espionage Action

"I heard about that, but I was too busy putting together an anti-drug lecture for the elementary schools that the station is forcing me to do. Were you making threats?"

I explained who I was as best I could, focusing particularly on the fact that I was working against the vampires making threats.

"Well you did break a law since you weren't wearing your seatbelt. You guys were also going pretty fast back there. I'm surprised you're all still alive." We looked at each other, embarrassed. We would be in deep trouble if not for the obvious danger we were trying to escape from.

"Could I see your license and registration?" Amelia complied with his request. He cringed when he saw her license. "Oh! You're Captain Valentine's girl."

She nodded. He didn't look too happy.

"Look." he looked to his side as if the idea of vampires were tiring him out. "I don't know what the hell I just saw. I don't think you deserve a ticket, and, frankly, I don't feel like explaining this back at the station, so would you be okay if I just let you off with a warning?"

We three nodded.

He carefully wrote up the warning for speeding, underestimating Amelia's speed by 50 MPH. "I don't know why, but I have a feeling that I'll be seeing you all again. Try to stay out of trouble." He reluctantly went back to his car, trying to shake all that he had just witnessed out of his head.

11: Food and Family

"It's a wand." Will carefully examined the strange object I took from the vampires in the light emanating from the car's ceiling. We were parked in the driveway of my house.

"A wand? You mean like a magic wand?" With all the insanity that took place in obtaining this item, nothing would surprise me.

"And..." Will was silent for a moment.

"What?"

"My family's emblem?" The wand had one pointy end and one blunt end. He pointed to the blunt end. On it was an engraving of a bird—likely a crow or a raven—holding a knife in its foot.

Amelia was intrigued. "Your family has an emblem?"

"Yeah. It's magically charged and imbues whatever it's engraved on with an enchantment. But why would this..." I knew what he was thinking. The presence of that emblem served as some evidence that a member of his family—most likely his mother—was involved. He yawned deeply. Then Amelia did as well.

"You two need to get some rest."

"But..." Will seemed to really want to know more about the wand.

I took it from him. "I'll take it for safe keeping. It'll be safer here than at your place if your mom really is involved. You can examine it tomorrow after you get a good night's sleep."

He nodded.

I stepped out of the car and waved to my friends as they drove off. While I felt exhausted, I wasn't quite ready to sleep yet. As soon as I went inside my house, I exchanged my damaged glasses for my spare pair, which had a slightly older prescription but still allowed me to see just fine. Then I called Allen.

FOOD AND FAMILY

"Hey…sis…what's up?" He sounded drunk and half-asleep. Did I care? No.

"Yeah, 'bro,'" I emphasized "bro," saying it the way his fraternity brothers would. "You called me at a very bad time before. You could've killed me."

"Huh, wha?" He seemed to be too inebriated to listen very well. "Hey, are you a…y'know?"

"Yes. I'm a vampire."

"Woah, what? Really?" He suddenly sounded more awake.

"Yes."

"So you have fangs?"

"Yes."

"You drink blood?"

"Yes."

"And this isn't all a load of crap?"

"No, I'm seriously a vampire. I burn in the sun and everything."

"Oh man, I—I saw you on YouTube it was at a…a…"

"Concert?"

"Yeah, that. That was you?"

"Yes."

"Oh…" He finally seemed to accept that it was me in the video. "What…what do mom and dad say? Nobody answered the phone before." Just like the principal, my brother could only assume that mom and dad were still around. No one beyond Will, Amelia, Lupia, and I knew about their disappearance. *Should I tell him?*

"Mom and dad…don't know what to think." I didn't know what to say at this point, so I lied like I did with the principal. I also figured that if I kept working to solve the mystery of what was going on, I'd have mom and dad back very soon. I just hoped that my lies wouldn't end up killing me.

"Can I talk to them?"

"They're, uh, both asleep right now." Considering how late it was, I'm sure he was willing to believe that.

"Oh…alrigh—" I heard him pass out and start snoring.

"Have fun with your hangover." I hung up. *Now what should I do?* My hunger decided for me. I was tired out from the combination of sun exposure during the day and extreme stress at night coupled with my lack of ability to obtain blood besides the bit I stole from Buford. *That's right! I was going to*

Blood on Fire

experiment. I just remembered that Buford and the principal both gave me an idea.

From my room, I went over to the kitchen. I was the only one making noise in the entire house. I heard no sounds at all coming from Lupia's room, which wasn't unusual since she was a fairly quiet sleeper. The house was also dark. I didn't bother turning on any lights since I didn't need them, but the darkness still felt strange and unnatural in a house that I always remembered being so bright and cheerful.

In the kitchen, I walked up to the freezer and was suddenly reminded of the horrific sight that I saw in BioLogic's freezer. The thought made me afraid of opening my own fridge as I half expected to see the same sight inside of it. I had to shake my head hard to dispel the thought from my mind. The food that was left in there since before the whole vampire thing started was still there. Lupia was mainly living off of the long-lasting leftovers from the fridge and pantry, not the freezer, though her supplies would soon need to be restocked depending on how long she stayed.

I took out the same package of beef that I opened in order to try my first taste of blood. A bit more blood and two whole steaks remained on the Styrofoam tray. I removed one of them, put it on a plate, and shoved it into the microwave, setting it to defrost.

I stared at the microwave. It shined brightly as the only source of light in the room. It glowed yellow, as if it were a supernatural force acting upon that meat. *Maybe microwaves are actually magic.* I found this thought intriguing even though I knew it was probably false. I had a few minutes to spare, but I wanted to know the result of this experiment as soon as possible. I started pacing around the kitchen while I waited. That was when my eyes came across something I'd never seen before.

I picked the strange object up. It was a pill bottle that looked like it could only be obtained through a prescription. I certainly didn't have any prescriptions, and I only knew of my parents taking multivitamins. I turned the bottle around in my hands, reading the text on it. It was hard to decipher since I knew nothing of prescription medications, but one word stood out to me. "Estrogen?" *Why would there be estrogen, of all things, in my kitchen?* I looked for a name on the bottle and found "Esau White" listed on it. *Who's Esau White?* It wasn't a name I'd ever heard before. It didn't even register as having a gender to me, so I assumed that this individual must be female due to the contents of the bottle. *Does Lupia have an estrogen deficiency?* Someone who looked as good as her didn't seem to need to look any more feminine, so the bottle left me confused.

The microwave let out its usual long beep to tell me in was done defrosting, thus distracting me from the pill bottle. Now, despite my extreme clumsiness, I was never particularly bad at cooking. Granted, I burned and cut myself accidently on all too many occasions, but I was always pretty good at actual food preparation. After setting the bottle down, I went over to the microwave and popped it open. The meat was still cold, just as it should be, but it was defrosted and tender.

I took a knife and cut the steak into two halves. I remembered Buford at lunch time eating his big pile of meat. Perhaps vampires could eat meat as an alternative to blood. It seemed like something viable that I could try. The meat he ate was cooked, so I took out a pan and coated it with some cooking spray to lessen burning or sticking. Sautéing seemed to be the fastest and simplest option.

I turned the heat up just enough to bring the pan to a decent simmer and then added one of the two pieces of steak, leaving the other on the plate. I cooked the piece for several minutes until it became medium-well, just the way I preferred it as a human. I didn't bother adding any seasonings as they would represent a complication to the experiment.

The moment of truth came when the steak reached just the right level of cooking perfection. I grabbed a two-pronged grilling fork from a nearby drawer and stabbed the piece of meat. I lifted it up toward my face and sniffed it. It smelled perfectly normal, just as a steak should. I lowered it to my mouth and took a bite.

Never before had I ever thought that I would taste sand twice in the same day. I mean, sand was only something I tasted on accident at the beach or in the sandbox back in elementary school. It wasn't something that a Hershey's Kiss or a steak should ever taste like unless somebody were playing an extremely cruel joke.

I spat out the bite I took into the kitchen sink, not really relishing the idea of coughing up blood again. *So is eating meat something only daywalkers can do?* I remembered the term Will used to possibly describe Buford. I was so confused. *Is blood really the only thing I can consume?* I thought about the way I took Buford's blood. *Wait, didn't Will say something about how drinking*

Blood on Fire

vampire blood turns people into slaves? But I didn't feel any desire to serve Buford in any way. Therefore, he couldn't be a vampire at all, right? Yet he still did some weird mind thing to those reporters, according to Will. Nothing made sense.

I turned my sights to the other slice of steak, freshly defrosted, that I hadn't cooked, and wondered what I should do with it. I didn't have much confidence that I'd be able to eat it. I stared at it. Blood coated the plate all around it, blood that I could smell. *No...* An idea I didn't quite want to consider trying crept into my mind. *Should I try eating it...raw?*

First of all, let me state that I do not condone the unwarranted consumption of raw meat. The risk of the bacterial infection is simply too great. In other words, for the vast majority of the human race, doing what I was about to do would be an extremely bad idea that should never be attempted by anyone ever.

I wasn't confident, especially with what the principal said about the possibility of spreading sickness by bite. Was it true? Only later through later research and experimentation did I learn that I could spread blood-borne illnesses like AIDS or Hepatitis. My saliva killed most bacteria, and I could always brush my teeth (although toothpaste wouldn't taste quite the same).

I picked up the slimy, raw piece of meat and held it up. The pan was still hot, so I very briefly exposed both sides of the steak in the hope of killing any bacteria that may have been living on the outside of it. It dripped with the same blood that I had already tried eating. I knew that it was disgusting, but for my own sake, to make my undead life easier, I had to make this attempt. I quickly bit off a piece and started chewing.

I rushed at first, ready to spit the meat out at any moment, but then I slowed down. My eyes widened upon my realization of, *It's...not bad.* By no means did it compare with the taste either source of human blood that I had tasted thus far, but it was more than tolerable. I dare say that it was actually pretty good. It was like ordering a steak at a mediocre restaurant. It wasn't the best but it was tasty enough. Like any raw or undercooked meat, it was extremely chewy, but the razor tips of my fangs and the increased strength with which I could chew helped to take care of that issue. I almost rejoiced when I discovered that I was actually able to swallow it.

Still hungry, I defrosted another whole steak and ate that one too. I couldn't believe what I was doing, but it was far more satisfying than simply going hungry and risking a dangerous outburst at school the next day.

FOOD AND FAMILY

Animal flesh wasn't as satisfying as human blood. In fact, instincts inside of me gave me the feeling that I wouldn't be as powerful if sustained in this way.

So I can eat flesh...does that make me a zombie? I vowed to never eat human flesh. Blood was one thing, but biting a chunk out of a living person was something I definitely couldn't do.

Awkwardly satisfied, I made sure to discard the remains of the meat package and then clean and put away the kitchen utensils. I put the half of the steak I cooked into the fridge in case Lupia wanted it later (no need to waste food, right?). I then took out an old lunch box that I hadn't used since elementary school (it had an old version of *My Little Pony* on the outside) and left it open on the counter. I put another steak into the fridge to let it defrost by the morning. Knowing that the school cafeteria would never serve me raw meat, I would pack my own lunch.

I then went back to my room, sat down on my bed, picked up the wand, and examined it closely, looking particularly at the emblem Will pointed out. *What does this thing do?* I pointed it at a random object—my dresser, actually—and flicked it as if I were a *Harry Potter* character casting a spell.

"*Accio* dresser." Nothing happened. "*Petrificus Totalus.*" Again, nothing happened. "*Avada Kedavra?*" Still nothing. Believing that nothing else would happen, I made one last vain attempt at casting a spell. "*Incendio.*"

When I tried this last spell, *Harry Potter*'s spell for producing fire, something unexpected happened. I found myself with a similar sensation to what I had when using my pyrokinesis. The top of dresser caught on fire. "Oh crap!" It was small at first, and I managed to run to the kitchen a few times to grab glasses of water to put it out before it became out of hand. The smoke detector was silent. *That'll have to be fixed.*

When the fire was completely gone, I surveyed the damage. Due to my lack of organization, I had multiple objects randomly strewn about on top of the dresser. "This bra's toast." I tossed the damaged article of clothing aside. "Aw damn it! Not you, Pikachu!" My small plush of the popular Pokémon was roasted.

I picked up the wand and very carefully put it down on my desk, not wanting to accidently set off more magic. *I really need to figure out how this thing works.*

Blood on Fire

In order to avoid damaging any more of my possessions, I decided to use the remaining hours of night before I would need to go to sleep to do homework and read more of *Dracula*. I made an interesting observation as I read. *Wow, this guy really has a thing for pretty young women.* Bethany Davis and Carla Evans were both young and pretty. Melanie Steyer was a bit chubby but looked decent enough. The Ogre Queen, however, stood out. Were we really dealing with Dracula? I was young. I supposed that I was pretty, but I wasn't really sure.

I lost track of time while reading. Since I finished my other homework and was tired from that night's ordeal, I dozed off. The time I had left before the start of my next school day would be short, so getting some sleep would be best. That was when I could see me. I could see Amy. Her neck was free of strange marks. In fact, she seemed to be her sprightly self. But something was off. Something, or someone, was keeping her and me from being the same person.

After school, a few days following dad's return from Eastern Europe, Amy walked in on him checking over receipts on his desk, mumbling. "I can't believe that I spent that much money shipping boxes full of dirt from Romania. Why the hell does Acula need those boxes, anyway? And why does the cost have to come from my pocket? How can I even write that off as a business expense?"

"Uh...hey dad." Amy curiously eyed the receipts from far away.

"Oh...I...uh...hi, Amy!" He was extremely nervous, even in front of his own daughter.

"Mom said to tell you that dinner would be ready in ten minutes."

"Um...right..." He was cut off by the ringing of his nearby telephone, which was connected to the landline that Amy almost never used anymore since she had her cell phone. He picked up the receiver. "Oh, hi doctor...yes...right...what?...Really?...Um...okay, fine, I'll let them know." Amy had been standing there awkwardly, curious about her father's conversation. "Please tell your mother that a coworker of mine will be stopping in during dinner time. He won't be eating anything, though."

"Okay..." Amy didn't seem to know what to think. Her father bringing coworkers to the house was a highly unusual occurrence.

She did as he asked. "Dad's going to have a guest here for dinner."

"Who is it?" Mom stood over the sink, a skeptical look on her face.

"He didn't say."

FOOD AND FAMILY

"That's fine I guess." Mom didn't sound very happy about this turn of events. "Set up another place at the table."

"Dad said that his guest won't be eating."

"Why? Did he already eat?"

Amy shrugged, not knowing the answer.

Only mere minutes later, the doorbell rang, and Amy answered it. Now I could see a man who looked the way that I imagined Dracula to look while reading the book. He had that telltale pale skin along with enormous bushy eyebrows and curly hair. His lips were oddly red, considering how pale the rest of his skin was. He also had long, sharp white teeth and a pointed chin. I knew this man was Dr. Acula. Amy, however, had no idea who he was.

"Greetings, you must be the lovely daughter of my compatriot, friend Erick."

Amy's raised an eyebrow, struck by this man's odd appearance. "Dad! There's a strange man here to see you!" She was awfully blunt.

Dad ran in to greet his coworker, motioning him to come inside. Acula complied with this invitation.

Through the still-open door, Amy could see the last rays of the sun dying away outside. She then closed it. She seemed to find something about this man disturbing.

Mom came from the kitchen to greet this visitor. "Ah, friend Erick, what a beautiful wife you have. She still looks so young for being a mother of two children. I am absolutely charmed by her."

"I think I like this guy already." Mom seemed impressed. "So did my husband meet you during his trip to Romania?"

"Indeed he did."

"He says that you live in a castle."

"Ah yes. It has been in my family for generations. So many of my ancestors have made it their home." The two of them struck up a short conversation about Romania (mom was always well-read on various subjects).

Amy became increasingly wary of Dr. Acula's presence as time went on.

"You have put together such a fine house, friend Cassandra, and such a lovely daughter you have." He turned to Amy. "Please do me the honor of introducing yourself to me."

Amy reluctantly put out a hand to shake his. "Um…my name is Amy Able. It's, uh, nice to meet you, Mister…" She didn't know what to put after the title. Dad hadn't told her this man's name.

Blood on Fire

"Doctor," he corrected her, "Dr. Acula."

"Right..." Amy only became more uncomfortable.

The three family members and their guest sat around the dinner table, although, as requested, Acula's place wasn't actually set, but he did join in the dinner conversation. Dinner itself consisted of mom's garlic chicken, which, as usual, Amy couldn't get enough of. Acula, however, seemed repulsed by it, though he was as polite as he could possibly be. "Please, my nose is a bit sensitive. If you could keep the chicken on that side of the table, it would be much appreciated."

"Suit yourself." Amy voraciously tore the meat off the bone as she ate. How she stayed so tiny with her ravenous appetite was a mystery to everyone, even her father the biologist. The only explanation he could think of was the lack of massive amounts of junk food that infest so many diets.

Mom seemed to enjoy conversing with the guest. "So, Dr. Acula, do you have any particular focus in your studies?"

"I mostly work with blood myself."

"What do you do with blood, exactly?"

"The usual things. I study its properties, its potential, its diseases."

"Interesting."

Acula glanced at dad as if to make sure that he didn't have any sort of comment about the work they did. He kept his mouth shut. He was oddly quiet.

"Friend Amy." Acula turned to her after his conversation with mom.

"Huh?" Amy hadn't expected the doctor to address her so suddenly.

"Do you have many friends at school?"

"I have a few, but I'm not exactly what you would call one of the popular girls. Not like some of other bitches I know."

"Amy!" Mom didn't like her daughter talking like that. It didn't bother dad too much since he was hardly any different at that age—and so was mom.

"I see that you have a will of your own." Acula smiled. "That is a good thing to have indeed. You must stand out from the others at your school."

"I suppose so..." Amy sounded like she wanted the conversation to end, but she didn't want to leave a rude impression on a foreigner.

"Tell me about some of the other girls at your school."

This was a very awkward question that made mom and dad glance at each other inquisitively, but Amy nonetheless gave a generalization of the other girls

FOOD AND FAMILY

in her school without naming names, though clearly one of was Shelly and another was the Ogre Queen. She avoided describing Amelia.

By the time dinner was done, night had set in outside, and Dr. Acula seemed to know not to overstay his welcome.

He stood by the front door, smiling jovially. "Ah yes, I must be going now. I greatly appreciate you allowing me to meet your family, friend Erick. I hope that we can have many great times together as we work."

"Um, you're welcome. Do you need a ride anywhere?"

"No, thank you, I will be able to reach my destination on foot." Considering the layout of the town, this was a strange statement.

"Are you sure?"

"Goodbye for now, friend Erick!" He gave dad an absurdly strong handshake and rushed out the door, slamming it behind him and shaking the whole house.

"Well, he seems like a nice guy," mom said, "if a little weird."

Amy didn't say anything; she only stared after him suspiciously after he left before going back into her room.

The rest of the night went normally, but on the next morning Amy woke up with two strange circular marks on her neck.

12: Protested Existence

Wednesday morning was partly cloudy—a welcome shift from the completely clear and sunny days of Monday and Tuesday. This slight change in weather, however, didn't make being outside very much more bearable.

After Lupia awoke me, seeming more lethargically than she had at any point previously, I hastily packed my lunch and the items I would need for class that day into my bag. I couldn't see Amelia yawning as she drove since I kept myself covered up as much as possible, but I could hear her. I couldn't exactly blame her for being tired. The night before had held all too high of a possibility that all of us could have died during The Ogre Queen's onslaught.

"Did your parents notice the new damage to your car?" I managed to squeeze out a question. I of course referred to any singing or melting I caused or any dents from our attacker.

She yawned while speaking. "They were asleep." She really needed to focus on the road and I really needed to focus on not burning to death. She would likely somehow get a hold of an energy drink sometime before class.

Soon, the drive to school was finally done and I arrived in Mr. Royal's class. That wasn't when the trouble of that day began, but it was the time that I first knew about it.

"Miss Able..." Mr. Royal's tone indicated that something was wrong. "...You're here..."

"Why shouldn't I be? I made it through yesterday and the day before alive."

"Well, yes. It's just that I'm surprised you made it through."

"Through what?" The only outside witness to any of the previous night's events was Officer Freeman, so I figured that Royal must have been talking about something else entirely.

"How did you get inside the school?"

PROTESTED EXISTENCE

"Through the junior parking lot. My friend drove me."

"That explains it." Apparently something just clicked in his mind, but I was still confused.

"That explains what?" I wanted to be in the loop of whatever my teacher was talking about.

"How you got past all the protestors outside the front entrance."

"Come again?" I knew that I just heard something I didn't want to hear.

"There are protestors outside the front of the school."

"And what, exactly, are they protesting?" Somehow I already knew how he was going to answer, but I hoped against all odds that he would say something different.

"They're protesting against you." He said exactly what I expected him to say. Even though I hadn't had the time to watch any news reports the previous night, I couldn't think of anything else they could be protesting besides, of course, the sad state of the American—and particularly Floridian—educational system, but the ignorant masses don't care about that.

"Well, I guess I'm, uh, lucky that there are multiple entrances to the school." I said this halfheartedly while I sat down, dreading whatever this day was going to ultimately bring me.

"If you want my suggestion, just stay away from the front entrance." Royal turned back to the chalk board and continued writing that day's lecture outline.

Seriously, can my life get any more stupid? Now I had to deal with protestors, of all things. *Should I go outside and face them or should I just avoid them?* I decided to avoid them.

More of my classmates made their way in and took their seats. "So Lamy," Shelly stood over me like she was high and mighty, "it looks like everyone really does hate you. I guess nobody will ever like you and your ugly pale face." I wondered if she believed that her continued insults would get me to say more about the Ogre Queen. I didn't respond. I only sat back in my chair with the knowledge that this day would be a difficult. All the students gave me different looks from what they gave me on either previous day. I felt like I was the cancer that was killing their normal school lives.

"Is she really as evil as they say?" I heard one boy ask.

"I heard she's trying to fight the others," one girl said.

Of course, when Ella walked in, the atmosphere took a turn for the stupider as she whispered loudly (it's possible) to herself. "It's a good thing that none of those people know about vampires. Otherwise they might tear Buford apart and burn the pieces." I just rolled my eyes as she passed.

The bell rang and Royal called the class to attention. "Alright everyone, I realize that there are some people outside expressing their First Amendment rights, but that should not be a reason to turn our sights away from algebra today."

One boy interrupted. "But what about the fact that the vampire is right here—"

Royal ignored him and started teaching. He really did have a knack for shutting the class up to begin his lesson, which lasted for the entire class period with very little interruption from the students.

I wanted to experience as minimal strife, so when going to my next two classes, I took a more roundabout route that would expose me to more sun (albeit a bit less intense thanks to that day's clouds) but would bypass areas with easy access to the school's front entrance. My reception in both of those classes was much the same as in math, and I managed to avoid any confrontation. I survived until lunchtime unscathed.

The cafeteria wasn't far away from the main entrance of the school, which was exactly where the protestors were. Luckily, like many places on campus, it had multiple entrances, so I managed to continue my exercise of avoidance. When I sat down at my usual table, Will and Amelia looked exceedingly worried.

Will stared in the direction of the front entrance as if he could see the protestors. "I guess we must've missed something serious last night."

"Obviously." Amelia seemed to be on her guard.

"So did you guys just miss the news or something?" Doug sounded like he knew what he was talking about.

"You could say that." I wasn't planning on telling him why.

Doug turned to Amelia. "What were you up to, anyway? I thought we were supposed to go out last night. Your phone kept going to voicemail." I assumed that his comment meant that Amelia had turned her phone off during our infiltration, which made me feel incredibly stupid for leaving mine on.

Amelia seemed nervous about answering that question. "Well, I—my father took my phone away last night because he said I wasn't focusing enough on my homework." This explanation was enough for Doug to believe since, as

PROTESTED EXISTENCE

Amelia's boyfriend, he knew firsthand exactly how scary Robert Valentine could be.

Will didn't seem as tired as Amelia (after all, he wasn't the one driving) but he still looked exhausted. However, Will didn't seem to be worried at all about what happened in the past. His mind was on the protestors. I supposed that, as witches, his family likely had a history with witch hunts. Was I now the target of a modern-day witch hunt? Would these people stop at nothing to burn me at the stake?

James stared at me flirtatiously. I wondered if he would ever return to the real world.

I had my bag next to me, and I could feel the hard lunch box inside of it. I knew that with the strain of the day that lay ahead of me, I would grow desperate for sustenance at some point. This time, however, I was prepared, but I would inevitably gross a ton of people out. *Is this going to be worth it?* Even I was disgusted by the possibility. "Okay guys, what you're about to see is going to be incredibly disgusting, and it's probably going to reduce my social status around here to an even lower level than it's at already, but just bear with me."

"What are you talking about?" Will looked at me, skeptical.

"Remember how I became desperate for blood during the last two days of school?"

"Yes." Will, Amelia, and James all answered at the same time. Vanessa, Kim, and Doug looked on, curious.

"Right. Well, I did a little experiment last night and found that while it isn't quite as good, I do have an option other than blood."

"Really?" Will seemed very interested.

I took a deep breath. "Alright." I pulled out my lunch box.

"That old thing?" Amelia laughed. "You haven't used that in years."

"Wait till you see what's inside." I opened the box and pulled out the bag that contained my raw steak, which practically glowed a deep shade of red.

Will almost cringed, but he seemed to appreciate my thinking ahead in this matter. "Amy, truly this is the most disgusting thing that you have ever done. But I admit that it's pretty damn smart."

"Thank you." I smiled. After lining the table with napkins, I opened the bag, pulled out my lunch, a chomped off a huge piece from one side of it.

Amelia didn't seem to care that I was eating raw meat and James was locked in his trance, but Doug seemed absolutely disgusted. "Ew! How could you…I mean…that's a…I…Ammy…" He used his pet name for Amelia, which looks and sounds a lot like my name, so he generally wouldn't say it around me. "…Could…could we please go sit somewhere else?"

"Why?" Amelia knew why, but she didn't see the point of moving.

"But that's so disgusting." Doug's face looked like it was turning green. "I mean, it's absolutely vile. I don't care if she's a vampire; as a vegetarian, I don't want to be a part of this." Doug's lunches, which he brought from home, were usually such elaborate-looking leftovers that I couldn't tell he was a vegetarian.

I continued eating my steak, licking the blood from my hands every so often. "I'll be the first to admit that this is pretty damn disgusting," I said between bites. Quick glances around the room revealed both disgusted and intrigued faces.

"Then why are you still doing it?"

"Because the sun is painful and I need blood to heal." I kept eating even as he grew more and more uncomfortable.

Will seemed to be in favor of my new food source. "Just make sure you get meat from a decent source. There's nothing to kill any bacteria when it's raw like that."

"Maybe I should've brought a tooth brush with me. Or some Listerine."

"I—I can't take this anymore." Doug stood up, looking like he was about to faint.

Amelia rolled her eyes. "Come on, man up. You watch me eat cooked meat all the time."

"But…it's not…"

Amelia looked downright annoyed, as if Doug's complaining had finally snapped something inside of her. "Doug, can I have a word with you outside?" She stood up and motioned to him to follow her.

"Anything to get away from this sight." He readily followed her, keeping his eyes off of me as I nibbled the last bit of red meat from the bone.

"Huh…" Will looked off in the couple's direction. "I wonder if that's a bad sign."

"I don't know." I tried wiping off my hands with a napkin, which was difficult since they were very sticky. "Hold on, I'm going to need to wash my hands." I stood up, ready to head to the nearest restroom, which was right

Protested Existence

outside the front entrance to the cafeteria, but I stopped when I heard a collection of sounds that served as an ill omen building up from that entrance.

Will was already looking in the direction of the ruckus. All I could see at the moment was Buford throwing away his lunch tray after having eaten nothing from it besides meat, but the sound quickly came closer, and I could see people carrying signs with huge letters on them entering the cafeteria. Administrators rushed up to try to stop them, but were forcibly pushed out of the way.

I couldn't make sense of what the protestors were saying because they all yelled different words very loudly, creating a jumbled mess of sound that didn't mean anything to anyone.

Buford stood in their way and said, "You do not understand the peaceful nature of a fellow vampire!" but he was quickly knocked aside, hitting the ground quite hard.

Just about all of the people in the crowd seemed to be of the ages of parents or grandparents, and they consisted of an even spread of men and women. Their faces were all angry. However, their signs were what hurt me the most.

"SCHOOL IS NO PLACE FOR BLOODSUCKERS"
"PROTECT OUR CHILDREN FROM SATAN"
"RED-BLOODED AMERICANS AGAINST VAMPIRES"
"DON'T TAINT MY CHILD'S WHITE BLOOD"

That last one was disturbing though not surprising since we were in the American South. That guy probably wouldn't recognize a vampire like me as actually being white despite the fact that race has nothing whatsoever to do with vampirism. Also, that second sign didn't seem to me like it belonged, as I wasn't aware of any association between vampires and Satan. I guess it must have made sense to the evangelical mind. They probably also thought that video games, movies, TV, and books (with the exception of the Bible) were made by Satan.

The rest of the cafeteria became silent and stared at the spectacle. They had already spotted me. My skin and clothing made me stick out, so hiding from anyone would be futile. The small group of about seven (maybe eight, maybe six) people stopped in front of me, and then I could recognize their leader. The other protestors became quiet to allow him to talk. "That there's the vamp girl what attacked me at my house!" Tower's father pointed at me. He didn't hold anything, not even a sign. I was thankful that he didn't bring his shotgun.

Blood on Fire

Still, his face was one that I most certainly never wanted to see again. "I didn't attack you! I just wanted to ask you about your daughter! You attacked me!"

"Shut up with your lies, vamp girl!" I had lied on a few occasions, but I wasn't lying then. The other protestors all looked ready to attack.

"Guys, maybe we can work this out. I'm just a student here." I started to panic. I really didn't want a confrontation.

"Yer the one what made my daughter a vamp!" Mr. Evans definitely sounded more insane every second. Perhaps he wouldn't be so insane had his daughter not turned evil, but blaming her transformation on me was ridiculous.

"I never knew your daughter until she attacked Lupia! I don't mean you any harm!" *Seriously, what did I do to deserve this?* I started backing slowly toward the nearest exit.

"Shut up, vamp! Let's git 'er!" Several of the protestors pulled out crosses and garlic and came toward me. I didn't want to take my chances facing off against a mob, so I did the only sensible thing I could do—I ran.

With no shadier option, I went straight outside. Unlike the night time, when I could run continuously while barely becoming tired at all, trying to run at full speed during the daytime was like trying to move my legs through molasses—I had the power to put behind them but not enough energy to actually move them fast enough.

The screaming mob kept close behind me as I ran into the nearest building, which was full of classrooms. Escaping the sun was essential since the crackling of my skin as it burned made running that much more difficult. Classroom doors opened and teachers and students alike peered out into the hallway as we passed due to the huge amount of noise the protestors made.

Why am I running? Can't I just overpower them? I thought about how satisfying hurting these people would be but doing so would probably have created even more hate for me.

A few of my chasers yelled louder than the others, and I actually heard them.

One sounded like a common soccer mom. "Anything with fangs must be evil!"

Another was an old man. "You can't be a little girl! Show us what you really look like!"

Then, of course, was Mr. Evans. "Gimme my little baby back!"

Protested Existence

That guy needs to meet Dracula. I quickly came to the end of that building's hallway where I found another portal to the outside as well as a set of stairs to the second floor. I then came to the realization that I had two choices—either stay inside the buildings and run through the linear hallways where I had no chance of escape or take my chances and run outside where I would burn but have a better chance of escaping.

I burst through the double doors into the daytime sun once again. Nobody else was around since classes were still going on at that time. *Crap! Crap! Crap!* Going outside of course meant sun exposure. I wanted to run through the courtyard because it was wider and less obstructed, but the sun would kill me.

I wish there were more clouds…why can't there be more clouds? What about some rain? Rain would be nice. But no more clouds and no rain came. Perhaps some vampires had the power to change weather, but apparently I didn't.

For once, I didn't trip, but I did fall. I just couldn't keep running. My energy was gone. Though eating raw steak was a good idea for gaining sustenance, its effects are nothing in comparison to human blood. It was, however, enough to keep me from passing out, but I could feel myself burning away. It was painful

I waited for the coming onslaught of people who hated me. Some time passed, and nobody came. My head was turned sideways on the ground with my glasses pressed against the concrete so that the nosepiece dug into my face hard. I could only see the hedges at the edge of the courtyard, but I could hear a ton of movement.

Then I heard a voice. "You all have the right to remain silent." It was a deep, familiar voice that I had heard in the past on rare occasions, a gruff man's voice that exuded authority. "Anything you say or do can and will be used against you in a court of law. Take it from here, Freeman."

I then heard the voice of the officer who inadvertently saved me and my friends from certain doom. He quoted the rest of the usual Miranda Warning in a less imposing and authoritative voice.

"Amelia," came the powerful deep voice again, "go help your friend up, I'd like to have a word with her." I knew that the voice's owner was none other than Captain Robert Valentine, Amelia's father.

Blood on Fire

"You can't stop us!" Mr. Evans was beyond angry, and he ignored the Miranda Warning, "We have the right to speak out against blood sucking demons like her!"

"You have the right to do that but you don't have the right to force your way into a school and then endanger the life of a student, vampire or not. Take 'em to the wagon, boys." Valentine seemed to enjoy his job.

I was quickly cooking in the sun. My only saving grace had been that day's cloud cover. I could feel two people gathering around me, and I could see one of them at my side, though I couldn't make out who it was. "Let's get her to some shade." It was Will's voice. The two people picked me up and carried me. Sometimes weighing so little has its advantages.

They propped me up against a wall with my head resting against my left shoulder some distance away where I could no longer feel any sunlight. With my head turned upward, I could see ceiling tiles above me. I knew that I was safely inside. I could see both Will and Amelia kneeling in front of me. "Triple A?" Amelia sounded horrified.

I tried lifting my head, but it barely budged. Moving any part of my body hurt. My skin felt charred, and it didn't feel like it was healing at all. I couldn't see myself, of course, but I apparently really looked like the living corpse of a burn victim. "Come on, Triple A, get up!" Amelia became more frantic.

I tried to say something, but all I could get out was a moan.

"I'm guessing you're out of juice." Now I could see Captain Valentine's legs in front of me. I only very slightly nodded since doing so was rather painful. He tossed something into my lap. "Drink up. It's from the ambulance we called over in case someone got hurt." I slowly managed to move my right arm to the object, which felt like a plastic bag that was squishy since it was filled with liquid. I lifted it into my line of sight. The plastic had some white letters etched onto it, the most prominent of which was a big letter A. The liquid inside the bag was a deep red.

Upon realizing that Captain Valentine had thrown me a medical blood bag, I shoved it into my mouth, sank my fangs into it, and drank deeply. It had no taste, likely since it had been separated from its original owner for a while. I felt my skin properly reform as soon as I started drinking. The bag didn't satisfy me, but it was enough to get my body moving.

"So now that you're awake, I'd like to ask you some questions so we can figure out exactly what happened here, if you don't mind." Captain Valentine

Protested Existence

took a small notepad and a pen out of his pocket. I looked up at him. I had seen him before several times because of Amelia, but I had never actually met him when he was on duty. He was a bear of a man. Just one look at him and it was obvious that he played football in both high school and college. At about six and a half feet tall, he would tower over me even if I were standing up, so from the ground he looked like a mountain. I still had a hard time believing that he was married to a tiny Japanese woman whose height was closer to mine. He had short black hair and a thick black mustache, both of which matched his dark sunglasses.

"Um...okay." I had no reason not to comply since he had practically just saved my life.

"Did you do anything at all to incite those rioters?"

"No...although I talked to their leader previously in reference to his daughter attacking Lupia."

"And where is Lupia now?"

"I don't know." I shouldn't have mentioned her name, but I wasn't thinking straight. This time I had to lie to protect her.

"Now, Amy, we've met before, and you've always seemed like a good kid. My daughter pretty much adores you." I could tell from his voice that his compliments were going to culminate into something uncomplimentary. "But I have to ask you...have you been up to anything unlawful ever since this whole vampire business started?" He seemed eager to know.

I wasn't sure how to answer this question since I was still in shock over what I had survived and since I was intimidated by the colossal police officer.

"Don't worry, there's currently no law against drinking other people's blood, as long as you do it consensually." Amelia looked away. Valentine tried to reassure me but I still wasn't sure what to say. He didn't seem to know that I had drank his daughter's blood. "Look, ever since last Sunday, right after the events at that concert happened, strange damage has been appearing on my daughter's car. Furthermore, Freeman wrote her a warning late last night. What were you kids out doing?"

I staggered upward, using more strength than normal to lift myself. Compared to Valentine's height, though, I was practically still lying on the ground. "I—um." I couldn't respond. I couldn't think of what to say. What does anyone say in such a situation?

"We just went—" Amelia tried to answer for me.

Blood on Fire

"Amelia," he cut her off, "you already told me. I want to hear it from her mouth. Miss Able, look, you're the friend of my pride and joy, so I want to trust you." From his lofty height, his authoritative gaze pierced into me. Then I realized why I couldn't say anything. Not only was what we did the night before completely illegal, having this police officer standing over me was completely scary. I had precious little energy and I had just outrun a crowd of crazies who wanted to kill me. Why couldn't he just leave me alone?

I felt myself starting to shake out of fear. "I...I...I..." I could barely form a word. I just wanted to be somewhere else. Will looked like he wanted to talk for me, but he also looked intimidated.

"Dad! Stop it!" Amelia shouted at her father. "Can't you see she's stressed out?" She came over to me and put her arm around my back to help keep me steady.

Valentine sighed. "Fine, Amelia." Then he turned to look at me sternly and his tone became much darker. "Just remember, I'll have my eye on you." He left to rejoin Freeman and the violent protestors outside.

I couldn't tell whether Sergeant Valentine was trying to help me or whether he was actually trying to find a reason to arrest me. He did give me that blood bag, but he left me in a bad mood. His questioning coupled with my run from the protestors just gave me the feeling that the world was against me. When I finally managed to stand up, I walked slowly to my next class with my friends at my side. I had very little energy.

"Thanks a lot, Amelia." She saved me from that situation.

"Don't mention it, Triple A. I'll—uh, I'll do anything to protect you."

Will raised an eyebrow since that wasn't something that she would normally say.

I tried to collect my wits, but I had trouble getting my mind straight. "A few days ago, nobody cared who I was. Now everyone wants to kill me. Humans...other vampires..." I felt like I could cry, but no tears came out.

Will and Amelia both looked like they wanted to console me, but they had trouble getting the words out. Finally, Amelia spoke. "I'm really sorry about my dad. He just takes his job too seriously sometimes. I'm sure everything will work out."

"Amelia," I said through gritted teeth, "I don't blame you and I hardly blame him. I just have to accept the fact that the world is out to screw me right now."

PROTESTED EXISTENCE

Will tried to stay optimistic. "Don't forget, you have both of us here for you."

"And pretty soon people will probably start randomly hating you guys too just for hanging out with an evil vampire." I felt pretty much defeated.

"You are definitely not evil. Trust me. I should show you some of the crap I've read about."

I wasn't quite in the mood to further discuss this matter. Not only did I feel awful, I figured that I probably looked awful too, so I headed into the nearest restroom. Amelia followed me in while Will waited outside. When I lowered my hood and took a look into the mirror, I saw that my burns were almost completely healed, but my hair was messed up. I reached for my bag to grab my hair brush, but then I realized that I didn't have my bag at all. I had a panic attack over the possibility that I had left it in the cafeteria after the protestors attacked, but Amelia then handed it to me. She had been holding the whole time. "Thanks a lot."

She smiled and gave me a quick nod. I grabbed my brush and put my hair in a state somewhat close to presentable. Then I straightened out my clothing as much as I could.

"All things considered," Amelia said, "I think you look great."

"Um...thanks," I appreciated her compliment, though as long as those red eyes looked back at me from the mirror, I couldn't quite agree with her. I put some finishing touches on my hair. I couldn't quite get it perfect, but it was the best I could do with the limited time I had. "I should probably just get to class."

Amelia nodded.

We eventually arrived at the door to English class where some other students were arriving. As they saw my haggard figure, I thought I may have seen a sign of sympathy in some of their eyes, but I figured again that I was just seeing things.

"Will you guys be okay without me?" Amelia wanted to stay around, but she would inevitably have to be in class elsewhere.

"We'll be fine," I said with obvious weariness in my voice.

"Alright." Amelia then gave me a tight hug, and when I say tight, I mean it. Our difference in height put my head right above her breasts. She held me there almost lovingly for nearly a minute. For some reason, I felt no desire to object. Will looked on, even more surprised than I was. "Please take it easy," she said to me in a low, somewhat sensual, voice before releasing me and turning to walk in the opposite direction. It looked like she put an extra swing to her hips as she went on her way.

"Well, uh," Will was almost speechless, "let's just head inside." I gave a quick nod and followed him. The usual students, including Ella Spawn, also went inside.

As the substitute had said the day before, Ms. Perth was absent. Rather, a woman who looked rather young, likely in her late twenties, stood at the head of the class. She had brown hair, a bit darker than mine, as well as a light complexion and soft features. She wore the sort of brown dress that doesn't stand out at all, the sort anyone would expect any normal female school teacher to wear.

"Okay class," she had an obvious British accent, "your old teacher, Ms. Perth, decided to take her leave from teaching at present for her health."

"I wonder why." I heard one student whisper to another.

"She had her reasons." The new teacher seemed to have good hearing, at the very least. "I will be your new English III Honors teacher. You may call me Ms. Hacket."

This name wasn't one that I was familiar with.

"Now, I am told that you all started reading Dracula." Most of the class around her nodded. "And I see that we have a real vampire in class with us." She turned to me, much to my dismay. "I'm sure that you know firsthand the horrors of such legendary beings."

Sick of being singled out, I didn't respond. I knew so little about this woman, but she had just made a poor impression on me.

"Don't worry, with time you'll come to understand that your curse is truly a blessing." She smiled. Then she picked up copies of her syllabus, which was a revised version of Perth's, and passed them around.

As I waited for my copy, my mind raced. *What did she mean by 'a blessing'?*

"You will notice that my syllabus is a continuation of Ms. Perth's but with a few personal changes." Indeed, the page contained more British texts than before, but it was still normal for a high school literature class. "So, as per Ms. Perth's last assignment, you will still be reading *Dracula*. It is a fine text that I know extremely well. I suppose that I might even fancy myself a *Dracula* scholar." She gave a quick chuckle. "Now, those of you who actually bothered to read it surely have realized that Dracula himself enjoys preying on young

Protested Existence

women—women not far removed from those here in this classroom." She stole a quick glance at me. "You will notice that with the brides in his castle and his later victim of Lucy Westenra," she paused at the mention of this character's name, "Dracula has changed these women into beings just like himself. Essentially, he 'corrupted' them, so to speak, infecting their bodies and minds and changing who they were. Just as the role of a formerly good politician can be changed through corruption by the desire of money, they retained their human appearance and memories, but the manner of their existence remained permanently altered. Now, this does not mean that all of our real-life vampires have become evil monsters. I understand that we have an exception, a good vampire, in this very room." She smirked at me. I locked my eyes on her. The woman seemed to have some sort of significance to me, but I couldn't figure out what it could be.

She continued with her lecture, occasionally asking for feedback from the mostly inattentive class until the end of the period. "Now, you all should continue reading tonight and be prepared for a quiz tomorrow." The bell rang as soon as she finished talking, as if she had an indubitable sense of time.

"Good afternoon to all of you." She waved goodbye to the class, who quickly stood up and left the room without a second thought, as students generally did. Then one of her students received an unexpected request. "Oh, Miss Able, could I speak to you for a second?"

So she wanted to talk to me. I wasn't sure what to expect because I didn't quite trust her yet, but I wasn't one to disobey the immediate request of someone who potentially controlled my future through the distribution of grades. After collecting my possessions, I went to her.

"I apologize for singling you out today; I only wished to explain to the class that a vampire is still, essentially, human."

"Um…okay." I suppose that I should have appreciated having a teacher make a concession for me, but admittedly I hated the idea of being singled out in any way, especially after the day's riot.

"Just remember, you now have the power to accomplish things that no one else can. All you need is a little bit of creativity."

"Creativity?" I looked at her quizzically.

"Yes. Creativity is like a magic wand. If you simply take the time to wave it and see what happens, you can accomplish great things."

A wand? Her use of that metaphor was an odd coincidence.

Blood on Fire

"Many people are expecting certain things from someone like you. Why don't you wave your wand and give them something unexpected?"

"Alright." Her words seemed to linger in my mind. They seemed to be important to me even though I knew that this woman was probably just a normal teacher. She began to turn away, indicating that our conversation was over, but I still had something to ask her. "Ms. Hacket?"

"Yes?"

"We just met today…why are you trying so hard to help me, as you say?" The situation didn't sit quite right with me.

"Oh, no real reason." She shrugged off my question easily. "I suppose I'm just interested in vampires, that's all."

"I see…well, thanks, I guess."

She turned away from me and back toward her books.

I joined Will, who had been waiting for me by the exit. "What did she want to tell you?"

"Nothing important, really. I guess she just wants to provide me with some support." Her mention of a wand didn't seem like anything worth pointing out.

"That's good, though something about her bothers me." This statement confirmed that I wasn't the only one who might be paranoid.

"Did you detect any sort of magic at work?"

"It's tough to tell when so many people are around, but I didn't sense anything like that. It's just that the way she was acting bothered me, and I'm not quite sure why. That and the fact that the school replaced Ms. Perth so quickly. I mean, she was here two days ago and now we have this new woman in her place. That's strange."

"Any stranger than everything else that's happened?" I was being sarcastically.

"Point taken."

"Well, keep your magic eyes open for me." I smiled at him.

He gave me a thumbs-up as he turned and went on his way to class. I did the same.

I wasn't quite sure how I survived the rest of that school day. I was too exhausted to re-invoke the blood-stealing spell that I used the day before and I didn't feel like risking the use of my fangs, so I remained weak throughout the rest of my classes. I was lucky that the steak and blood bag could sustain me for so long.

Protested Existence

The protestors who attacked me were only a few of those in front of the school, and while several of them stayed around for the entire day, their numbers dwindled as many didn't want to be associated with the crazies.

13: Wolf's Bane

"Ugh...damn it." For once, I found still found myself tired even when night fell and I got some sleep. I jumped into the shower, wanting in vain to wash away the stress.

When I was done, I wrapped myself in a towel and went into the living room, which was unusually quiet and dark. Even though this was only the third night since she had moved in, I already expected to find Lupia watching TV. However, she was nowhere to be found. "Lupia?" I got no response. I went over to her bedroom door with my brother's poster of a Porsche on it and knocked. Still no response. I opened the door just a little bit and peeked inside. "Lupia." Again, I received no answer. Then I opened the door wide. "Lupia!"

My voice echoed through the house. Since I could see through darkness, I could tell that nobody was in Lupia's (or rather Allen's) bedroom at all. It was so eerily quiet. I checked every room just to make sure that she wasn't in any of them, and surely enough she wasn't.

She didn't leave, did she? My eyes widened at this thought. The other vampires wanted Lupia, and, according to Will, she would be safe so long as she remained inside of my house. Yet she clearly wasn't there. *Crap!*

I flung my towel aside as I ran to my room to grab some shorts and a shirt. I took my keys and ran out the door, locking it behind me. I didn't need a flashlight. "Lupia! Lupia!"

It was a quiet night. Few cars passed across my home's cul-de-sac even during the daytime, so understandably, nobody would be around at night. The night was also rather brighter than the others I had experienced recently. I looked upward and saw the full moon lighting the sky, even amid the partial cloud cover. I took a moment to remark at how beautiful it was—I always liked looking at the moon.

"Lupia! Damn it...where could she be?" I wasn't sure of which direction to head in. *Is she even nearby?* My mother's car was still in the driveway, so she couldn't have driven off. *Maybe she got a ride?* But who would give her a ride? I ran back inside to see if she left a note of any sort, scouring the living room, the kitchen, and her room. All of the few possessions she had brought with her were still where they were supposed to be. They were easy to spot in her room amid all of my brother's crap. I found nothing that told me where she could possibly be.

I took out my phone and called Will.

"What's up, Amy?"

"Um...it's about Lupia."

"What's wrong?"

"I...can't find her." I was afraid of what his reaction would be.

"WHAT?" He sounded downright pissed off. "What happened? Did somebody come and take her? Did she leave? Why did you let her leave?"

"What am I? Her keeper? I was asleep all day since I got home and I just woke up to find her gone. We need to figure out where she went." I tried my best to keep a cool head, though it didn't really work.

"Right, right. Sorry I snapped at you. I'll head right over."

But I had a better idea. "Actually, call Amelia and have her pick you up. We may need wheels."

He seemed oddly disappointed by my suggestion. "Fine...I'll go ahead and give her a call."

"Both of you get over here as fast as you can."

"Got it."

I knew that Will and Amelia would take a while to arrive, so I searched around the perimeter of my house. I still didn't find Lupia, nor did I find anything out of the ordinary that could possibly point to wherever she went.

However, sight was not the sense that would lead me to where I needed to go. The more I stood outside, the more I noticed a very faint yet oddly familiar odor that I couldn't quite identify. It wasn't a bad smell, simply one that seemed out of place, and it was much stronger at the back of the house than at the front.

What could that smell be? I felt like a blood hound. I followed the olfactory signal, trying to find out where it emanated strongest. I followed it into the pine tree forest behind my house, and found myself surrounded by tall, skinny pine trees that only had branches and needles growing toward the very top of their height. Closer to the ground were the palmettos, those weird tropical plants with the spiky leaves that didn't grow nearly as tall as palm trees. I never realized before that the surrounding forests were so sharp.

My shorts left most of my legs exposed to the potentially vermin-covered wild. As I waded through the plants, I wondered, *Do ticks suck vampire blood?* They don't.

The forest didn't stretch very far. I soon came out the other side of it, onto one of Palm Coast's many golf courses—a large, open space of lush, green terrain that was wholly unnatural in every possible way. Florida has very few hills, but this course had many. It simply shows the efforts that companies will make in order to reshape the land in an attempt to appeal to the surrounding population of elderly and vacationers. I personally didn't know anyone who actually played golf with any regularity, though my father would go out with his coworkers on rare occasions.

My eyes could see only hills, flags, roughs, sand traps, water hazards, and trees all around. The smell, however, was definitely stronger here than it was around my house. "Lupia!" Of course I got no answer. Why should I have expected her to be hiding on a closed golf course?

I continued following the smell, my visibility in the dark aided not only by my vampire eyes but also by that bright full moon. I saw my surroundings more clearly than I ever had in the daytime as a human.

The smell led me toward one of the sand traps, which from a distance looked like it may have been one of the deepest ones on the course. I approached it, keeping my eyes open in case I saw anything suspicious. I saw nothing until I came right up to the pit. That was when something jumped out, leaping high into the air and leaving a cloud of sandy dust in its wake. It landed several feet behind me.

I was completely flustered, but I managed to spin around quickly to see what suddenly appeared. It was a tall and muscular figure. It was also completely covered in hair. The sight was oddly familiar.

"Why are you here?" The deep voice was also familiar.

It was the combination of that voice and the fur-covered figure that clicked in my mind and made me realize who I was looking at. "You...you're that werewolf from the mall, aren't you?"

"You shouldn't be here." He completely ignored my words.

"First, I want you to answer some questions for me: Who are you? Why did you show up the other day? Have you seen my friend Lupia?"

"Get away from here!" With blistering speed, the naked werewolf turned around and rushed toward me, claws bared. I sloppily dove sideways to roll out of the way, awkwardly landing in a sitting position. The werewolf turned to come at me again, but I managed to lift up one hand to prepare a fireball without actually throwing it. The werewolf stopped short.

"Attack me again and I'll kill you with fire."

Then he backed off, though, even with that dog face, he didn't look happy about it. "Please leave."

I stood up, managing to still hold the fireball. "Now I'm not leaving until you tell me why you attacked me."

"I'm...sorry. I just don't want you here."

"I'm not going to hurt you." As soon as I said this I accidently lost control of my fireball. It landed in front of the werewolf's right foot, burning the grass away. "Uh...sorry...that was an accident." I must have looked like an idiot.

The werewolf simply grunted and turned to walk away, replacing his huge front tail with his larger, actual tail in my view.

"Just wait a second, please." I was desperate for information. He stopped walking. "Do you know where my friend Lupia is? It's extremely important that we find her. Some bad vampires are trying to kidnap her."

He started walking away again, ignoring me. Then I recalled what I saw at BioLogic. "They've hurt at least one werewolf too. They slaughtered her." He stopped when I said this. "Look, we should work together. You're probably in danger too and my friends and I can help you."

"They killed another werewolf?" He didn't turn around.

"Yeah. They probably drained her dry for their weird experiments." This was just a guess on my part, but it was fairly convincing.

"Have you figured out why they're after your friend?"

"Well, no...unless she's..." I thought of the only logical conclusion I could make, considering what little information I had "...unless she's also werewolf."

The wolf in front of me stood still and silent.

"This isn't the first time I've met you. How were you in Daytona just a few days ago when you're here now? Have you been following us?"

"You should learn when to stop asking questions." He started walking away again.

Blood on Fire

Why was this guy so eager to help me before just so he can hate my guts now? He's just being a jerk. "Jerk" was seriously the first word I thought of, but then I somehow reminded myself of another insult, a word that I almost never uttered since I didn't like the meaning it held, but Will had said it only two nights before. I was put off by this naked werewolf, so I wanted to at least insult him before he left. "Geez, stop being such a faggot."

"WHAT DID YOU SAY?" He immediately turned around, baring his teeth like an angry dog.

I was taken aback; I didn't expect that reaction. It reminded me of how Lupia had reacted when Will said that word, suddenly becoming completely put off and depressed. *Why would someone like him be that insulted?* "Wait a second. What's your name?"

"Never, ever, utter that word in my presence!"

"Tell me your name!"

"Don't say that word!" We both shouted loudly enough for the whole neighborhood surrounding the golf course to hear, but no reaction came from anywhere in the area.

I closed my eyes and yelled "Faggot faggot faggot faggot faggot faggot faggot faggot faggot faggot faggot faggot faggot faggot faggot faggot faggot faggot faggot!" just in the hope of pissing him off enough to give in to telling me who he was.

Doing so turned out to be an incredibly bad idea. As my eyes were closed, the werewolf ran up to me and grabbed me by the neck, lifting me off the ground and digging his claws into my flesh. I couldn't utter any more profanity because my airways were blocked. He squeezed, trying to strangle me, and he probably would've killed any normal human.

If I said that his grip didn't hurt, I would be lying, so I won't say it. Just know no one deserves a one-handed strangle from a werewolf. Luckily for me, he lifted me off the ground just enough to attack his weak point for massive damage.

Achievement Unlocked: Ball Buster 40G

The werewolf suddenly was reeling. He looked like he had never experienced such a pain before in his life, and he completely hated it. He immediately dropped me and fell to the ground, grasping his not-so-private area. I took a few seconds to snap my neck back into place (I'd have only died if it were completely severed) and allow the pain of the claw wounds to subside.

"Are you ready to tell me your name?" I readied another fireball.

He breathed hard, working through the pain. Werewolves have balls of steel, but a vampire crotch kick is a force to be reckoned with. "Fine…my name…is Esau."

"Esau?" That was an unexpected name. "Esau White?"

The werewolf was surprised when I said that name "How…how do you know that name?" He actually sounded scared.

"From a bottle of estrogen tablets I randomly found sitting in my kitchen." It finally felt as if I would know who he was. "Why would there be female hormone pills prescribed to such a manly werewolf in my house?"

"I…I…oh what's the use." His tone completely changed, knowing that I finally had him cornered. "I guess a fake name would've been better if I truly wanted to hide."

"But I do appreciate your honesty." I smirked at him.

"Please forgive me for trying to harm you. The truth is that I really hate being in this form."

"'This form'? You mean that you're not always a werewolf?"

He sat up and nodded. "The rest of my family chooses to use their powers to live closer to the land in harmony with the planet, but I prefer to change the world with music."

"With music…?" His comment sent my memory into a flurry. I thought I knew who I was talking to, but I just didn't want to acknowledge it. Finally, I said, "Lupia?"

The werewolf nodded.

I could feel my hip shake, which I thought was due to the awkward situation, but then I realized that it was accompanied by the Super Mario Bros. theme. I answered my phone.

"Where the hell did you go?" It was Will's voice. "We're waiting at your house."

"Don't worry, I'm still nearby."

"What about Lupia?"

"Yeah…I found…her." It was hard to say the pronoun with the hulking werewolf on the ground in front of me. He looked back at me, almost imploring me not to tell Will. "They're going to find out eventually," I whispered.

"Okay, so you'll meet us back at your house soon?" Will sounded impatient.

"Of course."

Blood on Fire

"One more thing." Here, Will's tone was disconcerted.

"What?"

"Buford Mullen is standing on your driveway and staring at your house again."

"Huh...he must've just arrived." He wasn't there before.

"What should we do about him?"

"You guys are in Amelia's car, right?"

"Yeah."

It was after I made this next statement that I realized just how much of a bitch I really was. "Run him over." It was partly a joke and partly serious

"WHAT?" Will was nearly speechless at my suggestion. Lupia looked at me like I was crazy. He was probably right.

"He survived what I did to him the other night, right?"

Then I heard a series of odd bumping sounds over the phone. "Amelia! What the hell?" Will was alarmed.

"Something wrong?"

"Just meet us back here soon, okay?" He ended the call. I could only guess that Amelia followed through with my suggestion.

I turned back to Lupia, who had stood up and begun brushing the grass out of his fur. "Now how are we going to introduce them to you?"

The werewolf shrugged. We would just have to face our friends and hope for the best reaction from them. We began to walk back to my house along the same path I had followed to find him.

"So what you're saying is that you attacked me with no intent to kill; you just wanted me to go away so that I wouldn't know your secret." Lupia and I talked about his nature as a werewolf and our fight as we navigated the forest.

"Right." He nodded.

"What about when I said that word? You seemed pretty dead set on killing me."

"I'm sorry...I just really can't stand hearing that word."

"Hmm..." I still didn't appreciate being strangled. Since we had made peace, I decided to change the subject. "So during a full moon, you have no choice but to be in this form, right?" It was one of the most common aspects of werewolf legends.

"That's correct, but I can also shift into this form one time in between full moons." This explained how he was able to join the brawl at the mall.

"Furthermore, I can turn into a normal four-legged wolf any time I want unless I'm in this form."

"Cool." What else could I say? It really did sound pretty cool to me. As a vampire, I was supposed to be able to turn into a bat (or, judging by one of my opponents, a wolf) but I just couldn't.

"Trust me, it's not as cool as it sounds." He sounded like he was recalling some painful memories. "Personally, I hate this form."

"Yeah, I suppose that it's a bit too manly for someone who's usually so feminine. Speaking of which, what gives? What's with turning into a man-wolf with a colossal…you know?"

"Yes, I know." At least he was aware of his indecency.

"You're such a beautiful woman in human form."

He sighed. "Some would say that I've never been a woman."

"Please explain." My knowledge of Lupia's definition of gender was sorely lacking.

"When I was born, my father was so proud to have a son to carry on the family line. Our tribe has always been paternalistic."

"A werewolf tribe?"

"Yes. We live in various areas west of here, blending into the common people." Lupia's voice sank as he recollected his story. "But I was never interested in taking charge of the family or even in being my father's heir. In fact, I didn't even identify as a man. Both my parents expected me to simply take another werewolf as a wife and then take the mantle as pack leader. You see, there is so much expected from the Alpha Male of any pack, but all those traditions of masculinity just didn't interest me."

"So you became a woman? You're a transsexual, aren't you?"

"My family thought it was because I was gay, but that wasn't it. I just hated being a man. I hated my pack. I just wanted to travel and serve the planet with my real passion rather than just go through the motions expected of me."

"You mean you wanted to make music, right?"

"Exactly. I had the talent early in life, but my father would never hear of it. By escaping from him, I managed to form a brand new identity for myself, though I haven't quite had time to finish the job, as you can see."

"But why do you become so masculine when you take on your werewolf form?"

"How should I know? You really think anybody has done research on transsexual werewolves?"

"Will might know."

"Doubtful. Too bad he and Amelia will have to see me in this form. They'll probably hate me."

"Hey, come on, have more faith in them than—"

"Holy crap! What the hell is that?" As we finally arrived back at my house, Amelia looked completely disturbed at what she saw since she was probably reminded of the freezer of horror as soon as she beheld the werewolf. After all, she hadn't witnessed him at the mall.

"I thought you said you were coming back with Lupia, not the werewolf from Sunday night." Will also had surprise in his voice, though he wasn't as appalled as Amelia.

"Well, uh…" Now that I thought about it, I didn't feel right forcing Lupia to give up his/her secret.

"I…I am Lupia." That deep voice to saved me the trouble.

"WHAT?" Both Amelia and Will's jaws dropped at the same time. I had figured it out on my own. For them, however, it was a sudden shock.

"So you're a man?" was Will's next question.

Lupia sighed, "Not exactly." He explained everything he had discussed with me, but he particularly added a bit about how hormones have a powerful effect of altering the body and how he was basically a woman while in human form.

Will scratched his head. "Hm…That's odd…So you change into a man in werewolf form? I wonder why."

"Oh come on." I put my hands on my hips. "You mean you've never read about this in a book?"

"You really think anybody has done research on transsexual werewolves?" I thought I heard an echo.

I shrugged. "So it seems we have no explanation for the naked man werewolf who's actually a pretty woman." Lupia looked embarrassed, so I shut my mouth. I walked toward my house, but something was off. Amelia's Camaro wasn't parked correctly; it was sitting at an odd angle at the edge of the cul-de-sac, in front of my house's swales (for those who don't know, they provide drainage for the massive amount of Florida rainfall). I looked at the space in front of the car and saw something lying in the swale that shouldn't have been there. "Amelia…is that a body?"

"Um…about that…" Amelia broke her gaze away from the werewolf, the distraction having subsided, and looked toward me, terrified. "…I think I killed him."

I crept closer to the body and peered over it. Buford Mullen lay there, not moving at all. I stood above him and extended my right index finger. "Poke." I said the word and then followed through with that action. "Poke…poke…poke…Yeah, I think he's dead."

"You know, you'd make a great coroner," Will said snarkily.

I stood up. "There's a dead body on a vampire's lawn. This…is bad."

"We don't really know if he's dead, and your poking isn't going to help."

"Then how do we figure it out?"

"Well…" Will thought for a second, "When people die, they evacuate their bowels."

"They what?" I knew exactly what he said, I just hoped that he had said something different.

"They crap themselves."

"Um…" I didn't like where this situation was going, "How do you suppose we check for that?" I already knew the answer to this question.

"How do you think?"

"I'm not touching that!" Poop was never something I was very fond of.

"Okay then, check for a pulse." I made the motion to do so but was interrupted. "No wait, Amelia, you check for a pulse instead."

"Why me?" I was curious too.

"Because Amy's much stronger than you and might break him." That was fair enough, considering my clumsiness.

"Why don't do you it?"

"Because to be honest, corpses creep me the hell out." Indeed, Will looked uncomfortable.

Holding back her own uneasiness, Amelia went over and felt Buford's wrist, searching for a pulse.

I was a bit frazzled by the whole situation. "Jesus, what the hell did you guys do to him?"

"We ran him over, like you told us to." Amelia continued feeling Buford's wrist. Upon closer inspection, his legs were partially flattened.

"Oh...right." Now I felt bad for being so evil.

"I'm not feeling anything," Amelia's voice betrayed real fear.

"Try his neck?"

Amelia felt for a few seconds. "Nothing."

"That's very bad." Will knew that the situation was dire.

"What do we do...?" Amelia sounded desperate. "Daddy's going to find out...we'll never get away with this!"

"Wait!" I had a dumb idea. "If he's a vampire then he won't have a pulse, right?" I felt for my own pulse, which wasn't there.

"He is NOT a vampire." Will insisted on this point.

"But you're the one who said he had psychic powers." Will was silent. He couldn't quite account for that fact.

"Okay, okay, let's think about this rationally." Will covered his face with his hand, a sure indication that he was thinking hard. "Amy, you threw him halfway across town the other night and he came back the next day just fine, right?"

"Right." I nodded. "So he's probably going to come back to life and we won't be arrested, right?"

"Possibly, but we can't be sure about that."

"Damn it, he'd better not be dead. I mean, I didn't like the guy but I never meant to kill him." I definitely felt guilty.

"You say that even after you tossed him away." Will's sarcasm felt like a knife.

"Shut up about that."

"Anyway, if he is dead, we need to do something...Amelia, stop poking him!"

Amelia looked up from her distraction and then stepped back. The body made no response.

The entire time, Lupia was silent, standing there nervously.

"Well..." I had another dumb idea "...we have a terrifying werewolf here as well as a vampire...and we need to hide the evidence...maybe we should..." I shuddered with disgust that I would ever think of such a horrible notion, "...eat him?" They all, Lupia especially, shot me the most disturbed looks conceivable. "Just...uh...just kidding!" I tried to pass off the suggestion as a joke, but I think that the others just chose not to take it seriously for their own sanity.

Then I had one more stupid idea, but this one actually had some logic behind it. "Okay, okay guys, remember when this guy returned to school entirely uninjured the next day after I threw him across the neighborhood, right?" They seemed to be following me. "So, what if I did the same thing again? Think that maybe he'll just come back again?"

"And what if he's really dead?" Will didn't like this idea when I originally did it, so of course he wouldn't like it this time. "Do you really think that anyone around here would want a corpse suddenly landing on their roof?

"Well we don't have a lot of options, now do we?" I then heard Lupia give a deep sigh. I turned to him. "Do you have an idea?"

"I really don't want to do this, especially not to a friend." Lupia walked over to me and grabbed one of my wrists, putting a claw (I suppose it could be called his index claw) up to it. I quickly pulled my hand away, not in the mood to endure any more pain. "Please, just trust me," he said. I could sense the sincerity in his words and therefore relinquished my arm. He forcefully slashed my wrist, which was more painful than I expected it to be. He then held it over Buford's mouth as it started dripping blood.

"Oh, I get it," Will said.

"Mind explaining?" Amelia said.

"Vampires have supernaturally fast healing because of a property of their blood. When humans drink vampire blood, they temporarily gain that healing ability, albeit with several side effects."

"You were saying in the lab that the person usually ends up becoming a slave," I said.

"Yeah."

"In that case, should we really be doing this?"

"Do you think having him as a slave would be any worse than what he was doing before? What about just having him be dead?"

"No, I suppose not. Hey, wait a second, why didn't my wrist already heal?"

"It takes longer for a vampire to heal wounds from werewolf claws," Lupia said. I used my other hand to feel my neck where he had grabbed me before and it felt raw, as if it were still in the process of healing.

"Hey, wait Lupia." I was reminded of a question I had already asked but to which I hadn't received a proper answer. "Really, how do you know so much about vampires? You're a werewolf, not a vampire."

"Much like Will, I am well-versed in the ways of creatures of the night. My clan makes a point of instructing all children about beings like themselves."

"Vampires and werewolves, both creatures of the night." My mind put two and two together. I realized that what Tower said on Saturday night made sense. *"I am, but at the same time, I am not."* "Tower really is a vampire infused with the power of a werewolf. Maybe the others are as well. That would explain the corpse we found and why they would want you."

Will thought about my statement. "While the concept of such a hybrid is outlandish, it does make some sense." Then, addressing me directly, he said, "I can say with certainty though that you aren't a hybrid."

"How do you know?"

"You show no properties of a werewolf whatsoever."

A few seconds later, we heard Buford start coughing and sputtering, and we moved my arm away from his face, allowing him to regain his senses (what little he had, anyway). We all watched in awe as the seemingly dead walked again. I also held my wrist to minimize further blood loss. "Amy Able," he said between coughs.

"What?"

"I will alert our vampire brethren to this injustice you have committed!" With that odd statement, he dashed away, stumbling since his legs had not yet fully healed.

"You think anyone will come after you?" Amelia asked.

"Who cares? Let's just be glad he's not worshipping me. We're also no longer responsible for his murder anymore. Come on, there's four of us. Let's just go play some games or something." I was getting tired of all this madness and I just didn't want to be bothered for the rest of the night.

"Let me just park on your driveway first," Amelia hopped into the driver seat.

"Hold on Amy," Will said as I began walking to my front door, "don't we still have to examine that wand?"

He reminded me of all the questions I still had about that object. "You're right. Come on, let's take a look." I unlocked the door and motioned for everyone to follow me.

Lupia seemed indecisive about following. Will turned to him. "You coming inside?"

The werewolf looked glad to have friends looking out for him. "I'd love to."

Wolf's Bane

"Just please put some pants on when you get in." Embarrassment was obvious in Will's voice. "You can poke an eye out with that thing."

"My brother used to be kind of fat until his sophomore year of high school," I said. "You might be able to find something that'll fit you in his closet."

It was tough to see it on that face, but Lupia smiled.

After I dug through Allen's closet and pulled out an old pair of very large jeans, Will and I left the now partially and rather baggily dressed Lupia with Amelia, the two of them engaged in conversation. We went to take a closer look at that wand.

Will grabbed the strange object and fiddled around with it. He waved it around a bit. "That's strange."

"What?"

"I can't sense anything at all special about this thing."

I knew that wasn't true. "Well it lit my dresser on fire last night."

"Seriously?"

I pointed to the site of the blaze. Much of the dresser's top was still charred.

"Why didn't you tell me about this before?"

"I forgot." I was being honest. With the protestors and Lupia's disappearance, it was very easy for anything to slip my mind.

"How did you get it to work?"

"I tried a bunch of magic words from *Harry Potter*, and only the fire spell worked."

Will looked dumfounded. "That shouldn't have been possible."

"The fire or the *Harry Potter* stuff?"

"While Rowling did her research, this wand bears the seal of my family, and our magic doesn't quite work that way." Will sounded skeptical, as if he thought I was just making up what I said.

"Well, why don't you try it?" I attempted to sound confident.

Will pointed toward my dresser, and then said, "Grab some water, just in case."

"Oh right!" I felt embarrassed that I would forget something so critical. I ran into the kitchen and came back with a medium sized pitcher of water, filled to the brim.

Will nodded and then readied the wand again, but he paused awkwardly. "What was the magic word again?"

"*Incendio*."

213

Blood on Fire

"*Incendio!*" With a swish and flick of the wand, Will looked like a true warlock, except for the fact that nothing happened.

"Really? I know I didn't just dream about that working."

"Well the charring on top of your dresser is proof enough that something did happen—unless you just lit it on fire for the hell of it, which would be out of character for you. How about you try the wand again?" He handed it to me.

I took it and repeated exactly the same motion that I had the night before. "*Incendio!*" This time, the same flames rose up from the dresser.

Will scrambled to grab the pitcher and put out the fire. "Interesting...so it only works for you."

I scratched my head while looking over the wand further. "This doesn't make any sense."

Will started stroking the stubble on his upper lip, making the fact that he was trying to piece what little we knew together very clear. "Well it seems that it's responding to the pyrokinetic ability you have already."

Amelia peeked her head through the door. "Hey, we both smell smoke. Should we be worried?"

"Maybe," I said. "Apparently this thing makes fire whenever I reference *Harry Potter*, but it doesn't work for Will." Sometimes when I talk, I have a tendency to wave my hands around, as many people do. On a few rare occasions, it's gotten me in trouble, such as the time I accompanied my mom on a visit to my Aunt's house in Orlando, and I knocked over her favorite vase—which was also full of water since it housed flowers. It landed on her VCR (it was a while ago, and she also had a DVD player), which, luckily, survived. The vase, however, did not. Needless to say, I haven't seen my aunt since.

I made these unconscious hand motions as I spoke to Amelia. I was still holding the wand. The ceiling light in my room was turned on, as Will did need to see, though it was still fairly dim, as it always had been (my desk lamp provided better light). To my eyes, however, the red streaks slowly travelling from Amelia to me, like those I saw emanating from Buford, were clearly visible. A small ball of blood formed on the tip of the wand, and it stopped growing as soon as I noticed it.

Amelia twitched slightly, but she didn't seem too affected. "Is that blood on the wand?"

Wolf's Bane

The blood hovered on the tip, and it moved as I moved the wand. I moved it closer to my eyes. It was definitely blood. I licked it, causing my friends to cringe. Like Buford's when I obtained it similarly, it had no taste. I consumed the entire ball and threw the wand aside, onto my bed. "This thing is too unpredictable. First it sets my dresser on fire, then it steals Amelia's blood."

"Yet those are both things you could've done without it," Will said.

"Well, yeah."

"Think about it, Amy." He did that point with his index finger that people often do when they figure something out. "It didn't work for me. Maybe it's specifically for magic as used by vampires."

"That can be done?"

"It's magic. Of course it can be done." Now he sounded sarcastic.

"What was it used for at BioLogic, though?" All three of us stared at the thing. None of us knew the answer to that question. "I think I'm going to put it in a safe place until I figure out what to do with it. I then proceeded to throw it into a shoebox in my closet.

"You don't want to examine it more?"

"I'm done with that thing." I really didn't trust it. Stealing blood randomly and setting my dresser on fire counted as two strikes against it, in my opinion, and I didn't feel like striking out.

"But the more we know, the more we can figure out about how BioLogic used it."

"But at what cost? Burning the house down? Stealing all of Amelia's blood? Sorry, but I'm leaving that thing alone until I figure out more about my own powers."

Amelia seemed to understand, nodding in confirmation.

Will shrugged. "I suppose that's fair."

I let out a deep breath, shaking my head. "None of this crap makes sense to me." Then I looked toward my friends in the room. "I need to unwind a bit...you guys want to play *Super Smash Brothers*?"

"Sure," Amelia said.

"Why not?" Will said, shrugging again.

I led both of them into the living room, where Lupia was still sitting. "You want to play too?" I asked him.

"I would, but I've never played before and my hands would damage the controller." Looking at those claws, I could say that they certainly would.

14: Breaking Point

When Lupia came to my room in the morning to wake me up, she had returned the pretty form that I was used to. She also seemed to be somewhat sprightlier. Perhaps having friends who accepted what she was helped.

Thursday morning was overcast with grey skies all around. Whereas most members of the human race dislike such weather, I, being not quite human anymore, welcomed it greatly. It was about time that I would be able to go outside and not have to worry about dying within mere minutes.

I was in much less pain, though the sunlight and its wrath still pierced the clouds to attack me. When Amelia picked me up that morning, for once I actually felt like talking.

She spoke first. "So, are you doing alright?"

"Better. I never thought that grey skies could be a sign of a blessing."

"So you think that means school will go well for you today?"

"Probably not." I was so used to everything falling apart over the past few days.

"Well, you've come pretty far, Triple A. Don't give up yet."

She glanced at me and winked. And by "winked," I don't mean one of those corny "do your best" winks; no, I mean that it was a bit seductive. I thought I felt myself shudder, but I shook my head to banish the feeling.

"Amelia..." I thought about her encouragement.

"Yeah?"

"If everything really goes to hell, just promise me that you'll keep your cool like always." I glanced at the fang marks on her neck, which had faded a bit. I could only immediately recall her losing her cool twice: on Saturday after I had bitten her and on Monday after arguing with Shelly.

Breaking Point

She seemed to have trouble understanding what I asked her, but soon I saw that cool smile of hers forming. "Of course, Triple A, I'll be there for you."

When we reached the school, I made another request: "Amelia, could you loop around the senior parking lot for me?" As opposed to the junior parking lot in the back of the school, where Amelia would actually end up parking due to her class standing, the senior parking lot was right in front of the school and therefore had a view of whatever may be going on out front.

"Alright, but I'll still need to park in the back."

"That's fine. I just want to take a look." I tried my best not to look out the window too conspicuously. Another wave of protestors was there with signs denouncing the evils of my existence, but they didn't seem to be as possessed with the spirit of violence as the splinter group from the day before. "That's all I needed to know; go ahead and park."

Amelia swung around to the back of the school and parked in her usual spot—only something was very obviously different about that area on this day. "You have to be kidding me!" The junior parking lot bordered the back entrance to the gym, and in the shade by that entrance was another group with signs.

"I guess they caught on," Amelia said.

"Either that or there's another group posted over where the busses drop off." Surely enough, one was over there, but I wouldn't pass by that area.

"What are you going to do?"

"What else can I do? I'm going to keep my distance and go to class."

"Good luck."

"You know, they're going to be heckling you too for being my friend."

"It's not like I haven't been made fun of for being your friend before." Amelia was talking about middle school, that dark time in my life when I was a social pariah simply for being a pimply socially inept nerd. That time was still embodied through Shelly, who tried to perpetuate the stigma even though my appearance and mannerisms had improved. "Come on, you can get through this. Besides, if you stay in my car too long, you'll be too burnt to move." She had a point. Even though I'd experienced the least burning yet upon arriving to school, I was still fairly charred.

"Alright…here goes." I swung the car door open and stepped lightly onto the pavement, exposing myself to both the outside world and the views of everyone around. Nobody came after me, nobody moved from their spots, but I heard a growing sound of unrest in the crowd, which began to wave its signs more intensely. I tried putting on a fake smile (Was it even possible to have a real smile in this situation?) and waving, but that definitely made them madder. Considering the possible need for law enforcement if anything went wrong again, I decided that the best course of action would be simply walking away.

I didn't watch as I walked away, but Amelia shot the crowd her middle finger, which only aggravated them further. She, however, was amused to no end. Amelia was always the type to screw around with people she didn't like, regardless of who they were.

I made my way to class through the mostly empty hallway, but something was definitely out of the ordinary. I mean, I wasn't stupid. I knew that the fact that Shelly and four other girls (named Libby, Jessica, Jennifer, and Taylor if memory serves me right) standing on opposite sides of the hallway wearing identically-colored T-shirts spelled trouble for me. Shelly's presence alone was enough to put me on edge, but I decided to keep walking forward without stopping. After all, this hallway was the only direct path to class, and turning around from these potential adversaries would be showing a sign of weakness.

I looked upward to avoid eye contact as I passed by them. They started moving alongside me, walking at the same speed. I had two on either side and I was fairly sure that Shelly was right behind me. I kept walking until Libby and Taylor ran in front of me, blocking my way forward. They were close enough for me to read their shirts, both of which said "Team Buford" and were definitely made at home with iron-on letters.

I rolled my eyes. "Okay seriously, what's this about?" My patience wore thin.

"It's about you, Lamy." I heard Shelly's voice behind me, and I turned to face her.

"And what exactly did I do to deserve this little encounter?"

"Can it, vamp girl" Shelly had a smug, self-important look on her face. "Look, we've determined that you very clearly don't belong here. You...are a night vampire."

That sounded incredibly idiotic. "Well duh, all vampires are."

"But you just don't belong outside during the daytime with all of us *normal* people." She put a special emphasis on "normal."

"Your point?"

Breaking Point

"My point is that you don't belong here. This school only has room for one vampire, and he is far superior to you."

"Buford, right?"

"Wow, you're not as retarded as you look, Lamy. Word around the street is you've been abusing Buford."

"And who did you hear that from?" While her statement wasn't false, I wanted to know where she got her information.

"Ella Spawn."

"Of course." Ella and Buford had been inseparable at school, aside from when Buford randomly ran away.

"You've also been conspiring with Emily to destroy us all. We've long since cut all ties with her, so why haven't you?"

"I don't have any ties with her." I knew that she made up this story just to downplay her own connection with the Ogre Queen. "I'm trying to defeat her and the others."

"Is that really so?" She had that tone in her voice that implied that she was about to do something horrible. "I do hope that you don't plan on getting into too bad of a fight. You don't want to lose your fangs, after all." She sneered at me.

"Maybe you and I should switch places. Maybe then she'll beat the bitch out of you…or kill you. Either works for me." I sneered right back.

"Just let Buford handle it. He's the greatest vampire hero. I'm going to do you a favor that'll convince you to stay home. She reached into the expensive Prada bag she always carried around and pulled out a string of garlic cloves, shoving them into my face.

I really didn't know what she expected would happen. Maybe she figured I would die. Maybe she thought that I would just be tortured by the smell. Maybe she thought that I'd be so weakened that her girl posse would beat me up. But I don't think she expected what she got.

Upon catching a whiff of those cloves, I tried to resist for as long as I could, holding my reaction back, which in itself was torturous. I knew that I wouldn't be able to prevent what was coming, but I waited for the right moment. After a few seconds, Shelly pulled the garlic away, confused. "Why isn't it doing anything?" I had my opening. "Maybe you're not a vampire after—"

I gave up resisting and let the torrent flow, aiming specifically at her face, although I hoped to soak her clothes as well. If she was going to compromise what little dignity I had, then I would make sure to take away hers in the process. By the time I was done and feeling weak from all the blood that I had lost, she was practically drenched.

Her posse didn't know what to do. They stared in awe at their bloodied leader, unprepared as to how they should react.

"What—what is this?" Shelly started to cry. "Why would you…why…my hair…my shirt…my purse…"

I took this opportunity to shove Shelly out of my way, knocking her hard into a nearby locker. Moving a safe distance forward, I turned back to her and said, "First you make fun of me, then you sick that colossus of a woman on me, now you try to run me out of this school." Shelly stood still, speechless and utterly disgusted. "What did I ever do to become your enemy in the first place? Oh right, I existed. You think that you have the right to use me as a punching bag just because I'm not exactly like you. But this time, you got exactly what you deserved."

"But…but…garlic…I…but…"

"You really are pathetic, you know that?"

I should've paid more attention to her friends, though, each of whom pulled out a cross.

"Seriously?" I rolled my eyes.

"My dad said he'd buy me a car if I made you quit school," one of them—I think it was Taylor, or maybe Jessica—said.

"Let me guess, he's out among the protestors, right?"

"Uh…yeah. He also wrote to Governor Pott to ban all vampires in our state."

"Right…good luck with that." It would be like banning all Italian people because a few of them have ties to the mafia. I knew it was possible but I didn't feel it was likely in this day and age.

As students began entering the hallway, they were bewildered by the sight of Shelly covered in blood among all the girls holding crosses, but I just walked away. One of the girls tried to follow me and hit me with her cross, but I just lightly elbowed her in the chest and continued my remaining trek to math class unobstructed. I could hear Shelly yell out "I'll get you for this Lamy!" I only made one stop at the rest room to wipe the blood from my face.

When I arrived at Royal's class, he noticed how annoyed I looked. "It's been tough for you, Miss Able, hasn't it?"

Breaking Point

"You have no idea." At this point I was just sick of dealing with the treatment everyone else was giving me.

I had missed it because of needing to find Lupia, but apparently Rock Rivers decided to put on a special newscast the previous night. I was able to watch it on a later date thanks to Channel 45's YouTube page, where it hadn't been removed despite its factual inaccuracies—Channel 45 thrived on local controversy, so removing it wasn't in their best interest.

"Good evening and welcome to a Channel 45 special report with your host, Rock Rivers."

"Good evening, everyone. You've all probably heard about vampires, but what do you really need to know about them? The truth is that they are very real and hiding in your children's school waiting to prey on them."

He then proceeded to show interviews with people who protested in front of the school and who clearly knew nothing about who I actually was, talking about how I was openly harming students and how the administration was doing nothing about it. I suppose I was harming certain students, like Amelia, but firstly the administration wasn't even aware of it and secondly they practically said that I was killing students.

The report then returned to Rivers. "A vampire in one of our schools, ladies and gentlemen. Here's what you can do to protect your children. Vampires hate God and Christians because anyone with true faith has the power to repel them. Make sure to arm your children with the symbols of our Lord Jesus Christ by giving them crosses—and remember, the bigger the better. Garlic is also a good idea, but it's generally not recommended as it may upset others with allergies. Vampires are dangerous, but you can take the precautions to protect yourself."

This report aired at 11:00 PM. Not wanting to be outdone, Niles Granite and Delta Stone said the same thing during the morning news on their respective networks. Even though high school students generally don't watch the news, their parents do, so about half the students came in holding crosses and garlic. These crosses were rather large as well, and many of them looked cheaply fashioned out of fresh wood. Luckily none of them tried attacking me. Otherwise they may have ended up like Shelly.

Royal didn't call on me for the entire class period. He probably gave me some leniency because of what I had to deal with, which I appreciated hugely. The class dragged on for me. I couldn't say I was very interested in math in a place with so much hate for me. When the bell rang, I made sure to leave as quickly as possible.

Art class went very similarly, so nothing particularly important happened.

I had been sitting out of gym ever since I started going to school as a vampire, using the fact that class usually involved playing baseball, soccer, or flag football outside in order to avoid burning. However, during second period the sky started pouring rain, making outdoor sports impossible—or at the very least impractical. The heavy showers continued well into third period. Therefore, finally, gym class was to be held inside the actual gym. I arrived there drenched and only slightly burned. I sat down in the same spot in the bleachers I had every other day that week.

"Able, what are you doing?" Coach Bellows came up to me, acting like his crotchety self.

"Does anybody really know what they're doing?" Come to think of it, what I said here really didn't make much sense.

"You've been complaining of sunlight or some other hoopla all week. Come on, we're playing volleyball inside today." Indeed, the indoor volleyball nets had been set up. "Go smack around some balls with the other girls."

"Coach, I have the strength of five gorillas. Do you really think it's a good idea for me to 'smack around some balls' as you so eloquently put it?" I was already aware of the danger that taking part in such a sport with normal people would pose in my current state.

"Girl, I don't know what kind of crap you're talkin' about and frankly I don't give a damn. You need to put some meat on your skinny bones and be active so your grade can stop suffering."

"You know what, coach? I think I will join in on the ball smacking." The truth was that my patience was gone. I just didn't care anymore. School had exhausted me both mentally and physically, especially after I was attacked that morning. I stood up, made my way down the bleachers and walked right in to the girls' locker room.

Those I passed, who were still in the midst of changing, immediately turned, stopped whatever they were doing, and stared, surprised to see me, a vampire, walk into a place where they were so vulnerable. Perhaps they thought that their exposed skin would send me into some sort of bloodlust frenzy. I really couldn't say. I stopped at my locker, which was toward the back of the room, where Vanessa was stuffing the last bit of her wide torso into her undersized gym shirt.

"Amy?" She was definitely surprised to see me. "I thought you were sitting out of gym."

"It's raining today."

"Oh…okay then." Though I was never the most athletic student, at least I never finished last when running track. That was Vanessa's job. Physical activity wasn't her forte.

"Did you catch last night's *Fullmetal Alchemist*?" Anime was her forte.

"No, I didn't. I was busy. I've probably seen it before though." As I had previously seen the entire serious, I knew it was a rerun, and attending to Lupia was far more important.

She started describing how much she loved the episode, and I pretended to listen as I opened up my locker and pulled out my gym uniform, which had developed an interesting smell since it hadn't been washed in over two weeks (I had forgotten to bring it home the week before my memory went blank). I calmly took off my coat and hat and stuffed the mass of them into the tiny locker.

Normally I was uncomfortable undressing in front of other people, even if they were the same gender as me, but on that day I didn't care.

"Wow…your skin is so pale," Vanessa said.

"Of course it's pale. It's dead." Her skin was almost as pale, but that was due to lack of going outside. I didn't bother looking around, but I knew everyone was staring at me. My skin was almost the same color as my underwear, which was white, so it must have been a strange sight. It didn't last long, though, as I pulled on the required green shorts and dark grey shirt with our school's athletic logo on it. In the middle of the logo was a white oval where I had scrawled "Amy Able" with a black Sharpie. I then grabbed my purple scrunchie from my bag, which I also stuffed in my locker, and tied my hair into a pony tail.

"Oh yeah, I'm ready." I formed both of my hands into fists.

"Ready for what?"

"Pain."

Vanessa just stared at me quizzically as I steadfastly walked back out into the gym, where the students had assumed their lineup in the bleachers to prepare for the coach's initial lecture. About half of them, male and female alike, clutched garlic-covered crosses. I made sure to sit a safe distance away from these students.

"Okay you all." Coach Bellows addressed everyone on one third of the bleachers. Two other coaches handled the remaining thirds. "I'm not against Christianity. In fact, I love Jesus, I go to church every Sunday. But I want all of you to put those things away. You don't want them getting damaged, do you?" Some students complied and put their crosses away while others kept them out. Bellows didn't pursue the matter further. "Now, I want the girls on the left and the boys on the right. Y'all are going to form teams and play some volleyball. Now get to it!"

After everyone dispersed from the bleachers and did the usual routine of warming up and stretching, two circles, one of boys and one of girls, formed for the selection of teams. "Alright," Bellows said loudly enough for the whole class to hear, "team captains are Brad and Jesse for the boys and Jamie and Samantha for the girls." I didn't know Jamie or Samantha very well, but neither of them had crosses, which was a decent sign at least. They were both very physically fit, and Samantha was even fairly muscular. They both had brown hair; Jamie wore hers relatively short while Samantha had long hair tied into a bun. They both participated in after school sports.

Jamie and Samantha called out various names as they chose their team members. Jamie made the first call: "Ella." I hadn't even noticed that Ella Spawn was in the class, but considering her inexplicable popularity elsewhere, her being called first made sense. She awkwardly walked to Jamie's side, looking not at all confident in her athletic ability. The choosing of team members continued until Jamie called out, "Uh…Vanessa." Vanessa was the second to last person to be picked. Usually she was the last. This time I was. While my athletic skills were lacking and sometimes dangerous, I wasn't quite useless in sports. I was normally picked for teams after most others but before Vanessa.

"Amy, I guess," Samantha said, much to the dismay of her cross-carrying teammate, who would now be my teammate. I counted myself lucky, though, that she wasn't carrying garlic.

Six people were on each team. On my side was Samantha, one cross-carrier, myself, and three others. Our opponents were Jamie, Vanessa, Ella, two cross-carriers, and one other.

"Get to it ladies!" Coach Bellows called out, though he addressed the boys.

BREAKING POINT

Samantha had the first serve, which she performed beautifully. The ball sailed over the net, heading in the direction of a cross-carrier, who didn't hit it back very far, failing to even reach the net, because her cross naturally got in the way. "I wouldn't have to carry this if not for that monster."

I rolled my eyes. That comment bit at my brain. "You know, I'm immune to crosses!" She didn't seem to listen.

Samantha went for another serve, once again sending the ball sailing over the net. "Hey monster!" The other girl with a cross on the opposing team called out to me.

Whenever my brother was being an ass to me, my parents would always say "Just ignore him." I'm not sure why they said that. The truth of the matter was that when he hurled insults constantly, I could try to ignore them, but I could still hear them. I could hear all of them. Saying "Just ignore him" was just my parents' way to avoid taking any real action.

Therefore, as much as I didn't want to, I paid attention to this girl. "Go back to hell where you belong." As I was distracted by this insult, I didn't notice the ball being hit in my direction. It collided with my face, knocking my glasses off. Everyone who had a cross and a few others laughed. Apparently it was funny to see a "monster" fail in a test of physical prowess. "For a vampire your reflexes sure do suck."

"Oh that is it." Something finally snapped within me. It was on the verge of snapping during Shelly's attack on me that morning, but now a rage that I'd been holding back came to the forefront. After retrieving my glasses, I spoke in an eerily calm voice. "You want a monster? I'll show you a monster."

Since her team had just scored, Jamie made the next serve. Rivaling Samantha in athletic ability, she also made a beautiful serve. I took control of the blood in my body just as I would during a fight against another vampire. I dashed over to the ball, where my cross-carrying teammate was about to spike it back, shoved her out of the way, and hit it back myself. However, I failed to hit it over the net. Instead it went straight through the net, slamming the ground on the other side.

Jamie and her teammates had no idea what to make of this action. "Um...net ball?" Jamie really had no idea of what the ruling would be.

"Now that's the type of thing I like to see." Coach Bellows walked over, looking impressed. "Enthusiasm so strong it breaks things. Point goes to the vampire's side."

Blood on Fire

Jamie tossed the ball to Samantha so she could make the next serve, which she sent sailing in the direction of Ella, who actually tried to hit it back, only to be hit in the face.

This girl's clumsy too. She's clumsy yet popular while I'm clumsy yet unpopular. That isn't fair. As my irrational rage continued to build, I vowed to gain revenge on Ella Spawn.

After Samantha's next serve, Jamie hit the ball back (in case anyone is wondering, Vanessa had yet to move from her original spot on the court). I didn't know whether Jamie intended it or not, but the ball went in my direction. I ran to it, jumped up and slapped it back hard. It actually went over the net this time. It slammed into Ella's face, knocking her down.

"Ella! Are you okay?" Jamie and a cross-carrier ran over to help her.

"I don't know." She seemed to hold back overly-dramatic tears. "I'm not cut out for sports."

"We'll take you to the nurse's office, okay?" I didn't hate Jamie. In fact, I really didn't know her. I just didn't like the fact that she and everyone else seemed to give the transfer student special treatment.

"It's okay. I can go there myself." Ella walked sadly out of the gym.

I really don't like her. Then I caught something in the corner of my eye. I glanced over to the entrance of the gym, where Ella headed, and I saw Buford ducking out of sight. *Was she distracted by him?* I shrugged, not caring enough.

"Why do you have to be so mean, you monster? Someone needs to hammer a stake in your heart." The other team tried to intimidate me. I only became angrier.

I went up to Samantha as she was about to make her next serve and grabbed the ball from her. "I'm making the serve."

"What? I...okay." She backed off, seemingly scared.

"What are you doing, Sam?" said the cross-carrier on my side. "You saw what she did to Ella." Samantha didn't say anything in return.

Okay, I've never done a proper serve before. Now I'm going to do it right. I tossed the ball up high—insanely high. In fact, I think it bounced off the rafters. As it came down, I jumped up and sent the ball screaming to the other team. It hit one of my enemies in the face, making another gaping hole in the net.

"Hah! Take that!" I felt overly-accomplished. "Can a monster have such an awesome serve? I think not!"

BREAKING POINT

"Holy crap! Are you okay?" Jamie, Samantha, and most of both teams ran over to the girl I knocked out. "She's bleeding!"

I felt a sense of satisfaction at this accomplishment, having effectively taken my revenge against someone who would mark me as a pariah.

"Freeze!" I heard a deep and familiar voice far behind me. I instantly knew the voice.

Oh...crap. The world seemed to come crashing down around me as reality set in. The principal had warned me not to harm any other students, but his words completely slipped my mind under that day's stress. One girl was on the floor bleeding while another was on her way to the nurse's office.

I slowly tried to turn around.

"Freeze!" I stopped dead in my tracks. I still couldn't see who said it, but the voice, which came from behind me, sounded too familiar. "It's a good thing I decided to pop in. Your blood-covered friend already told me about how you were acting out of line." I knew it was Captain Valentine, and I suspected that he was pointing a gun at me. The gym had many entrances. He was easily able to enter without me seeing.

"I'll go quietly. I'm sorry." It happened so fast. My mind was back in the real world, and now I would have to face the consequences of my enraged actions.

"Girl, you have the right to remain silent, and I suggest that you use it." Valentine continued giving me my Miranda Warning before stepping up to me and applying handcuffs. I could have resisted very easily, but I didn't. I was in enough trouble.

15: She's Not Legal

Amelia scanned around the cafeteria, a disconcerted look on her face. "Where is Triple A?"

Will was also worried. "Judging by past events, she's either with the principal again or something very bad happened."

"I hope she's okay."

"Speaking of missing persons," Will peered around Amelia's vicinity, which seemed oddly empty, "where's Doug?" Vanessa and Kim also weren't present.

"Oh…" Amelia looked embarrassed. "I broke up with him yesterday."

"What? Why?" Doug and Will were fairly cool with each other.

"He was being a big baby for a while before this vampire business started and his whining about Triple A yesterday just tore it for me. I like my men…feisty."

Will wasn't sure what to think about what she said. He instead turned to James, who almost looked angry. "Where the hell is she?" He was focused on the cafeteria's front entrance. His fang marks were still much fresher than Amelia's. Will decided to leave him alone.

The bell rang and I still didn't show up. Will and Amelia packed up their belongings and proceeded out of the cafeteria together.

Amelia was frustrated. "Damn it! Where is she?" She was clearly angry at the world, not at me.

"Knowing her, I'm sure she's alive at the very least." Will was confident in that assertion. "We'll just have to wait and see. Who knows? Maybe she'll be in class."

"I guess I'll see you later then." Amelia waved to Will as she took her own path to class.

SHE'S NOT LEGAL

I wasn't in my seat. When Will arrived at English, he found only Mrs. Hacket writing vocabulary words related to *Dracula* on the chalkboard along with students discussing what seemed to be the latest rumor.

"Hey did you hear? They say Amy the vampire girl got arrested." Of course this caught Will's interest.

"Yeah, apparently she tried to kill a bunch of people," one guy said.

"I heard she was just throwing volleyballs at them," a girl said.

"No, she was punching them."

"Maybe it was basketballs."

"Why would she throw basketballs at them?"

"I don't know."

Nobody could quite get the story straight. Everyone seemed to have their own version of events as nobody from that class had been in the gym at that time. The only fact that Will could reliably glean from our classmates was that I was in police custody.

After the bell rang, Ms. Hacket turned to the class. "Alright everyone, I know that you are all interested in news of what happened to our local vampire, but you are in a class for literature, and that is what we will study." With her commanding voice, she managed to get her class in order and lead it. It didn't differ much from the day before, as it was a fairly standard academic coverage of *Dracula*. When the bell rang at the end of class, however, Hacket called Will forward. Not knowing what to expect, he approached her podium with only a little bit of apprehension.

"I know that you are friends with our young vampire, but don't worry. If she uses her creativity, I'm sure she can find a way out of this situation, and you can help her. Creativity is like a magic wand that any of us can use."

Will nodded uneasily. It was an odd thing for her to say.

"Dracula doesn't seem to be in control of her. Her actions are still her own. Now run along to your next class; I don't want to keep you too long."

Will did as she said, stepping out into the hallway, where he realized something strange. "Wait a second…how would she know anything about Dracula's possible involvement?" The most obvious answer was that she would just attribute the events to Dracula as a fan of literature. Will could think of no better explanation.

A few miles away, I sat at a white table in an otherwise empty room illuminated only by one florescent light on the ceiling. It was blindingly bright to me. The rest of the room was dark, and on the wall adjacent to me was a mirror—or so it looked. I was sure that it was a one-way window. Behind me was a camera that scanned the whole room constantly. I was still in my gym uniform, my hair still in a pony tail. The police had taken me through the rain between the gym and the squad car and between the car and the station, so my clothes were only starting to dry out. The sun couldn't reach me in this room, but I struggled to stay focused. They had left me in there alone with only some garlic resting on the knob of the only door. I probably still could have ripped it open, but I chose not to. I took off my glasses, laid them on the table, and tried resting my upper body next to them.

Then the door swung open. *Damn it!* Some sleep would've been nice.

Valentine stormed into the room, shutting the door hard behind him. He tossed a manila folder onto the table and took his seat across from me, an odd smirk on his face. "So, what's the deal here? What's with all the vampire funny business?"

I wasn't sure of how to respond, so I didn't say anything.

"We already received multiple reports of destruction of property from the Volusia Mall. That's what I was asking you yesterday, but you refused to say anything about it. Then, as we were stationed nearby the school today in case anything similar to what happened yesterday occurred, one girl came to me and told me about how you needlessly poured blood all over and then knocked her into a locker."

That was definitely in reference to Shelly. "But she was—"

"She was what? Making fun of you?" He said this tauntingly.

"Threatening and attacking me, and that blood was actually vomit because she assaulted me with garlic."

"A likely story. Then I find you willfully endangering other students in the gym." He took a sheet of paper out of his folder. "You have a laundry list of charges against you. Let's see..." He examined the page, though he spoke like he already knew what it said. "Breaking and entering, disturbing the peace, vandalism, assault and battery, sexual assault..."

"Wait, what?" I knew what most of those charges referred to—the way I broke into the mall, the damage to Amelia's car or Delta Stone's camera, the noise caused by my "chat" with Mr. Evans, and injuring Shelly and the other girls (perhaps even the other vampires or Buford)—but I had no idea what this charge of sexual assault was about.

SHE'S NOT LEGAL

"Oh come now Miss Able, you don't think I've noticed those marks on my daughter's neck? My little girl would never allow something like that to happen to her willfully."

You'd be surprised.

"And then there was that report that Freeman filed the other day. Apparently you, Amelia, and that boyfriend of yours"—what an awkward assumption for him to make—"were found speeding late at night. What exactly were you kids doing?"

No American History class I had taken quite gone over the Bill of Rights in any particular depth, so I wasn't aware of my rights under the Fifth Amendment, but I had a halfway decent idea as to how the system worked. Besides, I was scared and I wanted to at least have someone else there on my side. "Could I get a lawyer or something?"

"Does your family have a lawyer?"

"Um…" The matter had never come up with my parents. "I don't know."

Valentine wore a microphone on his shoulder that was wired to a walkie-talkie on his hip. He spoke into it. "Send in the public defender."

The door swung open again and a plain-looking brunette woman who appeared to be in her mid-20s wearing a grey skirt-suit was practically shoved inside. She seemed extremely confused.

"Now you two play nice." Valentine stood up. "I'm gonna go have a nice little chat…" he gave an evil smile "…with your parents." He exited the room quickly, leaving this new woman alone with me.

Well, he's in for a surprise. I knew that he was about to discover my parents' absence.

The woman stood where she was, staring at me awkwardly. She didn't seem to like being there.

"So…are you going to do something?"

"Right." She seemed to accept the fact that she wouldn't be going anywhere else soon. She took a seat in the same spot that Valentine had before. "Now, I'm sure you're aware that you have quite a few charges against you." I sensed no fear in her voice, but I sensed no confidence either.

"Believe me, I'm aware."

"You're going to get juvie at the very least here, unless they decide to try you as an adult. You're just lucky your charges don't include murder, although we do have a few charges of animal cruelty."

Blood on Fire

I knew that she was talking about the wolves. "But wait, that was in self-defense."

"I figured as much, and that wouldn't be hard to prove. But these other charges..." Her voice trailed off as she looked over the folder on the table. I waited for her, staring. Not long earlier I had been punishing hecklers at school. Now I had this strange woman supposedly trying to help me out of this bad situation.

When she looked up, she noticed my uncomfortable gaze. "Oh, I'm sorry...we haven't been formally introduced, have we? My name's Jenna Flynn." She gave a wry smile and put her hand out toward me.

I grabbed her hand and shook it very lightly, not wanting to take a chance of hurting her. "Amy Able."

"To be honest..." she rolled her eyes unconfidently "...I'm not even sure why I'm here. I mean, I'm 26 and almost straight out of law school. I haven't even taken a case to court yet. I was literally just hired as a public defender two weeks ago. Little did I know that I'd be working in the same area as Valentine. He and I have some history and he's probably just resentful." She made a fist in frustration.

"Um..." I gave her a confused look, "what about my case?"

"Oh, sorry, I'm just a bit frazzled here. Hey wait, just out of curiosity, does Valentine have anything personal against you?"

"Not because of anything I did before this week, but I think he doesn't appreciate the fact that I was involved with the damage to his daughter's car. I also drank her blood." I decided to be honest with her.

She stared at me wide-eyed, glanced at my file, and then back at me. "You really are a vampire, aren't you?"

I rolled my eyes.

"I'm sorry, I was just choosing not to believe that they would stick a greenhorn like me with a case like you. It's nothing against you, but frankly, I don't think I'm cut out to take on this case. Then again, none of my seniors would touch it with a ten foot pole." She looked extremely discouraged.

Seeing her so distressed, I realized something: I wasn't the only one being driven to madness by the recent events. This defense attorney in front of me was experiencing her own form of frustration, and I was sure that Valentine only treated me the way he did out of concern for his daughter. "Miss Flynn, you and I are going to get through this. A bunch of vampires are out there who

232

are harmful to everyone and I'm determined to stop them. If you're the only one on the legal side who's willing to help me, then so be it." I gave a relatively weak smile.

She gave one back, looking only slightly more confident. "Well, let's see what I can do for a vampire vigilante."

At her request, I told her about that day's events, focusing on the incident with Shelly and the heckling I received from the other girls during gym. She seemed very understanding of the sense of frustration I felt.

"I know how you were feeling, but you shouldn't turn to violence unless it's your last resort. The law really isn't going to look kindly on what you did."

"I know." I felt defeated.

"But don't worry too much. You didn't hurt them that badly." She tried to cheer me up. It worked somewhat. "Also, don't worry about those people with their crosses. I may not be the most devout, but I am a Christian, and I do think that they went too far."

She then asked me about the other vampires, and I was about to explain what I knew of the situation (leaving out my encounter at BioLogic), but we were interrupted.

Suddenly the door burst open again and Valentine stormed in. "You mind telling me why we can't reach your parents?" Valentine seemed almost furious. "Daytona State College told us that they haven't heard anything from your mom for over a week, and we got no answer from BioLogic or your home phone." I could understand why Lupia wouldn't answer. "Where the hell are your parents?" He gave me a stern look that pierced into my very soul.

As I did when facing this man the day before, I found myself unable to say a word, feeling an unshakeable sense of dread.

"Where are they?" He demanded to know.

I still couldn't say anything.

"Answer me!"

"Captain Valentine!" Flynn stood up, appearing much taller than she had when she first entered the room but still dwarfed by Valentine. I sensed a good bit of anger from her. "I will not have you addressing my client that way. It is her right to remain silent."

"But because she's a minor we need to contact her parents or legal guardians. Now is there anyone in your family you will allow us to contact?" This time he addressed me in a much calmer voice.

Blood on Fire

They were going to find out somehow at some point anyway. I stared downward at the table, my eyes clenched shut from the fear of what would possibly happen to my life if the police learned the truth. Would I be sent to foster care? Would foster parents even take in a vampire? I couldn't hold out any longer. "My parents…"

"What about them?" Valentine sounded eager to know what I was going to say.

"…are missing."

Both Valentine and Flynn seemed to be taken aback. "What did you do to your parents?" Valentine asked as if I were some sort of murderer. Flynn shot him a dirty look.

"I didn't do anything. I just woke up Saturday morning and found that I was a vampire and they were gone."

"And why didn't you notify the police sooner?" He did pose a good question here.

"I thought that I could find them myself." Except I still didn't know where they were.

Valentine didn't seem happy. "Is there anyone else in your family we can call?" At first I didn't have much of an answer to this question since any aunts, uncles, or grandparents I had lived far away—aside from one aunt in Orlando who didn't like me—but I quickly recalled that I had one family member over the age of 18 who lived within the state and wasn't missing, although I didn't quite want to mention his name.

"I need to call someone." Valentine was adamant.

I supposed that since I needed someone to act as a legal guardian, I really only had one choice. "Allen Able."

"And how is he related to you?"

"He's my brother currently attending college at UF up in Gainesville."

"And you know he's not missing as well?"

"No, he isn't."

After shooting me a skeptical look, Valentine left the room, presumably to contact Allen.

"Well this is a surprising turn of events." Flynn was flustered. "Looks like I'll also be acting as a custody attorney."

"I'm sorry."

SHE'S NOT LEGAL

She shook her head. "No, no, don't worry about it. So what do you think happened to your parents?"

"I'm still trying to figure that out." I still didn't say anything about BioLogic because I wanted to take no chance of possibly incriminating myself further.

"Well now that the police know, hopefully they'll be found." She then looked toward the door, scowling. "But with that idiot in the lead, I don't think you'll get much help."

We spent the next hour discussing my charges and recounting what happened to me. She was extremely supportive. Eventually, two officers came in to drag me off to my cell.

"I'll continue to work on your case and I'll see what I can do," Flynn said as we parted ways.

I must have passed out on the cheap cot in the cell as soon as I was transferred because I could hardly remember my arrival there. Instead, I remembered seeing me—I remembered seeing Amy.

Despite those strange marks on her neck, school went fairly normally for Amy that day, and she had already made plans for that night.

"Amelia, are you sure about this movie?" Will said in the car after picking up Amy. "I mean, it sounds pretty stupid."

"Hey, it's supposed to be a comedy from Russia. Maybe it'll be amazing or maybe it'll suck. We won't know unless we give it a shot." Amelia was a little bit more enthusiastic than him.

Amy didn't say much during the car ride, stroking those strange marks instead. She had mostly been doing homework since school let out. She and her mother had eaten dinner on their own, even though her father had come home. He and Dr. Acula stayed in the garage, talking. What they spoke about was anyone's guess.

The movie was, to put it lightly, strange. *The Adventures of Space Bear* mostly consisted of a bear wearing fish-bowl helmet in space mauling people. Apparently he was supposed to solve mysteries, but instead he mauled people. People would come up to him expecting him to help them solve a mystery in space, but he would just maul them...in space. This part was familiar to me. The shear ridiculousness of that movie was what kept the event from becoming hazy like the rest of what happened during the time leading up to my awakening.

Blood on Fire

"I told you that movie would be stupid," Will said after the trio walked out of the theater. They had stayed through the end of the credits as they tried to pronounce the complicated Russian names.

"It was still pretty fun though," Amelia said, holding back a laugh. She was often amused by exposing her friends to strange things. The night ended normally enough, with Amelia dropping Will and Amy off.

This next event, however, didn't feel familiar at all. "See ya later, Triple A!" Amelia drove away, leaving Amy in front of her house.

Something wasn't right. She could feel it. Those marks on her neck began to itch, and she couldn't resist scratching them. All of the lights in her house were turned off. She checked the clock on her cell phone. It only said 9:45 PM, yet all the lights in her house were off. The house usually would not be entirely dark at this time.

Other than her strange feeling, she had no reason not to go inside of her house, so she pulled her key out of her bag and approached the front door slowly. Her heart pounded, and she didn't know why. Placing her key inside the lock seemed like an absolutely monumental task. She paused. "Come on, Amy, what are you suddenly so afraid of?" She couldn't answer her own question. "It's okay...everything's going to be just fine." She took several deep breaths before finally putting the key where it needed to go.

She turned the key to the unlocked position and then turned the knob. Her anxiety quickly rebuilt. She breathed hard as the sense of dread overtook her. When she pushed the door open, a pale hand immediately grabbed her hard by the shoulder. It hurt. She looked upward, eyes wide open, and saw the now familiar face of Dr. Acula above her. She found herself unable to scream.

"You have been...chosen, my dear." He had a genuine smile on his face.

Then all went black. Her entire mind was consumed with horror and then...bliss?

Why did I feel bliss?

I could also hear voices. "You monsters! What are you doing to her? Let her go!" It was mom's voice. She sounded beyond desperate.

"Honey, please relax...they...they know what they're doing." It was my father's voice. He sounded unsure of himself, uneasy.

"Don't worry," said a third voice, "we have special plans for her." This voice wasn't Dr. Acula's. I couldn't tell whose it was at all, but it sounded like a woman.

236

SHE'S NOT LEGAL

"Able! You have visitors!" This voice was familiar, and it wasn't among the others.

I opened my eyes. I was in a small holding cell in the police station. I could tell that night had fallen, even though the small window toward the ceiling was covered, because I felt far more energetic. *What happened to me? Was that when I became a vampire.* Even though I had dredged up my other lost memories related to the event, I felt that whatever happened at my home that night would remain locked away indefinitely. I could feel it. It was something that I could barely even hope to imagine, let alone remember.

I still had my glasses on. Having passed out, I naturally never removed them. I didn't think about this until later, but regarding what Will said about not being able to sleep unless I had something from my room with me, I found out that simply having my glasses was enough for a nap like that one. I would need more to sleep longer. I looked toward the bars at the front of my cell and spotted Officer Freeman looking inside. Then I noticed some strange white objects all around him. I sniffed the air.

"Oh God! This has to be police brutality!"

"Huh?" Freeman looked around until his eyes settled on the garlic hanging on the bars. "Oh, that. It's just a safety precaution. I mean, as long as you're not right up against them, it doesn't hurt you, does it?"

"No, but the stench is horrendous!" A clove of garlic was also in front of the blacked-out window. The rest of the cell was made of cinder block. This was the police station's way of keeping me locked up. The cell contained only a cot and a toilet—not that I would actually need a toilet (I hadn't used one in days). "Seriously, what the hell?"

"It doesn't smell that bad." Judging by his voice, Freeman sounded weary.

"Well maybe to you it doesn't. You're still a human. Garlic is delicious to you."

"I'm not really the biggest fan of it."

"How could you not like garlic?"

"I was never really big on the taste."

"You sir, have to try my mom's garlic chicken."

"Speaking of your mom..." he shrugged and shook his head "...we still have no leads."

"I wasn't exactly expecting much."

Blood on Fire

"Anyway, like I said, you have visitors." He made a motion toward the nearby hallway, which was blocked from my sight by a wall, and both Will and Amelia quickly followed. Neither of them looked particularly happy, but they were certainly glad that I was safe.

I couldn't hold back a smile at their presence. "I'd hug both of you through the bars but I don't exactly feel like throwing up right now."

Will was the one who spoke first. "Well, Amy, what's new with you?"

"Oh, not much. Just got arrested and locked up like an animal. You know, the usual."

He sighed "Somehow none of this surprises me."

I sighed. "I know. At least I got to cover Shelly in blood though."

Through the bars, Amelia handed me a bundle wrapped in a green shirt of mine. "We brought you some stuff, Triple A. The police checked it already. Sorry, but there's no chisel or anything to help you break out, not that you'd need it."

"Yeah, super strength and pyrokinesis would tear this place down, but I'm in enough trouble."

"Lupia wanted to bail you out," Will lowered his voice to a whisper to not give away the fact that we knew where Lupia was, "but she doesn't have the money in cash." Unable to show up in person, Lupia would have had to give Will or Amelia cash to pay for bail. "I'm too poor, and, well, Amelia's father was the one who arrested you."

"Yeah, daddy seems to have it out for you." She looked toward Freeman, who sat behind a desk in front of my cell, reading a newspaper. "He doesn't know I'm here, right?"

Freeman nodded.

"Amelia, I'm sorry, but your dad's an asshole." I spoke through gritted teeth. Freeman let out a chuckle. "I mean, he did help me out with those protestors, but he only seemed to do that so he could interrogate me."

She rolled her eyes. "I don't know what's gotten into him. He did say that he wanted to be elected Sheriff. Maybe making a big spectacle out of anything vampire-related is all some big PR stunt."

Will looked around the cell oddly. "Amy, have they been feeding you here?"

The thought hadn't yet occurred to me. "No, they haven't."

"It's been a while since you've gotten blood, hasn't it?"

She's Not Legal

I hadn't realized it until Will brought it up, but I was extremely hungry—yet I didn't feel like eating. All the garlic scent must have been killing my appetite.

"We were wondering what we could feed you while you were here," Freeman said, hardly moving from his newspaper. "The hospital doesn't exactly look kindly on taking too much of their donated blood."

I had a good answer to this question. "Steaks…raw."

"I thought vampires were killed by stakes."

"Other kind of steak, smart ass."

"Hey, watch your mouth, girly. You're talking to the guy who can put you into solitary." Freeman said this jokingly. He didn't sound as if he particularly cared.

"No you can't," Amelia said. "This isn't an actual prison." She smirked at Freeman. "Believe me, I know how this works."

"Yeah, yeah, just spare me a lecture. I get that enough from your father." Freeman seemed restless.

I went ahead and took a look at the package Will and Amelia brought me. It contained two full changes of clothing (I assumed that Amelia handled that part), my Nintendo 3DS with some games, and a copy of *Dracula*. "*Dracula*, huh?"

"You left all your books at school," Will said. "That was the only one we could bring you."

"It looks positively ancient." The paper was a deep shade of brown and the yellow cover was extremely worn.

"It's mine." Will blushed. "An original edition."

"Cool. Thanks a lot, both of you." They both smiled.

The walkie-talkie that Freeman wore said something indecipherable. He said something indecipherable to it in response. He turned to Will and Amelia "Sorry, but your time is up. You two will have to leave."

Neither of them looked ready to leave. In fact, they both looked determined to never leave my side. "But can't we stay with Triple A a bit longer?"

Freeman shrugged. "Sorry, but I don't make the rules."

"I'll be fine," I said. "Don't worry about me. It's not like I'm going to be prison raped or anything—I'm not even in an actual prison." I was the only one in the cell, after all, and Freeman didn't seem like the predatory type.

Both of my friends nodded and waved to me.

Blood on Fire

"We'll get you out of this!" Will said as Freeman led them back down the hallway.

"Count on it!" Amelia said.

Freeman was only gone for a few seconds, and he returned alongside another officer holding a plate with two raw steaks. "You do realize that this is extremely disgusting, right?"

"Uh...yeah...Actually, could you turn around for a sec?"

Freeman gave me a skeptical look. "You're telling the guy who's supposed to be guarding you to turn around?"

"Well..." I pointed toward the clothes that Amelia handed to me. "I do want to change out of my damp gym uniform."

"You realize that the camera's still on you, right?"

"Well then I can only hope that the people watching the security footage of the women's holding cells are women."

"This is one of the men's cells, actually."

I tilted my head. "Why did you put me in a men's cell?"

"Do you see any other inmates? Does it matter? The people who attacked you at school have all been bailed. Don't worry, though, they all have court dates."

Only Freeman and I were in the room after the guy who brought the steaks left. "Fair enough...but I'm still changing, so turn around."

"Alright, fine." He was uneasy with the idea, but he complied. I searched for the cameras around the room and tried as best I could to turn my naughty bits away from them as I changed. I freed my hair from the pony tail. "Okay, I'm done." Freeman turned back around, shaking his head.

As soon as I was done, my mind was once again fixated on that one blank spot in my memory. *Why bliss?* I had to read more of *Dracula*. I had to know what the vampire did to his victims. Careful not to drip any blood on Will's old book, I ate and read at the same time. Although the stench of garlic bothered me, I trudged onward through my reading. I read until I found a description that could possibly explain what had happened to me:

"With his left hand he held both Mrs. Harker's hands, keeping them away with her arms at full tension. His right hand gripped her by the back of the neck, forcing her face down on his bosom. Her white nightdress was smeared with blood, and a thin stream trickled down the man's bare chest which was sown by

SHE'S NOT LEGAL

his torn-open dress. The attitude of the two had a terrible resemblance to a child forcing a kitten's nose into a saucer of milk to compel it to drink" (Stoker 282).

The author's name and number at the end of the quote is an MLA citation. The following is MLA bibliographic information:

Stoker, Bram. *Dracula*. UK: Archibald Constable and Company, 1897. Print.

I give that info to cover my ass. I learned it in school. Few other students actually bothered to learn the style even though it was expected, sacrificing many points of their grades to shear laziness. This section of the story was all that I had. Mina Harker—yes, apparently the very same Mina Harker whose charred paper and ring I inexplicably found in my mom's drawer, although that was likely just memorabilia of some kind—was compelled to drink blood from Dracula's chest after he drank her blood. Was this what happened to me? But the process wasn't finished. It only established a mental bond between Mina and Dracula. I wasn't aware of any such mental bond with me, although such a bond definitely existed for Tower, Strength, and Chariot. It likely did for Devil as well.

I also had to consider the people involved. Were my mother and father actually present? Or did I just imagine their presence? And who was that last voice? No such equivalents were in *Dracula*. Mina's husband Jonathon simply lay catatonic next to her and the other male characters interrupted the process.

Then I had to consider my father. Did he allow Dracula—or Dr. Acula—to do whatever he did to me? What sort of business did he conduct with the vampire? I didn't want to believe that he was up to anything evil, but I just didn't have anything to go on.

"Damn it!" I threw the book down on the cot. "None of this crap makes sense to me." I was just too frustrated, trying to find answers to my situation in a book that was well over a century old while stuck in a jail cell.

Several hours had passed by, and Freeman had fallen asleep in his chair. He woke up at the sound of my outburst. "Does literature really make you that angry?"

"Sorry, I'm just looking for answers and I'm finding more questions."

"Doing homework or something?"

"Well…technically yes." I did have an assignment of reading the book. "Have you ever read *Dracula*?"

Blood on Fire

"Oh yeah, great book. If that guy were really around, I don't care how dangerous it would be, you know I'd be out there with a hammer and a stake. That guy's not getting my wife and little girl." He said this in a surprisingly casual manner.

"Well he already got me."

"Dracula?" He was interested.

"He's calling himself names like the Fool and Dr. Acula, but it's probably him."

He came over to the bars of my cell and gave me a stern look with an eyebrow raised. "Seriously? We thought this whole thing was caused by a bunch of high school girls who were turned into vampires."

"Well who do you think turned them into vampires?"

"But Dracula? Really? This whole thing just gets weirder and weirder. How do you know this?"

"Just ask any of those high school girls you mentioned. They're not exactly being secretive about it. Then again, they'll probably try to kill you after you ask."

"But wait, how come you don't seem to be one of them?"

"Hell if I know. I'm just as confused about this whole situation as the rest of you." My frustration was downright tangible. I wanted answers, but I couldn't get them.

"Those other four are scary," Freeman said offhand, scratching his head. "Apparently most of them had no history of anything wrong with them, but that's just what Valentine's been saying."

Wait a second, what about them? For as little as I knew about my own situation I knew even less about theirs. The only one I had prior history with was the Ogre Queen. "What do the police know about them, anyway?"

"I suppose it couldn't hurt to tell you since this information's all public already anyway. Carla Evans was a high school freshman...and that's about it. She went to your school, had a few friends, and liked shopping at the mall. We really couldn't find anything special about her. Bethany Davis also went to your school and was a senior who loved animals and wanted to be a veterinarian. She also loved camping with her family and friends. That's it. Melanie Steyer's a university student from the Jacksonville area who was living with her mother and stepfather. Nothing else special about her."

"So nothing really stood out about these girls?"

SHE'S NOT LEGAL

"Nothing at all. Well, except for Emily Rogers."

"Oh believe me, I know." I pointed to the gaping hole toward the front of my top jaw. "That's some of her handiwork. If it weren't for my fangs growing in, I'd be missing a canine too."

He just shuddered in response.

"How much trouble has she caused for the station?"

"Well I haven't been working here that long, but the other officers say that she's gotten into some serious fights and abused her parents and—"

"Abused her parents?" This wasn't a topic that I'd ever heard much about.

"Yeah, apparently she hurt her parents on multiple occasions. Her father even divorced her mother because of it. She had a lot of anger problems and refused to seek psychological counseling for them."

"She instead chose to take them out on everyone else."

"Right. Apparently, several years ago, her uncle molested her and that drove her to violence."

Molested? Now that I thought about it, although the novel didn't exactly give all that much detail, the scene in which Dracula attempts to turn Mina into a vampire did seem sort of sexual when I read it. Furthermore, if what Freeman said was correct, sexual abuse had caused Emily Rogers to turn to anger when she was a human, and as a vampire, she was so angry that she couldn't even form a coherent sentence, meaning that it could possibly have happened again. I thought back to the blank space in my mind. *Was I...raped?* I didn't want to think of this possibility, and I quickly pushed it aside, having to hold back a violent shudder merely at the thought.

Still, I did have some new insight about my enemies. "Thanks. I think I understand a little better now."

"Hey, it's really not a problem." He gave me a very slight smile. "I know you're bored in here. But if you'll excuse me, I need to get back to my nap." He went back to his chair and almost instantly dozed off again.

I decided to finish reading *Dracula* that night. It didn't reveal anything else to me, but at least I knew the full story.

16: Taking Charge

Even though not a single vampire was present in the school, protestors still lined the entrances, and the student population was still uneasy. The day demanded for Lupia's delivery to Dark Arcana had arrived.

Amelia had become used to having a companion on her way to school. Even though she had only been taking me with her for less than a full week, she didn't feel quite right without a vampire next to her.

The situation felt even more unnatural when, on her way from her car to her first class, she found Buford Mullen shirtless behind the school, his skin glistening in the morning sunlight thanks to a fresh coat of paint. He didn't seem to notice her, keeping his eyes closed. Amelia shrugged and decided to ignore him, walking away. "Ella's in trouble!" Amelia turned around to see Buford dashing off in a seemingly random direction into a nearby forest. She was perplexed.

The vampire talk continued all throughout the day, and seemingly no two students could arrive at the same conclusion or decide whether or not to be scared of the potential attack that night. Like the day before the predicted doomsday date of a potentially false prophet or the supposed attack of a would-be terrorist, life mostly went on as usual, though quite uneasily.

English class went as normally as one could possibly expect on such a day as Hacket mentioned nothing with regard to vampires outside of *Dracula*. She didn't call Will forward to tell him anything, either. He still hadn't figured out the purpose of what she told him the day before.

Amelia had no lab partner in Biology, instead serving as a third wheel to a pair of students she had never even talked to before.

In history class, Shelly had returned after her traumatic blood drenching the day before. She remained quiet for the entire period, looking distinctly unhappy, until bell rang to end the school day. As soon as everyone in class began to pack up, she walked up to Amelia's desk, a scowl on her face. Only Amelia could hear her words. "Emily's going to tear Lamy in half, and I'll laugh when she does." She then promptly walked away.

Amelia wanted nothing more than to make sure that Shelly wouldn't be laughing.

Meanwhile, in the holding cell, I was jerked awake by an unnecessary ruckus, which was quite a feat, considering how deeply I slept.

"I told you, no one is going to talk to my client!"

"The police told us it was okay."

I could feel that it was daytime even without any light or a clock simply because my body didn't want to move.

"I am her lawyer, and I don't want reporters talking to her!" I instantly recognized Jenna Flynn's voice hurriedly following after some others that I thought I recognized.

"Hey, I'm the one who found her first, this should be my story!"

"You forgot about the amazingness that is Rock Rivers. It's my turn to interview her."

"Valentine!" I heard Flynn's voice again. "Don't you think you should do something about them?"

"What?" I heard that booming voice from far away. "They're just reporters; what're they gonna do?" He sounded smug.

I kept my eyes closed. *Go away...just go away.*

"What the hell? She's asleep?" The voice of Rock Rivers sounded disappointed. I suspected it was him even though I hadn't met him in person.

"Oh, that's right." Now I heard Niles Granite. "Vampires sleep during the daytime. I'll just let her go for now. The best interview will come tonight." Footsteps told me that he left.

Delta Stone sighed. "I've been trying to get this interview for days. Can anyone wake her up?"

"I'll wake her up!" Rivers yelled now. "Hey, vampire! Wake up!"

"You really are an idiot."

"Fine, then you wake her up."

"Hey, guys..." Now I heard Freeman's voice, "she may be a prisoner, but she has the right not to be barged in upon. I don't think she appreciates what you're doing."

"Exactly," Flynn said, "and she is not fit for answering questions at this time."

"It's just an interview," Stone said, "and she has the right to refuse."

"The hell she does!" Rivers had some extreme determination. "I've put in all this effort to get this interview and nothing's gonna stop me this time!"

I finally decided to open my eyes. "Seriously, guys, can't a girl sleep?" Freeman was at his desk while Stone, Rivers, and their cameramen eagerly peered into my cell. Flynn stood behind them looking angry.

"That's what I've been trying to tell them," Flynn said through gritted teeth, "but that idiot" (I assumed that she was talking about Valentine) "thought it would be funny just to send them straight back here unrestrained."

Rivers wasn't listening to her. "Girly, you have a lot of questions to answer, especially about that attack you're planning."

"What attack?"

"Your plan with the other vampires to destroy this town!" Rivers became increasingly frustrated.

"I recall making no such plan. Maybe you have me confused with those individuals on TV."

"But you're a vampire! You have to be in cahoots with the others!"

"She wasn't on that broadcast." Stone seemed ready to slap Rivers. Then she turned to me. "What, exactly, is your relation to the other vampires?"

I didn't move an inch from the cot, but I looked her straight in the face. "To be perfectly honest, I have no clue at all. Why don't you ask them?"

"But what about the fact that you're all vampires?"

"You're both white. Does that make you white supremacists?"

Stone seemed to be taken aback when I said this. Rivers only became madder. "There has to be more to this!" Now he yelled.

"Oh yeah, there's more to it, but I'm the wrong person to ask."

"Ask me instead," Flynn said while grabbing both their shoulders and trying to tear them away from my cell.

"Some two bit lawyer isn't gonna know jack about vampires."

"But I am her legal representative, and I am the one you may speak to." Flynn stood her ground firmly.

"Fine." Rivers started grumbling as he backed off from the bars.

"We apologize for disturbing you," Stone said to me, "but you will give us an interview, right? The world wants to know more."

Taking Charge

Instead of answering, I pretended to go back to sleep as the reporters were led away. Then I actually fell asleep. I couldn't recall any dream.

After night fell, my friends decided to meet up.

"I'm going to need your help. Can you meet me at my place?" After school, Will called Amelia, they needed to plan their next move.

"Triple A and I have never been inside your house. Would your mom be okay with it?"

"To hell with her. She's not even here." Will knew that he had more important matters to attend to.

As soon as Amelia arrived, Will set her to work helping him scour through every book on the arcane he had. "Amy came up with a fairly sensible idea for why Dark Arcana wants Lupia…" He of course referred to my theory that our enemies wanted to make more vampire-werewolf hybrids "…but I want to see if we can find any other sort of connection between vampires and werewolves. We need some kind of advantage over them."

After few hours of searching, they found nothing useful. They had almost entirely given up, despite having only lightly skimmed the main chapters of many books. They hadn't even touched so many others. They relocated to the couch in the living room to rest and keep an eye on the local news.

"How does that ridiculous library contain nothing of what we're looking for?" Amelia was impressed by the collection's size while also disappointed at its lack of anything useful.

"Well, we couldn't find anything other than the mild weakness of vampires to werewolf claws and teeth and the fact that both are classified as creatures of the night." Will was also disappointed. "Maybe there really isn't anything else to know. Maybe we're dealing with an entirely new type of enemy."

"Which would mean that we're S.O.L., right?"

"Probably, but at least they likely have all the same weaknesses as vampires and werewolves, so we have some chance."

On the Jadises' decrepit old television the 6:00 news continued onward. "We now turn to Niles Granite, reporting from Palm Coast." Granite stood in front of a street of houses. "I'm here in Palm Coast with the members of the local Sheriff's Office who earlier gave me permission to accompany them. In our station earlier this week, a set of four vampires stated that they would attack this town unless they received pop idol Lupia in exchange. They did not specify an exact time or place for the attack, but the police are ready for anything.

Blood on Fire

Neither the police nor anyone else has any idea where Lupia is currently, nullifying any potential for proper negotiations. Police and firemen are ready to minimize any damage that may befall homes. I have with me Police Captain Robert Valentine. Any words for those watching at home?"

"So daddy's on the news, huh?" Amelia was still angry at her father, but she hoped that whatever he had to say would be important or useful. The fact that he was on TV was nothing new to her—although it was rare in Palm Coast, whenever a serious crime occurred, he often volunteered to report it.

"Our main stance here is to protect homes." He sounded like he was doing routine work. "We already have one of the vampires in police custody and we will be working on taking in others. We have all of our officers at various points around town and we will not hesitate to use lethal force if necessary."

"He makes Triple A sound like some kind of criminal." Amelia was resentful.

Will shook his head. "Your father has no idea what he's doing. Taking down this set of vampires is going to be a hell of a lot harder than arresting Amy. No offense to her, of course."

"I tried to tell him that, but he wouldn't listen. He doesn't even think that military support is necessary."

"Knowing these beasts, it just might be."

Suddenly both of them heard the front door of the house slam. Within a few seconds, Will's mother had was in the room. "Will, what is this? I thought I said no girlfriends! You two better not be having sex in here!"

"We're not, mom! Amelia's just a friend of mine." Will only knew that his mother was present for the past few days because he would find her sleeping. The two hadn't spoken for entirely too long.

"You expect me to believe that with you two here alone?" She plunged her current cigarette into the closest ashtray. "You've been taking these opportunities when I've been gone, haven't you?"

"Mom, you're overreacting."

"Overreacting? The last thing I need is you getting some slut pregnant!"

"How rude!" Amelia stood up, facing the middle-aged witch eye to eye. "Do you have any idea what we've been going through this week? You haven't even been here to support your son through it."

"How dare you tell me how to raise my son! I'm working my ass off for his sake."

TAKING CHARGE

Now Will stood up. "Speaking of working, did someone hire you to create a wand with our family's emblem on it?" He was determined to know the truth.

"H—how did you know?" She clearly knew what he was talking about.

"Please, mom, just answer the question."

"Y—yes I did." She answered hesitantly, but she quickly became defensive. "But what does that have to do with anything?"

"Who asked you to create it?"

"I don't see why I should tell you."

"Mom, we're dealing with vampires making threats here, or are you unaware?"

"Vampires?" She seemed to actually be unaware.

"Five of them. One is our friend and she needs our help. The others are planning to destroy this town."

Minerva Jadis's eyes were open wide as a realization sank in. "It all makes sense…Why else would someone ask for a wand designed to manipulate blood?"

"And who was it that asked?"

"He called himself…Dr. Acula."

"That name!" Amelia looked toward Will, who nodded.

"Do you know something I don't?" Minerva seemed genuinely confused.

"Amy mentioned that name," Will said. "She suspects that he was the one to turn her into a vampire."

"She's a vampire?" Clearly she was unaware.

"Do you remember what he looked like?"

"I didn't see him very often," Minerva scratched her head, "but if I remember correctly, he was pale and had black hair and a pointy mustache."

Will thought back to the literary description he had read countless times. "It could really be Dracula."

"Dracula?" His mother hadn't expected to hear such a name. "What?"

"It's tough to explain. Did he mention what he planned to use the wand for?"

"It was for manipulating blood, and he said that he planned on giving it to someone special as a present."

"Someone special?" Will struggled to find an explanation.

"He could've meant Amy," Amelia said.

"I suppose so, but how was the wand meant to be used?"

"It's a conduit for blood magic meant to enhance its intensity, nothing more." Minerva bit her thumb. "I suppose it could also be used to aid in creating vampires."

Will stroked his light stubble. "It's beginning to make some sense."

Amelia rolled her eyes. "Whether or not it makes sense doesn't matter. We still have to fight a bunch of werewolf vampires. We need a plan of attack, but without Triple A around it's going to be almost impossible."

"That wand might give us the edge we need, though." Will looked sternly at his mother again. "Creating the want explains why you were gone last week. What about this week?"

"Dr. Acula asked me to create other enchanted items—a cup, a sword and some coins."

"The minor arcana suites of tarot!" Will knew the magical significance of this set of items, and their connections the names utilized by the vampires. Amelia would ask him to explain later. "That could indicate that Dr. Acula and the Fool are the same person. Have you finished them yet?"

"No."

"Then abort the projects! Don't you see, mom? You've had a hand in causing events that have pretty much ruined our friend Amy's life and could quite possibly destroy this town."

"We've gone through a lot of crap because of you," Amelia said.

Minerva Jadis took out another cigarette and lit it. "Will, I was making artifacts for the money. Frankly, I don't know what kind of show you're running here, but what the hell, I'll bite. Where's that wand now?"

"Triple A's house," Amelia said.

"Go there and get it. I have some preparation I need to finish here. Call me whenever the vampires show up."

The wand was at my house, but I still wasn't

The reporters were gone. I woke up a few hours later to a silent police station. Opening my eyes, I could see Freeman at his desk on the other side of the garlic-infested bars.

"Finally awake?" Freeman asked between sips of coffee.

"What time is it?"

"7:30." He seemed relatively calm.

I was curious about what was going on in the outside world. "Are there any other officers in the station?"

"Besides the office staff, just me."

"And why's that?"

"Because I get no respect."

That wasn't quite the answer I expected. "But…what are the other officers doing right now?"

"Patrolling the streets and looking for vampires." That was the answer I expected.

"So they just left you here to guard me?"

"That's right."

"But I thought you were a patrolman, not a cell guard."

"I am, and I was on patrol on Tuesday night when I watched you pull yourself back together, remember?"

"How could I not?" Contorting my body into shapes that it was never meant to take was a memory that I wouldn't soon forget, but that, recent though it was, was in the past. I was more concerned about the present and I was curious about the man watching over me. "So why is it you who's here watching me? I mean, you seem to me to at least be a decent enough officer—although the few times we've met have been in kind of awkward circumstances."

"With Valentine in charge, I'll never be considered a 'decent' officer."

"Please don't tell me that it's because you're black." I didn't want to believe that my best friend's father might be a racist.

"Nah. There are plenty of black guys on the force who get along fine with him."

"Then what's the reason?" Now I was even more curious.

"Because I'm clumsy."

*Because I'm clumsy…*As soon as he said that, it continued playing in my head over and over. "Clumsy, huh?"

"Yeah. A few months back some teenagers with marijuana got away all because I dropped my handcuffs and tripped over them. I mean, how does somebody trip over handcuffs? Only I could screw up that badly." His otherwise calm and cool demeanor was broken now as he sounded frustrated.

"Hey."

"What?"

"You're talking to someone who took her homework into the shower with her." He failed at holding back a chuckle when I said that. It was subtle, but he was smiling. I suppose I presented him with a means by which we could actually relate. "Look, Officer Freeman, do you have anyone who's special to you?"

"Well, there's my wife and my daughter." His spirit sank again. "Who I can't protect from Dracula right now all because that ass in charge won't let me."

This attitude of his didn't suit me. "Freeman, I have some friends out there who are determined to stand up to these vampires and figure out why I've been caught up in this madness. They understand the dangers involved. One of them is your boss's daughter. With my parents missing, they're all I have right now." Freeman listened intently. "Look, the only reason you guys could take me in so easily was because I complied. I didn't want to cause any more trouble than I already had. But these vampires don't have the same sense of morality I do. I knew one of them when she was a human, and back then she had no qualms about knocking teeth out. Just think of what she could do to houses, let alone teeth, now. The police can't handle this. I'm the best weapon you have."

Freeman sighed heavily. "You know, Valentine's probably going to take my badge for this, but I don't really give a damn." He grabbed the key to the cell. "I know they're not prepared. He thinks the police of this two-bit town can handle something like this? I've seen what you can do." He came up to the bars, pointing the key toward the lock. "Do you promise not to run away? You're still under arrest until we say otherwise, which means I'm sticking by you."

"You have my word." I gave him a very serious look. I wanted him to know I was honest.

He sighed again. "He's gonna kill me, I just know it." He unlocked the cell. He also pulled off some of the garlic lining the door as he opened it. "Well, what are you gonna do now?"

I gathered my belongings walked out of the cell. "I need something else from you."

"Just say what it is."

"A ride. I need you to drive me to my house, and fast." I wanted to go home for two reasons. The first was to retrieve the wand. I figured that having that in my possession would give me a slight edge over my opponents, who seemed very protective of it before I stole it. The second was to check on Lupia's status.

Freeman shook his head. "This could all go horribly wrong." He then grabbed another set of keys and motioned me to follow him.

Taking Charge

Palm Coast never did have the most crowded roads in the world, but aside from early morning hours, the roads were generally never empty. That night, however, the only cars on the road were other police cars, which, judging by the radio chatter, were out patrolling the streets to keep an eye out for vampires.

Our ride wasn't exactly smooth. Freeman had to stay alert while driving "Sorry, this car's been having transmission problems. All the good ones are part of the patrol."

"Sir, we could be travelling on a rickshaw. As long as we get to my house on ti—i—i—me!" As I was trying to say "time," the car stalled nastily while changing gears. "Okay, maybe it is a problem after all."

"Good thing we're here." Freeman parked the car on the curve of the cul-de-sac near my house, where I spotted only my mother's car in the driveway.

"I'll be right back!" I swung the door open and dashed out of the car. I had some business to take care of, and the sooner I did so, the better.

When I entered my house, it was entirely dark, but Lupia was present, sitting quietly on the couch in the living room.

"Lupia!" She didn't say anything. "Lupia?" I ran up to her and she didn't move, sitting on the couch, legs crossed, head down, eyes closed. "Um...so the vampire attack may be starting soon."

"I am aware." She barely moved as she spoke.

I wasn't sure what to do with her. "So are you planning to just stay here?"

She finally looked up at me, her girlish face smiling. "What are you planning to do?"

I thought that we had already established what I would do. "Fight, of course."

She gave a quick nod. "That's what I wanted to hear."

"How do you mean?" I was curious about where this conversation was leading.

"Amy...I have to thank you."

"Hey, it's nothing." I really had no problem with protecting her. I'd do the same for any other friend. When we met, I was just her fan. Now I gladly called her a friend.

"No, I'm serious." She looked down again. "I never liked fighting, and I suppose it was because that was what all the boys in my tribe did. Fighting was always sort of a guy thing...but you...you're a girl."

"Well obviously." The ironic thing was that she was much curvier than me.

"You fight to protect what's important to you. And you can accept me as a woman even after seeing me in my other, horrid form."

"Lupia, it doesn't matter what gender you are. What matters is that you have the ability to fight and something to fight for. I fight because I have friends I want to protect and because I want to reach out to the truth of what's happened. It has nothing to do with the fact that I'm a girl. Even if I weren't a vampire, I would still at least stand up for myself" (although I knew the dangers of going too far with such resistance—I was reminded of it every time I opened my mouth in front of a mirror).

"And that's why…" She stood up. "I'm going to fight too!"

"Awesome!" I clapped. I liked the fact that another combatant would be joining my side of this battle. It certainly tipped the odds more in our favor.

"Although…" Lupia scratched her head. "I don't really like transforming in front of other people. Could you leave the room, please?"

"Oh, of course."

"Able!" Freeman was at the front door. "Hurry your ass up! I'm getting some weird stuff on the radio!"

"Oh crap, sorry!" I dashed into my room and grabbed the wand from my closet. My skirt didn't have any pockets, so I put it in that special spot where girls can hide stuff. (I mean my chest, of course. I may be unusual, but I'm not a pervert. Unfortunately, I didn't have all that much space there, but it would do for a wand.)

I stepped out of the front door again, and another car was in the driveway—a red sports car that I knew very well. "Amelia! Will!" They began to emerge.

Freeman was still stood near the door, where he sighed. "Seriously? Valentine's daughter is here too?"

"Amy!" Will seemed delighted that I was out of the holding cell.

Amelia ran toward me to give me a hug. "How'd you get out of prison?"

I pointed toward Freeman with my thumb. "This guy just happens to be awesome."

Then, at that moment Amelia's phone rang, playing a song from Lupia that we all knew. All of us stopped moving and stared at her. Something about the fact that she was even receiving a call at this time just didn't seem right to any of us, including her. She pulled out her phone and checked it. "Daddy's calling." We knew that whatever this was, it couldn't be good at all.

"Answer it," I said.

254

Taking Charge

"Hello..." She seemed to freeze in place as she listened to the call. "It's him," she covered the microphone as she addressed the rest of us, "but something doesn't seem right."

"How so?"

She listened more. "He's demanding that I tell him Lupia's location and his voice sounds all monotone and he's speaking in a very roundabout way."

I turned to Will. "Hey, you don't think—"

He cut me off. "That the vampires got to him first? Oh yes I do think that."

Lupia stepped out of my front door, still untransformed, wearing my brother's oversized jeans and a cheap men's undershirt. Her lack of a bra made her look a bit raunchy. "If they want me, they can have me, but only if they can catch me."

Amelia looked increasingly worried. "Guys, he's saying that this is our last chance. We have one hour before they destroy the town."

"One hour?" I had an idea. Whether or not it was a good one, I couldn't say. "That's just enough time...to lay a trap for them."

"A trap?" Will and Lupia both peered at me. I grabbed both of them and we went into a huddle. The others looked on curiously.

"Amelia, tell him what we're about to tell you."

17: First Kill

The gym seemed empty. It was almost creepy. The lights were turned on low, and the moon brought little illumination from outside. The wooden floor glimmered in the low light, accentuating the usual markings of the basketball court.

A lone person treaded the gleaming wood. Despite the creepy atmosphere, she would not be deterred. She came there for a purpose and she would fulfill it no matter the cost. Her feet squeaked as she strode through the gym, but that sound didn't matter to her.

What did matter was the voice she heard. "No! Please don't do anything to me!" It was a woman's voice. She was looking for a woman. "Leave me alone!" She turned to face the source of the voice, but she had trouble tracking it. Where was it? The she saw it. Another person was there, far away, sitting on the first row of bleachers. The person almost seemed to glow for some reason. "No! No! Stop it! Please!" This woman was definitely in trouble.

She could feel it; this was the person she was looking for. She approached. "You better not do anything to me!" Finally, she could see a small person wearing glasses holding an electronic device with two glowing screens. "Why won't you let me go?" The voice came from the device. This girl was not who she was looking for. She took a step backward.

"Oh no you don't!" Then she found herself pinned to the ground—by me. "Did you really think we'd hand over Lupia so easily?" She didn't even struggle, I barely had to put forth any effort to hold her in place. My plan actually seemed to be working.

"I should have known that this would be a trap." I recognized the girl's voice, but she was not who I expected her to be. "Vampires are the greatest of hunters."

First Kill

I looked down at my prisoner. "Ella Spawn?"

She seemed to have given up all hope of resisting, ready to accept anything that I would do to her. Her head was tilted away, her eyes closed.

"No, seriously, what the hell are you doing here?" Truly, this situation wasn't going as planned.

"The vampires said you kidnapped my mother."

"Your mother?" I thought about how my own mother was missing. This could have been a very serious turn of events. "Do you know where she is?"

"Safe at her home in Phoenix."

"Come again?" If she meant Phoenix, Arizona, then her mother was very far away.

"You vampires tricked me into thinking she was kidnapped."

I stood up from my pouncing position, releasing her. She didn't move. "And you believed that?" She didn't answer. I glanced back at my Nintendo 3DS, its twin screens still glowing in the dark gym. We had recorded Lupia's voice on its sound application. "Does Lupia's voice really sound like your mom's?"

She didn't have the chance to answer this second question, as a man dashed into the gym "Ella!" It was Buford. "What did you do to her?"

"Pinned her to the ground and released her. That's it."

Buford wasn't in the mood for talking, with his hands balled into fists. He looked like he would do anything to protect Ella. He was about to attack, but then I heard growling.

It seemed to come from all directions, and it was a sound that I recognized all too well. At least ten wolves must have encircled the spot on which the three of us stood. They were all showed their teeth.

"Amelia!" As soon as I called out that name, I lifted my right hand into the air and produced a bright fireball, making the figures of the wolves very clear as they began to pounce on me. They ignored Ella and Buford for some reason. Then they dropped to the ground one by one. Amelia's shots were accurate and fast, but nobody could've fired fast enough to hit all of them in time. I had to throw off several of them. I could feel the deep gashes that they inflicted on my arms and legs healing quickly.

"Behind you, 20 feet!" Since it was part of a public and taxpayer-funded high school it was almost impossible, magically, to determine who owned the gym, so Will couldn't cast a warding spell. We had to make do with magic that would work in public areas. Will and his mother had covered the gym with a detection spell that caused the sheet of runes that Will kept in his pocket to glow differently depending on where intruders were in the building. The two mages and Amelia were all well behind me on the second floor of the gym, which housed extra space for sports practice and P.E. classes as well as an additional set of bleachers for larger events.

The gym was actually kept locked at night, but we broke in. It was my idea to go there. It was a wide open spot far enough away from any major residences. I knew of the colossal chance for collateral damage, but I would rather have buildings and objects destroyed rather than people.

Will's mother met us there after we arrived. At her request, she wanted a part in this battle. She didn't say anything to Amelia or me before the fight.

When we arrived we found an ambulance in front of the school accompanied by EMTs placing injured police officers on stretchers. They wouldn't tell us why the officers were injured, but they offered me a blood bag in exchange for leaving them alone. They definitely seemed afraid of vampires. Will suggested that I drink the blood since the steaks I ate probably wouldn't be potent enough to get me through a battle. Otherwise, my friends each would've made a small donation by cutting themselves, but that luckily wasn't necessary. Freeman decided to wait outside on standby in case anyone else entered the area or we needed to find additional help.

I spun around 180 degrees, as Will told me, to see a wolf-like creature much larger than the others approaching. Several of Amelia's bullets hit it, but they did nothing to stop the snarling beast's approach. In an instant, I wasn't even looking at said creature anymore, but at the face of the girl formerly known as Carla Evans, now Tower. "Did you honestly expect us to fall for some sort of trap?"

"I wasn't sure what to think." I was actually being truthful. "Perhaps you'd have actually fallen for it if Wingus and Dingus over there didn't get here first for whatever reason." Ella and Buford shared an awkward embrace and made no reaction.

"The Lovers have served their purpose in creating the new world order." She smiled evilly. "Now it's time for you to fulfill yours."

"You want Lupia?" Now it was my turn to smile evilly. Just to look cool, I also outstretched my arm and pointed at Tower. "You can have her!"

First Kill

Fully transformed into a werewolf, Lupia dashed out of the shadows enshrouding the girls' locker room at the back of the gym, straight at Tower. He ran on all fours at a pace that would put any bipedal creature to shame. Tower instantly transformed in response and the two of them pounced on each other simultaneously, colliding in midair. They hit the ground clawing and biting.

"So like the cornered prey you are, you've finally decided to fight." Now I heard the voice that once belonged to Bethany Davis. I turned to face the gym's back entrance, from which Strength approached, accompanied by two of her wolves. She snapped her fingers, and the wolf corpses on the ground slowly turned to dust and faded away into the air.

"What the...?" I had never seen anything like that.

"The Fool has placed an endless supply of wolves at my command. Do you really wish to face my army?"

I wouldn't find out why the wolves faded away until sometime later, when Will, who would find out the information from his mom's continued investigation into the matter, would explain to me that the wolves were actually homunculi, or beings artificially created through a combination of science and magic. Strength had full control over their existence. Exactly how, we could only guess since the creation of homunculi differs between individual mages and scientists. After learning these facts, I felt much less guilty about killing the wolves since they weren't actually real wolves and therefore not endangered. Homunculi, likewise, rarely live beyond a few days. At that moment, though, with Strength standing right in front of me, guilt was the last thing on my mind.

"No matter how many wolves you have, they still fall to Amelia's bullets." My voice now had more bravery to it than it ever did before. Then I then heard several gunshots fired off, but neither of the wolves accompanying Strength fell. I also heard more growling, but I couldn't see any more wolves approaching. I looked up toward the second floor, where I could see movement.

"Your pack mates seem to have expected an attack from mine, but they still stand no chance."

I sighed. "You know, you keep talking some crap about 'pack this' and 'pack that,' but you were a high school student just last week. Do you even remember what it's like to have real friends?" I had to hope—no, believe—that Will, Amelia, Lupia, and Will's mom would be fine.

"These are my friends." She bent down and scratched the ears of one of her wolves. It wagged its tail. "And besides, the Pack is always growing." Each of

Blood on Fire

the gym's entrances burst open, and police rushed inside, keeping their distance to avoid the dangerous battle between Lupia and Tower. They all had their guns out, pointed at me. The police were then joined by more wolves. Several of the officers fired warning shots at Lupia, who leapt away from Tower to stand back-to-back (although considering our height difference it was more like back-to-head) with me. Tower changed back into a girl and took a spot by Strength's side.

Captain Valentine was among the officers. "Freeze." His voice was a monotone.

I knew that we were in some serious danger. "You can command humans, too?" Her power over wolves was obvious, but having an entire police force against me was downright ridiculous.

"Do you not remember Devil?" I knew that Strength referred to the fourth member of their team, as featured on TV.

"Where is Devil now?" I tried to bide my time.

Tower gave a sickening sneer. "One need not necessarily be present for the creation of the new world order to have a part in it."

"This is bad," Lupia whispered to me.

"Why's that? We only have about 60 opponents. I'm sure we can take them all at the same time." Somehow sarcasm made the situation a little less scary.

"You yourself said that they are infused with werewolf blood. As pack animals, werewolves draw spiritual strength from their allies."

"Spiritual strength, you say?" It was an interesting notion, but not one that seemed like our main concern. "I don't think these two have souls anymore."

"Furthermore, as vampires, they have a near endless supply of blood from these people."

"Now that's a problem."

"It is just as you say." Tower apparently heard us talking (then again, how could she not?). "Together, we are far more powerful than we are separately. Now, Lupia will be ours so that the Fool can create more like us, but you, Magician, have one opportunity to escape death."

"And what's that?" The longer I could keep them talking, the longer I had to think of something useful.

"You stole it from me," Strength said menacingly. "Return it. Unless you want to keep it. We will let you if you join us."

First Kill

Even though I had been keeping it against my chest the entire time, I had forgotten about the wand. The truth was that I just didn't trust it. I pulled it out slowly, keeping a steady grip on it while making sure not to even think of any of the things that it could possibly do. I didn't like either of the options Strength gave me. "Tell me, why is this thing so important?"

"To us, it bears no importance at all," Tower said.

"What?"

"But to you, it is a weapon, an item created to the Fool's own specifications with the specific purpose of allowing you to reach your full potential, but only if you open your mind to his guidance."

"My full potential?" I stared at the object in my hand. It seemed so harmless visually, like a mere costume prop. "So it's really intended to enhance my magic?"

Tower grinned, showing her fangs. "The fool commissioned its creation to use his power as he saw fit to both increase the power of magic and allow the creation of new vampires like us. It is his wand and he has ultimate control over it, but he will let you use it if you side with him. You were not supposed to obtain it early; that was Strength's blunder."

Strength shot Tower a dirty look.

"So you're saying that every time I use it, I invoke his power?" This seemed to be what she described.

"That is correct. He knows that you have tested it. You can invoke its immense power because he allows you to do so."

While still holding the base of the wand in my right hand, I gripped the tip of it with my left. "Something that could add his power to mine...I must admit that it's a cool concept, I'd be invincible, wouldn't I?"

"Amy, no!" Lupia didn't like these words, sensing the slightest hint of possible betrayal.

Tower grinned wider. "You would indeed." She held out her hand to motion me to join her.

"Awesome." I snapped the wand in half. Doing so took some effort and the full strength of both my arms, even though it was just a piece of wood. I threw both pieces sideways in opposite directions. They exploded into blue flames upon hitting the ground and quickly fizzled out.

"You idiot!" Tower and Strength were both absolutely appalled.

Lupia definitely seemed relieved.

Blood on Fire

I held out my hand much like Tower had, only I prepared a fireball in it. "The Fool gave me my power, but I'll use it however I want to. I won't let him control me!"

"Why do you defend the old order of humanity?" Tower seemed sickened. "The ignorant masses will never learn to accept you."

I sighed. What she said did strike a nerve after my ordeals at school that week, but I wasn't too concerned. "No, they won't, but you know, as a geek, I've never been accepted by everyone. All that matters is that my friends accept me."

"Your friends are nearly dead." Strength seemed certain.

"If you're so sure of your new world order, then come at me."

"There's no need." Strength made a signal with her hand that looked like a gun pointed at me. I quickly guessed about what would come next and prepared to keep a grip (figuratively speaking) on my fireball. I knew that bullets might not kill me, but I feared for Lupia. The sound that came only a second after Strength's signal was absolutely deafening. Every one of the mind controlled police officers fired their guns at the same time, and they continued firing until their magazines were empty. The sound echoed as an annoying and persistent ring.

Wait, shouldn't I be full of holes? I glanced downward at my body, which was completely fine. I then looked to Lupia, who shrugged, also having sustained no damage at all. Seeing such small objects was tough, but on the floor a few feet away from the circle of officers was a circle of discarded bullets. *A shield?* I knew who casted it.

"Your master may have had the help of Jadis family magic in creating you," said a voice I knew from high up in the gym, "but he didn't expect that I would find out about his little game."

I managed to look upward and saw, standing at the top of the bleachers, the figures of a two women and a man. One of the women was adorned with the glow and smoke of a lit cigarette.

"Sorry to keep you waiting," Will shouted, "but she didn't exactly make it easy for us."

Strength seemed to quake with fury. "My pack mates…how dare you!" She and Tower simultaneously leapt straight at me. Lupia was ready to help defend me, but I still had to dodge quickly. Unfortunately, I went in the wrong direction, tripping on Lupia's foot. He managed to keep his balance as he braced for the incoming attack, but I couldn't. I toppled downward, losing control of my fireball just as the two vampires were over me.

In science class at school, on the few occasions on which we used Bunsen burners, the teacher would always tell all the long-haired girls—and a few guys—to tie their hair back to prevent it from catching on fire. I always complied since I didn't want my scalp burned off. For some reason, the teachers always emphasized the fact that burning hair smelled terrible.

Apparently, they had a very good reason. *It smells like a fat guy's feet after gym class being dipped in rotten eggs.* By some strange twist of luck, I managed to avoid my opponents' next attack, but not in any normal way. Both of them were above me and very close together when I released my fireball, and their hair caught on fire, starting on opposite sides of the heads, near the top. *Ooh...should I try cutting my hair just in case?* I seemed to be immune to my own fire at least until it left my body, so I figured that I'd be fine.

Both of the vampires screeched in pain and fell to the ground, rolling around in an attempt to put the fire out. I took this opportunity to shoot several more fireballs at them, which heavily damaged the floor of the gym but made their attempts at extinguishing far more difficult. Strength's wolves let out wailing howls. "Damn you!" The desperation in Strength's voice was oddly satisfying.

Not wanting to expend too much of my energy, I stopped shooting when they had mostly their fires. They were left almost bald with burn marks on their heads that visibly healed.

When I saw those bald heads, I couldn't help myself. "You two look ridiculous." I laughed, but they didn't.

"We were willing to let you join us," Tower said, her evil smile long gone, "but someone like you has no place in the new world." She transformed, but something was definitely off.

Now Lupia laughed, which sounded like a series of deep grunts. "You're the stupidest looking wolf that I've ever seen." He laughed because Tower transformed into a mostly bald wolf. I joined in as well.

A few of the hypnotized police officers also joined in. "Hey, wait, what are we doing here?"

"Huh? What the hell?" Those who laughed looked around confused. "How did we all get here to surround the vampires?" Then they promptly fainted.

BLOOD ON FIRE

I quickly figured out what was going on. "Lupia, make them laugh!" Jadis witchcraft could provide us with protective barriers to guard against gunfire, but they had to concentrate to do so. We'd be much better off if we could snap the officers out of their trances.

"I may be an entertainer in my other form, but I'm no comedian." I couldn't think of any jokes at the moment either.

Tower leaped at me, snarling. She knocked me down, claws digging into my shoulders. This attack felt different than it did the last time that it happened—I now felt cold skin instead of fur. Lupia freed me by grabbing Tower, biting her, and pulling her off of me. Lupia seemed to move more sluggishly. His early skirmish with Tower had tired him out a bit. I could only hope that he would be able to hold up until the battle's end.

As the two of them fought, Strength seemed delirious. "I...I must avenge my pack mates." She and the surrounding wolves both rushed toward the trio atop the bleachers.

"I don't think so!" I ran after Strength. Lupia continued to grapple with Tower, throwing her forward, right between Strength and myself. *Don't fall down! Don't fall down!* In my attempt to not fall down, I ended up punting Tower forward and then falling down face first. She slammed into Strength, knocking her down as well.

Tower didn't skip a beat. She immediately jumped off Strength and at Lupia. The two resumed their struggle.

Strength, however, seemed frazzled as we both simultaneously stood up. "Why can you stand against us even when you're falling down like the oaf you are? What did the Fool ever see in you?"

"I don't know, you tell me. I'm just a scrawny geek from Florida; you're the great and powerful pack leader." That last part was a taunt.

"Shut up! Shut up! Shut up!" Strength held her head, shuddering.

"You know, for someone named Strength, you're being mentally broken pretty easily." Something about my constant thwarting of all her strategies drove her insane, and my snark definitely made it worse.

Strength screamed as loud as a banshee piercing the heavens. All of her wolves went berserk and leapt up the bleachers. Amelia fired at them as fast as she could while Will and his mother readied another spell, but the animals seemed to move faster than ever before.

First Kill

I rushed toward Strength, who was too distracted to react. Tower tried to stop me, but Lupia stopped her. I punched Strength in the collarbone, sending her flying over the circle of officers and into the base of the bleachers. I ran over, kicked her in the shin, and punched her in the face. "Call off your wolves!"

Though my attacks seemed to faze her, they didn't leave any visible marks. "You should have joined us when you had the chance."

I could see the wolves were closing in much faster than Amelia could shoot them. I grabbed Strength hard by the arm. I guessed from her lack of reactions that she was putting all of her energy into commanding her wolves to attack. "I'm not going to tell you again! Call them off!" Now I was the one becoming enraged.

She made no response at all.

I began channeling my blood into my right hand, the hand that held Strength's arm. I could feel the heat building up. I knew what I was doing. I was creating a fireball inside her arm. Strength became more and more strained with every passing second. Her wolves began to slow down.

Finally, strength screamed, but the wolves were only barely fazed, and they launched themselves at the Jadises. The mother and son were unaffected, finding protection from a shield that they managed to cast around themselves. The wolves scratched at the shield, trying to break it, frustrated at their inability to catch their prey. The Jadises had to concentrate hard. The wolves seemed completely focused on trying to break the shield, likely as a result of me torturing their master.

Taking an obvious risk, Amelia used this opportunity to dash down the steps, away from that frenzy, right past me and Strength. Tower spotted her, but Lupia was relentless despite the blood obviously soaking through his fur—his skin was torn up pretty badly. After winning a grapple, Lupia threw Tower through the gym's south exit, knocking down two police officers. He followed. Amelia kept running until she reached her father.

And she punched him.

I was looking away from Strength now, although I still kept a firm grip on her and kept building up heat. I couldn't believe what I had just seen. In my 16 years of life, I never imagined that I would see a daughter giving her father a beating that hard. "Now that's insubordinately badass." I couldn't recall my father ever doing anything that deserved such a strike, though recent events may have warranted it.

Blood on Fire

Every single one of the police broke into a hearty laugh. Their hypnosis was broken.

"Amelia, why did you just hit daddy?" Valentine asked in his usual patriarchal voice that stood out its previous monotone. He sounded like he wanted to be angrier but couldn't since he was talking to his daughter.

"Two reasons. One: you've been a jerk to my friend Amy. Two: you were hypnotized by a vampire."

"I was what?" Then he looked around. "Able, what are you doing out of your cell?"

"Um..." I really didn't have a chance to answer because the vampire I held suddenly became much lighter. I looked back at where Strength should've been, and she was gone. "What?" I then felt her arm crumble in my hand. I looked down and saw a severed hand and forearm lying next to small pile of ashes. I stared at it in horror. *Did I just do what I think I did?*

"Ella! No!" During the entire fight, Ella and Buford had just kept up their awkward stare into each other's eyes with all others present avoiding them. Now Strength, with one arm, had grabbed hold of Ella and actively sucked her blood, fangs deep in her neck. Her other arm consisted only of a stump the end which was charred to ashes. "Let her go!" Buford tried to pry Ella away but failed.

"Freeze!" Many of the police pointed guns at Strength, but one by one they began to faint.

"Amelia..." Valentine fainted as well.

Strength let go of Ella, who Buford ran to embrace. "I have to suck out the poison!" Were vampires really venomous? No.

"It's over, Strength!" I tried to sound tough, but I couldn't hide the fact that I was horrified about burning her arm off. She dashed toward the gym's north exit while her wolves stopped attacking the Jadises and followed.

I wasn't going to let her get away, so I chased. Amelia followed me. I didn't stop her.

The parking lot outside the gym was unusually foggy, even though we had seen no fog at all along the way there earlier. Almost every direction was a dim shade of white. Overall visibility was quite low. I could tell that the parking lot was empty aside from the faint glow of red and blue lights flashing slowly in the distance, revealing the presence of police cars.

"She did this before," Amelia said from behind me, "at the mall."

First Kill

"So this fog really isn't natural."

"No."

"I can't see anything. Can you?"

"Nope."

It was eerily quiet, far too quiet even for that time of night.

"You..." I heard Strength's voice, though I couldn't tell where it was coming from. "You ruined everything. This town was more useful to the Fool standing than it will be destroyed. But you are the one responsible for its destruction, not us."

"Me?" I didn't like this accusation. "None of this would've happened if you bozos hadn't started making threats."

"You've seen the power that we possess. Lupia was the key to making us unstoppable. Her blood would have made Tower and myself as powerful as our sister, if not more so, and perhaps she would have gained even more power herself."

"Your sister?" Even though they most certainly weren't sisters in the technical sense, I knew who she was talking about.

"She absorbed more blood than the rest of us...so much more that she destroyed our previous source and became unstoppable enough to demolish this town. Our previous orders were to keep her restrained...but now, thanks to you, she has been set free."

A colossal shadow approached. It was a shape I knew only too well. "Her again," Amelia said. She sounded scared.

"The Chariot approaches."

The shadow let out a thundering roar and charged forward like a train—but not at me or Amelia. The Ogre Queen ran straight past both of us.

"This school will be the first structure to experience her wrath."

"Damn it!" I began to run after her, but I was quickly stopped.

"You aren't going anywhere." Strength's voice was followed by the usual set of growls. The shadows of her wolves became visible through the fog, surrounding us on all sides.

Amelia and I stood back to back, keeping our eyes on all of the wolves. I cracked my knuckles. "You ready for this?"

"Do we have a choice?"

"Nope."

Blood on Fire

One by one, they all began to attack. Surrounded as we were, Amelia and I could each only defend 180 degrees around us. We had bullets on one side and fire on the other, but after only about four of them were dead could we tell that we were at a distinct disadvantage. Amelia would have to reload only after a few more shots.

This mist... It really got in the way. Eliminating it would make the whole fight easier. *Maybe...just maybe.* I closed my eyes and focused on that mist, even ignoring the sharp pain I felt in my arm and leg (yes, I had been bitten several times). I could almost feel the mist as if it were something that I could grab in my hand and just move aside.

"Got you!" I opened my eyes and I saw her. Strength was some distance away, standing in front of the police cars. I had cleared a path to her, a straight line with mist on either side.

I could feel the pain of repeated bites tearing away at my flesh, but my focus was on Strength. More wolves dashed down the path that I had cleared.

"Amelia!" I wanted to call her attention to our real opponent. The wolves' attack let up significantly, as so many of them gathered in the path that I cleared to their master. Amelia spun around, reloaded, and started pumping lead down the path. Several wolves fell quickly.

"Damn it!" This outburst came from Amelia. I suddenly could smell chocolate. She was still shooting, but not as quickly. I knew that she had been bitten.

I could feel my body shudder. I couldn't even think. Amelia was injured. I knew who was responsible, and thanks to Amelia, I had a clear path.

I ran, leaping over the dead wolves. I put my hand outward and unleashed a torrent of flame the likes of which I never had before. Strength screamed. I couldn't even see her through the smoke I produced.

"Call off the wolves!" I wasn't playing around.

"They will feast on you and your friend!" She wasn't either. The smoke began to clear. Her skin was charred badly, but it healed.

Ella's blood. It was sustaining her. Otherwise the damage that she had already taken wouldn't have been healing so quickly. I imagined that I had that blood instead.

A red ball started forming in my hand.

"No! What are you doing?" She panicked.

First Kill

I heard five more gunshots. Amelia breathed very hard. Then I heard silence. No more wolves came. I had a huge ball of blood in my hand. I felt tired after using the spell, but I had no time to rest.

"I—I..." Strength seemed broken. "Why won't they respond?" Though she tried hard to summon them, no wolves came.

"If your powers are anything like mine, you need blood to use them." I held up the red ball in my hand. "And I've got your blood right here. Give up, please." I practically pleaded with her. This fight was going too far.

Strength herself growled at me like her wolves would. She broke her gaze from me and locked it onto the smell of human blood.

"Don't even think about it!" Now I yelled. "You're not killing Amelia!"

I would say that she ran on all fours, except she only had one arm. Fixated on Amelia, she wouldn't be stopped.

I already had the blood in my hand. All I needed to do was empower and ignite it. "Shinkuu..." I said a word that was somewhat familiar to a *Street Fighter* player like me as I poured as much power as I could into this attack. "Hadouken!"

My hand turned into a flamethrower. Not literally, of course, but that was basically what happened. The fire continued pouring out of my hand for what seemed like an eternity. Strength screamed at a deafening volume, and her voice became increasingly strained until she only let out what sounded like a choke, and then nothing at all. When the smoke cleared, only a few charred bones surrounded by ash remained. Strength was gone. The surrounding wolf corpses all turned to dust.

I stared at the skeleton, my eyes wider than they'd ever been before. "She's dead..." The realization dawned on me. "I killed her." I stared in horror at what I had done. "I...I...I..." At sixteen years old, I took my first life. How does one deal with such a realization? I was absolutely horrified. Although I had considered the nature of the power I had, the thought that I could really, truly take a human life had never even occurred to me.

But I did it in defense of someone important to me, and I was quickly reminded of that.

"Triple...A..."

"Amelia!" I ran up to her and knelt down. She was lying on her back with two open wounds, one on the left side of her torso and one on her right thigh. The smell of chocolate was distracting but not unbearable.

BLOOD ON FIRE

"You saved me, Triple A." Amelia smiled at me.

"You're hurt. I have to get you to a safe place." I didn't want her dying on me.

She shook her head. "You have more work to do. Just reach into my right pocket." Amelia's jeans were fairly tight, so the rectangular bulge of her iPhone was obvious.

I grabbed it and called 911 for her. An ambulance was on its way. They were apparently prepared for such a call. "Are you sure you'll be okay?" I was extremely worried.

She nodded. "I've helped you as much as I can, but you still have a job to finish." She reached upward and grabbed my shoulder, pulling herself up. She looked deeply into my eyes "I believe in you." Then she moved closer, and our lips touched.

I kissed a girl...and I liked it.

I really wasn't expecting to receive my first kiss right at that moment. I also really didn't expect my first kiss to be with another girl, let alone my best friend. What I felt, though, I liked. Was I in love with her? I couldn't decide.

She really went in deep, too. Was her tongue longer than others? Whether she did so accidentally or not, she scraped it on one of my fangs on the way out, leaving the taste of chocolate. Her body dropped back to the ground when she finished. She breathed hard, but she seemed as relaxed as she possibly could, considering the circumstances.

For the record, her fang marks were gone.

I took a life to save the life of a friend who just kissed me. I had to take a few seconds to get my bearings together. I still had a duty to perform, and figuring out the reason for this kiss would have to wait.

"Uh...stay safe." I stood up and waved goodbye to Amelia before running after the Ogre Queen.

18: Falcon's Fire

As I ran across the flat, grassy field behind the school, I heard a voice. *"Amy, can you hear me?"*

I stopped and looked around "Will?" I didn't see him anywhere.

"I'm not around you, but don't worry, you're not crazy." I could hear his voice clearly even though he was nowhere near me.

Wait, you're psychic now too? I thought, expecting him to hear me. I was still surprised enough at the fact that Will was a warlock. I didn't think that he would have psychic powers as well.

"If you're trying to just think something to me, you're going to have to speak up. Our minds aren't linked."

"So wait, you're psychic now?"

"Not exactly, it's a spell my mom cast that enables her to act as a medium and allow me to examine the area and communicate with you. I see that you've defeated Strength and that Amelia is injured."

"Uh...yeah..." I wondered if he had seen that kiss. "What about Tower?"

"We dealt with her."

Perhaps I should interrupt this little exchange to talk about exactly what happened between Lupia and Tower. As I pointed out before, the two of them viciously fought, locked in a constant state of biting and scratching. They had moved their fight outside of the gym as well, but on the opposite side from where Amelia and I had chased Strength. The two were locked in near equal combat, but Lupia was tiring out, lacking the supernatural healing ability of a vampire. He already had several wounds across his body, and his stamina would only hold out for so long.

Blood on Fire

When Strength ran outside, her wolves had stopped attacking the mother and son Jadis team. Will was ready to run after me and Amelia, but his mother stopped him. "I think the vampire has a better chance than the werewolf."

After considering her statement for a second or two, he nodded. Vampires were inherently stronger than werewolves after all, and these hybrid creatures that we were up against were as dangerous as both combined.

The wolf-on-wolf melee had taken its toll on the area, uprooting grass and bending the poles that held up the covered walkways into awkward shapes. The two of them fought in the small open field that was surrounded by the gym, the music building, and the building that housed several classrooms for underachieving students. In the very center of the field, Tower had Lupia pinned down, her teeth ready to sink into his neck.

Minerva Jadis uttered a few magic words and with a wave of her hand, an arcane circle appeared on Lupia's neck, and within that circle appeared some cloves of garlic.

Completely repulsed, Tower jumped off of Lupia, freeing the werewolf, who grabbed the garlic and kept a tight grip on it.

Will wondered where that garlic had been summoned from, but he didn't have time to ask as his mother began chanting again.

Seeing the extreme danger that she was in, Tower sprinted in the opposite direction, toward the road, but instead crashed headfirst into an invisible wall.

Will could see that his mother struggled to remain standing after all her casting, so he would have to be the one to aid Lupia from here.

While Minerva Jadis was about to collapse, Lupia really did collapse. His body could no longer take the continued stress, and it transformed back into the body of a human. She kept her grip on the garlic.

Tower turned away from the invisible wall and approached the now-vulnerable Lupia, growling. She most likely would have pounced if not for the garlic.

Lupia's loose clothing barely clung to her now much smaller body, making moving awkward. She was battered and bruised, with blood staining both the undershirt and jeans that she took from my brother's room. "Man or woman, it doesn't matter. I will never give in as long as I can still fight."

Will began a chant under his breath, trying to anticipate exactly when it would be needed. That was when Tower decided to change targets. She looped around Lupia, aiming at Will instead.

272

FALCON'S FIRE

Will knew he was in danger and that he would stand little chance against this beast. He tried to leap out of the way, but fell to the ground as he felt something like a blade pass across his arm.

He was bleeding, but not as much as he thought he would. He looked up to see Tower's mouth locked on his mother's ankle. "You can do whatever you want to me or to this town," she said, "but when you try to hurt my son, there's going to be hell to pay." Arcane circles were under both her and Will. The two had switched places at the last moment, leaving Will with only a scratch. Minerva looked like she was right on the verge of fainting.

This turn of events seemed to catch Tower off guard, so Will finished the chant he began before being attacked. Tower's four legs spread outward as her whole body was forced to the ground, causing her to release Minerva's leg. She was strong, and Will struggled to keep her pinned down.

Lupia stood up, garlic in hand, and staggered toward the ground-bound wolf. Will had to exert his entire mental prowess just to keep his spell enacted and prevent Tower from moving. He was quickly about to fail as Lupia shoved a few cloves of garlic into Tower's mouth and one in her snout.

Tower coughed and sputtered. Blood leaked out of her mouth. She lost her focus, retaking her human form and making Will's job a bit easier.

Tower spat out as much garlic as she could. "This world shall fall!" Her mouth leaked blood as she spoke. "It shall become my Master's soon enough!" Lupia stuffed the garlic back in.

"Looks like I didn't even need that silver dagger," Minerva said before lighting up a cigarette and taking a seat on the ground to rest (silver prevents werewolves from transforming, so it would have helped).

"We didn't have any way to actually kill her, so she's here tied up with garlic in her mouth."

"You guys are cruel, you know that right?" That certainly wasn't a fate that I ever wanted to experience.

"At least now we can turn her over to the police once they wake up...which is more than I can say about Strength."

"Um...right." The fact that I took a life really weighed on me.

"Anyway, stop standing around. Chariot is in the cafeteria."

"Uh, right!" I resumed my sprint. "Are you guys coming to help me?"

"Amy, I'd hate to break this to you, but she's too dangerous for anyone but you to fight. She could tear a human apart with minimal effort. Furthermore,

Blood on Fire

Amelia, Lupia, and mom are too injured and I would just get in the way. I'm sorry, but aside from my vocal support, you're on your own."

I sighed. "That's just fan-freaking-tastic."

"Don't worry, all of us are sure that if anyone can beat her, it's you."

I didn't respond. I tried to focus on the battle ahead of me. I ran my tongue through the gap in my mouth. *I have a tooth to avenge.*

I ran as fast as I could. The campus was empty, but the town wasn't. I couldn't let the Ogre Queen escape. I could see from the outside that she had already destroyed several classrooms, mainly art rooms since those were the rooms she came to first. The walls were almost completely torn down. When I reached the cafeteria, it was practically non-existent, as it was quickly turning into a pile of rubble. Tables were torn apart while the walls were in shambles. I saw her trashing a cash register—the very same register at which my teeth had been knocked out.

The amount of damage would only increase until I got her attention. "Hey! Midnight Meat Train!" I began charging energy in my right hand. She stopped mid-destruction and turned around. "So you traded what little brain you had for more brawn. You made the wrong choice."

She started growling in response.

"You were a mindless monster as a human and you've only become worse as a vampire."

Her rage mounted.

"Shelly used you before and Dracula's using you now. You are and never have been anything but a tool."

Now she roared and started charging, which sounded like a train. I kept my eyes fixed on her. To be honest, I was scared out of my mind, but I had accepted this encounter as inevitable. I remembered the feeling of that hand grasping the back of my head and the pain of my face being beaten into the ground. *I have to do this!*

I shot fireballs at her repeatedly during her charge. None of them fazed her. She grabbed me, catching me in a bear hug and dragging me along in her continued charge. I felt my body impact the cafeteria wall and then pass through it. It was followed by another wall, which led into a classroom. My legs repeatedly smashed into desks. Needless to say, I was in pain.

"Come on, you can get out of this. You just need a bit more power." I could only hope that Will was right. A test of brute strength was out of the question,

so my only real choice was to use magic. The only problem was that my hands were stuck near my waist. Chariot's arms were wrapped around my upper body, including my upper arms.

Here goes nothing! Instead of my hands, I channeled blood into my upper arms (where skin was exposed; the last thing I needed was clothing damage), hoping to form flames there. Chariot roared in pain as she slammed into yet another wall. My new trick seemed to work. I kept channeling. I wanted the pain to be too much for her. *Thank God for tank tops!* For good measure, I repeatedly kicked her shins. Finally, the heat became unbearable and she let go of me—by throwing me across the classroom.

I stood up and straightened out all of my bones while wiping the ash off of my arms. My new trick had actually done some damage to her.

The Ogre Queen's eyes actually glowed red. They were fixed on me as she growled. "Lamy..." She uttered her first word (that I was aware of) since becoming a vampire.

I braced myself for another attack. "I'm not the weak little nobody Shelly would want you to believe I am. I'm protecting both myself and my friends. I'm not afraid of you anymore."

"That's the spirit! Kick her ass!"

She roared and charged again. I leapt onto the teacher's desk nearby and then leapt over her. I almost landed on my feet this time, but a sitting position was still a perfect one from which to throw repeated fireballs at her back. I burned a hole in her body suit.

She turned around and began a new charge. I tried to slide underneath her, but I ended up being stomped upon. I felt ribs crack, but I didn't have any time to deal with that. She flipped around and stomped once again. I immediately grabbed her leg after she missed and rapidly channeled fire into it. She tried flinging me from her leg, but I let go, rolled sideways, and stood up. She roared in disdain and frustration. The outer part of her leg was charred.

Chariot grasped her head, as if something were trying to invade it. She shook around violently before bursting through the nearest wall back outside. She ran off at an unbelievable velocity.

"Is she giving up?" I secretly wanted this to be true.

"I'm not sure...hold on a sec." I waited a few seconds in silence, examining the gaping hole in the wall that the Ogre Queen had left behind.

Blood on Fire

Only then did I realize that I knew that room. It was Mr. Royal's classroom, and I stood near the remains of my own desk. I looked for Shelly's. It was untouched. *Why did it have to be my desk and not hers?*

"She ran into the library!" Will sounded frantic. *"She's already started tearing it down."* Considering his love of books, I couldn't very well refuse to save the library.

"Got it!" I bolted in the proper direction, knowing the path that I should take offhand.

"Go easy with the fire in there, okay?"

I was surprised by the amount of destruction that Chariot had already wrought by the time that I arrived—and I hadn't taken very long, all things considered. She threw an entire bookshelf, books and all, into a table of computers, smashing all of them.

She hadn't seen me enter. "Not much of a reader, are you?" I wanted her attention to be on me to minimize destruction.

She seemed to try to ignore me. She threw another bookshelf the check-out counter.

"You got a paper cut as a kid, didn't you?"

She still ignored me as she smashed yet another bookshelf with her fist.

"Or was your uncle an avid reader?" I recalled the information about her background that Freeman told me.

Now I got her attention. I didn't like striking nerves of that nature, but Will would kill me if I didn't save those books.

"Look, I'm sorry about whatever happened in your past, but is that really any reason to take out your anger on these books or my teeth?"

She only became even angrier, which I didn't think was possible. She stepped away from the bookcase, toward me. She towered over me.

"Do you think it's at all possible that after everything that's happened, we could just be friends?" Despite the strides that I had made in the fight, I would still have preferred not fighting at all.

I attempted to dodge, but she grabbed me by both of my arms. She pulled them in opposite directions. I resisted as best I could. I didn't have the fortitude to charge any fire as I did so. I felt like I was about to be torn apart.

"You still have a chance! Come on!"

As she stretched, she moved her arms further outward, which brought my body closer to hers. My mouth was aligned with her neck. Will had warned me against drinking vampire blood, but desperate times call for desperate measures. I bit her.

I wasn't sure what vampire blood was supposed to taste like, but hers wasn't pleasant at all. It was bitter, extremely bitter. I couldn't even bear the thought of swallowing it. A bit of it went down my throat, and then I saw an image.

A middle-aged man—perhaps in his 40s—towered above, an odd smirk complementing his bare and hairy chest. I could feel pain, helplessness, and a desire to be stronger than him. Then the man's face changed. It became paler and more rigid. His hair became darker. His face became one that I had seen before. I felt helpless. Then I felt blissful.

My mind returned to the real world and I realized that I was still being pulled apart. I let go of her neck, her nasty blood still in my mouth. I spat it into her eyes, but not before infusing it with some of my own fire power. She roared in pain as the boiling blood covered her face. Then she threw me across the room. I hit a computer, toppling it onto the ground. I landed flat on my stomach, and I could feel that the table was cracked under me. I couldn't see the Ogre Queen, but I heard her run away.

I felt woozy. I tried to sit up, but I had some trouble. Something was wrong with my right arm, so I had to use my left, which itself felt dislocated to gain leverage. I peered my right arm, and then the extreme pain set in. "Oh...my...God...my...my arm." I felt like I should've been crying, but I couldn't for some reason. "My arm is gone!" I started breathing rapidly. I was in a state of complete panic. The open stump on my shoulder neither bled very much nor healed. It just remained as a sort of open wound in limbo, unable to decide what it should do.

"Amy, relax!" Will certainly didn't sound very relaxed, and I don't think anyone would after watching someone's arm being torn off. *"Your arm is over by that smashed bookcase in the back. You should be able to reattach it."*

I decided to take his advice. My arm stood out amid all the rubble. I ran to it immediately, grabbed it with my left arm, and shoved the torn end of it into my right stump. I screamed in pain as the nerves and muscles began to automatically reattach themselves. Never in my life had I ever felt anything more physically painful. I still didn't cry, no matter how much I wanted to. To me, the process felt like an hour, but it was actually more like a minute before the pain subsided and I had full control over my right arm again.

Blood on Fire

"I can't even begin to imagine the pain that you just felt, but it's going to be alright."

The rest of my bones and organs were also back into their proper alignment. I felt beyond exhausted. "I don't want to fight anymore. Please tell me she ran away for good this time."

"I'm afraid not."

"Somehow I knew you'd say that."

"She's off campus now. She ran to the shopping center."

"The shopping center?" I checked the clock on the library's wall. It was just past 11. "It's late, but there might still be people there."

"Yeah. That might be why she's heading that way."

I sighed. "Alright, I'm on my way." I ran even though I didn't feel like it. As I did, my mind wandered to what I saw when I swallowed some of the Ogre Queen's blood. *Powerlessness...* I thought back to how I felt in that last memory that I dredged up. *Bliss...What does it all mean?*

I had lived in that town for a long time, so I remembered what the area next to my high school used to be like. It, like several other areas, used to be a forest. Now it was a complex of several stores that served as the alternatives to Wal-Mart that the town desperately lacked in the previously.

I passed by the back of gym again, where I found that Amelia was absent. I was relieved to know she was most likely safe. I kept running and had to turn onto the road that connected the school and shopping center.

I found the Ogre Queen sitting on top of a car in the mostly-empty parking lot, which made the whole thing tip downward. She grasped her head, and I couldn't see her face. She didn't seem to notice me.

"Hey."

She made no response

"Do you not want to kill me?"

Still no response. In fact, she didn't seem to move at all. Something was definitely off. When she ignored me before, she had been destroying something.

"Are you ready to stop destroying things?"

"Shel...ly..."

"What about Shelly?" I found the fact that she would bring up that name now very strange.

"Friend..."

Falcon's Fire

"She wasn't your friend. She was just using you as her personal tank so no one would threaten her as queen bee."

"Drac...u...la..."

That was a name that I hadn't heard the others utter. I felt an extreme sense of dread. I knew something was off about her. "It's okay. Just come with me. If you're willing to make peace with me, I'll protect you from him. We can work together. Come on, Emily." I wanted to avoid fighting. I'd never had the chance to try being friends with her, and I'd have much preferred that over further risking my life.

"Amy! Something's wrong! Tower just went berserk and we're having trouble keeping her tied up!"

"That doesn't sound good."

The Ogre Queen uncovered her face, which was still slightly charred from my last attack "I...must...serve!" She leapt off of the car, picked it up with one hand, and threw it at me. I had never dodged something so huge before and I was taken by surprise, so I took the hit straight in the torso. It was upside-down and I was pinned underneath it.

Strength also went berserk earlier. I tried to lift the vehicle. I managed to free myself easily enough, all things considered, from such a heavy object, but I didn't have nearly the level of strength that she did in order to throw such a thing. Chariot was already a berserker, but something had snapped within her. She wouldn't let me get away. I also couldn't expect much help from Will since he would have his hands tied up keeping Tower in line.

By the time I stood up again, Chariot had grabbed the car with both hands. I ran away across the parking lot. She chased, swinging the car like a weapon. I was more scared than ever. If she could tear my arm off before going berserk I could only imagine what she would do to me afterward.

I couldn't outrun her. She hit me, sending me flying far across the pavement. I could feel my clothing and skin tear on the rough surface as I landed on my side. She still came at me, gripping the car tightly.

I panicked. Then, for some reason, I remembered something. *"All you need is a little bit of creativity."* I heard Ms. Hacket's words clearly in my head. I didn't know why.

But those words did get my mind moving. *Creativity...She has a car.* I could see the underside of it as she ran, and I had only mere seconds before she would arrive. *Cars run on gasoline!* I put my right hand outward and targeted a spot near the tail pipe, which just so happened to be near where she gripped the car.

I shot out a continuous blast of fire. I didn't care how much of my power would be used up; I only wanted to ignite that car.

I had never heard an explosion before. Movies tend to downplay exactly how loud they are. All I could really hear was a loud and continuous ringing. The light was also too much to bear looking at, and I had to turn away. I could feel my skin drying out from the intense heat. Then I felt something huge stab my left thigh. "Damn it!" When the light had subsided, I could see a huge piece of metal, too broken and twisted for me to know what it was, lodged in the upper part of my leg. I yelped in pain as I pulled it out.

Through the smoke, I could see Chariot. She was on fire. All over her body were small protrusions. She was covered in shrapnel. She was also still coming toward me. She let out a continuous beastly roar.

I wouldn't be able to escape in time. I took the metal that I had pulled from my thigh, and, swinging it like a club with all of my strength, I aimed at the best target that my position on the ground would allow me to: her leg.

I don't know how I managed to do it. She had been moving so fast, but I still managed to knock her off balance. As she was about to fall on top of me, I rolled to my side and then scurried off to avoid further harm.

I wasn't quite thinking, and I ended up running toward the nearby stores, and I found myself at the entrance to the Books-A-Million, where I found a young man in the store's employee garb, holding the door open with one hand and holding a key in the other. He stood there frozen, staring agape at the fire and shrapnel-covered Chariot. "My...my car..." His voice was weak.

"Sir, if you don't want to be torn limb from limb, then I would suggest you get the hell out of here." I pointed toward the school and motioned him to run. He complied.

Then I quickly felt a burning impact to my back as I was pushed through the store's glass front doors. I landed in a bin of discount books.

I could smell smoke in the air. I leapt out of the bin to face Chariot, who stood in place roaring.

"First the library and now a bookstore. Do you just hate authors for their creativity?" That word was on my mind again. *Creativity, right...*

My body was really starting to tire out. I wasn't sure how long I could keep going.

Falcon's Fire

Chariot picked up an entire stand of books and threw it at me. Several of the tomes caught on fire as she touched them. Though I stumbled a bit, I dodged the attack. The stand crashed into another, and more books caught on fire.

"Stop it! The whole place'll burn down and kill both of us at this rate!" She didn't care. She just kept throwing more heavy objects at me. Next came a table and a cash register, the former of which just added to the fire.

I ran to my right. *She's blocking the only exit.* I wasn't sure where the back door was. *I have to lure her away. I need to reach a spot where she has no choice but to move to attack me.* With her level of strength, she could probably throw objects all the way to the back of the store. Seemingly, my only choice was to attract her attention by making myself difficult to target.

I dashed to my right, toward the mystery novels, using as many bookshelves as I could fit between myself and her for cover. She kept up her thrown assault, tossing all of the heaviest possible objects at me and continuously spreading more fire. I had enough cover for the moment, but I was concerned about how long it would last. "I'm sorry, Will. I wish I could save these books."

"I forgive you."

"Will!" I was glad to be reconnected to his voice.

"Sorry about that. We had to beat Tower pretty badly before she would finally calm down."

I started to tremble as the smell of smoke became sickening. "I don't know how long I can hold out. Nothing'll stop her." The sprinklers on the roof activated, dowsing the whole store with water.

"You've already damaged her very badly."

"I just want her to go away."

"This is a risk, but you look like you're badly hurt, so I'm going over there."

Another table just missed my head. The fire spread dangerously close to me. "Are you crazy?"

"You need blood!"

"Will, don't do it! Will!" Now he didn't respond. I wasn't sure how he would survive with that beast around.

The next bookcase that came at me was the largest and heaviest she had thrown yet. In the second in which I could see it, I noticed that it was lined with the oversized hardcover editions of teen romance novels, too many of which were about vampires. Most of my cover was destroyed, so I clumsily rolled out of its path. It grazed my leg and crashed into the wall, causing cracks that let out a light brown dust. *The wall's cracking.*

I stood up, ran full speed at the wall, and slammed into it with my shoulder. It crumbled easily and I stumbled into the Payless Shoe Source next door. I stepped away from the hole as another book case flew through it and slammed into the opposite wall. The shoes lining it were destroyed. *What a waste of good shoes.* The wall, however, like the one before it, was on the verge of collapsing. I leapt into it and staggered into my local GameStop. I was on the far side of the main desk, standing atop a pile of green Xbox 360 game cases that I had dislodged from their shelves. I knew that the cases were empty and no actual games were damaged. *Now's my chance!* I bolted toward the front door.

My spirits sank again. The wall in front of the checkout counter, which was covered in Nintendo DS games, crumbled, and Chariot, still covered in fire and shrapnel, emerged.

"You have to be kidding me!"

She roared louder than ever before and began approaching me. Her arms were held apart, as if they were ready to grab me and make another attempt at tearing me apart.

I wanted to defeat her. I thought about how I defeated Strength. Then I thought about all the copies of *Street Fighter* that were inevitably around me. "I'm sorry, GameStop." I put my hands together. I didn't have much energy left, but I would need all of it. "Shinkuu…"

The Ogre Queen looked ready to pounce.

"…HADOKEN!"

I covered her with as much fire as I could possibly put out. I continued even when my body told me I couldn't anymore. *I just want her gone!* I felt desperate. Chariot was covered in a constant onslaught of fire so thick that I couldn't even see her anymore. I heard her fall backwards through the glass doors. Less and less fire soon began pouring from my hands until I just couldn't release any at all. I couldn't see what happened to my opponent as my vision became blurry.

I was ready to pass out. I fell to my knees. *Did I defeat her?* My body felt limp.

Then I felt a pair of hands under my shoulders. They were gentle, and feeling them there was comforting. They held me up. I didn't fall to the ground.

"Not yet, Amy." Will's voice wasn't projected from far away. It was right behind me. "I'm sorry, but you still have a job to finish." He lifted me to my feet and helped me stay balanced. "You're almost there." I could only assume that he came in through the ruined Books-A-Million, braving the smoke and fire. Perhaps he knew some magic that helped him, but that didn't matter. All that mattered was that he was there for me.

I felt ready to cry again, but this time it wasn't because I was in pain.

When I regained my balance and stood up he stepped in front of me and pulled his shirt collar aside. "Take as much as you need." He gazed into my eyes. I knew that he was serious.

"Thank you." I said these words from the bottom of my heart. Will risked his life to be there just so that I could succeed. He smiled at me. It was a caring smile.

I kissed him. I wasn't sure what drove me to do it, but it felt like something I had to do. It didn't last very long and I didn't use my tongue, but I felt him relax as I put my arms around him.

When my lips released his, I gave him a smile, weak though it was. He smiled back. Then I sank my fangs into his neck. *Apples.* That was what I tasted. After a night filled with so much pain, I couldn't have asked for a more pleasant sensation. Will had supported me throughout the entire ordeal ever since I first became a vampire and there he was at a moment when I needed him most. *Don't worry. I'll protect you too.*

Perhaps I took too much blood from him, but I knew that he would be okay. He was still smiling when I let go. His eyes were closed. He was unconscious but at peace. I laid him down gently next to the shelves of PlayStation 3 games.

All of my strength had returned. I looked upon my opponent, who was now back on her feet, standing on the far end of the sidewalk in front of the store. The fire had disappeared from her body.

Her body itself, however, was an absolute mess. Most of her skin, hair, and clothing had burned away, revealing a horrendous mix of charred bones, organs, muscle, and layers of fat. Her face was nearly unrecognizable. This image was quite possibly the most disturbing that I had ever laid my eyes upon. It was certainly worse than the werewolf husk in that freezer. I didn't want to look at it long enough to be able to describe it in gory detail. Parts of her body were in the process of regenerating. I couldn't let her fully heal.

Blood on Fire

She roared louder than she ever had before, and this time it sounded absolutely inhuman—like the howl of a demon.

"I want you to go away." I walked forward, approaching the store's entrance.

She looked ready to charge.

"I want you to go away, and I'm going to do whatever's necessary so that you do."

I had only mere seconds until she began her next attack. I needed an idea. Then something caught my eye. Near the entrance were the shelves full of Wii games, and one of them had been knocked loose and was lying on the ground.

I knew that game, and it made me remember something useful. Many months earlier, I had been playing that game together with Will, Amelia, and James. I sat on my desk chair while the others sat on my bed, huddled around the tiny TV in my room. All of us gripped our controllers tightly

"I'm so terrible as Super Smash Brothers," Amelia said as her character, the cute yellow Pokémon known as Pikachu, was sent flying off the stage, which was a stone bridge that ran over the mythical land of Hyrule under a sky lit by a beautiful sunset.

"You just have to practice," Will said, "it's all about building your skills."

"How do you do that when you don't even have a Wii?"

"He's always mooching off of mine," James said right before Will, as the blue-haired swordsman Ike, knocked his character, mullet-wearing stealth specialist Solid Snake, into next week. "Aw dude, what the hell?"

"You left yourself open." Will sounded cocky. Only he and I were left on the stage, and I wasn't nearly as skilled at that game as he was. In fact, I wasn't as skilled as James either.

Will's character was on the right side of the stage while mine was on the left. Will held left on his control stick and held down his B-button, causing Ike to charge up an attack that would send him careening toward me with a powerful sword slash.

I could have easily just made my character jump over his, but I felt creative, so I hit the B-button of my controller to charge a powerful attack of my own. I knew that this plan was foolhardy and would probably cause me to lose the battle, but I was just having fun.

"Holy crap, that was awesome!" When my plan worked, and I won the match, I was filled with the sort of glee that only such an amazing outcome, whether fluke or otherwise, could give.

Will stared at the TV screen agape. "How the hell did you…?" He was nearly speechless. "You know that that would never work again in a thousand years."

Seeing my character in his tight racing suit and cool helmet in a victory pose on the post-battle results screen filled me with satisfaction. I had defeated a powerful opponent in an amazing way.

When my mind returned to reality and I could see the heavily damaged Ogre Queen starting to charge, I realized, *I want to do that.*

She came at me like the fist of an angry god as I took a big step backward and pulled my right arm as far back as it would go. My hand was clenched into a tight fist.

Even though I likely hadn't digested all of Will's blood yet, I put every bit of power that I gained from it into my fist. I could feel it. The blood that he gave me was potent, and it was exactly what I needed to fuel my magic.

I normally was immune to the heat that my fire produced, but I could feel this heat as it built up to an untold magnitude. I could feel the absurd level of strength that my arm possessed. It was more force than anything of that size should ever have been able to exert.

I stressed each syllable as I spoke, letting out a shout that overpowered even Chariot's roar.

"FALCON…"

My eyes were fixed on her. Each second seemed like an eternity. If my heart still beat, I knew that I would feel it pounding hard. I wasn't scared. I was determined. Everything came down to my fist, the same fist whose weak punch had cost me my teeth.

The ground shook with each step Chariot took. In her grotesque face, I could see that she wanted to tear me limb from limb.

She was very close, mere inches from contact when I thrust the entire right half of my body forward. My arm extended forward as far as it would go, digging straight into her gut. Fire surrounded it, glowing bright orange like the sun. The flames were huge. They looked like a bird.

"…PUNCH!"

Blood on Fire

I felt like that moment would last forever. What I truly wanted was to just curl up in a quiet place and just read a book without any other worries. I thought that perhaps now I'd be able to do that.

The Ogre Queen screamed in agony while her body went flying away. She sailed forward at constantly increasing altitude. Her entire body was engulfed in flames, which burned at a blinding intensity. She flew just over the nearby McDonald's and across the street, impacting the top parts of some tall pine trees on the other side, knocking them down. She kept flying, farther and farther, higher and higher, until she disappeared from view.

I stared in that direction, frozen in my punching position. My body trembled. Suddenly my legs buckled and I fell to my knees. I held myself up from the ground with my left hand since my right felt numb. I still kept staring in disbelief.

Many minutes passed. Then the realization set in. "She's gone." I felt a colossal weight lift from my shoulders. My arm buckled, and I fell to the ground. I closed my eyes. I felt like I could finally rest. Time passed. I wasn't sure how long I lay there.

Then I heard clapping. It came from one set of hands at first and then more joined in. I turned my face upward. At the ruined doorway, several figures appeared. I could see Amelia, Lupia, Minerva Jadis, Robert Valentine, and Maurice Freeman. They were accompanied by other police officers, firefighters, and paramedics. Amelia, Minerva, and Lupia were all wearing bloody bandages. All of them looked impressed. The firefighters diligently worked to extinguish any remaining flames.

I sat up. "What are you all doing here?" My voice was strained.

Amelia spoke for the group. "Will's mom kept all of us informed of the status of the battle. Then when daddy regained consciousness, I explained to him exactly what you were doing to protect all of us. We knew it was safe to come see you here when we saw that fire ball flying away. We all wanted to congratulate and thank you."

"I have to say, Able," Valentine said with sarcasm in his voice, "You did a bang-up job here." He looked around the store. "I just wish that you could cause less property damage. We may have to discuss this little matter with your lawyer."

"With all due respect, Captain, what the hell?" Officer Freeman vehemently protested. "This girl just saved the lives and property of everyone in this town.

Thanks to her, only the school and these three stores were damaged. If anything, you should give her a medal.

Valentine sighed. "Fine. I'll let you off the hook this time, girl. You still have those other charges against you, but for now, you're free to go." He didn't look happy about it, but he also didn't look like he would change his mind.

Amelia smiled at me. I smiled back.

Suddenly four more people fought their way through the crowd. Two of them were carrying huge cameras. The other two were Rock Rivers and Delta Stone.

"Are we too late for the battle?" Stone seemed disappointed. "Damn, that would've made a great story! Oh well, would you care to do an interview?"

Rivers shoved her, pushing her into the Wii games. "Back off, bitch, this evil vamp's mine!"

Injured though she was, Lupia stepped forward and tapped both reporters on the shoulder. She was wearing much nicer clothes than the ones she wore when she arrived—a shirt and shorts that complemented her frame. I figured that she must have put them in the police car when I wasn't looking, but I was still amazed that she found the time to change despite that night's events. That lady had some style.

"WHAT?" Neither reporter liked being touched.

"Look, the vampire's a little frazzled right now, but if you want someone to talk to, I think all of us would be willing to vouch for her."

Amelia, Jadis, and Freeman all nodded. Captain Valentine didn't.

"You know what?" I said, "I'll give you that interview. Both of you. Everyone knows who I am by this point anyway. We'll just have to schedule it for a different day, okay?"

Both reporters looked surprised—and satisfied. Lupia successfully led both them away.

Then an interesting thought entered my mind. "Wait a second, wasn't there a third reporter?"

That statement triggered something in Valentine's mind "Crap…Granite was with us when we were hypnotized." He turned to the walkie-talkie mic on his shoulder as he walked away. "Um, yeah, I think with might have a missing person to find…"

Freeman gave me a thumbs-up and followed him.

Blood on Fire

One of the paramedics beckoned Amelia to come to him. She complied after waving to me. She looked like she wanted to remain by my side, but she knew to tend to her injuries.

Minerva Jadis stepped inside the store, walked over to where Will lay, knelt down, and propped him on her lap. She sighed. "I guess I raised a good boy after all."

"Yeah, you did."

She lit up a cigarette despite the fact that smoking was most certainly not allowed in the store. "I just wish he weren't so reckless. I don't want him making the same mistakes I did." I wasn't sure what she was talking about and I didn't feel that asking would be appropriate. I still didn't know her very well and this was really the first time that I had ever spoken to her. "Just promise me one thing."

"What's that?"

"Don't get knocked up."

Now I felt awkward.

"You seem like a good girl. Perhaps I should've trusted Will's judgment in picking his friends. Please take care of my son."

"Don't worry, I will." Then something else crossed my mind. "Oh, about that wand...I know you're the one who made it, but—" I was going to say that I was sorry for destroying something that she must have worked so hard on.

She shook her head. "Thank you for destroying it. It was important to my client, that much I know, but you're strong enough without it. Besides, that Fool already paid me." She laughed. She definitely used the word "Fool" in its negative sense.

I nodded and stood up. I walked slowly out the front of the GameStop and breathed in the cool night air. I didn't know exactly how I would get home that night, but I didn't really care. I had a whole weekend with no threat of vampires ahead of me to recover.

Then a car screamed through the parking lot and came to a quick dead stop right in front of the curb. It was a black Honda.

I know that car.

Out of it emerged a figure I hadn't seen in months. "Geez Amy, why do you have to break everything?" He had an obnoxious smirk on his face. He had my same light brown hair, only it was cut very short. His face was rigid, similar to dad's, and he was far taller than me. He didn't wear glasses, instead insisting on contacts.

"Oh…Allen…hi…"

My brother shook his head. "So mom and dad leave you alone for a few days and you've already made this much of a mess. What's wrong with you?"

I rolled my eyes. "I don't know, Al, maybe the fact that I'm a freaking vampire."

He motioned me to his car. "Get in and tell me about it."

I knew that he wasn't going to leave me alone until I complied, and telling him about everything that occurred would be a chore with his usual insistence that nothing I said ever mattered. I waved goodbye to Minerva Jadis, who waved back. I had won a tough battle, but another very different battle was about to begin.

19: The Fool's Warning

My life was still strange and awkward, but it was quieter. I was free from danger but not from my other problems.

I still had too many questions and not enough answers. First and foremost on my mind—and on my brother's—was figuring out what happened to mom and dad. I told Allen just about everything I knew during our meeting at home after the battle.

"How could you let this happen?" he said accusingly.

"Me? I already told you that Dracula did it."

"You can't just blame this on a literary character. You were the one home at the time so it's your responsibility."

"How the hell am I responsible for something I had no control over?"

"You're always making excuses."

"Piss off."

"I mean, you were the one always complaining about being made fun of at school—"

"And at home."

"—so maybe you've always just been doing something wrong."

I looked away from him and sighed. "But I've always tried to do something about any problem I've ever had. I just wish you could see that."

"You just want people to feel sorry for you."

I felt powerless to get him to see things from my perspective. "Look Al, I know it's not going to be easy, but I'm old enough to take care of myself until I find mom and dad. I just need someone to serve as my legal guardian until I turn 18."

"I'm not dropping out of college for you." He was quite prone to such accusations.

The Fool's Warning

"I never said that I expected you to. I just need you to come home occasionally on weekends to sign things for me or do whatever I might need done that the law won't let a minor do."

"You're not going to be able to handle anything on your own and you know it."

I rolled my eyes. "Al, I just Falcon Punched a berserker who had not long earlier torn off my arm—which I reattached by myself, by the way."

"You'll have bills to pay, and you don't even have a car."

"I'll find a way. After all, I have friends."

After many hours of arguing, I finally convinced him to leave the next morning. He was angry at me for letting Lupia sleep in his bed and keep "all her crap" (which consisted of only one bag) in his room.

Lupia stayed out of our conversation and slept on the couch that night. "You and your brother don't have the most pleasant relationship do you?" She and I talked the next evening as she held a bag of ice against her head with one hand and drank a steaming cup of tea with the other.

"What clued you in?"

"My own brother would probably kill me if we ever ran into each other again."

"Resentment over you becoming a fine lady?"

"More like he was a lazy bum who didn't want to inherent the clan's responsibilities."

"But you didn't want them either."

"Only because of the masculinity involved."

"Well you're still tough enough to keep Tower off me. Thanks."

She sighed. "I don't like that form, but if I can use it to help a friend, I won't hesitate to transform."

"What did you guys do with Tower, anyway?"

"We turned her over to the police."

"I wonder what they're doing with her."

She shrugged. "Maybe we'll be able to ask."

"Oh, speaking of asking, how did your interview with those reporters go?"

"We just told them about how you risked your life to save everyone."

"Did they even realize that they were talking to Lupia? I mean, you didn't tell them the truth, did you?" I wasn't sure if coming out as a werewolf (and, furthermore, a transsexual) would be the best career move at the moment.

"They did. I managed to convince them that I really had no idea why they were after me. Then I told them that I wouldn't run away if any more vampires came after me."

"I'm happy for you."

"It was all thanks to you."

"So what's next for you, Lupia?" As much as I wouldn't have minded, I didn't see any reason for her to continue staying at my house.

"I guess I should call my agent. He's probably really pissed that I never told him where I went."

"And you had some concerts and signings you didn't do."

"I do need to do something to apologize to my fans."

Lupia ended up rescheduling her cancelled concerts and giving free merchandise to all attendees. She personally reimbursed anyone who couldn't attend at the rescheduled time and sold more tickets to make up for the extra open seats.

She still hung around my place for a few days—until that next Wednesday, specifically. With Amelia undergoing treatment for her injuries, I needed someone else to drive me to school for a while. She drove my mom's car. She left the house once she had set all of her affairs in order and Amelia reached a state at which she could safely drive. As soon as Lupia left, I missed her. I realized exactly how alone I was. I felt lucky whenever I would have a visitor.

Even after surviving that battle, a weekend of rest was all I needed to refresh myself for school. I had no remaining injuries at all. The school, however, wasn't nearly as lucky. The district brought in some portable classrooms to replace the ones that were destroyed, and the library and cafeteria were inaccessible as they were repaired. Food had to be served in the hallway.

I couldn't tell whether people had started to respect me or if they were just too intimidated to mess with me, but my Falcon Punch had an effect, for better or worse. Those who didn't know me really just shied away. Another week of school came and went, and though surviving the sun was still an ordeal, the entire experience just seemed easier.

During that subsequent week, I would run into Valentine as he stopped by to make sure everything at school was in order. I decided to ask him about what the police did with Tower.

He raised an eyebrow as if I were crazy. "You don't need to know."

The Fool's Warning

I raised an eyebrow right back. "But if she escapes, she'll probably try to kill me."

"We have top men working on it right now."

"Who?"

"Top...men." As much as I cared about his daughter, I could safely say, once and for all, that I didn't like Captain Valentine.

All things considered, classes were mundane.

"Alright," Mr. Royal said during first period that Friday," I want you all to take a look at the problems on page 297 and please turn in all of the even ones on Monday." He wrote the assignment on the board as he spoke. "Don't forget to show your work." Since his classroom had been destroyed, we had relocated into one of many trailer-like portable classrooms.

I began to gather up all of my belongings even before the bell rang. Shelly had largely left me alone during that week, leaving the room almost immediately after the period ended. I wanted to catch her this time.

As that familiar sound of the bell played over the loudspeaker, I saw that usual head of long blond hair immediately heading to the door. I jumped out of my chair and slung my bag over my shoulder. "Hey Shelly!" I tried to sound neither friendly nor confrontational. I wanted to know something, and I felt like only she could tell me.

She stopped dead in her tracks and slowly turned her head toward me. Her face was locked in a scowl. "What?"

"Tell me, exactly how did you and Emily first meet?" I figured that using the Ogre Queen's real name was the best choice. "And what do you know about her past?"

Her facial expression didn't change. "As if I would actually tell you." She rushed out the door and out of sight.

I shrugged. "Hell, it was worth a try." I suspected that she wouldn't tell me anything. She was a bitch, after all.

With regard to the Ogre Queen, further investigations also revealed no trace of her body. Firefighters worked long into the night to make sure that areas she passed over didn't flare up into brush fires, but her remains were nowhere to be found. They probably just burned away, but no one could be sure.

Mrs. Hacket seemed to be a permanent addition to the teaching staff, and she seemed like a worthy replacement for Mrs. Perth. "Alright class," she said that Friday, "you should all be about two-thirds done with *Dracula* by now.

Blood on Fire

Please keep in mind that I will test you on the book one week from today." The entire class groaned. "Oh come now, it won't be that painful."

When class ended, she called me forward to speak to her. "I just wanted to congratulate you on your victory against the vampires last week." Few people at all had made any comment on the matter.

"Uh, thanks." I was a bit glad to get some positive recognition.

"You must have relied on some very creative methods in order to win such a battle."

I recalled hearing her words in my mind during the fight. "Yeah, creativity definitely helped."

"Have you had any luck in finding your parents?"

That question seemed odd to me. "Wait, how did you—?"

"Everybody knows. A missing person alert was put out and the news reported on it."

I hadn't even bothered to watch the interviews that my friends gave. I was just glad to be rid of the other vampires. "Oh. No, I haven't found any clues."

She had a warm, caring smile. "That is a shame. If you need any help with anything at all, please don't hesitate to let me know. I like to aid my students in any way I can."

I wasn't sure what to make of that offer, so I just nodded and said "Well thank you very much; I'll keep that in mind."

"You're welcome." She sent me on my way.

Overall, school wasn't much of a concern. I still had other matters that I wanted to attend to.

Amelia was out and about relatively quickly even with her injuries. The fang marks on her neck were gone. She didn't mention anything about the moment she and I shared on Friday night, but I could somehow tell that it was on her mind.

Will had fang marks for a while, but he acted much differently than James did, and by that I mean that he didn't act any different at all. By the end of the week, the marks were gone. He didn't mention anything about the moment he and I shared either.

As for James, he returned to normal as soon as his fang marks faded.

I still had some of Will's blood left in me, so I could sustain myself by eating steaks that week since I didn't need to fight.

THE FOOL'S WARNING

That Friday, Will, Amelia, and I decided to go on another, albeit much less dangerous, adventure. If one thing continued to bother me, it was the fact that I had actually taken two lives. I found myself at the front door of an unfamiliar house, ringing the doorbell. It was still early night time. The door opened. A stern looking man with short brunette hair and an unkempt beard now stood in front of me.

"Uh…hi…you must be Mr. Davis, right?"

The man didn't answer; his gaze just narrowed into a scowl.

"Um…I came here to offer my condolences and to tell you that I'm sorry. I did it to defend a friend of mine, but that doesn't change that fact that I…I killed your daughter."

The man began to shudder and I spotted tears beginning to stream out of both of his eyes. He slammed the door, and I heard it lock.

"Well at least he didn't pull a gun on me like Tower's father did." I got back in the car and pressed my face against the window. "Why can't they just see that I'm trying to be nice?"

"It's not your fault, Amy," Will said from the passenger seat.

"I know…I just wish it could've gone better than that."

"What about the other sets of parents?" Amelia asked. "Do you still want to try talking to them?"

"Well…let me think about this." I considered the other vampires. "We don't know jack about Devil, so we can rule out anything involving her. We didn't even fight her. As for Tower, her father tried to kill me…twice. Besides, we didn't even kill Tower. That just leaves…"

"The Ogre Queen." Amelia finished my sentence for me.

I fell silent. I couldn't see any good coming out of anything involving her.

"You don't have to do it if you really don't want to," Will said.

I sighed. "I'm scared to death of facing her parents, but I have some questions that I need answered. Let's give it a shot."

Thanks to Will's brilliant ability to find nearly anything on the Internet (or a book), we already had an address.

Again, it was just me, the front door, and the doorbell. *Come on Amy, you can do this.* I reluctantly pushed the glowing button. Then I waited several seconds before the door finally opened. From behind it emerged a meek middle-aged woman with cropped salt and pepper hair. She didn't look anything like I expected, and she was almost as short as me.

Blood on Fire

"You must be Amy." She had no apparent malice in her voice whatsoever.

"Um...yes."

"Somehow I knew you would come here. Please, come inside."

She invited me inside. It was certainly a surprise. I wasn't sure whether to trust her.

"Don't worry, I'm not going to shoot you or anything. You did want to talk to me, right?"

"Yeah...um, I have two friends in the car. Do you mind if they come in as well?"

"Not at all."

She sat the three of us in her living room around a small coffee table. The room was decorated in a simple fashion and everything was spotlessly clean.

"Can I interest you kids in any coffee, tea, or hot chocolate?"

"Coffee please," Amelia said.

"Hot chocolate," Will said.

"Nothing for me, thanks," I said.

She disappeared into the kitchen for a few minutes.

"Do you really think she's not mad at me?"

"Who can say?" Will said. "She doesn't really seem like the vengeful psychotic type, though."

She came back into the room, holding two mugs, which she distributed to my friends. She sat down in a small chair across from us. She faced me. "Now, I know you're the one who killed my Emily, but don't worry, I bear no ill will against you."

"Thank you." That was something refreshing to hear. "I'm extremely sorry about what I did, but I didn't have much of choice. She was destroying everything."

"Don't worry, young lady. I understand. You see, Emily had a very violent streak to her. She even knocked out another student's teeth at school a few years ago."

"Yeah. Unfortunately, I know that firsthand." I pointed toward my missing tooth.

She smiled. "You must understand that Emily wasn't always like that." She turned to a nearby table, on which stood the photo of a rather normal-looking girl. "It all happened when she was in the 7th grade."

Two years before the tooth incident.

296

THE FOOL'S WARNING

"She had a few friends back then, but she was closer to none more so than Shelly."

I nearly choked at the mention of that name. "She and Shelly were best friends?" Shelly always did have a girl posse, and all of its members were always pretty. Its members shifted every so often, but I never remembered that hulking beast being a part of it. I glanced at the photo again. The younger Emily looked so normal. I thought I recognized her, but I couldn't recall interacting with her at all. Perhaps she, unlike Shelly, had left me alone.

"Yes. Those two were inseparable...until it happened."

"Until what happened?" I had my suspicions since I had already learned from Officer Freeman, but I wanted to hear it from a primary source.

"My husband's—ex-husband's—brother, Emily's uncle..." She became chocked up. I could see tears forming on the edges of her eyes.

"Say no more. I can guess where this is going." I didn't want her to break down after so kindly inviting us in.

"She hardly even knew him. After that happened, she just became violent and obsessed with becoming stronger. Her father and I couldn't control her anymore, which was why he left. She grew to hate everyone except her one remaining friend."

I already knew who she meant. "Shelly."

"The two weren't really friends in the traditional sense anymore, but I always had the feeling that Shelly wanted Emily to change back into her old self. And that's how things were until the week before last when Emily suddenly disappeared." She struggled to talk at this point.

Will and Amelia both stared into their cups, silent. They, like me, had seen Emily Rogers as more of a beast than a person.

I took a deep breath. "The tragedy that happened to her may have also happened to me, but if it did, somehow my mind blocked it out. It...really isn't something I want to think about."

I hadn't mentioned this to Will or Amelia before, and they looked exceedingly worried. Amelia was about to say something, but I shook my head. I didn't want to talk about it, at least not yet. Mrs. Rogers remained silent.

I stood up. "I think we've bothered you enough. Thank you, Mrs. Rogers."

"It's fine, dear. You're always welcome here should you choose to stop by. You really do seem like a kind-hearted girl." She was looking down, so I couldn't see her face, but I knew that she had a sad smile. She was glad to have visitors who could show her some empathy.

I asked Amelia to bring me home. "I don't see any more reason to stay out tonight."

I handed Will the key to the front door when we arrived. "Go on inside; I have to go check the mail." I seemingly had no reason to be concerned while going outside my house anymore as Buford hadn't shown up all week, though he was at school. Will and Amelia went inside while I checked inside the mailbox at the front of the driveway. I found a few thin envelopes inside. *Probably just more junk mail for mom and dad.* Most of the mail I received since they disappeared had consisted of offers for credit cards. The envelope at the top of this pile, however, stood out to me. It was addressed to "Amy Allison Able," written in beautiful calligraphy. *What is this?* It didn't have a return address. I decided to open it inside the house.

As soon as I stepped in, Will called me to the living room, sounding frantic. "Amy, you're going to want to see this!"

Delta Stone was reporting on the news. "We have sad news from Palm Coast tonight, which just last week survived a potentially catastrophic vampire attack. Apparently former high school English teacher Eleanor Perth was found dead in her home late this afternoon."

"What?" I couldn't believe my ears.

"Forensics analysts examining the crime scene say that her body had been lying there decomposing, drained of all blood with vampire fang marks in her neck. She was last seen entering her condo one week before Thursday, apparently cowering in fear of an unknown source. Known vampire Amy Able has been dismissed from the list of potential suspects due to a strong alibi, having been in police custody at the time. She has also never been seen in that area."

"Well that's a tiny bit reassuring, but still, what the hell?"

"Perth was a widow with one adult son and lived alone in her two bedroom house. She had quit her job teaching at Flagler Palm Coast High School only a few days prior to her death and has since been replaced. If you have any leads as to any suspects, you are encouraged to call—"

I grabbed the remote control and shut the TV off. I was too creeped out.

"I don't like this," Will said. "I can't think of any connection that Perth may have had to the vampires."

The Fool's Warning

"Maybe it had something to do with Hacket replacing her," Amelia said, shrugging.

I shook my head. "That makes someone else who had to die...just what is going on? And where are my parents?" I peered down at the envelope in my hand.

"What's that?" Amelia seemed curious about it.

I opened it. Inside was piece of paper folded up. I unfolded it. "A letter, apparently."

Will raised an eyebrow. "Who writes letters anymore?"

It was typewritten. I decided to read it out loud:

Dear Illustrious Miss Amy Able:
It has come to my attention that a week has passed since you slaughtered Strength and Chariot and placed Tower in captivity. I must congratulate you on your victory, which only one with your level of creativity and strength of willpower and heart could achieve.

However, I am afraid that the opponents you defeated as well as yourself were merely the beginning of Project Arcana—an experiment to produce vampires and minions of a new type, three of whom were hybrids with a certain other powerful creature of the night. You and your friends so elegantly defeated them. I had even created a new source of power just for you, and you decided to spurn it, yet you still managed to emerge victorious. I must say, I never expected that you would possess this much power.

You are different from the others. You are special, and you have proved as much with your performance in combat against them. I am very impressed and very proud of you.

Although you did succeed in foiling my plan of testing more werewolf hybrids, please know that it was not you who made a Fool out of me. I will be watching you.
Yours Truly,
The Fool

When I finished reading, I felt a lingering sense of dread that simply wouldn't go away. I sat down the couch, holding the top of my head with my right hand. I could feel reality sinking in—the reality that I was far from free.

Will remained silent.

Blood on Fire

"That's...really creepy," Amelia said.

"The Fool's watching me?" I looked around the room. "He didn't plant cameras around this house, did he?" This was the first time that the Fool ever contacted me directly.

Will shook his head. "Definitely not. He's just trying to intimidate you."

"Well he's doing a good job."

Amelia pointed at the rest of the pile of envelopes that I held. "What about the rest of those? Did he send you anything else?"

I picked another envelope at random and tore it open. Inside was another folded sheet of paper. I unfolded it. Toward the top, I spotted the logo for our local electric company, Florida Power and Light. It was followed by a complicated chart with a bunch of numbers on it. At the bottom of that chart was a horrendous looking number with a dollar sign next to it. I quickly realized what this was.

"It's the electric bill." My spirits sank. "How the hell am I going to pay this?"

I wondered if anything else would come along to complicate matters. *I miss mom and dad.*

About the Author

M. P. DePaul was born on Staten Island, New York and grew up in Palm Coast, Florida. DePaul holds an M.A. in English from the University of North Florida in Jacksonville, Florida and currently teaches writing to college freshmen and sophomores there. None of them sparkle.

Made in the USA
Lexington, KY
24 July 2012